WHEN SMILES FADE

PAIGE DEARTH

Dirt On The Author

Born and raised in Plymouth Meeting, a small town west of Philadelphia, Paige Dearth was a victim of child abuse and spent her early years yearning desperately for a better life. Living through the fear and isolation that marked her youth, she found a way of coping with the trauma: she developed the ability to dream up stories grounded in reality that would provide her with a creative outlet when she finally embarked on a series of novels. Paige's debut novel, Believe Like A Child, is the darkest version of the life she imagines she would have been doomed to lead had fate not intervened just in the nick of time. The beginning of Believe Like A Child is based on Paige's life while the remainder of the book is fiction. Paige writes real-life horror and refers to her work as Fiction with Mean-ing. She hopes that awareness through fiction creates prevention.

Connect With Paige

Find all of Paige's books on Amazon

Sign up for new book releases: paigedearth.com

Follow Paige At:

Facebook: facebook.com/paigedearth

Instagram: paigedearth

Goodreads

Twitter: @paigedearth

More books by Paige

Home Street Home Series:
Believe Like A Child
When Smiles Fade
One Among Us
Mean Little People
Never Be Alone
My Final Breath

Rainey Paxton Series:
A Little Pinprick
A Little High

In loving memory of Dell, my brother from Seattle: I'll miss you always.
Hugs and Kisses,
Paige

~

For my daughter, whose hard work and dedication to people is nothing
short of amazing. You inspire me in many ways.
I will love you until the day I die.
~Mom

Acknowledgements

Thanks to my hubby for being there with me every step of the way. It is your unfailing belief in me that has helped me to carry on and continue to write, confident in the knowledge that one day, it will all make a difference.

Much love and appreciation to Aunt Barbara for your review and edit of this book. It means the world to me.

My deep appreciation to a great artist and childhood friend, Boo-Boo. You have captured my soul with your God given artistic talent and understanding of who I really am. Check out her incredible work at www.disantoart.com

My deepest gratitude to Gina: your devotion to my work and success means everything to me – hmmmm.

Big E: I love you as if you were my very own.

Many, many, many thanks to the wonderful book-blogging community! You're all incredible people!

~Paige

Just Listen

"When your mind is quiet and you listen closely, you will hear the children weeping silently. If you can't quite hear their cries, then listen with your eyes. These are the children of the streets, who have learned pain and suffering before they ever had a chance to experience life. Do not ignore their cries for help, for all they wish is that you will rescue them. They do not have a family that wants them, they don't know how it feels to be loved and they've never lived anywhere that felt like home...the streets are where they find their voice and relief from all of the suffering.

Just listen and you'll see them."

~Paige Dearth

The Seed Is Planted

"**E**mma! Get your ass down here, you stupid little bitch! What the fuck did I tell you about not living like a pig?" Pepper screamed.

Panic-stricken at the thought of what would happen next, Emma rushed her younger sister, Gracie, over to the bedroom closet and pushed the tiny child inside. Before shutting the door, she said, "Don't move or make any noise." Then in a softer whisper she warned her younger sister, "You have to be really, really quiet. I'll be right back. I promise."

That was code for "be invisible." Gracie obeyed her older sister, tears of fright silently dribbling down her cheeks.

Emma rushed into the hallway and stopped to look at her mother, who was standing just inside her own bedroom. "What the hell did you do now?" she accused. "How many times do I have to tell you to do what you're told? You brainless idiot!"

Gracie listened from the closet to the rapid patter of eight-year-old Emma's feet as she ran down the stairs. There was an eerie silence during which she unconsciously held her breath. Then the first blow was struck. Followed by others. Gracie cringed at her older sister's muffled shrieks of torment as she imagined the scene downstairs with telling accuracy. Emma, she knew from past experience, had once again been transformed into her father's punching bag. She wondered why their mother didn't go and help Emma. Resisting the urge to run downstairs, Gracie stayed hidden upstairs in the bedroom closet as she was instructed, waiting for the beating to end, scared that her father would come for her after he was finished with her older sister.

Down in the kitchen, Pepper Murphy lurched around, unsteady on his feet. He towered over his young daughter, contemplating her stricken face for several minutes and deriving a sickening enthusiasm and fresh energy from her growing terror. She stood before him, whimpering from the fear that was planted in her heart, wishing, as always, that her father's love for her would overpower his fury. That never happened. When she had worked herself up into a frenzy of fear, Pepper punched her in the eye. Emma lost her footing and hurtled back into the doorframe. Almost immediately, her face began to swell at the site of impact.

Snatching her up by the collar of her shirt, Pepper slapped Emma across the face with such force that he split her lip open. Blood gushing into her mouth and down her chin, she watched as her father walked over to the stove and turned on the burner. When the cold black coil began to glow a scorching orange, he shut the burner off and stood glaring at his daughter. Her body involuntarily shook as she wondered what he was going to do to her. Huddled in the corner of the kitchen, Emma wished the walls would open so that she could crawl inside of them and find the needed protection from her father's wrath. "Please, Daddy. Please don't hurt me. I'm sorry," the child begged.

His eyes bored into hers, undeterred by her fear and pain. Emma watched in terror as the corners of his mouth curled up, until he was smiling like a sadistic monster. She trembled visibly in anticipation of what was to come. Her father suddenly pounced on her. Grasping her by the arm, he dragged her, kicking and screaming, over to the hot burner. Then he seized her left hand and ordered her to unclench her teeny fist. After she opened her hand, Pepper slapped her palm down on the hot burner in one swift movement, holding it in place for a couple of seconds and letting the young, tender skin boil and blister from the intense heat that still remained. Then he bent down, his face close to his daughter's, and snorted, "Oink! Oink! Oink!" into her ear.

All through the ordeal, Emma's shrills of agony sliced through the silence of the house. Valerie lay on her bed upstairs. Her mind filled with raw horror as she imagined what would happen to her if Pepper killed the child and was sent to prison. She prayed that he wouldn't take it too far this time. She didn't give a thought to the suffering that her older daughter was enduring at the hands of her husband. It was as if she had ice water running through her veins in place of blood.

As Emma collapsed on the floor, Pepper stood over her threateningly. Speaking in a tight, cold voice, he said through clenched teeth, "You are a worthless piece of shit. I don't know why I just don't kill you right now. I'm giving you another chance to act like a human being. You can forget about eating dinner tonight. I don't see why a little pig like you should be fed. Consider yourself lucky that I don't beat you to death." He began to leave the kitchen, but turned back at the doorway and bellowed, "You better have this place cleaned up before I get home from the bar!" With that final warning, Pepper grabbed a beer from the refrigerator then stormed out of the kitchen and left the house.

Emma remained sprawled on the floor, paralyzed by the depth of her own despair, her eight-year-old mind trying to recover from what her father had just done to her. Then she scolded herself for failing to wash that one dirty fork that Valerie had left in the sink when she had gotten home from school. Maybe if she had washed it, none of this would have happened, she tried to rationalize, looking for some reason why she deserved such harsh punishment. She sat staring at her blistered, deformed palm. The pain the burn caused was only secondary to her overwhelming despair at being unloved.

This year of her life was when Emma became acutely aware of the possibility that Pepper might actually kill her. The years prior had been hard for her, but now that she was getting older her thoughts and senses were on high alert and she could no longer deny them. She grappled with finding different ways to behave that would stop the abuse, not because she was afraid of dying, but because she was afraid to leave Gracie alone with her parents.

After Pepper had burned her hand on the stove, she did everything in her power to fly below his radar. She made sure to clean the house after school every day and took special care in making his meals. But nothing lightened his fury. It was a Wednesday night and Emma was sitting at the kitchen table doing her homework after she had finished cleaning up from dinner. Her father staggered back into the kitchen to get himself another beer. He opened the can and took a long, hard swig. His head hung as if it were too heavy for his neck to hold as he eyed her with disgust. "I don't know why you bother with dat school shit; you're never gonna 'mount to nuttin' no matter how hard you try," he babbled through his drunken daze.

Emma looked up at him, her heart pounding in her chest. "My math teacher thinks I'm really smart. She told me that if I wanted to, I could be an accountant someday," Emma said, hoping to make him feel proud of her.

Pepper stomped over to the table and picked up one of her pencils and thrust the point into her forearm. The pencil stood at attention as she looked on in shock. She quickly yanked the pencil out of her arm and ran to the sink to wash off the blood with soap and water. "See dat! Now you're not so worried 'bout pretending like you understand anything in those books of yours. Let that be a lesson not to leave your stuff all over my kitchen table. Now get this shit out of here!" he bellowed.

Pepper was tireless in his violent treatment of Emma. To her, the slaps, punches, and kicks came from a bottomless pit of hate that burrowed deep in her father's soul. The endless bruises he left on her made Emma feel hopeless and ashamed. Alone in the bathroom, Emma would study the wounds and scars that Pepper gave her. She was consumed by her sense of loneliness and lack of power to change her circumstances. She was completely at his mercy and knew he could do whatever he wanted to her, regardless of how broken she became.

It was a warm morning in August and the two girls were jumping rope in the backyard. Pepper got annoyed because they were making too much noise while he was nursing a burning hangover with vodka. He flung open the back door and stood holding his aching head. "You two shut the fuck up. You hear?"

They immediately went silent and stood perfectly still. He turned and went back into the house, and Emma was lulled into a false sense of security as they began running through the yard, playing tag. Moments later, the rotted screen door burst open and Pepper barreled down the cement steps into the yard. He grabbed Emma under her arm and pulled her into the house. She began to plead with him, knowing she was in for something terrible. "I'm sorry, Daddy," she cried, "I swear, we'll be quiet. OK, Daddy? Please don't hurt me," she cried.

Pepper grabbed the soft flesh under her upper arm and pinched as hard as he could. Emma went to her knees as she tried to get him to release his hold. He dragged her into the living room where there was an old wooden trunk. "You want to disobey me? Well then, there is a price for that," he said calmly.

Pepper pushed the glass vase filled with dusty plastic flowers off the chest. It slammed to the floor and shattered into a million pieces. Emma's eyes bulged as she frantically wondered what he was going to do to her. As her father lifted the lid to the trunk, she shrunk away from him trying to run and escape. He lifted her around the waist, her feet flailing as she tried to break away from his tight grip. Her movements made it impossible for him to get her legs into the trunk. Growing more irrational by the moment, he clamped his teeth on her shoulder until he could taste her blood in his mouth. Then he twisted her arm behind her back until he heard the pop as it dislocated at the shoulder. With excruciating pain in both shoulders she stopped fighting and sank into the trunk. After he slammed the lid shut and locked it, he left her and went to find Gracie. Ignoring her own painful injuries, Emma's gut twisted as she heard her father slapping Gracie around the living room. I wish I were a superhero, she thought, so that I can break out of here and help my sister.

Inside the trunk her body was twisted in an unnatural position. Her legs were folded at the knees behind her and her torso was bent at the waist so that her nose touched her knees. There was not enough room in the small space for her to reposition herself, and after a couple of hours her limbs went numb.

After the first twenty-four hours had passed and he hadn't let her out, all she wanted was to die. She reveled in the idea of leaving her measly existence and finally being free of her tormentor, believing that death was a much more appealing option than her current living conditions.

During her imprisonment, every so often her father would flip the trunk on different sides, smashing her dislocated shoulder and twisted body against the walls of the wooden box. Two days later, when he finally opened the lid and let her out, Emma could barely walk.

She literally crawled, with Gracie's help, over to the sofa where she lay for another four hours. Finally she managed to get to her feet. As she headed toward the foot of the stairs to go up to her room, Pepper put his foot in front of her. Unsteady on her feet, she crashed down onto the floor. She broke her fall with her hands before her face hit the floor and she scurried like a wounded animal to get away from her father. He stood over her and began to laugh. He laughed so hard that tears streamed down his face as his daughter watched him, humiliated and defeated.

Her stomach twisted into a tight knot as disgust for her father overcame her anguish. She felt a surge of hatred so profound that no one could stop it from taking complete control of her. It shook her entire being. Emma grappled with an idea so horrifying that it took her a while to accept it: she now believed that her father was the devil himself in a man's body. This conviction would mark a new beginning for her, eventually determining who she would become. The seed had been planted.

Chapter One

It was a cold November night a little more than a year later and the temperature had dipped into the low thirties. The family was having dinner in the small, dimly lit kitchen. Valerie's eyes were fixed on her plate as Pepper grumbled about his boss and how much he despised the man. That evening, like most others, his drinking had started before he even got home and only ramped up the moment he walked through the front door.

Emma had just spooned some peas onto Gracie's plate. The six-year-old reached for her glass of water and accidentally caught her father's freshly opened can of beer with her small arm. Pepper erupted. His face looked like a twisted mass of bumpy, pulsating flesh as the veins in his temples stood out and he turned bright red. Clenching his fists, he put them up against Gracie's dainty face and yelled, "You fucking little whore! You spilled my beer! You're an idiot, just like your sister!"

In a swift motion, he yanked the terrified child out of her chair and flung her down on the floor. Before she could recover from the shock, he bent down and slapped her in the face, sending her flying across the kitchen floor. Her body seemed weightless, like a rag doll, as she tumbled head over heels and landed on the other side of the room. Pepper trudged over to her, buried his fingers in her hair, and closed his fist over a handful of strands. Then he pulled her upright until she was standing. Gracie's face twisted with pain as she let out a blood-curdling shriek.

Her father ground his nose against hers. "You fucking maggot!" he yelled. "I never wanted you! You belong to that stupid bitch over there!" He gestured toward Valerie. As Pepper released his daughter's hair, she fell back to the floor.

Stunned by what had happened, Emma ran to her little sister. She desperately hoped her mother would protect them, even though Valerie had proven time and again that she wouldn't. She now snapped at her father. "Why don't you leave her alone? You bully!" she screamed.

Outraged by what he considered to be the ultimate form of disrespect, Pepper snatched a frying pan from the top of the stove and whacked the side of her face with it, knocking her unconscious. When Emma woke up, she found herself lying on the cement steps that led from the back of the house into their small yard. Dressed only in the jeans and sweater she had worn to school that day, she felt the cold seeping into her bones, clearing the cobwebs of confusion that had clouded her mind. Emma picked herself up and knocked softly on the back door.

Pepper, who had been waiting for her to wake up, immediately flung open the door, startling her. "You think you're smart?" he snapped. "You think you can talk to me like that? Nobody tells me what to do in my house! Tonight, you'll sleep outside and learn never to talk back to me, girl!"

After he had slammed the door in her face, Emma huddled into herself, trying to keep warm. The wind slashed through her worn clothing, increasing her desperation to find shelter. Afraid to go too far, she decided to seek refuge on their front porch. There, she remembered, was a broken-down sofa that had never made its way to the trash.

Mrs. Tisdale, her elderly neighbor who lived across the street, was looking out her window as Emma made her way to the front of their row home. The old woman watched the child move slowly up the front porch, trying to step as lightly as possible so that the creaky boards wouldn't betray her presence. Then her eyes widened in alarm as the little girl crawled under the worn cushions on the sofa and completely vanished from sight.

Mrs. Tisdale kept her eyes glued to the sofa for more than fifteen minutes before she put on her coat and went across the street to find out what the hell was going on. She approached Emma with great care, so as not to startle her, and gently lifted the cushion covering her face. "Child," she murmured, "why you out here in the cold? Where's your mama?"

Her eyes red from crying, Emma replied, "My father is making me sleep outside tonight. He was hitting my little sister and I yelled at him to stop. So he hit me with a pan and put me outside. This is my punishment."

"Well, I'll be dipped in shit if a little child like you is gonna sleep out here in the cold!" the elderly neighbor said in a huff. "Come on, baby, you sleepin' at my house tonight."

Emma's body stiffened with resistance. "No, Mrs. Tisdale," she protested, "I have to stay here so I can get up in the morning and get out back before my father goes to work. If he finds out I didn't stay on the back steps during the night, I don't know what he'll do to me."

Mrs. Tisdale gave her concern due consideration. "Okay then," she conceded, "you'll come sleep at my house and we'll set an alarm so that you can get up before he does. That way, you can go back on those steps before that bastard goes off to work. okay, baby?"

Comfortable with Mrs. Tisdale's proposition, Emma dug herself out from beneath the cushions and followed her across the street. Once inside her own house, Mrs. Tisdale wrapped Emma in a warm blanket and made her a steaming cup of cocoa. The chocolaty milk warmed her insides, filling her with a sense of security. Emma was grateful for Mrs. Tisdale's kindness as she lay, warm and cozy, on her neighbor's sofa waiting for sleep to provide a temporary release from her life.

This was the first real encounter that Emma had with Mrs. Tisdale. From here on the relationship grew, and over time, the girl came to rely on her for the support she needed to make it through each treacherous day. Mrs. Tisdale was well aware of how Pepper treated his two daughters. As a result, she tried to compensate by showering the children with the love their parents couldn't seem to find for them. Mrs. Tisdale failed to understand how Valerie could allow her husband to beat their own children. If it were her husband, the old lady told herself, she would surely have set things right. Hell, she thought, I'm gonna try my best to set things right and I ain't even married to that no-good dirty, rotten bastard.

Chapter Two

A voluptuous black woman, Mrs. Tisdale had short salt-and-pepper hair that fell about her head in large curls. Her eyes were such a light brown that people mistook her eye color for hazel. Her bright smile lit up her jolly face, and her hands, although extremely large, gave Emma tender comfort when she needed it most. Mrs. Tisdale's loving ways filled the girl with joy, and when the old woman laughed, a rumbling sound rose from deep within her belly, making the child's heart soar and offering her a temporary reprieve from the darkness that enveloped her life.

From the time she had gotten to know Emma, Mrs. Tisdale often brought up the issue of Child Protective Services, explaining to the girl that they offered a way out of her predicament. The old lady wanted to alert them so they could take Emma and Gracie away from their brutal father, but the child had pleaded with her to keep the secret. Not understanding how the system worked, Emma feared that they would take her away and leave Gracie at home to become the new target of Pepper's abuse.

"Mrs. Tisdale," Emma had sobbed, "it won't be any use. My mother will just stick up for my dad and tell them I'm lying."

Against her better judgment, Mrs. Tisdale had let it go. Instead, she had turned to prayer, asking for peace and love to be bestowed upon Emma.

At home, Emma lived in fear, but with Mrs. Tisdale, she always felt safe and secure. Life was sweet with her elderly neighbor, regardless of how short-lived those moments of happiness were. When Pepper was at work or drowning himself in booze at the bar, the child helped Mrs. Tisdale fold clothes and do small chores, listening intently to the stories the lady shared of her own youth. Emma would pretend that her neighbor was her real mother, knowing that if she were, her life would be very different.

In the neighborhood, Mrs. Tisdale was regarded as a tough old black woman. Nobody in Norristown fucked with her. She had three grown sons. They were big and they were mean. When it came to protecting their mama, they were ruthless. Her sons were always nice to Emma, because their mama had explained to them, "The poor child has to put up with brutal beatings from her papa. He's a sorry excuse for a father. We need to give her as much lovin' as we can, so she knows people care for her. Otherwise, she's likely to turn out just like him. Children become what they know. You hear me now?"

Rather quickly, Emma secretly began to wish that Mrs. Tisdale's sons would stop Pepper from hurting her. But just like Valerie, they never came to her rescue. Emma had no choice but to carry the burden of her sickening youth alone

Chapter Three

Pepper Murphy's mother had died in childbirth, leaving his alcoholic father to raise the boy. The man often beat his small son, berating him time and again for killing his mother. The boy's destructive temper evolved over time, fueled by his anger and helplessness as he endured daily rounds of abuse from his father. When he was still a young boy, Pepper had taken to hiding behind bushes and cars and either throwing large stones at other children as they walked by or whacking them on the back with thick tree branches. He did these things in an attempt to release his own anger.

In middle school, he acquired quite a reputation as the class bully; he would hit and verbally abuse his classmates for no good reason, leaving them defenseless and humiliated. As a young teen, Pepper's explosive anger at his peers escalated to intolerable levels, often leaving his weaker prey with scars and bruises from his boiling rage.

By the time he reached high school he was drinking and smoking and had only a couple of close friends. However, when he entered eleventh grade, Pepper's shop teacher took a liking to him. The teacher realized that with some encouragement the boy could be saved from the fate that he was heading toward. He thought Pepper could someday be a talented home builder, a dream of Pepper's from the time he was small and had used his homemade wood blocks to build houses.

Pepper's whole attitude changed with the positive attention he received from his shop teacher. He made the teenager believe that he could actually do something good so that he would become a man that others respected. For the first time in his life, Pepper was filled with optimism. He quickly became likeable to many of his peers. He enjoyed the last two years of high school—making new friends, going to parties, and becoming the guy that all the girls wanted as their boyfriend.

When he graduated from high school, he had big plans of setting up his own construction business with his closest friend. They talked with excitement about getting contracts for building houses for a large company. The two friends mapped out how they would start out with smaller construction jobs before branching out to build homes on their own. They agreed to save a portion of their earnings from each job to purchase their first company truck.

Only four months after they graduated high school, the two young men signed their first contract. They believed that all of their dreams were coming true. "We need to celebrate! We're on our way to the big time," Pepper boasted. "Let's go to the bar and have a few beers."

They had only been at the bar for an hour when Pepper raised his beer. "Here's to building houses, buddy!"

As they banged glasses and chugged their beers, a beautiful woman named Valerie walked in front of them. Pepper and his friend stared at her, along with every other man in the bar, as she made her way over to a table of friends. That was the night Pepper and Valerie first met.

Pepper and Valerie were almost immediately infatuated with each other. Her beauty stirred a sexual hunger in him that he couldn't control and she was smitten by his apparently strong, protective nature. The two made an attractive couple. Pepper was tall and full-bodied and his intimidating stature matched his burly character. Pepper's jet-black hair and thick, dark eyelashes set off his blazing green eyes. His full lips complemented his long, slender nose, and his rugged features and square jaw made him appear fearless.

Valerie was equally attractive, but what she possessed in physical beauty she lacked in brains. She had long, straight blond hair that fell to her shoulders like strands of golden silk. Her eyes were stunning, almost royal blue, and her pale pink pouty lips were plump and inviting. She was tall and thin with full breasts, a tiny waist, and curved hips.

Valerie's parents had died suddenly when their car slid off of a bridge on an icy winter night two days before Christmas. She was just thirteen-years-old with no other family, and spent the next five years of her life being raised in various foster homes. She carried an unrelenting resentment towards her parents who died and left her alone. Moving all the time annoyed the shit out of her and she hated having to adjust to new families and different rules.

By the time she was fourteen-years-old the other foster girls had taught her how to use her body to get men to do whatever she wanted. These girls influenced her into being manipulative and self-absorbed. Her mannerisms and good looks often created tension between each of her foster parents. The men took her side while the women resented that she stole all of the attention that rightfully belonged to them. Valerie lied and cheated to her foster parents, teachers and anyone else who stood in her way. The once sweet child had grown into a despicable young woman. Finally, when Valerie turned eighteen, she and another girl who she knew from foster care moved into a cheap, rundown apartment over a pizza shop in Pottstown.

Pepper and Valerie were inseparable at first. He took her to the movies where they sat in the very back row, kissing and groping each other. When the weather turned warmer, Valerie made picnics with egg salad sandwiches, potato chips, and homemade blueberry pie. They would spread a blanket out in Valley Forge State Park where they ate their lunch and talked about how much they liked being together. Since their conversations lacked substance, they spent most of their time together kissing and sexually teasing one another.

They had been dating for six months when, after Pepper had one too many shots of whiskey, he forced himself on Valerie against her will during one of their usual make-out sessions. Valerie was devastated that he had stolen her virginity. When she found out she was pregnant with Emma, she threatened to tell the police that she had been raped by him if he left her.

When Pepper turned to his old high school shop teacher for advice, he told him in no uncertain terms, "Good men take care of things when they make mistakes. If it's true that what you did was a mistake then your only choice is to marry her and raise the child together."

Pepper's attraction to Valerie had always been a physical one and he had never planned on spending his whole life with her. But between his shop teacher's advice and her threat of lying to the police, he grudgingly agreed to stay with her. Pepper, for his part, was forced to work on an assembly line at the local auto factory in order to feed his new and unwanted family. Abandoning his friend and the dream of his own business made his heart heavy and filled him with bitterness.

By the time Emma was born, Pepper already resented the baby who, he firmly believed, had destroyed his dream and stolen his life. It was inevitable that she would never know a father's love. She only knew the man as a large and frightening creature she had to please at any cost. But no matter how hard she tried, she was never successful. She clung to the only option available to keep his violent temper at bay—obedience. It might, she hoped, help to lessen the intensity of the physical and emotional pain he caused her.

Despite her dismal circumstances, Emma was still a sweet-natured child, respectful toward everyone she met. People took to her easily, and those who knew her well sensed a deep sadness about her. They couldn't help being moved to pity. A beautiful girl, she seemed to have the perfect combination of her parents' good looks. Blessed with her mother's blond hair and her father's piercing green eyes, she was taller than most nine-year-olds, her height alone leading people to believe that she was older than she actually was. She worked hard every day to keep her spirit intact in the unhealthy, dysfunctional place she knew as "home." While her father abused her physically and emotionally, her mother constantly blamed her for Pepper's rotten temper. "The two of us were doing fine," Valerie would explain as if it were really true, "until you came along and ruined everything we had."

Three years younger than Emma, Gracie was an average-looking girl with curly black hair and deep-set brown eyes. Her nose, a bit too large for her long face, merely accentuated the thinness of her lips. Although far less attractive and more timid than her sister, Gracie was equally sweet-natured. The child's only asset in life was her sister, who acted as her protector and was the only one to stand between her and their heathen father. As Emma grew older, she often spared her younger sister from their father's beatings by pushing herself forward as a buffer. When Gracie was old enough to understand her sister's sacrifice, her emotions were set in turmoil between guilt and love.

The so-called Murphy family lived in a small home on Chain Street in Norristown, Pennsylvania. They lived largely on bare essentials; sometimes even those were lacking. Their row home was a run-down shack that appeared on the verge of collapse. The wood porch had rotted and its roof was supported by four-by-fours sloppily nailed in place to prevent it from crashing down. The floorboards creaked when walked on, their mushiness giving a bit beneath their feet.

Inside, the once white walls were yellowed from Pepper's chain-smoking. The long shag rugs were old and so matted down with overuse that their fibers felt perpetually soggy under their bare feet. The furniture was secondhand with pieces of foam peeking out from the ripped upholstery in several places. The absence of adequate lighting made their home feel like the inside of a cave; but for the glare of the small television that stood on a battered table, there was almost no light at all.

Valerie and Pepper earned so little money that putting food on the table took great effort. The family rarely owned anything new and relied on handouts that were offered at local churches. Of the little that the couple earned, a major chunk went toward supporting Pepper's addiction to booze. The financial strain that the couple lived under only brought more tension into the home. Pepper knew they were destined to be poor white trash and for this he despised his family.

Emma and Gracie were submerged in dreariness day after day. They didn't enjoy the small gestures of affection like most other children that didn't cost anything to give, like a hug or a tender pat on the back. With no relief from their dismal circumstances in sight, they clung to each other to save themselves from the misery that threatened to swallow them alive.

Chapter Four

O ver the next three years of Emma's life, Pepper's brutal beatings had become an almost daily occurrence. By the time she was twelve years old, Emma had suffered three concussions, two broken arms, three fractured ankles, and 250 stitches over her body. She bore several scars, all inflicted by her father, including the one on her left palm, a memento from the time he had held it forcibly against the hot burner of the stove when she was eight.

In that same period of time, Gracie had to be taken to the hospital twice. The first time was because she had left a dab of toothpaste in the bathroom sink. As a punishment Pepper bit the top of her hand until a deep purple bruise appeared. He was further annoyed with her when she wouldn't stop crying because of the throbbing pain he had caused. As she descended the stair case, with Pepper closely following, he kicked her down the last three steps breaking her ankle. Gracie's second visit to the hospital was to get stitches because he had shoved her into a wall face first with such force that her two front teeth tore through her lip. Other, less severe injuries sustained by Gracie and Emma were sneakily tended to by their mother.

Valerie was always ready with a stream of concocted explanations for the nurses and doctors who tended to her daughters' frequent injuries. She claimed that her girls were little tomboys who liked playing rough. A variation of that lie was her argument that their innate clumsiness led to "accidents." The most inventive fabrication of all was when Emma broke her ankle for the third time. Valerie insisted that the child had been playing dress-up and had fallen when she attempted to walk in her mother's high heels. Valerie never took the girls to the same hospital within the same year. She would drive for hours, when it was necessary, to bring them to a different hospital in order to harness their dirty little secret.

The daily violence that Emma endured seemed all too normal, no more than a routine part of her life—until the night that changed her forever. It was Christmas Eve and their father was drunk, as usual. "Embracing the yuletide spirit," he had slurred as he tried to coordinate his tangled feet into a celebratory dance. Their mother had made them TV dinners for supper and they sat in the living room, watching the blinking colored lights on their small aluminum Christmas tree. Nothing else mattered to the two little girls and for that night, at least, they were happy.

Once dinner was over, Valerie called her older daughter into the kitchen to help her clean the dishes.

"Emma," she told her, "this is going to be a great Christmas, so don't fuck it up. After we finish cleaning up here, I want you to take Gracie upstairs so the two of you can take a bath. Daddy's been drinking and I don't want anything to piss him off tonight. I'm looking to make this a great night for him and me, so don't fuck it up."

As instructed, Emma quietly led her sister upstairs and prepared for their bath. The two girls bathed together, splashing about in the water and chattering excitedly in anticipation of Santa's arrival. They were hopeful that Santa wouldn't skip their house again this year, as he had in previous years because they were "rotten little shits," as their father had put it.

When Emma and Gracie came out of the bathroom, they heard their father screaming and Valerie trying to calm him down. She didn't want to spend her time mending her daughter's wounds on Christmas Eve.

"Pepper, please!" they heard her beg, "It's Christmas Eve. Please, not tonight."

He yelled, "I don't give a shit what night it is! Get your ass out to the store and get me a six-pack of beer or someone is gonna get it!"

Emma knew that "someone" was her. It always had been.

Still wrapped in their towels, the girls heard Valerie leave the house. Frightened at being home alone with their sloshed father, they rushed into their bedroom. Emma quickly helped her sister into her pajamas. After getting dressed for bed herself, she drew Gracie into the closet and there the two children sat in tense silence, pretending to be invisible as they waited for their mother to come home. Just moments later, they heard the stamp of angry feet on the stairs. Both girls knew at once that it wasn't their mother.

Terrified, they clung to each other, the magic of Christmas Eve quickly fading away. Although they anticipated the inevitable, the girls couldn't suppress an audible gasp as the closet door abruptly swung open. Pepper stood there, scowling at them. His hair stood on end and his jaw was clenched so tight that the sharp angles of the bones below the skin's surface were clearly visible. Sensing her father's fury, Gracie peed on the floor in fright. Pepper grasped her by the arm and hauled her to her feet. She was so tiny and fragile that Emma feared he might break her in two pieces. Instinctively she held onto Gracie's other arm as their father tried to yank her younger sister out of the closet.

"Who do you think you are, pissing on my floor, you little brat?" Pepper yelled.

Seized by terror, Gracie screamed and sobbed, trying to break free of his grip.

Emma grasped her sister tightly around the waist in a desperate attempt to resist their father's efforts to drag them both out into the hallway. Having managed to have his way, Pepper paused as he reached the top of the stairs and stood staring at Gracie with revulsion.

Through her sobs, the little girl pleaded, "Please, Daddy, I'm sorry! I didn't mean to pee on the floor!"

Pepper looked at her, then at Emma. His eyes blazed with unadulterated rage. "I didn't mean to pee on the floor, Daddy!" he mimicked his younger child, distorting his voice to sound absurd and menacing. "Wah! Wah! Waaah!" He looked at Emma again. "The problem with the two of you is that you're spoiled rotten!"

With mounting dread at what their father might do to Gracie, Emma forgot herself. "Leave her alone!" she screamed at him. "I hate you! You're nothing but a stupid drunk! We both hate you!"

Temporarily oblivious to Gracie's presence and his urge to punish her, Pepper scurried over to his older daughter, clamped a hand on her thick blond hair, and dragged her down the steps. Without uttering another word, her father took her down to the basement. Then he turned on her quickly and punched her in the temple. She fell to the floor, half-conscious. Despite the pain she silently wondered what she had done to deserve the parents she had been given. Why had God let her be born if she wasn't wanted? No matter how well behaved she was, Pepper always found a reason to show how much he hated her. He continued to beat her until she was senseless, her mind enveloped by blackness.

When she came to an hour later, she found herself sitting on a damp dirt floor, stripped naked, her arms tied to a pole behind her back. After several moments, she realized where she was: in the center of their basement. She could hear rats scurrying around her in the dark. Her bare bottom was chilled by the damp dirt floor. She opened her mouth to scream, but her voice came out muffled. She had been gagged. Scared and utterly alone, she focused on her breathing. She tried to pretend she was at Mrs. Tisdale's making the apple pie she loved so much. But Emma's mind kept going back to the dark, hazy space where something had happened before she fell unconscious. What had happened to Gracie? Where was her mother? Did anyone know she was down here? Why was she naked?

Chapter Five

As her eyes became accustomed to the darkness, Emma noticed the slightest of movements in the corner of the basement. Then she saw a cigarette tip glow bright as Pepper took a long, hard drag from its other end. The short hair on her forearms stood on end as she watched him make his way over to the spot where she had been tied up. Without a word, he bent down and stubbed out the cigarette on his daughter's upper thigh. Emma flinched violently and reeled back as the hot ash seared her exposed flesh. Her father relit his cigarette and poked it into her flesh again. Only, this time, he targeted her right nipple. He repeated his version of torture again and again, choosing a different spot on his daughter's body to singe each time before he stopped.

Pepper threw the light switch on. The bulb, which hung from two wires, cast an eerie glow over everything. He turned to the sink that sat next to the washer and dryer that hadn't worked in over five years and pulled from it a bucket of cold water to which he added several capfuls of bleach. A second later, he flung the contents on Emma's body.

"Just a little solution to help with those burns you have there, you pathetic animal!" he screamed at her. "Haven't you learned yet that you should keep your fucking mouth shut? You want to be the fucking hero of this family? No problem! How's it feel to be the hero now? Huh? How's it feel to be the hero now?"

Having had his say, Pepper turned, his feet pounding on every step as his went upstairs, but not before shutting off the light and plunging Emma into darkness. She spent the remainder of Christmas Eve tied to the pole, wet and cold, the cigarette burns throbbing with an acidy pain as the bleach solution ravaged the raw wounds. Throughout the long, silent hours, the rats and bugs in the basement tormented her. She kept kicking out with her feet to keep them at bay, but by morning, she was no longer able to fight them off. Overpowered by sheer exhaustion, she drifted into an uneasy slumber.

It was noon when Pepper brought Gracie down to the basement with Valerie lagging behind.

"Gracie," he said menacingly, "take a good, long look at her. This is what will happen to you if you think about giving me any back talk."

Gracie's eyes welled up with tears and her face crumpled as her horrified gaze swept over the cigarette burns that freckled Emma's body. Her impulse was to run back up the stairs as she watched the large insects dancing on the open wounds, stopping only to take a nibble of her sister's burned tissue.

Emma drifted in and out of consciousness, but at one point, she looked to her mother for help. "Please, Mommy," she pleaded in a cracked voice, "please help me!"

Valerie silently turned away and headed back up the stairs, dragging Gracie with her.

Pepper sneered, "Remember who the boss is around here! This is nothing compared to what I can do to you!"

Bending down, he untied Emma's hands, forcefully pulling her limp body up the stairs, and left her lying on the floor in the middle of the living room. Shortly after one o'clock that afternoon, Valerie approached Pepper, who had just finished his Christmas lunch of two shots of cheap whiskey and three beers. "Pepper," she said hesitantly, "I'd like to take Emma upstairs, clean her up, and get her into bed. Can I have your permission to do that?"

Valerie was shrewd and always worked to keep Pepper on her good side. Besides, she was tired of having to step over Emma's lifeless body as she ran to the kitchen to fetch her husband his beer.

Pepper eyed her for several moments. His hesitation made sweat break out on Valerie's body. "Yeah," he finally said. "What the fuck! Given it's Christmas and all, I guess it's okay." Then he added threateningly, "Don't any of you bitches ever say I'm cruel! See what I'm letting you do for that little shit stain after what she said to me? Who the fuck does she think she is, calling me a drunk?"

"Of course you're not a drunk," Valerie said quickly, trying to appease him. "You're a good father and husband. Okay, Pepper? Now I'm gonna get her out of here so you don't have to look at her anymore. I wouldn't want our Christmas to be spoiled because of her."

With Gracie's help, Valerie quickly got Emma upstairs and put her into a warm bath. The piercing sting of the warm water and soap against her fresh burns made her jump, but her mother held her in the tub, rubbing each of the sores until they were raw.

"You need to be still, Emma," she stated coldly. "We have to get these wounds cleaned out. There were bugs and rats in the basement and we wouldn't want you to get an infection. I don't want to have to bring you to the hospital looking like this. Besides, that would really piss off your father."

Weak and broken though she was at that moment Emma couldn't help asking, "What really pisses you off, Mom? What else would he have to do to me to really piss you off?"

Valerie averted her gaze, ignoring her question, and rubbed harder at the open wounds, hoping the increased pain would make her daughter shut her filthy mouth. Emma was always trying to make her feel guilty. She hated that about her oldest daughter, among other things.

It was Gracie who broke the silence. "I'm sorry, Emma," she said in a voice just above a whisper. "I'm so sorry he did this to you. It was all my fault. If I hadn't peed on the floor, he would never have hurt you." Gracie reached into the water and hugged her big sister, whispering in her ear, "No one loves me like you do, Emma. I hate him too. I hate him just as much as you do."

After her bath, Emma dressed and settled into her bed, pulling the covers up over her head in a feeble attempt to block out the world. When dinner was over that night, Gracie came up to their bedroom, reached into her jeans pocket, and pulled out a crumbling slice of bread. She handed it to Emma. "I snuck this in my pocket for you."

Without a word Emma grabbed the bread from her sister's hand and gobbled it down. Afterward, Emma managed to give her sister a small smile. Gracie went into the bathroom and got a cup of water for her sister to drink. When she had finished the last drop, she turned to her frail baby sister.

"It's going to be all right, Gracie," she whispered reassuringly. "I'll figure something out. And it wasn't your fault. He's the one to blame for this, okay?"

Gracie nodded, tears of guilt rolling down her cheeks. Emma was the only one who was willing to protect her. Emma loved Gracie as fiercely as she hated her father, for instinct told the twelve-year-old that what had been done to her sister and her over the years was not only cruel but perverse. They had to escape.

Chapter Six

B y the time Christmas break was over and school started again, Emma's burns had healed enough to be barely noticeable. Emotionally, however, she was mentally damaged and still recovering from the torment her father had put her through in the basement.

Over time, the girl seemed to grow numb to all feeling toward her parents, except for the seed of animosity that had been sown years earlier and had blossomed into an intense hatred for them. She found herself slipping into a morbid frame of mind. She felt isolated from the rest of humanity, and each morning she woke disappointed that God had allowed her to live another day. She often sat on her bed, where Gracie played next to her, wondering what it was about her that made her father hate her so much. She searched for an answer that would make Pepper see that she was worth loving.

Emma still spent what precious free time she had with Mrs. Tisdale, often taking Gracie along with her so that she, too, could enjoy the comfort and love the old woman so generously provided them. Mrs. Tisdale continued to instill in Emma the courage to go on, and when the child mentioned her hatred for her father, she heard her out patiently. In her infinite wisdom, Mrs. Tisdale did not try to persuade Emma to love a man who caused her such grief just because he happened to be her father. Of course, Emma kept much of her suffering to herself. Had she divulged the gory details of all the cruelties inflicted on her, Mrs. Tisdale might have felt compelled to alert the authorities. Aware of this risk, Emma disclosed only as much information as was necessary to explain the fresh bruises on her body to a concerned Mrs. Tisdale.

During an unusually long winter, Emma came down with a violent case of the flu. The virus was going around school and most of the kids were affected. Annoyed that she had allowed herself to get sick, Pepper started picking on her as she lay in bed with nausea and high fever. Listening to his ranting, Emma was suddenly overcome by a wave of nausea and jumped off the bed, stumbling over her father as she made a run for the bathroom to vomit. She was just short of the toilet bowl when her insides heaved. Unable to hold back any longer, she puked all over the bathroom floor.

Furious with her, Pepper demanded she clean the mess immediately. Gracie tried to step in and clean up for her sister, but their father pushed her out of the doorway and warned her not to intervene. Pepper stepped inside the bathroom, grabbed Emma by the hair, and pushed her face toward the pile of warm, smelly vomit.

"If you don't clean it up, you dirty little scumbag," he snarled, "I'll make you lick this floor clean!"

Emma's hands slid in the vomit as she tried to back away. Losing the battle against her father's brute strength, her arms slipped out from under her. Her face slammed down onto the tile and into the pile of puke. She knew from the searing pain that shot up her nose that it was broken; the pain from the fracture was more intense now than her nausea. Blood streamed from her nose and into her mouth, its sour taste mingling with that of vomit and threatening to make her throw up again. In a panic, she lunged at a towel from the rack and began to wipe up the puke with it.

"Alright, Daddy," she whimpered. "I'll take care of this mess. I'm really sorry for being such a pig and throwing up on the floor. I swear it won't happen again. I'm just going to clean up the bathroom. Then I'll go downstairs and make you dinner. I swear, Daddy? Is that okay?" she crooned, trying to make her voice sound as sweet as possible in an attempt to get her father to back off.

Satisfied at having established that Emma understood his lack of tolerance for her illness, he turned to leave the bathroom. "Hurry up!" he snapped on his way out. "I'm hungry. You've played this sick card long enough!"

Once he was gone, Gracie quickly stepped into the bathroom to help her sister. "Emma, are you okay?" she whispered. "I think your nose is broken. I think you need to go to the hospital."

Emma shook her head. "No, Gracie, I'm fine," she told her. "I need to clean up here so I can go cook dinner. I don't want him getting more upset than he is already."

While Pepper had been brutalizing Emma, Valerie sat in her bedroom, polishing her toenails and brushing her long, silky hair. She was selfishly grateful for not being the target of his rage. Besides, she thought to herself, if Emma would just do what he wanted Pepper wouldn't have to beat her so often.

Chapter Seven

For Emma's thirteenth birthday, Mrs. Tisdale threw a small party for her after school. She invited Gracie, of course, along with her three sons, who were there more for the cake their mother had baked than for Emma. Nonetheless, they sang "Happy Birthday" and enjoyed big slices of the homemade chocolate cake that Mrs. Tisdale had lovingly decorated with chocolate icing and served with generous portions of vanilla ice cream. The girls were ecstatic; cake and ice cream weren't something they often had the pleasure of enjoying.

While Emma was happy that Mrs. Tisdale had thrown a party for her, she was just as disheartened that no one in her own family had thought of celebrating her birthday at home. Neither of her parents acknowledged her birthday in the morning before the girls left for school. Emma's birthday was always an annual reminder of how Pepper's dreams had been stolen from him and his life reduced to nothing.

At four thirty the two girls left Mrs. Tisdale's house so that Emma would have enough time to get dinner ready for her parents. She knew how intensely her father hated her birthdays and the foul mood he would be in anyway. She did not want to provoke him further by not being right on schedule.

When Pepper got home from work an hour later, Emma had dinner ready for him to eat. Walking into the kitchen, he growled, "What the fuck is that nasty smell? What the hell did you make for dinner?"

A defeated Emma replied, "I made spaghetti with Ragu sauce. Your favorite, Daddy."

"Who the hell said that's my favorite?" he roared. "It smells like shit in here! Now you're trying to serve me shit? It's bad enough that I have to work all day so that this family of gluttons can eat. When I come home, I want to eat something that I like."

It was becoming increasingly clear which way the evening would turn. Emma started to back away from him.

"But you always liked this meal before," she protested timidly. "I thought it was your favorite."

With a growl, Pepper stepped forward and struck her with the back of his hand. Emma staggered back from the impact of the blow. Her father turned to snatch up the pot of burning hot pasta from the stove, swung back around, and flung its contents at her.

"Now clean up this fucking mess and make me something decent to eat, you ungrateful little slob!" he snapped.

Gracie, who had been watching them from the doorway, rushed into the kitchen to help her sister, who was now covered in pasta and sauce. As she leaned over her, Pepper hauled her up by the back of her shirt and shoved her away roughly.

"You think you're any better?" he snarled at his younger daughter. "What the fuck do you do around here to earn your keep?"

Shaking off everything that had just happened to her, Emma sprang to her feet. She was determined to save her kid sister from the agony and humiliation she'd grown to accept as a part of her own life. Protecting Gracie was the only thing she had left that made her feel like a human being.

"Gracie, go upstairs and get washed up," she told her. "I'm going to cook something else for dinner. Go now!"

Annoyed that his older daughter had dared interfere in his mistreatment of her sister, Pepper grabbed Emma under the arm and began pulling her up the stairs to her bedroom.

"I'm sick and tired of you thinking that you can say and do whatever you want, you little whore!" he yelled. "It's high time I taught you a good lesson!" He continued to scream at her until he had worked himself into a tizzy, like a rabid dog foaming at the mouth. Then his animalistic urge took over. "Get undressed now!" he screamed, standing there, legs apart, watching her like a hawk.

By now Emma was familiar with the "rules." They were the same every time her father took her up to her bedroom to hand out "punishment." She took off all her clothes, just as he had demanded, and stood naked in front of him. Now that she was older, she was more conscious of her budding breasts and the small patch of pubic hair that had appeared over the last few months.

In the meantime, Pepper had removed his belt. As Emma looked on, he went to the bathroom and placed the leather under the open faucet until it was soaking wet. Waiting for him to come back into the bedroom, she was consumed with dread. She knew exactly what he was going to do to her and prayed for her own death before he came back into the room.

When Pepper returned, he ordered Emma to lie face down on the bed. Then he lifted his belt high into the air and brought it down with force across her bare back. The pain was unbearable as he whipped her mercilessly with the belt, the wet leather tearing through her young, tender flesh. The louder the groans that escaped through her gritted teeth, the more frenzied the nature of the lickings she got. The more her father beat her, the more his rage appeared to intensify. Nearly half an hour had passed when, exhausted from the effort of whipping her relentlessly, Pepper left the room.

This was a ritual that Emma had grown accustomed to. But this time, he had beaten her so long and hard, it had taken its toll, robbing her even of the tiny shred of humanity she had clung to so far.

Emma's back and legs were bloodied and raw as she lay on her bed crying. Then she heard him scream at her to go downstairs and cook dinner. When she put her clothes back on, the fabric clung to her wet wounds. With each movement she made, it seemed as if layers of skin were being torn from her body. Barely able to walk now, she hobbled past her mother, who stood at the top of the stairs, a mute witness, as usual, to the atrocities being perpetrated under her very nose.

Emma stopped for a brief moment and looked at Valerie with burning eyes. "If you were a real mother," she whispered, "you would at least try to stop him, but you don't. I hate you almost as much as I hate him, but you probably disgust me more."

Valerie stood there, irritated by her daughter's harsh words. Her eyes followed the girl limping down the stairs to cook the family dinner. She prayed that Emma wouldn't give Pepper any shit. Once again, her fear mounted of Pepper being sent to prison for killing his daughter. She couldn't bear the thought of losing her husband.

After Pepper had filled his belly and the dishes had been cleaned that night, Gracie followed her older sister up to the bathroom. She helped Emma get into the tub and gently washed the fresh wounds on her back.

Gracie had never seen her sister subjected to such brutality before. As she helped Emma into bed, she said, "I love you, Em. Someday we're going to leave this stupid house and never come back. We won't ever have to see either of them again."

Gracie's words played in Emma's mind as she tried to fall asleep. There was nothing she wanted more than to never see her parents again. She didn't know exactly how or when, but she believed that one day they would break loose of the shackles that held them to their parents.

Chapter Eight

The next day, Mrs. Tisdale saw Emma hobbling up the street after stepping off the school bus. Gracie was by her side. The girls walked in silence until they reached her.

"Child, why are you limpin' like that?" the old lady asked. "What's wrong whit cha?"

"Nothing's wrong, Mrs. Tisdale," Emma lied. "I fell down the steps last night and hurt myself. I'll be fine."

Mrs. Tisdale placed her large hands on her hefty round hips. "Don't you give me none of that crap!" she huffed indignantly. "Get yourself in my house right now! We need to have a little chat. Come on, Gracie! You comin' too."

The girls followed her inside and Mrs. Tisdale guided Emma to a chair.

"Now, let me take a look at those injuries of yours," she commanded. "I want to make sure everything is all right."

Emma tried to squirm her way out of the situation, but realized it would do no good. Resigned, she gave in and raised her shirt so the old woman could see what her father had done to her.

Mrs. Tisdale's breath caught in her throat. "What the fuck?" she said out loud, not meaning to. As she studied the zigzag of thick slashes, with blood and pus still seeping from her blistered skin, she couldn't help blurting out, "Sweet Jesus! What the hell did that man do to you?"

Emma began to cry. Her chest heaved with great sobs and then with a feeling of relief that someone other than Gracie had confirmed what a cruel father Pepper was to her.

Mrs. Tisdale turned her attention to Gracie. "What happened to her, child?" she asked. "You're telling me right now!"

In a voice strained with the fear that she had done something wrong, Gracie replied, "My father beat her because she made spaghetti for dinner. But Mrs. Tisdale, the last time Emma made spaghetti for dinner, he said it was his favorite meal. She didn't try to piss him off. It was her birthday and she was trying to keep him from getting mad," she finished, gasping through her sobs.

Mrs. Tisdale took Gracie in her arms. "It's all right, baby," she soothed. "We're gonna get Emma taken care of here. Need to be sure there ain't no infection in those cuts. Come on, now. You can help me."

Mrs. Tisdale had Emma lie down on her sofa as she gently bathed the wounds with soap and water. Then she went to the kitchen and came back holding a jar of honey.

Emma was startled. "Wha-what are you going to do with that?" she asked apprehensively.

"Don't cha worry none, child. See, this here is honey, and it's gonna do lots of good things for ya. It's gonna take away some of dat pain you have and take down that there swelling. It's like putting a seal over the top of your exposed flesh; it'll catch all the dirt and fibers from your shirt and keep those deep wounds moist while they heal. We'll need to put this on every day until that raw skin gets better. Okay, baby?"

Emma nodded. She trusted Mrs. Tisdale and believed she knew what she was doing. And she was grateful to have such a kind and caring person in her life. Maybe she wasn't so damned after all, Emma thought. She did have Mrs. Tisdale and Gracie in her life, didn't she? She just wanted to stay there forever, with both of them as her only family. And she longed for the day she would never have to see her parents again.

That night, after the girls were asleep, Mrs. Tisdale strode across the street and softly tapped on the Murphys' front door. Valerie was surprised to see her elderly neighbor standing outside when she opened the door. Mrs. Tisdale deliberately looked at Valerie from head to toe, as her expression turned to a slow simmer, finally locking eyes with her. Valerie found herself squirming under the old woman's judgmental gaze. At that precise moment, Pepper stepped up behind his wife.

"Yeah, what do ya need?" he asked gruffly.

"What I need is for you to keep your goddamn hands off that child of yours!" the old woman growled with all the ferociousness of a lioness protecting her cub. "She don't know I'm here and if I find out that you laid one finger on her because I came over here, you'll have to deal with my sons. You listen real good now. I want you to stop what you're doing to that poor child or I'll call the cops."

Pepper snorted, "Shut the fuck up, you old bat! No one tells me what to do with my own kids. Mind your own fucking business! I ain't afraid of you and those bastard children of yours. Get the hell off my porch before I call the cops! And stay the hell away from my kids!"

Pepper slammed the front door shut and walked into the living room.

"Valerie!" he yelled. "Bring me a fucking beer—and be quick about it!"

Valerie hurried off to the kitchen, boiling over with annoyance at Emma for having gone to their bitch neighbor and telling her all their personal business. She thought about waking her eldest daughter so that she could tell her what an idiot she was, but decided to stew on it some more and tell Emma in the morning.

Mrs. Tisdale kept the incident to herself, never telling her sons, but kept a closer eye on Emma and Gracie. It seemed to her as though Pepper Murphy didn't beat his older daughter after she had confronted him, for the child was more upbeat and happier. Emma's back was healing nicely and the honey treatments had worked like a charm. She and Gracie were spending an hour every day at Mrs. Tisdale's after school. The old woman gave them homemade cake or cookies she baked for them every morning. It was her own way of doing what she could to make the girls feel loved and wanted.

Chapter Nine

O ver the next three months, Pepper seemed to back off from beating his daughters. While he still slapped Emma around, he refrained from indulging in the brutal beatings she had come to dread, especially after Mrs. Tisdale had, unbeknownst to Emma, confronted him. She still hated her father with a passion, and the daily slaps and blows were an ever-present reminder to her of the evil spirit that had infested his heart, mind, and soul.

On the Tuesday before Christmas break, as the girls strolled down to Mrs. Tisdale's house from the school bus stop, Emma was surprised to not see her neighbor waiting on her porch for them as usual. She must be inside, she thought, busy getting a snack ready for us. The girls climbed the porch steps and knocked at her door. One of Mrs. Tisdale's sons answered it. He looked disheveled and lost.

"Is Mrs. Tisdale here?" Emma asked.

"No, Emma," was the reply. "My mama died last night in her sleep. She had a heart attack. The doctor said it was massive. She probably didn't see it coming."

Emma stared at him. She willed him to take back the words he'd just spoken. She wasn't prepared to lose the old woman. Rejecting the thought that Mrs. Tisdale was gone, she took a small step toward the front door, but the large man blocked her from entering. "No, baby. She's gone," he said gently, "Mama ain't here no more."

Emma's eyes fixed on his for several moments, and time stood perfectly still, then she dropped to her knees at his feet and burst into tears. She began to rock back and forth. She felt as though someone had reached down her throat and ripped out her heart. Gracie dropped next to her, and the young sisters clung to each other for a long time, feeling utterly lost, as if they had been orphaned. Finally Emma looked up at Mrs. Tisdale's son whose eyes also glistened with tears from the deep loss they all shared and feeling useless in his ability to ease their pain.

"Listen, girls," he said after composing himself, "I know things ain't right for you with your papa, but you need to stay strong. My mama tried to help you as best she could, but now it's up to you. Mama loved you a whole lot and she'd want you to be brave. Now go on home and do the best you can. Make my mama proud of you."

Then he stepped inside the house and gently closed the door, leaving the two girls drenched in sorrow. Emma felt a hollowness inside that she had never known before. Mrs. Tisdale had provided her with the courage to face her demon and now she was left to battle him alone. The emptiness in the pit of her stomach made her long for the comforting arms of the old woman who had stood by them through thick and thin. Emma's deep sadness filled every space inside of her as she realized that she had just lost the only person who loved her, apart from Gracie. In many ways, Mrs. Tisdale had been the mother she never had.

After slowly coming to her senses, Emma took Gracie by the hand and went home to start dinner. When their parents came home, Emma told them what had happened to Mrs. Tisdale.

"Decrepit old fool!" Pepper gurgled through a swig of beer. "I couldn't stand that old bat!" Then, as he noticed Emma's grief over their neighbor's death, her father started to laugh, loud and hard. The sound grated on Emma's nerves and made her want to stab him with the blunt butter knife she was holding.

"You brainless moron!" her father taunted her. "What, did you think that ancient hag was going to live forever and protect you from me?"

Disgusted by the words he had spewed, Emma couldn't help retorting, "How could you be so mean? She was the only person who ever cared about Gracie and me!"

The look of fury that came over her father's face prompted Emma to try and flee from the kitchen and race up to her bedroom. But Pepper was already blocking the doorway. Emma recognized the familiar evil look on her father's face. She suspected that with Mrs. Tisdale gone, things would go back to the way they had been earlier. As Pepper towered over her, she tried her best to stand tall against the bogeyman who threatened to destroy her. But her bravery was short-lived. His first blow was aimed at her temple.

She awoke a short while later on her bed, naked, face down, arms and legs tied to her bedposts.

Pepper waited until she was fully awake so that she could see him pull his belt from the bucket of water he had placed beside her bed. With each thrashing, he dipped the belt into the water, getting ready for the next lash. When he was done, he grabbed a handful of her long blond hair and hacked it off close to her head. She watched in a stupor as he scattered the strands across the room. As he finished, he sat on the floor next to her bed, breathing hard as he took several long swigs from his coveted bottle of vodka.

He wiped his mouth on his sleeve and struggled to his feet again. She watched as, swaying drunkenly, he began to move closer to her. When he was right next to her bed, Pepper unzipped his pants and stepped out of them. As he removed his boxers, her heart began to pound so hard in her chest she thought she, too, was having a heart attack. She considered calling out to Gracie for help, but stopped short, fearing that their father might harm her sister. Emma screamed in pain as Pepper climbed on top of her and raped her, his fingers digging roughly into the open flesh on her back. She knew her mother heard her screaming and had no hope that she would rescue her from the madman.

When he was done, Pepper rolled off the bed, got back into his clothes, and guzzled more vodka.

"You just remember who the boss is around here, girlie!" he warned. "You're a fucking little whore! All you care about is making men do whatever you want. Well, we'll see about that, you filthy pig!"

When he had left, Gracie snuck into their bedroom and untied her sister, who was in a state of shock and could barely speak. As the memory of what Pepper had just done to her plagued her thoughts, Emma raced over to the trashcan in the corner and vomited. Unaware of what had happened, Gracie looked at her, bewildered. She noticed that Emma's beautiful hair had been hacked off from the back of her head.

"What the fuck did he do to your hair?" she asked her sister. Then she saw the trail of blood running down the inside of Emma's legs. "Emma? Emma, what can I do? Oh, Emma, what did Daddy do to you?"

Emma remained silent. She had nothing to say and certainly didn't want Gracie to know what had just happened. She felt humiliated and afraid. To make matters worse, Mrs. Tisdale was now dead, leaving her on her own to face this fiend and his new form of torture. Her breathing became labored and she felt dizzy. She couldn't bring herself to believe what the devil had just done to her. Until that horrifying moment, Emma hadn't imagined her father could cause more trauma in her life than he already had. Now she knew there was no end in sight—unless she herself did something about it. But what could she do to stop him?

Chapter Ten

Mrs. Tisdale and Gracie were the only friends Emma had ever known. Partly because she was an outsider among her peers and worked to keep a low profile, but also because the other kids just didn't seem to like her. She wanted more than anything to have a friend her own age. She watched the other girls at school sharing their clothes and gossiping about which of the boys they liked. She longed for a relationship with someone she could laugh and share secrets with. Someone she could call her best friend.

Her classmates enjoyed tormenting her, because with her higher level of tolerance for bullying, acquired through the ordeals she endured at home, Emma seemed an easy target. The kids in her class picked on her because she wore all the wrong clothes and was socially inadequate. She sat by herself at lunch and was pummeled by morsels of food her schoolmates threw at her when the aides weren't looking. Eventually she started eating her lunch in the girls' bathroom. She locked herself in a stall and sat on the toilet seat, gobbling down whatever sparse meal she managed to bring to school.

As the months passed, Pepper's abuse escalated in new and different ways. Emma's detachment from the people around her grew. She felt it was taking forever for her to turn fourteen. Finally she did, and with her new birthday came a glimmer of hope. A woman and her daughter moved into Mrs. Tisdale's old house. Brianna and her mother, Pam, had moved to Chain Street from New York City. Emma was really excited at the opportunity of getting to know someone from a place like New York. To her, it seemed like another country.

Brianna was bold and sassy, to say the least. Although she was tiny, standing five feet tall and weighing just one hundred pounds, she wasn't afraid of anything and didn't take shit from anyone. Emma liked that about her. Brianna had brown hair that fell to her shoulders and brown eyes that seemed able to cut through all the bullshit in the world. She was a ballsy fourteen-year-old who had grown up in New York with an alcoholic mother who made her money selling her body. She had learned to defend herself against predators and to tolerate her mother, who stumbled through life, drowning herself in liquor with men who were willing to pay for sex. Other than that, Brianna's mother was harmless. In fact, Pam's lifestyle had put Brianna in a position of power in her own house.

Brianna took to Emma right away, partly because she was so enamored by her ways, but mostly because she connected with Emma on so many levels. Brianna, who was quick-witted and capable of losing her temper in less than a second, could tell there was trouble brewing inside of her new friend. It wasn't difficult to see; Emma looked the part—a torn-down, shattered girl.

They started eating lunch together at school. Emma was thrilled to have someone to sit with. After school, Emma and Gracie hung with Brianna at her house until it was time for Emma to go back across the street to Hell Central and cook for Satan and his wife. For Emma, being friends with Brianna was almost like having Mrs. Tisdale back again. She made Emma feel special. She said things that made her feel as if she wasn't the piece of shit her parents always told her she was. She made her feel normal.

A month after Brianna moved into Mrs. Tisdale's house, and after spending every free moment with her, Emma was granted her wish: she finally had a best friend.

After school one day, the two girls were sitting on the porch helping Gracie color in a poster board for a science project that was due the next day. Her crayons were in an old cigar box, stripped of their labels and broken into small pieces. The three of them were talking when Brianna lifted the blue crayon to her mouth and began scraping it against the inside of her lower teeth.

Emma looked on in horror. "What are you doing?" she said. "That's gross!"

Brianna laughed. "Oh yeah? Have you ever tried it? I think it tastes great!"

Emma thought it a little odd, but went back to her chatter, simply accepting her friend as someone different from anyone she'd ever known and glad that she lived across the street from her now.

As the two sisters lay in bed that night, Emma told Gracie, "I think Mrs. Tisdale sent Brianna to us. She's wild, isn't she? I like her a lot."

Gracie agreed with her, but deep inside, she was a little jealous that her sister liked another kid besides her. For the first time in her life, Emma had a friend and she basked in the fun they shared. The only thing that made their relationship uncomfortable for Emma was Brianna's acute insight into people. She kept asking Emma to explain every fresh bruise and scar that appeared on her body. Brianna suspected that Pepper was a big asshole, and only three months into her friendship with Emma, she had asked her, "So, Emma, what's up with the bruises and shit, man? What the fuck is goin' on?"

"Oh, I'm just clumsy, that's all," Emma had deflected somewhat weakly.

Brianna's annoyance had flared at the obvious lie. "You're not clumsy when you're with me," she declared. "How come you turn clumsy when you go home? Your father is a dick, isn't he?"

Relieved that her friend had opened the door for her to trash Pepper, Emma, trusting Brianna, began to tell her everything. "See these marks on my hand? That's where he pressed it down on a hot burner when I was eight. He has broken my bones so many times that I've lost count." Then she explained in detail the horrifying Christmas Eve when Pepper had left her in the basement. "All these dark round marks are from the cigarette burns he gave me," she explained, showing her arms and legs to Brianna. When she had finished, her friend sat back on the front step and looked at her.

"Who the fuck does your father think he is?" Brianna said indignantly. "You don't have to put up with that shit!" She quieted down as she considered the life Emma was living, physically and verbally abused by her father on a daily basis. A mother who blamed all of his violence on her two daughters, telling both of them that it was their fault their father beat them. She addressed Gracie next. "So does that motherfucker do all the same stuff to you?"

Gracie shook her head. "Not as much. Emma protects me. She gets him pissed off at her so he leaves me alone. Sometimes he beats me even after he beats Emma. My dad hurts me a lot, but he hurts Emma more. I don't know why my mom and dad hate us, but they do."

Brianna started to giggle. If the girls hadn't known her, they would have thought her reaction freakish. But that was Brianna—a young girl who marched to the beat of her own drum. Laughter was her way of releasing anxiety when her nerves got the better of her. While this coping mechanism might look inappropriate to outsiders, Emma and Gracie took no offense. They knew that Brianna was processing what she had learned and was scheming to find a way to help her friends get the freedom she believed they deserved.

Chapter Eleven

Now that the three girls had shared their stories, their bond grew stronger. The older girls kept Gracie close to them and Brianna became a second older sister to her. They had no friendships outside of the one they shared with each other. Emma knew Brianna wanted to have other friends; it would have been easy for her with the way the kids at school were always trying to get her attention.

Brianna snuck around school one day searching for Emma. When she finally found her she gushed about the party they had been invited to. "Yeah, Kelly, you know the one with the huge tits, she told me there's a party at some construction site. The Conshy Keg Kickers are having it."

"The Conshy Keg Kickers? What the fuck are they?" Emma asked, bewildered.

Brianna laughed. "They're kids from Conshohocken that drink kegs of beer. When a keg of beer is empty it's called kicked," she explained.

Emma watched Brianna with a confused look.

Brianna started to giggle at her friend. "What?"

Cocking her head to one side, Emma stated sarcastically, "So you've been living here for what? Two fucking minutes and we're invited to a party? I've lived here my whole pathetic life and none of these assholes have even talked to me."

Brianna's face lit up. "It's my charming personality. What? You don't see it? I'm adorable. Who wouldn't love me? Em, the only reason they're into me is because I'm new and I'm from New York. The kids at our school are such a bunch of dorks. You're way better than any of them."

When Saturday night arrived, Emma walked over to Brianna's house. "So we never talked about how we're going to get to this party," she stated.

"No worries, Em. I have everything covered. Come on, let's roll," Brianna responded, pulling her friend outside by the hand.

Brianna enjoyed the privilege of driving her mother's car, something she had done since she was thirteen years old. The girls got into the car and drove to the construction site where the Conshy Keg Kickers' party was being held. During the entire car ride Emma marveled at how well her friend could drive.

Emma was surprised to see several dozen kids milling around the dirt-covered site. The girls walked with intention up to the keg of beer and were approached by a pudgy teen. Her belly protruded beyond where her breasts stopped and all of her clothes looked tight and uncomfortable. "Two bucks if you wanna drink the beer."

The two girls looked down at the ground so they wouldn't laugh in her face. Brianna reached into her jeans and gave the girl four dollars. After she'd handed them each a cup and walked away, a boy approached. "We call her Two-Bucks Burkey. Her name is Daisy Burkey. She dates the old guy over there." He gestured to a man who looked to be in his early twenties. "He's the guy that buys the kegs. My name is Funky, by the way."

Brianna looked him over and Emma was as uninterested in him as she was in Two-Bucks Burkey. "Funky?" Brianna asked him, her tone clearly stating that it was a stupid name.

"Yeah, it's my nickname," he explained, feeling a little intimidated by the two good-looking chicks, "my real name is Francis."

"Yeah, well, whatever. We're just here to drink some beer. Isn't that guy a little old for Daisy?" Brianna pressed him.

Funky laughed. "Yeah, he's a little old, but hey, it works for the rest of us 'cause he's over twenty-one so he can get served."

"Oh," Brianna said, then looked over at Two-Bucks Burkey. "By the way, who the fuck names their kid Daisy?"

An awkward silence hung in the air. "Well, I'll catch you guys later." Funky offered.

As he walked away Brianna leaned in to Emma. "And who the fuck names their kid Francis? Oh, and the only thing that's 'funky' about him was his breath."

"Man, you are one tough bitch," Emma toyed. "I don't want to be on your bad side."

An hour after they'd arrived, while they were sitting on cinder blocks, they were approached by three teenage girls. "Hey, Brianna!" the popular girl sang.

The two girls were still giggling at a rude comment that Brianna had whispered to Emma about one of the boys standing near them. "Oh, hey, Kelly," Brianna shot back without the same excitement the girl had shown toward her.

"So, you brought Emma with you, huh?"

"Yep, looks like it," Brianna responded, her guard going up.

Kelly looked at her friends. "So, Emma, I didn't know that the white trash look was back in style," she remarked.

Brianna stood up abruptly. "Fuck off, Kelly! Since when did you become the fashion czar with your cheap Walmart jeans? What? You think you got fuckin' style? Or do you think because your tits are so big that it doesn't matter what you wear?"

Kelly stood stunned and looked to her friends for backup, but the girls looked away because they were afraid of Brianna. She was from New York, and because of this, all of the kids at school assumed that she belonged to a gang.

Emma gently placed her beer on the ground and stood. "Fuck you, Kelly. You and your stupid little friends are sickening."

Brianna shot Emma a quick smile. She liked that Emma was sticking up for herself. The group of girls walked away, retreating back to the boys who desperately wanted Kelly's attention.

"Let's kill these beers and get the fuck out of here," Brianna told her.

Emma was grateful that Brianna had stuck up for her. However, between her pent-up childhood anger and the beer she had drunk, she was on the verge of punching Kelly in the face. As they drove back to Chain Street, they vowed that was the last time they would go to a party thrown by a group of assholes from school.

Instead, on the weekends, after Pepper had left for the bar, the girls would pile into the car and cruise around Norristown. On several occasions, they drove to the Plymouth Meeting Mall, where Brianna taught Emma how to shoplift. They would leave Gracie on the bench outside the store, assuming she didn't know what they were up to, but she did. At other times, Brianna would stand outside seedy bars in the area, talking twenty-somethings into buying them a six-pack of beer with her undeniable charm. Then the girls would drive around, drinking their beers and singing along to familiar songs blaring on the radio. They were content in the world they shared together without outside interference.

On a hot Friday night in July, Emma and Brianna went out for a joy ride. Gracie didn't come along that night because Valerie had taken her to the church, where she and some of the women she worked with were meeting to play bingo. Gracie didn't mind. She didn't really care for the car rides and was petrified when Brianna solicited people to buy her and Emma beer. As usual, the girls hung outside a local bar until they were able to persuade someone to buy them a six-pack of Budweiser. Then they drove to Fairmount Park, where they drank their beer and talked about how much they hated school.

Inevitably, the talk veered to how much they hated Pepper. Emma constantly told Brianna how much she wanted him dead. Her friend clung to the idea, believing that a man like Pepper had no right to live. Alone, after her beatings, Emma fantasized about him being mugged and getting his throat slit. It got to the point where the only comfort she derived in her young life was from the thought of her father dying a cruel and unnatural death. Now that she had Brianna in her life, she wanted more than ever to escape him.

The beatings had continued for Emma and Gracie. Valerie continued turning a blind eye to her husband's treatment of their daughters, often accusing Emma of being too dramatic about how her husband treated them. Emma wondered if she could figure out a way to end this nightmare. How could she make Pepper suffer the way he made them suffer? She prayed for the answer.

When Emma got home that night, she walked into a shit storm. Gracie was alone, sitting on the kitchen floor and crying. She rushed over to her, not needing to ask why she was in that state. The kitchen had been torn apart and her sister's face was swollen and bruised. For the first time in her life, instead of hurrying to clean up the mess, Emma sat down next to her sister and held her while she cried.

Gracie finally looked up at her. "It was awful, Em. He came home early, right after we got back from bingo," she said. "We ran out of beer and he was really mad. He said it was my fault."

"Well, he's a fucking idiot, Gracie. He's a drunk and an awful father. What did Mom do? Walk upstairs?"

"Yeah," Gracie confirmed, "after she told me that I was a bitch for pissing him off."

Over the next fifteen minutes, Emma worked the whole story out of Gracie. Her sister and Valerie had come home and Pepper had lost his temper. When their mother saw how mad he was, she had scurried up to her bedroom like a slimy weasel, leaving Gracie to answer to her father. He began hitting his younger daughter with his fists. When that wasn't enough to appease his rage, he'd dragged her into the living room, taken off her shirt, and whipped her with an extension cord that had been left there from their cheap Christmas tree the year before. He pulled her into the kitchen using brute force and made her sit at the kitchen table while he tore the room apart, leaving her to clean up the mess as he stormed out of the house, heading for the bar.

"Let me see your back," Emma said gently.

Gracie lifted her shirt. Her bare back looked like a highway that had split off in a million directions—leaving the imprint of the plug belonging to the extension cord Pepper had beat her with. Emma picked up a jar of honey and took Gracie upstairs to tend to her cuts, just as Mrs. Tisdale had done for her.

After she had nursed her sister as best she could, she went downstairs and turned her attention to the kitchen. She began cleaning it up as quickly as possible, aware that the fucking bastard would be home any minute.

By the time Pepper came through the door shortly after two in the morning and fell asleep on the sofa, Gracie was in her bed, sleeping, and Emma was sitting next to her, feeding the hate she nursed in her heart for their father. She was increasingly firm in her conviction that one day she would escape him. No one, not even Brianna, understood the nature of the untamed beasts lurking in Emma's soul. Before she went to sleep each night, she prayed to God to kill her father. But He seemed deaf to her prayers and she knew it was ultimately up to her to ensure that her father paid for all the pain he had caused them.

The next day was just like any other in the house of horrors. Down in the kitchen that morning, while Emma was making breakfast for the beast, a rat scurried across the floor just in front of her feet. The girls were accustomed to small mice and bugs; it came with the territory, the neighborhood. However, this particular rat was as big as a cat. Emma screamed when she saw it and jumped up on a kitchen chair.

Pepper came thudding into the kitchen with Valerie following, infuriated that his sleep had been disturbed. When he saw the rat, which didn't seem scared of them at all, he grumbled, "Holy Christ! Where the fuck did that thing come from?" Grabbing the broom, he swung at it. The rat shuffled off under the kitchen door from where it had originally appeared.

Pepper turned on Emma, his favorite scapegoat. "If you weren't such a fucking pig and knew how to clean like a real woman, we wouldn't have this problem!" he yelled. "Now make my breakfast, will you? And when you're done, I want this place spotless. Then take your fat ass down to the grocery store and buy some rat poison, you fucking idiot!" He looked at Gracie, then back at Emma. "You two are useless! Now get moving!" he screamed sharply, making them both jump.

After breakfast, Emma scrubbed every inch of the kitchen. She emptied drawers and cabinets and rewashed clean bowls and dishes. She knew Pepper would inspect her work when she was done and also knew the consequences that awaited her if he found even a speck of dirt anywhere. While her father looked over her work, Valerie handed Emma a five-dollar bill and told her to run down to the grocery store for rat poison.

Emma knew she was leaving Gracie in a vulnerable situation alone upstairs in their room. She went upstairs to see her before she left and instructed her to stay in the bedroom and not to come out until she was back. She ran to the store as quickly as her feet would carry her. Pepper was impossible to satisfy and always found something to complain about. Emma was anxious to get back home in case he went after Gracie again. Her sister was so broken from the night before that Emma believed another beating might kill her. If it didn't kill her, it would most certainly leave permanent scars on her already swollen and bruised body. Having made it to the store, she quickly found the rat poison and hurried to the cashier to make her purchase. Then she sprinted back to the house.

She had been gone less than twenty minutes, but the moment Emma stepped through the front door she knew violence had erupted in her absence. The stillness in the house, combined with the smell of fear and anger, gripped all of her senses. She hurried into the kitchen and found Gracie unconscious on the floor. Blood oozed from her nose and mouth. Her eyes had fresh bruises, in addition to the ones inflicted on her the night before.

After checking for her sister's pulse and finding one, Emma went to see where the son of a bitch was. Unable to find him in the house, she went back to her sister. After cleaning the blood from Gracie's face, she brought her to the sofa and placed a bag of frozen peas over her swollen eyes.

"Stay here," Emma told the battered child. "Don't move. I'll take care of everything. I won't leave you again."

The kitchen was a wreck. All the work she had just finished had been undone in ten minutes of unchecked rage. From habit, Emma proceeded to do her normal clean-up. When she was through, she sat at the kitchen table and reaffirmed her deep hatred for her father. Noticing the rat poison on the kitchen counter, she got up and took it out of the bag. If she didn't use it, Pepper would subject either Gracie or her to another beating for not doing what he had ordered. As she removed the container from the bag, she noticed the skull and crossbones that accompanied the warning on the label. Underneath the image was the word, "TOXIC."

For the first time in her life, Emma felt a surge of pure power sweep over her. She read through all of the warnings on the label and grew more delighted by the minute. She knew then that God was finally answering her prayers. The information on the container warned that if ingested by humans, the poison could be fatal. Emma did a happy dance in her head for her newfound secret. She knew she had to be careful and not get ahead of herself; if she got caught by Pepper, he would surely kill her. It was difficult for her to contain her excitement and even more difficult not to tell Gracie or Brianna.

Hours later, Pepper came home, drunk and smelling of cheap whiskey. He demanded to know when dinner would be ready. In less than fifteen minutes, Emma told him. He grabbed her by the hair at the base of her neck, pulling her face close to his. "Did you take care of the rat poison like I told you to?" he growled.

Afraid that he would go after Gracie again, she answered, "Yes, Daddy. I placed the poison on both sides of the door so the rat doesn't come back."

He looked down to check and was satisfied at the sight of the thin line of white powder on the floor. Still grasping her hair in his hand, he snarled into her face, "If I see that thing in here again, you're going to be really sorry. Do you understand me?"

Emma nodded.

Just then Valerie walked in and slithered up to the beast. "Dinner is almost ready, Pepper," she crooned. "Let's get you washed up."

He turned and staggered out of the kitchen with Valerie following him. Emma took out four bowls. She filled three with the stew she had cooked and placed them on the table where she, Valerie, and Gracie sat. Then she filled her father's bowl. Emma set the bowl down on the counter, picked up the rat poison, and stirred in a heaping tablespoon of the lethal ingredients.

As she watched him eat his stew laced with the tasteless, odorless poison, Emma rejoiced in what was to come. She had never felt so good in her life. Adrenaline raced through her veins. She almost felt high. She was euphoric. Paybacks are a bitch, she thought to herself.

Chapter Twelve

O ver the next week, Emma fed her father large doses of rat poison every day. Slowly, he started showing signs that the poison was taking an effect on his body. It began with uncontrollable nosebleeds. Halfway into the second week, and to add to his horror, his gums began to bleed. By the end of the second week, Valerie mentioned her concern over his condition to Emma. Her mother had seen blood in his stool and was worried he might be really sick. When Valerie mumbled something about taking him to the doctor, Emma assured her that it was probably nothing more than a bad bug he had caught from somewhere. Valerie, always content to put herself first, relented. She didn't want to lose a day of pay to take him to the doctor, and Emma gave her the perfect reason to put up with her husband's "temporary" health condition.

During the first two weeks of Pepper's "illness," he rarely raised a hand to her; a few lame slaps was about all he could muster. He was lethargic and weak from bouts of dizziness and nausea. All the while, Emma quietly gloated over his misery, knowing that the stupid motherfucker hadn't suspected a thing. By the end of the third week, Pepper could no longer get out of bed. His body was shutting down, bit by painful bit. Considering how gravely ill the man was, anyone would have felt bad for him, particularly a daughter. But Emma didn't. He deserved everything he was getting and she wasn't going to stop until he was dead. The truth was, if she could have physically tortured him even more, she would have. But she didn't want to arouse any suspicions when they came to remove his dead body from the house.

After five weeks of ingesting the rat poison Emma's father died. That night was the happiest moment of her life. She and Brianna took two of his beers out onto the front porch to celebrate.

Emma raised her beer in the air. "Here's to people getting what they deserve!"

Brianna smiled brightly and they clanged beer cans and took a long swig.

The ambulance workers and the police who came to the house to take Pepper's body away didn't suspect any foul play. The police were unconcerned at his death. People in their neighborhood died all the time. The authorities had better things to worry about than the untimely death of a notorious drunk. Just to be certain that no doubts remained about the nature of her father's death, Emma pretended to console Gracie in the presence of the policeman who had been sent to their home. "We always knew that all the alcohol he drank would catch up to him some day," she said mournfully.

Her younger sister played along. In bed that night, Gracie asked her sister, "Why did Dad hate us? We never did anything to him."

Emma took her hand. "Dad hated himself because he was a total loser and he took it out on us. Dad was a dick."

The night of Pepper's funeral, Emma lay on her bed and relived the moments leading up to his slow and horrible death. She smiled broadly, remembering how good she had felt lacing his food with that amazing powder. Even toward the end, she had been slipping large doses of poison into his soup. She was truly proud of having killed her father. In her mind, she had killed her father to save herself and her sister from his sadistic behavior. She was finally free of the son of a bitch. He had beaten her unmercifully and now he was finally dead.

Valerie was sad and pitiful, which annoyed Emma. It made her sick that her mother was so self-centered that she had allowed him to do all those horrible things to Gracie and her, always blaming it on something that the girls did or didn't do. In her mind, Valerie was as much to blame for all the brutality in their life as Pepper.

With Pepper gone, Emma and Gracie began to lead a normal life. Emma spent most of her free time with her younger sister and Brianna, while Valerie hung out with the women from her workplace. Emma still hated her mother, but decided she could always be disposed of as easily as Pepper had been, if she tried to give her or Gracie any shit. The next year was peaceful for the sisters. Gracie even managed to make a couple of her own friends at school. The girls had become closer in the year after Pepper died. Mainly because Emma had more freedom to come and go as she pleased.

The year Emma and Brianna turned sixteen was exciting. They threw themselves a joint birthday party at Brianna's house. They invited Gracie and Pam. Valerie was excluded since she hadn't celebrated her daughter's birthday before. The party turned out to be a lot of fun and Pam bought two six-packs of beer and let the girls drink them until they threw up.

Brianna had grown into an attractive sixteen-year-old. She had a small face that suited her small, thin body well. Her brown hair hung in loose curls, which made her look exotic. Her brown eyes still had a mischievous glint to them, which Emma loved. She had a sweet smile, offset by her brazen personality.

Emma was five feet eight inches tall. She was thin, with full breasts. Her silky blond hair set off her emerald-green eyes and she had a perfect set of straight white teeth. Stunningly beautiful though she was, Emma remained blind to her own looks. The other kids in high school had tormented her so much that when she looked in the mirror, all she could see was ugly. Regardless of how they were treated by their peers in school, the girls loved the freedom they shared and enjoyed being teenagers. Gracie was now thirteen years old and quite the little social butterfly. It pleased Emma to see her so happy, and she felt vindicated for having committed murder to remove the thorn in their lives. She had done the right thing by killing her father.

Everything seemed perfect—until a quiet Saturday night, when Valerie brought home a man, she'd been secretly dating for six months. A man named Jake.

Chapter Thirteen

Jake was a dick from the start. When introduced to Emma, he took her hand on the pretext of shaking it and squeezed it a bit too tightly for her comfort, yammering all the while about how nice it was to finally meet "Valerie's girls." But it was the way he shook Gracie's hand, holding on to it for an uncomfortably long time, that made the little hairs on the back of Emma's neck stand on end. The moment her younger sister turned away to get Jake a beer at Valerie's insistence, Emma noticed the pervert checking out the thirteen-year-old. She suspected that Valerie had seen how he looked at Gracie with longing, but her mother gave no indication that she had caught on. Emma shot her a scornful look as Valerie nervously moved closer to Jake and put her arm through his.

Later that night, as the girls lay in bed, Emma told Gracie firmly, "You stay the fuck away from that asshole Jake. I didn't like the way he looked at you. Do you understand?"

Alarmed by her sister's gruff tone, Gracie immediately agreed to steer clear. "Emma, why does Mom have to let him sleep here tonight?" she inquired. "We just met him. What's wrong with her? When I grow up, I'll make sure I don't turn out like her. I'm going to be like you."

Emma rolled over and gathered her sister in her arms, holding her close. She couldn't sleep for most of the night, sensing that something bad was looming. Anger welled in the pit of her stomach. She didn't like Jake and intended telling her mother about her feelings in the morning. If Valerie wanted to date him, then fine. But Emma didn't want her bringing him home again.

The next morning, after Jake had left, she confronted her mother. "Why did you let Jake sleep here?" she asked. "This is our house! Haven't you put us through enough already?"

"Listen, Emma," Valerie retorted, "this is my house, not yours. I like Jake. He thinks I'm beautiful and sweet. He's also good to me. Do you have to be so mean about him? This is exactly why you always made your father angry. It's your bad attitude. You want everyone to feel sorry for you."

Emma shot back, aghast, her temper flaring. "You saw the way he checked out Gracie last night. Don't pretend you didn't! Get your fucking head out of the sand, Mom! You're a selfish woman. You helped Dad torture us. I'm sick of you!"

Valerie gasped. "What the hell are you saying, Emma? What does that mean? You know I had nothing to do with how your father treated you girls!" she argued.

Emma retorted, "Yeah, sure. You had nothing to do with it! That's why you locked yourself in your bedroom while your husband was hurting us! You're as much to blame as he is!"

Beyond irritated, Emma stormed out of the house and made her way across the street to find Brianna. She couldn't wait to tell Brianna about Jake. The two girls got into Pam's car and drove off so that they would have privacy.

"He's not even good-looking like my asshole father!" Emma snorted contemptuously. "Bri, you should have seen the way he checked out Gracie! I wanted to rip his fucking eyes out of his head! The problem is, my moron of a mother does whatever men want and just pretends everything is normal. She's always told me the shit my father did to me was my fault. God, I hate her!"

The negative energy emanating from Emma fueled her friend's anger. "Well, fuck him, Emma!" Brianna said. "If he dares try anything with Gracie, he'll wind up just like Pepper!"

Emma gaped at her friend in shock. She had never confided in Brianna about her role in Pepper's death.

Brianna broke the momentary silence. "I'm not an idiot, Em," she said quietly. "You told me what Pepper was doing to you. I also know how much you hated him for it. What I haven't figured out is how you did it. Doesn't matter, though, I'm just happy he's gone." She quickly added, "You need to do whatever it takes to be happy. And don't worry, I'll never tell anyone."

Emma believed her wholeheartedly, because she knew Brianna meant every word she uttered.

Within a week, Jake had moved in with them and taken over the house as though it belonged to him. A familiar pattern emerged. Within the first couple of weeks, he came home and asked Gracie when dinner would be ready the moment he walked through the door. Unluckily for him, Emma still cooked dinner for the family and she wasn't about to let her sister fall into the same trap as she had with Pepper. Jake was less demanding of Emma, because, she believed, he knew better than to fuck with her.

Despite how cautious he was with Emma, his pure dislike for Gracie led him to bully the young girl. There was something about her monotonous voice and her dreary, sluggish manner that just pissed him off. She lacked the spirit, the fire he saw in girls her age and Jake thought he could fix that right from the start. Pathetic as he found her, he also thought she had the potential to be an attractive little thing, if only she knew how to make the most of her charms. All he figured he had to do was get Emma on his side, like he had with Valerie. Then all these women would be his to command. Jake liked the idea—of being the man of the house.

Chapter Fourteen

A lmost two months to the day that Jake had moved in, he beat Gracie for the first time. Emma wasn't home, having stopped at Dunkin' Donuts on her way back from school to have a cup of coffee with Brianna. When she entered the house almost an hour behind schedule, Jake's voice reached her from upstairs.

"You're such a stupid girl!" she heard him yell. "When I tell you to come into the bathroom and do something for me, I expect you to do it promptly! Do you understand me?" There was the distinct sound of a slap, followed by another and yet another.

Emma raced up the stairs, taking them two at a time, until she had reached the bedroom she shared with Gracie. She shoved herself between her sister and Jake and screamed, "Don't you fucking touch her, you motherfucker! I'll fucking kill you if you do!"

Jake laughed heartily at her threat. "Shut the fuck up, slut!" he sneered. "I'll do whatever I want to in this house. You don't see your mother in here, putting her nose in where it doesn't belong, do you?"

"That's because my mother is a fucking cunt!" Emma retorted. "Now get out of our room!"

Jake strolled out slowly, still chuckling to himself, as if the girl had told him a really good joke.

Emma slammed the bedroom door behind him and ran over to Gracie. "What did he do to you?" she asked her sister anxiously. "What happened?"

The side of Gracie's face was red and swollen from Jake's slaps. "He was taking a bath and called me into the bathroom to wash his back," the younger girl explained. "And I said I didn't want to. I don't want to wash his disgusting back, Emma. Besides, he was naked. I just don't want to live here anymore! Can't we go live somewhere else?" Gracie begged, wanting to be as far away from Jake as possible.

Emma held her sister in her arms for a long time. Then she went over to Brianna's, taking Gracie along. She explained to her friend what had happened as they sat in the living room with a drunken Pam slouching nearby and mumbling incoherently, her slurred words running into each other.

By the time Emma finished her story, Brianna had put a comforting arm around Gracie. "Don't you worry, little sister," she soothed. "We'll protect you."

Feeling safer now that she was with Emma and Brianna, Gracie began to relax.

"Here's the deal," Brianna began, looking at Emma. "You and Gracie are going to live here with me and Pam." She looked over her shoulder at her mother. "RIGHT, PAM?" she hollered.

Brianna's mother looked at her. "Yeah, sure, Bri, whatever you want," she mumbled passively. "Just don't call me 'mom' in front of my johns. Otherwise they'll think I'm over the hill."

The girls already knew why Brianna had called her mother Pam from the time she was a small child. She had told them when they first met how Pam always lied to her clients about Brianna, claiming that the girl was the daughter of her dead sister. The motherless child, she explained, had no one else to take care of her and Pam had volunteered to take her in and raise her as her own. During one of the rare moments when she was sober, Pam had explained to Brianna that knowing she had a daughter would be a turn-off for her clients.

"Nobody wants to fuck an old lady," she had said matter-of-factly. "I was very young when you were born and I could probably pass you off as my sister, but we'll just tell them you're my orphaned niece. In fact, some of them might actually get turned on by my kindness and fantasize that they are fucking a real Florence Nightingale!"

Brianna's plan for her friends was finalized, and Emma and Gracie headed back across the street to pack some clothes. They found Jake at home, sprawled on a recliner he had brought from his apartment and placed in front of the television.

"Where the hell did you two go?" he demanded.

"None of your fucking business!" Emma shot back. "You don't belong here. This is our house. So if you're staying, we're leaving. Fucking asshole," Emma mumbled as she turned to walk away from him.

Jake sprang up from his chair, grabbed hold of her neck, and jacked her up against the living room wall.

"Who the fuck are you talking to like that?" he snarled. "I'm the man of this house, sugar bottom. You might talk to your mom like that, but there ain't no snot-nosed little bitch gonna talk to me that way!"

He looked over at Gracie, who was mortified as she watched the horrors that were unfolding. "And what the fuck are you looking at?" he barked at her.

Emma kept silent, pushed him off her, and led her sister upstairs. While they were in their room, stuffing their clothes into a grocery bag, Valerie walked in.

"What's going on, girls?" she snapped. "Where do you think you're going?"

"Since you insist on having that asshole live here," Emma told her, "we're leaving. You may want to live with that toxic prick, but we don't have to. We're going to stay at Brianna's. Her mom's fine with it."

"Actually, Emma, you're not leaving," Valerie said authoritatively. "You are not old enough to live on your own, and even if you were, you would definitely have no right to take Gracie with you. So settle down and stop being such a drama queen. Haven't you caused enough trouble for this family already? It's always about you, Emma! It was the same way with your father. You just don't know when to stop. Do you?"

Emma couldn't believe her ears. She was convinced now that her mother was the bride of Satan. "My God," Emma grunted, "you're fucking delusional! Seriously, Mom, you're as far from reality as anyone can be. You're living in some fantasy world that you made up. What the hell is wrong with you? We hated Dad! He was a total dickhead that beat us for no good reason."

Valerie chose to ignore her accusations. Instead, she warned her older daughter a second time against leaving home. Emma disregarded her as she finished packing their clothes. As the girls made their way for the door, Valerie moved to block it. Emma forced her way past her mother, holding fast to Gracie's hand.

"Really, Mom," was her parting shot, "you are a sorry excuse of a person!"

The moment they were out of the house, Jake confronted Valerie upstairs in her bedroom.

"What's your problem, woman?" he sneered. "You just let your kids shit all over you!"

He inched closer to her, making Valerie uneasy. Then, taking her by surprise, he backhanded her, sending her crashing to the floor. The moment she was down, he pounced on top of her.

"You dense half-wit!" he yelled, punching her in the face and upper torso. "I uprooted my whole life to come and live here with you and those rotten kids of yours! I did it so that I could have a real family. And now you've gone and chased them away!" Grasping a fistful of her hair, he yanked her head up and banged it on the floor. "You get those two back here tomorrow or you'll see how ugly I can be!" he ranted through clenched teeth.

Valerie lay still on the floor. It was the first time any man had ever hit her so hard. She didn't like it, but she didn't know what to do about it. She waited until morning to give Jake time to calm down. Then she called 911 and reported her children missing.

"I know where they are," she said to the person who answered her call. "They're living with a prostitute across the street. It's my older daughter that's to blame. She took my younger one along with her. I need you to send an officer over right now, so he can help me bring them back."

Valerie hung up the phone and walked into the bathroom to cover her fresh bruises with makeup before the police arrived. Jake had reminded her that all the guys on the Norristown Police Force were his friends and he wanted her to make a good first impression. As she slathered on makeup, she thought, this will never happen again. My daughters will come home and give Jake whatever he wants. He will love me again.

Chapter Fifteen

Within thirty minutes, the police were knocking at Brianna's door. Roused from sleep and only half-awake, she opened it and stopped short. Her eyes widened with shock when she saw the police standing on the porch.

Pam hurried up to the door and peered out from behind her daughter. "Yes, Officer," she said politely to the first man, "how can I help you?"

The larger of the two officers sized them up before answering, "We received a call that two young girls from the house across the street are staying with you. Is that true?"

Pam looked at Brianna questioningly. Shit-faced drunk the night before, she had no recollection of who the hell was still sleeping in her own bed. She had no idea if one of her daughter's friends had slept over.

"Yeah, Emma and Gracie are here," Brianna acknowledged. "Why?"

"Well, they have been reported as runaways. We want to come in and talk to them," the officer said with authority.

By then the two sisters had come out into the hallway that led to the front door. The moment she saw the police, Emma realized that Jake had bullied her spineless mother into calling them. Putting a protective arm around Gracie, she led her into the living room with the policemen following.

"You're Emma and Gracie, right?" the burly officer asked.

"Yeah, that's us," Emma replied in a voice that did not hide her resentment.

"Your mother has reported you missing," the officer told her. "In fact, she said you were a runaway and that you had taken Gracie with you. I want you to understand that's considered kidnapping. Now, I doubt your mom would press charges, but I hope you recognize the gravity of the situation.

What you did was very wrong and could invite serious repercussions. Can you tell us why you ran away from home last night?"

Emma was unfazed by the officer's threats. "Well, let's see," she said coolly. "My mother is a piece of shit who lets the men in her life beat us up and then tells us it's our fault. Oh, and right now, she has a man living with us who is a complete asshole. He's trying to take over our lives. Let's see, what else?" Emma did not hide her sarcasm as she tapped her fingers on her forehead. "Yes, he's a big dick who likes to pick on little girls. I think that about sums it up."

The officers were not amused by Emma's cocky performance. They were used to tearful stories that emphasized the helplessness of the victims being questioned. This young girl seemed far from vulnerable and her rebellious stance failed to gain any sympathy from the two men. The impression they gleaned of Emma was that of a smartass troublemaker. The officers stood and firmly escorted the girls back across the street to their house.

Jake stepped out onto the porch when he answered the door and saw his friends.

"Ed, how are you, buddy?" he called out to the burly officer. Turning to Ed's colleague, he said, "Mack, how's it going?" He shook hands with both men.

Valerie stood in the doorway in full view of the officers, acting the role of the worried mother, but more concerned that Ed and Mack should notice how beautiful Jake's girlfriend was.

"We're doing good, Jake," the officers replied. "I guess you know that your girl Valerie here called about her daughters. We're assuming she won't press kidnapping charges against the older one."

The girls pushed past Valerie and went into the house without another word. Their mother quickly followed them in, after Jake gave her a look that said, "Scram!"

Alone with the officers, Jake tried to act nonchalant. "Nah!" he said. "Valerie just wanted to give Emma a good scare. She's a handful, that one."

Ed laughed. "Yeah, she has quite the mouth on her! She was swearing up a storm over there!" Then his expression became serious as he leaned in closer to Jake. "Listen," he said, "I think you need to sit those two down and have a serious talk with them. Going by our conversation with the older one, it seems to us that she isn't too fond of her mother. You know how teenage girls and their mothers can get! I'm sure you can help them straighten this mess out. They're lucky to have you here, pal! Good luck to ya, Jake."

When the police car had pulled away, Jake went back inside. Emma and Gracie were sitting on the old sofa, just as Valerie had instructed them to. Jake stood before them with a mean, twisted smile plastered across his face.

"Yeah," he said, "you're pretty stupid for trying to be so smart. You never asked me what I did for a living, did you? I work for a counseling service and deal with juvenile delinquents. So I know all the police around here. They know what a great guy I am, and thanks to your big, fucking mouth, Emma, they now know what a handful you are for your mom and me. We decided not to bring kidnapping charges against you, but if you push us, we can change our minds and put your sorry ass in jail." He leaned in really close to Emma. "You got that, sugar bottom?" he said in a stage whisper. "It means you would be locked up and we would be here to take care of Gracie all by ourselves."

Emma swallowed the rebuttal rising in her throat. She didn't want to push him, not now. She had to consider her sister first. The time would come when she could make things right again. For now, she would go along with his game. He had shown her his hand. He wanted to provoke her into fighting with him over Gracie. The anticipation of friction gave him as much sadistic pleasure as his assumption that, given the odds stacked against Emma, he would emerge victorious. The thought of the ensuing stress and chaos warmed him. So did the excitement of the hunt. Well, Emma was ready for battle. Jake was a piece of trash and she would throw him out of their lives the way she would any other garbage. As for Valerie, well, she was another story altogether and Emma would deal with her in a different way.

Chapter Sixteen

Over the next several weeks, the girls were forbidden to go over to Brianna's. They had to come straight home from school, but Emma talked to her friend every day in school anyway. On a few occasions, they ditched classes and hung out at a local pool hall. They shot a few games, but mostly they obsessed about how to get Jake out of the picture.

The man hadn't hit Gracie again since the night the two sisters had walked out, but he had shoved her around a lot. Each time, Emma had stepped in and stopped him, but she didn't know how long it would be before he got to her little sister again. It was impossible for her to be with Gracie every minute of the day, but she tried her best. Jake had also started drinking in the house. While he was nowhere near the raging alcoholic that Pepper had been, he did drink every day, and Emma had noticed that he couldn't really handle his liquor. When he drank, he lost control of himself and staggered around the house, half-cocked, before falling asleep on the sofa.

One night, having polished off a pint of whiskey, he lay on the sofa, snoring and emitting strange animal sounds. As she observed him, it dawned on Emma that she had found his weakness. She tucked the information into the back of her mind to be used later if she needed to. As long as he kept his hands off the two of them, she would stand down, she decided, but the minute he caused them any harm, she would make sure he paid for it.

Three weeks later, Jake told Emma before he left for work, "Your punishment is done today. Let me warn you that you better keep yourself out of trouble, sugar bottom. If you don't, you may find yourself locked up. Now Gracie, on the other hand: who would ever lock her up, innocent and naïve as she is? Mind your business and keep your fucking mouth shut! Understand?"

Emma smiled at him tauntingly and hissed, "Fuck you, Jake!"

He cackled scornfully and was still laughing as he left the house and went off to his job that involved "helping" children.

When Jake arrived home that night, the girls were setting the table for dinner. He sat down in his usual chair and gawked at them as they scurried around the kitchen. He liked his new home, which he could enjoy thanks to his beautiful, stupid girlfriend. He liked thinking dirty things about the girls. His mind lingered on Emma as he imagined her giving him a rough ride on that long, lean body of hers. While Gracie, with her overwhelming fear of him, turned him on so much, he had to keep fucking Valerie to prevent his balls from exploding. The woman wasn't a half-bad-looking broad either, but compared to the promise her two young daughters held, she was nothing.

After dinner that night, Emma scooted over to Brianna's house and Gracie went up to their bedroom to finish reading a book for a report she was doing at school. Emma had only intended to be gone for half an hour or so, since she and Brianna were pulling their money together—what little they had—to buy fake IDs from a kid at school. With their counterfeit IDs, they could buy their own beer and get past the bouncers at night clubs. Emma was surprised when she looked at the clock on Brianna's nightstand and realized that she had been at her friend's place for almost three hours.

When she hurried home and walked through the front door, Valerie was sitting on the sofa alone, staring into space. She looked startled when Emma asked her where Gracie was.

"Well, um, Jake took her out to get ice cream," Valerie stuttered. "They've only been gone a short while. I'm sure they'll be back soon."

No sooner had the words left her lips, Jake walked in through the front door. Gracie was not with him.

"Where is Gracie?" Emma demanded.

Jake sized her up, obviously amused by her outburst. "Little bitch ran off," he said casually. "I took her to buy ice cream. She was sitting at the table, and when I came back from getting our stuff, she was gone. I looked for her, but I couldn't find her. I figure when she gets hungry enough, the little whiner will come home."

Emma made the mistake at that moment of taking a swing at Jake. He dodged her fist and landed a powerful punch on her nose. Blood splattered everywhere. She remembered then, in that one moment, all the physical pain she had endured at the receiving end of Pepper's hands. She reached up and grasped Jake's hair, holding onto it as if for dear life. He lunged at her breasts and grabbed them, pinching the flesh so hard the pain forced her to release his hair. When she was able to focus again, she charged at him. In one swift motion, he punched her in the throat.

Emma was down for the count. She lay on the floor gasping for breath, fearing that Jake had broken something and she would suffocate to death. Slowly, she began to feel air entering her lungs and eventually she was able to sit upright on the floor.

Jake had been sitting in his chair the whole time, watching her. While the scuffle was on, Valerie had turned on the television to divert her attention from what was happening right in front of her.

When Emma was finally able to get up, she walked over to Jake. Although she was barely able to force the words through the insane pain in her throat, she managed to say, "I want to know where she is, Jake. If you don't tell me, I'll call the police."

Jake handed her the phone with a leisurely gesture. "Go ahead," he challenged with winning confidence. "Call the police and see if I care. It's not like they would believe you over me anyway. Let's not forget that I happen to know them well. Besides, with that scene you made with them a while ago, shooting off that filthy mouth of yours, they'll just think you're being a troublemaker. Better yet, maybe I'll just tell them that you left with Gracie and I'm concerned that you have her hidden somewhere. Yeah, they would believe that. You did kidnap her earlier and we didn't press charges, remember?"

Defeated, Emma turned and went up to her bedroom. She sat on the edge of her bed and cried for a long time. She thought about Gracie and how dumb she had been to leave her sister at home with her obnoxious mother. Why had she done that? If only she had kept track of the time! The self-accusations went round and round in her mind, tormenting her endlessly. The regret that gripped her was relentless. If only she could turn back time. Just this once.

Early the next morning, not being able to resist sleep anymore, she drifted off. In her dreams Gracie was calling to her, asking Emma for help, but there was something between them, something that Emma couldn't get through to reach her. She woke suddenly with her heart thudding in her chest. She had an unnerving sense of doom. Emma needed a plan to find Gracie. She needed it now before it was too late!

Chapter Seventeen

E mma heard the front door shut and knew that Jake had left for work. She ran into her mother's room.

"Where's Gracie, Mom?" she asked frantically. "What did that motherfucker do to her? What did you let him do to her?"

"Emma, do you have to be so melodramatic about every little thing?" Valerie said casually. "Calm down. I'm sure she'll come home soon. Besides, Jake's in a very good mood today and I don't want you spoiling it all with your big mouth."

Emma lunged forward, seized the neck of her mother's nightgown, and backed her into the closet door. "Let me tell you something, you worthless piece of shit!" she hissed through gritted teeth. "Thanks to all the shit I've put up with in this house while you stood watching silently, I have perfected the art of hating. If anything happens to Gracie, I will make sure that you suffer more than you could ever imagine. See these bruises on my neck? This was where your boyfriend punched me last night while you sat five feet away and pretended that it wasn't happening. These will seem like nothing compared to what I do to you. Someday I will get even with you for being such a lousy, nasty, stupid person."

Clearly frightened by her daughter's threats, Valerie retreated into her own little make-believe world, where nothing unpleasant ever happened to her. Speaking like the victim of a crime, she said softly, "It saddens me to see that you have become such a mean person. I am your mother, after all, Emma. Sometimes I think you're just jealous because I always have men in my life that love me. You seem to provoke anger in men because of how you act. Maybe if you took a little more time to make yourself look nice, you could find a boyfriend too. It might be good for you."

Realizing once again that she was wasting her time talking to a complete idiot, Emma swung around and left the room. She had real things to worry about, like finding Gracie. She quickly dressed and left for Brianna's.

The moment her friend opened the door, she knew something was wrong. "What the hell happened, Emma?" she asked. "What's wrong?" Then she said jokingly, "You look like someone just killed your best friend, but since I'm standing right here..."

Emma cut her short. "Gracie is gone, Bri! Jake claims he took her out for ice cream and she ran off. You know she would never willingly go anywhere with him alone. She was scared to death of him. I never should've left her there alone."

As her face crumpled and she gave in to her pent-up emotions, Brianna wrapped her arms around her. "It'll be all right, Em," she said soothingly. "We'll find her. Don't you worry. We'll find her. I'll get dressed and we'll take my mom's car and go look for her."

Within ten minutes, the two girls were in Pam's car and on their way to find Gracie.

"Where did he take her for ice cream?" Brianna asked.

Emma's mind was racing. "We only ever go to Joe's Water Ice on Johnson Highway, the one with the picnic tables outside."

The two girls drove for hours, looking for Gracie. They went to the local malls, delis, and other places where a thirteen-year-old might seek refuge. There was no sign that Gracie had been at any of those places. They talked to a couple of Gracie's friends, who said she had been in school on Thursday, but that was apparently the last time they saw her.

The next day Emma and Brianna drove over to Elmwood Park Zoo. Many of the teenagers from Gracie's school hung out there, and the girls hoped to gather information from them that might help them find her. They walked around talking to all the teens they came across. Some of them knew Gracie, but no one had seen her since school on Thursday. She had been missing for thirty-six hours now and Emma was on the verge of panic. All kinds of morbid thoughts took shape in her imagination: what if Jake had killed Gracie and dumped her body somewhere? What if he had her locked up somewhere and was torturing her?

Disappointed that their efforts had provided no useful information, Emma and Brianna drove home. Emma stepped out of the car and blasted her way through the front door. She found her mother slouched on the living room sofa, watching a rerun of some stupid reality TV show.

"Mom," she said firmly, "you need to call the police. Gracie has been missing for almost two days now."

"Emma," Valerie said, annoyed at being disturbed and letting it show in the tinge of exasperation with which she enunciated her name, "Gracie will come home when she's ready. I mean, really, don't you think you're over-the-top with all of this? I can't call the police about her yet, because they won't let you file a missing person report until a person is missing for forty-eight hours. That's on TV all the time."

Emma nearly imploded. "She's a thirteen-year-old kid, Mom! So I'm pretty sure you don't have to wait for forty-eight hours before informing the police. Or don't you care? Are you really so self-absorbed that you don't care about your daughter missing for days? What's wrong with you? You sent her off with that asshole, Jake, and he didn't bring her back home. Did it never occur to you to consider what the fuck he might have done to her? Or do you already know what he's done to her?" Emma ranted hysterically.

Had Emma blinked, she might have missed the familiar expression of forced denial that crossed her mother's face for a fleeting moment. Far more perceptive than Valerie, she knew right away that her mother held the secret, but Emma pretended not to notice. She was confident that she could yank the truth out of her mother, but held back, fearing Valerie would tell Jake and jeopardize her chances of finding Gracie. That was her mother, Emma thought, a completely self-centered cuntress.

Emma ran across the street to Brianna's again, leaving her pathetic mother to watch her equally pathetic reality TV show. She needed a plan to find Gracie.

"Is she home yet?" Brianna asked the moment she opened the door.

"No," Emma sighed. "My brainless mother won't call the police either. I was about to call them myself when I freaked out on her. I asked her if she knew what Jake had done to Gracie and she said no. But I can tell she was holding back something. I'm taking that as a sign that Gracie is still alive. I need a plan that will force Jake to tell me where Gracie is."

Brianna smiled slyly. "Oh yeah? What kind of plan?"

"Bri, I need to seduce him so that he'll tell me about Gracie. He's such a perv he would jump at the chance to have sex with me. The other thing is he can't handle his alcohol. So if I can convince him that I want to have sex with him and get him drunk first, I can get him to tell me where Gracie is. After that, he'll pass out and that will be that."

Brianna giggled, "I'm in! When?"

"We can't wait any longer. It has to be tonight," Emma stated with a sense of urgency that, for the first time, made Brianna feel scared.

Chapter Eighteen

E mma went home and showered. Then she waited tensely in her bedroom. She knew that Jake always came home right after lunch on Saturdays. It was his day to check on his young clients and their parents. Sometime later, she heard the front door open. Jake had returned. As he closed the door and started up the stairs, Emma's stomach began to twist in anticipation of what she was about to do. She opened the door of her bedroom and stood leaning against the jamb. As Jake reached the top of the stairs, he glanced at her.

Emma smiled at him sweetly. "What's up, Jake?" she asked in the sexiest voice she could muster.

"What's it to you?" he said sullenly. "I'm gonna take a bath." Then a small smile played on his lips. "Did you find Gracie?"

Emma resisted the urge to lunge at him and rip his fucking head off, but with the greatest difficulty, she kept her contempt for him from showing through.

"No," she answered, trying to keep her tone even, "I guess she must have run off and is hiding at a friend's house. I'm kind of pissed off that she hasn't called me. I figure she'll come home when she's ready."

Jake was visibly amused over all the chaos he had caused. "Maybe you'll learn to believe me from now on when I tell you something," he quipped. "She's a typical thirteen-year-old. I deal with this shit all the time."

He went into Valerie's bedroom and Emma could see him starting to undress. When he came into the hallway again on his way to take a bath, he was wearing nothing but his boxers. Emma scrutinized his revolting body. He was covered in hair from neck to navel. His bloated belly made him look as if he were six months pregnant. His arms had lost their tone, but were thick and bulging, mainly because of his excess weight. When he turned away from her to enter the bathroom, Emma almost threw up at the sight of the hair that covered his back like a furry rug. She held herself together, wondering if she could execute her plan without the small amount of food she had managed to eat that day rising up her gorge and splattering all over him.

Jake had left the bathroom door ajar, just enough for Emma to see what he was doing. She saw him drop his boxers and step into the tub. She paused at the top of the stairs, alert to every little sound. When she heard the television blaring Valerie's mindless entertainment, she moved into action. She slipped into the bathroom and looked down at Jake.

"What the fuck!" he said, startled. "Get the fuck out!" Then his lips twisted in a clever smirk. "Unless, of course, you want to join me!"

"Shhh!" she hissed softly, putting her finger to her lips. "I don't want my mother to hear us. I was just wondering if you needed me to wash your back." She knelt down at the tub next to him, took the washcloth gently from his hand, and lathered it with soap. With tender movements, she rubbed the rag through the tangled nest of hair crawling over his back.

Emma was relieved that Jake wasn't suspicious of her sudden change in behavior toward him. Being the perverted pedophile that Jake was, his lust for the beautiful teenager overcame any common sense that he was born with.

"You know, Jake, maybe I've been harsh," she whispered. "I mean, maybe you're not such a bad guy."

Then she leaned in and kissed him on his neck, running her tongue softly over his folds of fat. She reached into the water and ran her hand over his man boobs. Quickly aroused, he reached up her shirt, his damp fingers crawling like slugs under her bra, and fondled her breast. The feel of his hand on her flesh was so revolting, Emma thought she could probably drown him right there. Her hatred for him was so intense that she had to fight it back so as not to ruin her plan.

"Jake, not here," she protested faintly, "my mom is downstairs. How about if we meet up tonight at the George Washington Motor Lodge in Norristown? You get us a room. I'll meet you there around nine o'clock. Meet me out back by the pool and you can take me up to the room. Okay?"

So aroused he could barely think straight, Jake readily agreed. He reached up and pulled her head down to his. Closing his eyes, he opened his mouth to kiss her. She hesitated and he quickly opened his eyes.

"I've been waiting to have you since the day we met," he confessed.

Emma smiled thinly. She needed to keep her composure. She needed to find Gracie.

"It's just that I've never been with a man before, Jake," she said, pretending to be bashful.

"Oh, baby, it's gonna be so fucking good!" he promised her. "I'll make you feel like you've never felt before."

Then he pulled her to him again and they kissed, his tongue plunging into her mouth with such raw force she thought she would suffocate and die. But she forced herself to play the game, using her so-called virginity, which Pepper had stolen years ago, as the excuse for the slight resistance on her part.

Emma pulled away from the kiss and stood. "Well then, it's all set," she said. "We'll meet tonight at the pool. But Jake, please remember I've never done this before. I mean, I really don't even know what to do. I just know I want you to be my first."

She left him in the tub and went back into her bedroom, forcing down the bitter bile that seemed ready to spew out of her mouth. She could still taste his acidy stale breath on her tongue, and his smell made her nostrils shrink in repulsion.

Jake lay back in the tub, masturbating as he thought about having Emma, a virgin. He wanted to last a while so he could fuck her all night. Half an hour later, he masturbated again just thinking of her. He was getting himself ready for the event. In an effort to build his stamina for the evening with Emma that lay ahead, he needed to blow a few loads.

Chapter Nineteen

At seven thirty that evening, Emma went back over to Brianna's.

"We're ready to rock," she told her friend, adrenaline pumping through her veins. "We need to get some whiskey so that I can get him drunk."

"No problem," Brianna said, reaching into a kitchen cabinet and coming out with a bottle. "No problem at all. I guess there's one advantage to living with a drunk." She giggled.

"Perfect, Bri!" Emma exclaimed. "Let's go."

While driving to the other side of Norristown, the girls went over their plan once more. Emma would meet Jake at the pool, get him drunk, find out where Gracie was, and coax him into drinking enough to pass out. It was pretty simple.

Brianna parked the car in front of the motel. It was a run-down, dumpy place that was dark and depressing. The motel doors were painted in dreary shades of orange, yellow, and brown. The brick front gave it an eerie appearance. The hotel was known for being used by prostitutes and their clients. As Brianna put the car in park she shot her friend a worried look.

Emma smiled. "Stay here and don't come back to the pool," she directed her friend. "If he sees you, he'll know something's up."

While Brianna waited, Emma made her way around to the back of the building where the pool was located and leaped over the short fence. She stood for a moment looking around her. The place gave her the creeps. The metal lounge chairs, with their cushions put away for the winter, sat stark and uninviting. The surroundings were bare and isolated. A low cement wall surrounded by bushy evergreens providing a blanket of coverage and kept the pool area contained from every angle. The pool itself was empty, and Emma looked down into its depths at the stained and cracked cement. The scene sent chills up her spine. What if he came and just forced himself on her right there? Her anxiety grew by the moment.

At nine o'clock, Jake showed up as planned. He struggled to hoist his excessive body mass over the short wall and walked over to where Emma was sitting. Without uttering a word in greeting, he leaned down and kissed her hard.

She pulled away from him.

"What the fuck!" he snapped. "I thought you were into this."

"I am, Jake," Emma replied, faking an innocence she did not feel. "I told you, I've never done this before. I'm nervous."

Jake was clearly pleased to be reminded of her about-to-be-violated virginity. The very thought made her seem more beautiful than ever in his eyes. "Well, let's go," he said. "I have a room for us."

"Can we have a couple of drinks here first, Jake?" Emma pleaded. "I think it would help me to unwind a little. I brought a bottle of whiskey." She pushed the bottle in his direction.

"Sure, that works for me," he replied enthusiastically. "I want my little virgin to loosen up. But I don't want you loosened up everywhere, if you get my drift," he said, his tone and expression sleazy.

Emma threw him an innocent look. "I think I get your drift. God, Jake, don't be so weird!"

She poured each of them a healthy portion of whiskey in red plastic cups. As he gulped down the contents of his cup, Emma continued to lift hers to her lips, but refrained from actually drinking the whiskey. By the third cup, it was obvious that Jake was getting good and loaded. Emma kept pouring.

"You are one fuckin' good-looookin' chick!" he slurred. "I can't wait to fuck you. Your mother, she's good-looking. But fuck me—she's all stretched out and dry from having you kids. You, on da other hand, I fink you'll be like fuckin' a greased-up vise. Come on, let's go b'fore my balls esssplode!"

The drunker he got, the more repugnant he became to Emma.

"No, not yet. Just a little more whiskey, Jake!" she cooed. "Besides, I like talking to you when you're like this. It turns me on."

He gave her a half-cocked smile. "Fine," he said obligingly, moving over to her lounge chair and collapsing into it beside her. "But I need a little somethin'-somethin'...pull up that skirt and let me see your panties."

Emma stood and pulled her skirt up just enough to show the elastic at the top of her legs. Jake immediately reached up and slid his fingers under the elastic around her ass. When she sat back down next to him, he leaned over and began kissing her neck. She arched her neck, her head rearing back, pretending to be into it. But what she was really doing was holding her breath so she didn't have to smell his bitter odor. He grabbed her by the hair and pulled her face to his, sloppily searching till he found her mouth. Licking her mouth like a dog, he finally pushed his tongue through her lips until he had her in a full open-mouthed kiss.

Jake grasped both her breasts hard and started kissing the top of her cleavage at the V neckline of her sweater. Emma pushed him back. Realizing she needed to buy more time with him, she placed her hand on his crotch and rubbed hard. Then she pulled away from him.

"I think we need another drink," she suggested. "I'm really starting to get turned on. Are you?"

"Are you fuckin' kiddin' me?" he shrieked in excitement. "My dick is so hard right now it feels like it's going to break!"

Emma got up, poured another drink, and walked over to hand it to him. He accepted the whiskey and, still holding it, pulled her onto his lap with his other hand. Then he raised the plastic cup to his lips and chugged down the brown magic. Slamming the cup down, he slid his hands up and down Emma's inner thighs. Jake was so drunk by then he no longer cared about anything except getting laid. Emma could sense that he wanted to fuck her right there. She moved off his lap and pouted.

"What the fuck's wrong with you? Ain't you turned on?" he asked groggily.

"Are you fucking kidding?" Emma said, using his kind of language to hold his interest. "Of course I'm turned on! It's just that I know you think Gracie is sexier than I am and, well, I've always been jealous of how much attention you give her. I feel like you only want me as a second choice." She tried to sound needy and appealing, suppressing her desire to spit in his face.

"What the fuck!" Jake said. "I don't like her half as much as I like you! I like how scared she gets, if ya know what I mean? That really fuckin' makes my dick hard. She's a little fuckin' whiner! Ya shoulda heard her a couple of nights ago." He paused, moving closer to Emma and starting to rub her knee. "'Nuff about her! You're da one I want. Now come on and give me some of dat!" he exclaimed, moving his hands up her inner thighs.

Emma needed to keep him talking to find out where he had taken Gracie. She leaned down and handed him the bottle of whiskey. He took a long swig and gave it back to Emma, who pretended to drink from the bottle.

"Well," she began, careful to seem barely interested, "what happened the other night when you took Gracie out for ice cream? Where did she go?"

"Oh, 'nuff of this fuckin' bullshit!" Jake mumbled. "Fuck it…I don't wanna talk 'bout her anymore!"

With her irritation and anxiety festering in the pit of her stomach, Emma did the only thing she could do. She started kissing him passionately. He slid his hand up her skirt and put his fingers inside of her. She no longer felt as if her body was her own. She let him finger her for a few minutes as he grew increasingly aroused. He began panting and started to lay her down on the metal chair.

"Wait, Jake," Emma interrupted. "One more drink and we'll go to the room." She handed him a drink as she stood over him. "So tell me what happened to Gracie," she cajoled. "I need to know that she won't come back and steal you from me."

"Fine!" he screamed in frustration. "If that'll make you shut the fuck up and we can get to this! I put Gracie down in the fuckin' basement. But I hid her real good! She won't be a problem. She might even be dead by now! Who the fuck knows?"

He stood up unsteadily and weaved his way toward Emma who was, by now, standing at the edge of the pool.

"What the fuck are you saying, Jake?" she gasped. "Gracie's in the house?"

"Yeah, she's in the fuckin' house!"

"Does my mom know this?" she demanded.

"'Course the stupid bitch knows! Now come on!"

In his drunken stupor, Jake reached for Emma. With the overpowering desire for revenge she now felt toward him and her mother, her natural instincts took over and she shoved him with all her might into the empty pool. The look on his face was priceless as he tumbled into the dark, cement-lined depths. Wracked with fear, Jake flailed his arms in midair, trying desperately to get a hold and clawing at the air in a vain attempt to break his fall. Emma watched without emotion as his fall was broken, twelve feet below her, by a wonderfully resonant crack—the sound of his skull smashing into the pool's cold cement bottom. She stood for a moment imagining the Grim Reaper collecting Jake's wicked soul and propelling him to hell.

Having witnessed Jake's death, Emma felt invigorated. It was a feeling she wanted to hold on to forever. She stared down at his broken body and watched as the blood gushed from behind his head and spread in a circle around it. Her heart raced and she felt like an angel soaring through the sky. It was the same euphoria she had experienced when she told her father about the rat poison she'd fed him over the preceding weeks and watched his eyes widen with horror as he sucked in his final breath. Then she pushed all her feelings aside and focused on finding Gracie.

Chapter Twenty

Emma quickly picked up the bottle of whiskey and the two plastic cups they had used and raced around to the front where Brianna was waiting for her. She slid into the passenger seat of Pam's car.

"Floor it!" she urged her friend. "We need to get back to my house as fast as possible. Gracie is in the basement."

"How did you get him to tell you?" Brianna asked, intrigued. "Where is he?"

"There's no time for that now, Bri!" Emma scowled, unable to hide the panic in her voice. "Gracie may be dead. Just drive and hurry!"

Brianna knew that Emma wasn't messing around. She drove as fast as she could without losing control of the car. She had barely parked when Emma jumped out and started running toward her house. Brianna followed her inside and down into the basement.

At the bottom of the rickety stairs, Emma came to a halt.

"What? Do you hear something, Em?" Brianna asked, unable to mask the fear in her voice.

"No, I need to get a flashlight. We have no idea where she is down here."

Emma reached down to a shelf that hung at the bottom of the stairs and found the flashlight. Its beam of light made everything appear spooky as it shone across the dirt floor. Emma flashed the light around the walls of the basement, but saw nothing that gave an indication of her sister's whereabouts. All of the old appliances, furniture, and damp boxes seemed untouched. As they began walking to the other side of the basement, Brianna hung onto Emma's arm. Suddenly she stumbled.

"Watch where you're going, Bri."

"I can't help it, Em. I can't see a thing."

Emma shone the flashlight on the floor in front of Brianna and noticed a piece of garden hose sticking out of the ground. "You must've tripped on that," she told her friend. "Be careful."

Emma took a couple of steps forward, then stopped abruptly. She turned back to the garden hose and dropped to her hands and knees. She put her ear to the hose. She could hear a faint sound. Not a movement, but a sound so soft she couldn't know for sure if it was indeed a sound. Frantically she began digging at the dirt with her bare hands. Brianna quickly joined her, beginning to panic as she realized what they were digging for. They kept removing the dirt over a small area until they hit a piece of plywood that was buried about four inches under the surface, the hose sticking out through a hole in the wood. More frantic than ever, the girls began clawing the dirt from the six-foot-long piece of wood. After what seemed an eternity, they pried the wood up.

Underneath it, in a shallow grave, lay Gracie. She was utterly still, her face drained of all its natural color and her eyes closed.

Emma leaped into the grave and felt for a pulse, her fingers racing around her sister's body, feeling her wrists and moving up to her neck. There, she felt the slight bump of a pulse beat against her finger. She put her face close to Gracie's mouth and felt a tiny puff of breath tickle her skin.

The girls picked her up gently and carried her over to Brianna's. They placed her in a tub of warm water, gently removing all the dirt from her nostrils and her mouth. Then they cleaned up her face carefully and gently bathed the rest of her body. The two-day-old wounds on her body revealed how severely Jake had beaten her before burying her alive. As they bathed her, they gave her small sips of water, most of it dribbling out the sides of her mouth. When they were finished, they put Gracie in Brianna's bed and stayed awake all night by her side, making sure she sipped water and willing her to live. They didn't know it then, but they had saved her life. Badly wrecked though she was, Gracie would survive.

Once things were under control, Briana asked, "So what happened with Jake?"

Emma was blunt. "He got drunk. He slipped and fell into the pool. The pool was empty, so he sunk pretty quickly." She grinned from ear to ear. "I doubt he'll be a problem anymore."

Briana leaned over to give her friend a high-five. "Fucking asshole, Jake!" she exclaimed. "I guess he decided to mess with the wrong family."

Shortly after three in the morning, Gracie opened her eyes and gave Emma a small but encouraging smile. Emma started to cry. Her sister was still fragile, but at least she was alive. As Gracie closed her eyes again to embrace sleep, Emma and Brianna did the same, lying on either side of her and keeping her safe.

Chapter Twenty-One

The next morning, Emma went over to her house and found Valerie sobbing.

"What's wrong with you?" she asked, her voice devoid of feeling.

"Jake didn't come home last night," she bawled. "What if he's left me for another woman?"

Her hatred for her mother almost unbearable by now, Emma lashed out, "You stand here crying over that dick, Jake, but you aren't worried about Gracie? You're pathetic! And you call yourself a mother? You're a conniving bitch!"

"Oh, the only thing you ever think about is Gracie. She is a very unhappy girl. In fact, she's miserable most of the time. Maybe she's happy now. Did you ever think of that, Emma?" Valerie asked weakly, trying to be manipulative.

Emma put her hands on her hips and squared off against her mother. "Hmm, let's see," she said, pretending to ponder. "I have to think about Gracie because you never do. You didn't ever think about either of us. All you did was sacrifice us to keep your men happy. And what else? Oh yeah! You're rotten to your core and only care about what you think is best for you! You're well aware of the horrible things that have happened to Gracie and me since we were born. Yet you continue to worry about how your man feels. You're as much to blame for everything as they are and you know it!"

Emma turned her back on her mother and went upstairs to shower. She would deal with Valerie, but not until Gracie was well enough to be moved. She and Brianna needed to figure out what they were going to do next. They would run—that was for sure—but they hadn't decided where they would go. The good news, they had told each other while holding vigil over

Gracie, was that they had gotten those fake IDs, which would help them get started.

The next day, while Emma was in her bedroom sorting through the clothes she would pack for Gracie and herself before they left, a loud knock at the front door made her pause. Coming down the stairs to investigate, she froze at the sight of two policemen standing just inside the door.

"We aren't really sure what happened," one of the officers was telling a sobbing Valerie. "His blood alcohol level was point two nine. He may have lost consciousness or tripped. That level of alcohol would severely impair his motor skills. Best we can figure is that he didn't realize he was at the edge of the pool and toppled over when he took a step forward."

Valerie went on whimpering as she collapsed against the officer's chest and hung onto him. Embarrassed, he looked up at Emma, silently imploring her to come down and take charge of her mother. To stifle her laughter, Emma bit the inside of her lip until it started to bleed.

"I guess Jake is dead?" she asked the officer, prying loose her mother who was clinging to the police officer like a barnacle.

"Yeah, it's really tragic," he replied gravely. "Sometimes the good ones get taken. Jake was a good man. He helped a lot of kids in this area. He'll be sorely missed."

Emma nodded and nudged her mother over to the sofa. Then she went back to the officer. "Is there anything else?" she asked politely.

"No, honey," he said gently, "we just felt we owed it to Jake to let all of you know. You take good care of your mom now."

"No worries, Officer. I will definitely take care of my mother. Thanks for coming," Emma convincingly stated.

Emma had every intention of giving Valerie the kind of attention she deserved when the time was right.

Over the next two days, Gracie began to regain her strength. She was on her feet now, walking around Brianna's house. She was also eating regular meals that Emma cooked for all of them, and watching her get back to normal comforted Emma and Brianna. By the time Gracie was feeling better, their plan was fully baked. There was only one other thing to deal with before they left home and started their new life.

Emma walked with purpose as she went back over to her house to say goodbye to Valerie.

Chapter Twenty-Two

Valerie was in the kitchen making herself lunch. Emma walked in and sat down at the table, her gaze unwavering as she stared at her mother. Valerie sat down across from her and took a bite of her sandwich.

"What's wrong with you? Why are you staring at me?" she asked.

Emma smiled. "Well, I was just wondering how a woman, a mother, actually, can sit here like everything is normal and gorge herself on food, when she knows that her child is buried alive in the basement in a shallow grave. Not knowing if she's still alive."

Valerie's eyes bulged with fear. "It-it wasn't me, Emma," she stammered. "Jake was just trying to teach her a lesson. He warned me that if I went down and dug her out, he would put me in there and make sure that no one ever found me."

Emma shook her head slowly in disbelief. "Right, I should have known that he'd threaten to do something to you. After all, you've sacrificed the two of us your whole pathetic life. It never mattered to you how sick or twisted they were as long as you could go on living in Bizarro World! Well," she continued, "now that Jake has been dead for almost three days, did it dawn on you once to go and get her? Make sure she's still alive?"

Valerie quickly rationalized in her head that her youngest daughter wouldn't have been punished if she'd just behaved. Gracie was forever trying to avoid Jake and she knew that he hated being ignored or disobeyed. As Emma's words began to sink into her thick head her nervousness started to rise to the surface. Emma enjoyed watching her mother squirm.

"How did you know that she's down in the basement?" Valerie finally asked.

Emma leaned up on her elbows. "Jake blurted out everything when he was trying to have sex with me. I don't know, he said something about you being a dried-up prune and how he wanted young girls. You remember Jake, the fucking saint? The great guy who helped kids all the time? Well, you see, when he thought I was going to let him fuck me, he told me where Gracie was and I dug her out just in time or she would have died. Now here's what's going to happen, so listen carefully. Gracie and I are leaving and you will not look for us. You will never tell the police that we ran away, because if you do, I will tell them the things you let Pepper do to me. Also, Gracie will tell them how you stood by silently as Jake beat the fucking shit out of her, then buried her alive in your own fucking house! So unless you want to spend the rest of your miserable life in prison, I suggest you keep your mouth shut. Forever. Do you understand what I'm telling you?"

"Yes," was all Valerie could whisper.

Emma got up from the table and moved away until she was behind Valerie and beyond her range of vision. Then she picked up the wooden cutting board from the kitchen counter and brought it crashing down on her mother's head. Emma stood for a few moments, staring down at the woman lying unconscious on the floor. Then she took out their sharpest steak knife from the kitchen drawer and ran it over her mother's face in several directions, each cut about an inch deep, enough, she knew, to leave her scarred for life.

Emma got down on her hands and knees. While Valerie was still unconscious, she whispered into her ear that was now filled with blood running down from the cuts on her face, "You thought you could use your beauty to escape the life you forced us to live. Well, now you will never be beautiful again. You left your baby down in the basement of your own home to die. You really don't deserve to live. These cuts on your face will be a daily reminder of the ugly, ugly person that you really are!"

She stood, grabbed the clothes she'd packed, and left the house that had been a prison her whole life. Emma believed everything bad that could happen to her and Gracie was being left behind them.

Chapter Twenty-Three

E mma and Brianna hustled Gracie into the car. They had decided to drive toward Philadelphia and see where the road took them. They had over $400, most of which Brianna had stolen from Pam's secret stash of money. As they left Chain Street, Emma felt renewed. She had her best friend and her sister by her side. As the car merged onto the Schuylkill Expressway the girls turned up the volume on the radio and sang along with Madonna to "Like A Virgin."

They drove down the expressway with no specific destination in mind and found themselves on I-95 North. In a short time, neighborhoods began to appear. They turned off the highway and onto Somerset Street, driving until they reached Kensington Avenue. It was obviously not the best part of town. They noticed many kids roaming the streets, some of them their own age. The three girls were shocked at the way many of the girls strolling the streets were dressed. One Latina, for instance, who looked no older than fifteen, was wearing shorts so skimpy that her whole ass hung out of them. She had teamed them with a barely-there shirt and worn-out calf-length high-heeled boots. Considering that it was no longer summer and the slightly cool weather didn't warrant revealing clothes, Emma and Brianna figured she was a hooker. Despite their misgivings about the neighborhood, they decided this was one place where they could blend in and not draw attention to themselves. Their luck, rather than their sense of direction, had drawn them to the heart of Kensington.

As they turned right onto Kensington Avenue, their awed gazes were caught by the massive steel tunnel that ran the length of the street as far as they could see. They would later learn that this seemingly endless prehistoric-looking centipede was the Market-Frankford Line of the subway that was elevated above the ground; everyone called it the El.

The underbelly of the El harbored prostitutes and drug addicts. Brianna drove by slowly, and as the three of them took in their surroundings a man suddenly stepped in front of their car. Brianna slammed on the brakes to avoid hitting him, but the man never even looked up. He just kept walking, as if in a trance, and they watched intently as he continued his conversation with himself.

They pulled over on the side of Kensington Avenue and asked a teenager who appeared somewhat sober where they could find a motel.

The homeless boy bent down and looked them over. "Sure, I'll tell you where you can go, if you give me a dollar."

Emma pulled a bill from her pocket and handed it over. "Now where the fuck is it?" she snapped.

The boy was amused by her outburst. She had a fiery nature and he thought she might just make it here. "Go up and make a left on Tioga Street," he directed. "There's a place called the Trenton Inn, a big white building. Maybe I'll see you around."

Although they were somewhat uncertain about his recommendation, they followed his advice, given that their options were limited. Before they knew it, they had pulled up alongside the Trenton Inn. The place made Chain Street seem almost respectable. The building was of white brick. The windows on the first floor were glass block—harder to break into, Emma realized. The second-floor windows were all covered with white boards to ensure absolute privacy, she concluded.

They went in through the sole entrance, the bar, and approached the bartender.

"We need a room for the night," Emma stated assertively, worried that if she was perceived as weak the man would know they were underage and wouldn't rent them a room.

The bartender, a rugged older black man with short gray hair, looked at them over the top of his glasses. He wasn't fazed by the girls' tender age or their need for a room. In Kensington, he was used to it. It was a way of life in this part of hell on earth—young girls and boys, running from family, hooked on drugs, and making money by selling their bodies. More violence was born and bred in Kensington than in any other part of Philadelphia. It was infamous for the cruelty with which everyone who lived there treated life, regardless of the consequences.

"Sure," the bartender replied. "I need some ID and forty bucks. I can put you in the back of the building, away from the bar, so it'll be a little quieter."

Brianna handed him her fake ID and the money. He held the ID up and pretended to scrutinize it. He couldn't give a shit who they were. They needed a room, they had the money, and it was better than staying on the street all night. He handed Brianna a key, and they headed to the back of the bar, where the staircase leading to the second floor was located.

When the girls unlocked the door to their room, they were met with filth. There were two double beds with old brown bedcovers. When they pulled the covers down, they found wrinkled, soiled sheets that were dull yellow and worn so thin they could see the mattress design they were meant to cover. Watermarks patterned the nightstand where glasses and beer bottles had sat too long. The green carpet was worn down near the door to the dingy bathroom, exposing the wood underneath it. There was, of course, no television set. The window was completely boarded up, and the only source of light in the room was a lamp that sat on the nightstand. The bathroom was starker still, with a sink, a toilet, and a moldy tub. Forget about little bottles of shampoo or soap for the room's occupants to use; there wasn't even a mirror.

The girls settled in, tired from the events that had led to their flight from Norristown. Knowing they would eventually have to find something to eat, Emma suggested they venture out while it was still daylight to buy dinner and a newspaper so they could look for an apartment to rent.

As they walked toward a take-out place, they had noticed on their way to the hotel that specialized in fried chicken, an older man, covered in grime, approached Gracie and asked her if she had any money she could spare. "No, I don't have anything," she told him.

Emma was quickly at her side to find out what the man wanted with her sister. "Oh," she said, looking at the man with pity. "Here you go. A dollar is all I can give you."

"Thanks, sweetheart," he replied and smiled at Emma with three rotting teeth in his mouth.

After he walked away from them, Gracie turned to her older sister. "Em, I'm scared. There are a lot of strange people around here. What if someone asks us what we're doing here?"

"No one is going to ask us anything, Gracie. And you know, just because a lot of people here are poor doesn't mean they're bad. We're poor and I think we're the coolest fucking chicks on earth," Emma teased her sister and made Gracie smile.

After they returned to the dump they were staying in, they sat on the bed, side by side, and looked through the newspaper. They found nothing in Kensington. That struck them as odd. Emma went downstairs to the bartender.

"Yeah, um," she ventured, "we can't find anything for rent in the paper. We're looking to stay in this area and thought you might know of something."

The bartender laughed. "Missy," he said, "there ain't nobody gonna pay to advertise in the paper 'round here. Tomorrow, go down to Potter Street. I seen a 'For Rent' sign on one of the doors when I was picking up my grandbaby the other day."

Hoping they had a good lead, the girls finally settled into their room for the night, but Emma slept lightly. She was awakened every so often by the shuffling and curses of drunks stumbling to their rooms and the shriek of women's laughter echoing through the hallways. She knew they couldn't stay there more than one night. Besides, she was eager to find a permanent place to live that the three of them could call home before they found themselves in more trouble.

Chapter Twenty-Four

When the girls woke up next morning, they washed their faces and quickly left the shady motel, almost relieved to be back out on the dirty streets of Kensington. At least the sun shone outdoors and the world opened up around them. Before they got back into the car again, Brianna stopped at a pay phone to call her mother, knowing that if she were gone for more than a day, Pam might call the police.

"Ma," she said, "it's Bri. I'm gonna be away for a while. No big deal. Just trying to figure some things out."

It was early for Pam to be woken up. "What do you mean 'away for a while'? Where are you?"

"Ma, stop already, will ya?" Brianna said in exasperation. "I'm in Philly. It ain't a big deal. I have your car and I'll take care of it until I come home. Alright?"

Pam nudged the stranger who was stretched out in the bed next to her. She had met him the night before. He sat up and she motioned for him to leave. Then she put her hand over the phone's mouthpiece. "See you again sometime, baby," she whispered to him.

The man, whose name Pam hadn't bothered to find out, staggered across her bedroom. "Yeah, whatever," he mumbled. "But next time, for seventy-five bucks, you're gonna need to get a little more creative." He threw the money on the bed next to her.

"Sure! Whatever you want, baby," Pam promised with the sweetest smile she could manage that early in the morning. She needed good clients, and this new guy was a half-decent person. She wanted to hang onto him for a while.

"Mom!" Brianna huffed impatiently at the other end of the line. "What the fuck! I'm talking to you! So that's the deal. I'll be away for a while and I'll take care of your car. I'll try to check in once a week. Okay?"

"Yeah, okay," Pam agreed, giving in to her daughter. "But I want a call from you once a week. Don't do anything stupid."

"Yeah sure, I'll talk to you later!" Brianna hung up the phone quickly before her mother could ask her anymore questions.

Having settled things with Brianna's mom, the girls set out to explore Potter Street. They quickly found the row home that the bartender had mentioned. They knocked on the door, and when no one answered, they wrote down the phone number that was on the handmade sign in the window. Back at a pay phone, Emma dialed the number.

"Hello?" a gruff voice breathed into her ear.

"Yeah, hi," she responded. "I'm interested in renting your house on Potter Street."

"Oh yeah?" the man said. "Well, it's four hundred a month, plus utilities. I need the first and last month's rent up front. If you can do that, I'll show ya the place."

"You mean eight hundred dollars?" Emma asked, shocked.

"Yeah, eight hundred dollars. What? Are you stupid?" the man accused.

"Fuck you!" Emma yelled and slammed the receiver into its cradle.

She went back to the car and explained to Brianna and Gracie how the renting thing worked. "We're fucked. We need eight hundred dollars just to move in. Then it's four hundred a month, plus 'utilities,' whatever the fuck they are. We have three hundred and forty-four dollars left. We'll have to figure out something else. Until we get jobs, renting isn't an option for us."

They parked the car on a side street and made their way toward Kensington Avenue to look for work. As they walked along, taking in the circus around them, Emma became increasingly apprehensive and disheartened. From what she could see, there were plenty of drugs and people who were strung out on them. Hookers practically lined the streets and sleazy men seemed to slither up from the gutters. The three girls were approached by a couple of men who asked them if they wanted to get high. The prostitutes eyed them up, making it clear that if they even thought of hooking in their designated spots, they would rip their heads off. There were no "help wanted" signs in the store windows, and Emma even went into pawn and coffee shops to inquire about a job, but it was apparent that no one needed help.

After two hours of futile searching, the girls bought hot dogs and sat on the curb at Kensington and Somerset to rest. A couple of minutes later, a girl in her early twenties approached them.

"Listen, bitches," she said belligerently, "if you're gonna work, find somewhere else to do it. Me and my girls here," she gestured toward a pack of strung-out, slutty types, "work this area. So fuck off!"

Emma stood quickly, dropping her half-eaten hotdog on the ground, and stepped into the girl's comfort zone.

"Fuck you, bitch!" she said nastily. "Who the fuck do you think you are? We're not here to steal your business. We're trying to eat our lunch. So mind your own fucking business!"

Brianna and Gracie looked on in surprise, amazed at how aggressive Emma had become in a few days. The other girl stood for a moment sizing Emma up, and sensed she wasn't kidding.

"Fine," she conceded, "but don't let me catch you trying to turn any tricks or I'll fuck you up real good!"

The girl went back to her friends and exchanged a few words with them. Then they all scattered to stake out their territory.

Emma sat back on the curb between Brianna and Gracie, picked her hotdog off the ground, brushed the grit off it, and finished it. Brianna had considered herself a tough ass all her life, but seeing her friend stand up to the girl on the street made her realize she wasn't that tough after all. Emma was actually the tough one. Gracie couldn't take her eyes off of her sister.

"Ah, Em, what the hell has gotten into you? Are you trying to get our asses beat?" Gracie asked.

Emma put her arm around Gracie. "No," she said, "but nobody is going to fuck with us ever again. I will fucking kill anyone who thinks they're going to bully me. I've had my share of that shit. Fuck that bitch!"

Following her heated exchange with the prostitute, adrenaline was pumping through her body, making her feel alive. After a long, tense silence, she spoke again. "Here's what we're going to do. We're going to sleep in the car tonight, until we figure some shit out. We need to spend our money on the right stuff so we can get by until we earn more money. Let's find a market and buy some things to hold us over."

The girls walked back to the car feeling a sense of failure because they were unable to find jobs. The only jobs available to them, as far as they could tell, involved either drugs or sex. Neither was something that Emma wanted any of them involved in, but she also knew that there are times when you have to do things that you don't like. She had spent most of her young life learning that lesson. Emma hoped there weren't more lessons she'd have to learn.

Chapter Twenty-Five

After paying another teenager a dollar for information, the girls drove over to the Save-A-Lot on Lehigh Avenue. They bought water, cans of tuna with pull tops, crackers, cornflakes, powder milk, a loaf of bread, and peanut butter. They also purchased some cheap plastic bowls and utensils. This was enough to see them through several days, until they found a way to earn money.

Next, they bought blankets, pillows, and a couple of dark-colored sheets. They would use the sheets to cover themselves at night so that no one knew they were sleeping in the car. Emma was happy that they had been able to buy so much for only fifty-seven dollars. Of course, she had to bargain hard with the guy at the bedding place, but she had managed to talk the slimy young salesman into selling her displays at a deep discount.

Once back in the car, they set out to find a place to park for the night. Emma realized quickly that given the overwhelming number of drug addicts, dealers, and prostitutes on the streets, it would be difficult to find somewhere safe. Driving down Kensington Avenue, they came upon a street without sidewalks. Emma quickly told Brianna to turn onto it and park. She figured that on a street without sidewalks, there would be less foot traffic, making it somewhat safer—if the word had any relevance in a place like Kensington.

The first night the girls spent in the car seemed endless. Emma found herself wide awake for most of the night, alert to the sounds and sights around her. She was prepared to battle every possible threat if she had to. At daybreak, when Brianna woke up and ended her vigil, an exhausted Emma let herself sleep for a few hours.

By noon, the girls were back on Kensington Avenue, trying to come up with a way to earn money. Again, they had to ward off pimps, who approached them disguised as drug dealers and trying to get them high. These propositions were in keeping with the way things worked on the streets. At first, the pimps would offer girls drugs for free. As their prey steadily increased their intake, they became dependent on the drugs. And once the girls were totally hooked and at the mercy of the pimps, the bastards would turn them out to prostitute to pay off their drug debt and keep themselves high all the time. Confronted with the ugliness of the streets, Emma thanked her foul childhood for having taught her a valuable lesson: trust no one.

Walking down Kensington Avenue under the El was depressing. The steel monstrosity that loomed overhead always blocked the sun out and cast a cloud of gloom over the street, day and night. It was as if night never came to an end and the sun never rose below the underbelly of the El. All one saw in its shadows were hapless souls who stumbled through life, dismal and hopeless.

As Emma looked around, she realized that as young as they were they had an important decision to make: find a way to live here or live to find their way out of this hell hole. There were so many people and she wondered how they could all have been so unlucky in life, including herself. Maybe she belonged in Kensington with the other misfits of the earth. She felt like nothing more than a throw-away person. Born. Abused. Taught anger and hate. Then thrown away to make a life on her own.

Still, she wanted the best for her sister. So over the next week, Emma began collecting information from the other teens on the streets, valuable information that would help keep them safe. She learned to park the car in different places so that no one could identify it or pinpoint its exact location. They rotated parking lots at churches, hospitals, and anywhere that public parking was allowed. Their biggest problem in moving the car around was the money they had to spend on gas.

Ten days had passed and the girls were still living out of Pam's car. They desperately wanted a shower. They had used some of the water they had bought for drinking to wash themselves, but their unwashed hair had become lank and greasy and they were beginning to stink. It was at this point that Emma met Sydney, a teen who lived on the streets and gave her advice on how to "steal a scrub." Emma learned that they could steal a scrub by sneaking into the girls' locker room at Carroll Charles High School, but they had to be very careful and time it just right. The homeless girl had warned Emma to be cautious.

"Just pretend you go there and are familiar with the place," she had advised. "The janitors know that some of us go over there once in a while to take a shower. They won't bother you as long as you don't make any trouble or trash the place. Make sure you stay cool, because if you don't, you'll fuck it up for the rest of us."

Sydney had been born and raised in Kensington. Her mother had abandoned her at birth and her father was a drug-dealer-turned-addict. By the time she was seven years old, her father was in prison and Sydney had taken to the streets to survive on her own. Emma liked the young girl and was intrigued by her courage and ability to survive the mean streets of Kensington on her own for four years. She stopped to talk with her every day, and as the girls confided in each other about their traumatic backgrounds, they were able to connect on a level that was quite different from the one Emma shared with Brianna or anyone she'd ever met.

Emma was quick to share the news about the showers at the high school with Brianna and Gracie. They went to the store and purchased the cheapest bath products they could find.

"We can't afford towels," Emma explained. "So we'll have to use the two sheets we have to dry ourselves."

As they left the store Gracie started to whistle "Patience" by Guns N' Roses, so happy that they would be stealing a scrub the next day. The girls had grown up listening to music from all generations. They were quite familiar with the artists of the past and present. Emma looked at her now. "Patience? Yep, I get it."

Gracie stood on her toes and raised her arms to the sky, "I haven't been this fuckin' happy in ten days, you guys. Who would have thought that some water and soap could make me feel like I just won a million bucks? Hey, Bri, maybe you can wash some of that stink off ya!" she teased.

"Stink? You wanna talk about stink, your ass stinks," Bri bit back in fun.

It was in these special moments of being nothing more than teenagers that the three girls could release the anxiety caused by their hopeless living arrangement. The next day, just before school let out, the girls went over to the high school and, following Sydney's instructions, entered the girls' locker room. Emma felt the muck of days fall off her body as the water washed over her. With the funk of the last eleven days washed away, the girls emerged in high spirits.

It was just a few days later, as the girls were trying to settle in the car to go to sleep, that Gracie complained of a headache. "Emma, my head feels like someone is beating on it," she moaned.

"Alright, I'm gonna walk down to Kensington Avenue. I'll find a market and buy a bottle of aspirin. You two stay here. Make sure you keep the doors locked and the sheets over you. I'll be back quick," Emma told the two girls.

Emma left the car and made her way down the quiet street. She walked for over twenty minutes before she found an all-night market. Having purchased the aspirin, she tucked the bottle into her jacket and headed back to the car. She followed the same route she'd come, cutting through a long alleyway to get back onto Stouton Street.

Emma walked at a fast pace to make it through the alley as quickly as possible. She could almost feel the imminent danger of being in such an isolated spot. There were overflowing trash dumpsters, which seemed to be home to every rat in the city. Various abandoned household items lined either side of the brick walls. Spooking herself out, she began a slow jog, but was abruptly stopped when someone grabbed a handful of her hair.

Emma instinctively spun around and came face to face with the prostitute she had had the run-in with on Kensington Avenue when they were eating hotdogs. Before she knew it, she was surrounded by the four other hookers that Emma had seen with her that day. She immediately knew she was fucked. There was no way she would be able to take all five of them on. So she did the only thing she could do. "Listen, I don't want any trouble. The other day, well, you just caught me at a bad time. That's all."

The prostitute gave her an icy cold smile, exposing the few teeth she still had in her mouth. "You think we care that you havin' a bad fuckin' day? What-cha think, we livin' good and ain't never had no bad days? Ha! Every fuckin' day a bad day for us, motherfucker! Bottom line is, bitch, ain't nobody gonna fuck with Rock's girls."

As she finished her sentence, she threw the first punch into Emma's gut. She immediately doubled over holding her stomach. One of the other girls kicked her in the ass and she flew head first to the ground. It all became a blur as the girls punched and kicked her without restraint. Emma made her best attempt to cover her head; the beating was far worse than the crime she had committed by standing up to the girls days prior.

As Emma lay on the ground taking blow after blow, she resigned herself to the idea that she may die in that alley, beaten to death, and then she heard a young girl yell, "Rock, make them stop!"

"Why?" she could hear the man's voice responding. "What's she to you?"

"Come on, Rock. She's a friend of mine, okay? She got her ass kicked already, look at her," the young girl pleaded.

Rock told the crazed young girls, "K now. That's 'nough. This bitch just got lucky." Then he turned to Sydney. "You get her the fuck out of here before I turn them loose on her again."

Sydney rushed over and helped Emma to her feet. She half carried; half dragged Emma out of the alley. Once she had her on Kensington Avenue, she sat Emma down outside a drugstore. When Sydney came out, she was carrying a bag of ice and a can of Coke. "Here, drink this," she told Emma. "Sip it slow. You need the caffeine to wake you up. I need to get you back to your car."

After Emma finished the Coke and Sydney had iced her legs and ribs, she helped her up and practically carried her back to the car. The young girl knocked on the window, and a startled Brianna shot up from under the sheet. After her vision cleared and her heart rate returned to normal, she saw it was Emma.

Throwing open the car door Brianna gasped, "Oh my God! What the fuck happened to you?" She helped Sydney get Emma into the backseat of the car.

"Who did this to her?" Gracie screeched in a state of panic.

"Those hookers she stood up to the other day. They beat the shit out of her. They ganged up on her in an alley. She didn't have a chance. There were too many of them. By the time I got there they had fucked her up pretty good," Syd explained.

Emma was awake but not completely aware of what was going on around her. She finally spoke up. "Syd saved my life." Then she slid down on the backseat and fell asleep.

Gracie leaned into Sydney and hugged her. "Thank you, Syd."

Syd nodded at the two girls and headed off toward her home in the streets of Kensington.

"What are we going to do, Bri? I'm scared," Gracie asked, worried about her sister.

Brianna embraced her. "We're gonna stay in the car with Em. Tomorrow when she's awake we'll figure out what we should do," Brianna explained calmly, but inside she was terror stricken at the thought of being in charge. The two girls exchanged a worried look before lying down to try to sleep. It was as if they both sensed what was yet to come.

Chapter Twenty-Six

A couple of days passed before Emma felt like herself again. Luckily, the gang of girls hadn't broken anything, but almost her entire body was bruised. Emma told the other two girls, "Thank God for Sydney. If she hadn't shown up they probably would have beat me to death."

Now that she was feeling a little better the girls ventured out to look for a way to make a little money. As they roamed around the ghetto, Emma noticed Sydney standing with a group of teens on a street corner. She approached Syd, extending her arms to give her a hug. "Ah, she lives!" Sydney exclaimed.

"Yeah, thanks to you," Emma returned. "So how did you get them to stop?"

"Well, the hookers work for Rock. He's a drug dealer and pimp. Him and my dad used to work together dealing drugs. Then my dad got hooked on coke. Once my old man went to prison, Rock went solo. He's known me from the time I was born. After I told him you were a friend of mine, he called his bitches off. Don't get me wrong, Rock is a total asshole. I don't trust him as far as I could throw him. But he doesn't give me a hard time like he does the other girls around here," she explained.

Emma listened to the eleven-year-old, wondering again how she managed to survive on her own and grateful that she had been brave enough to speak up that night. "Well, listen, Syd, I owe you one. That was pretty fucking cool of you to step in and take that kind of risk for me. I mean, we don't even know each other that good."

Syd took a seat on the curb and lit a cigarette. "Yeah, well. You told me what you've been through. I get it. None of us asked for this shit life, so if we can help each other every once in a while, I figure what the fuck, why not? Right?"

Gracie sat on the curb next to Syd, and even though she was two years older, she felt like a weak child next to Sydney. "I wish I could be as brave as you are," she confided. "I'm with my sister and I'm scared all the time. Aren't you afraid that someone is going to hurt you?"

Syd took a long drag from her cigarette and offered it to Gracie, who shook her head. "Nah. I was born in Kensington. I mean, sometimes I get scared. Mostly that I won't have anything to eat, but other than that, being homeless doesn't scare me. I have my street family and we get along fine. When you're out here long enough you learn how to get by on whatever comes your way. You're lucky. At least you have them," she stated, gesturing toward Emma and Brianna.

Gracie nodded. "Yeah, Em has been protecting me my whole life. She's pretty much been my mom since I was really little. I guess I am pretty lucky, huh?"

"Yep," Sydney replied with a note of sadness in her voice. The worst part of her life was that she had no real family. Syd envied Gracie for having a sister like Emma and secretly wished that she could have been her little sister instead.

Gracie gently bumped her knee into Sydney's. "Well, thanks for helping Em the other night. I don't know what I'd do if anything happened to her. We'll see you around, right?"

"Sure," Syd said, her voice void of commitment.

A couple of days later the two older girls finally found temporary work at a deli. The deli was getting ready for its annual inspection by the FDA and needed to clean out the back of the kitchen area. The two girls were paid twenty-five dollars a day, under the table, for sorting through boxes and throwing away expired food.

While the two girls worked, Gracie hung out nearby. The owner said that she was too young and didn't want her working in his store. She was sitting on a curb watching in fascination all of the tattered people roaming the streets when she was approached by three boys. They were a couple of years older than she was, but that didn't seem to bother them when they stopped to talk to her. Within minutes the boys had her laughing, and since it was the first time that any boys had paid her attention, she felt giddy.

She sat with them for a couple of hours. In that time, Gracie forgot all about being scared of every living being that lurked over her shoulder. "So where are you from?" one of the boys finally asked.

"Norristown. We moved out here a while ago. You know, we just figured we'd come here and hang," Gracie told them, trying to be cool and appear more mature.

"Oh yeah?" the boy replied. "Where are you living?"

"Well, we haven't found a place yet. Right now we're sorta living out of our car," she said with shame, and pointed to Pam's car that was parked in front of the deli.

"Oh, that's cool. Do you sleep in it here? At the deli?" he pushed.

Gracie giggled. "Of course not! We move around to different places. Tonight we're gonna check out the lot behind that huge abandoned building off of Lehigh Avenue. You know where I'm talking about?"

"Sure we do. Sometimes we sleep inside that building. Just depends on how crowded it is. We like to move around too," one of the other boys told her.

"Why did you leave home?" Gracie asked, wanting to know their story and keep them talking to her.

"Ah, we all have different reasons. But we were all pretty much not wanted by our parents. We met up in elementary school and have been friends since then. Once we turned thirteen, we all decided to split together and come to Kensington to live a little," he said.

Gracie forgot that she was in the smelly armpit of Kensington, known locally as "the stroll." So captivated by the attention she was getting from the boys, she was blind to the fact that she was sitting on a curb in the heart of the city's heroin and prostitution scene. Drug users and hookers were all around her, yet she failed to notice them now. The boys had suddenly become the temporary relief she needed from her miserable existence.

That evening, after Gracie fell asleep in the car, the two older girls walked three blocks to meet up with a couple of teenagers that worked in the deli. They had agreed to hang out with a few of the girls with plans to drink a case of beer that one of them had scored from a dope head in exchange for five bucks.

Gracie was sleeping peacefully just a few blocks away when the rear passenger window smashed in on her. Her eyes flew open, her heart raced, and she froze. Unable to scream, her fear holding her voice hostage, she watched as an arm reached in and unlocked the car door. As it opened, she recognized one of the boys from earlier that afternoon.

"Hey, Gracie," he taunted her. "We know that you like us. Why don't you take your pants off and we can show you how much we like you?" he snickered.

She tried hard to form the word "no," but instead her whole body began to shake. She knew what they were talking about; after all, Jake had raped her before he put her in the grave he'd dug in the basement. As she stared at them with wide eyes, the first boy slipped into the backseat of the car with her. He pulled her pants off with ease and tore at her underwear, already tattered from age.

He unzipped his pants and pressed himself inside of her. She lay on her back without moving. She commanded her body to fight, but her legs and arms wouldn't budge. He was hurting her, and tears silently streamed down the sides of her face.

When he was finished the second boy climbed on top of her. Somehow, she found her voice and began to scream. The boy was much stronger than she was and grabbed a fistful of her hair, slamming her head against the car door. Gracie began to punch and kick at him. He straddled her, pinning her down so she couldn't get away. He picked up a pillow from the floor of the car and shoved it into her face. He held it in place until she had stopped kicking and lifted it only after she had fallen unconscious. He reached into the front seat and grabbed the gallon of water he'd seen sitting there. Then he poured some in her face.

She sprang back to life, gasping for air.

"Now, are you going to give us what we want?" he asked cruelly.

Before she could respond, he held the pillow over her face again. This time he didn't let her lose consciousness. He held the pillow just long enough for her to stop struggling, removed it so she could draw in a few gasps of breath, and did it again. After he'd done this to her several more times, causing her to pee herself, he unzipped his pants and rammed himself inside of her angrily.

By the time the third boy was finished raping her it was as if she was no longer in possession of her body. She couldn't feel anything. Not the pain from being raped or the fear that had plagued her in the beginning, making her such an easy victim.

When they were finished, they quickly left. Gracie lay staring up at the roof of the car, unable to understand what had just happened to her. They had been so nice to her earlier. Why had she been so stupid?

An hour later Emma and Brianna came stumbling back to the car. They were drunk and giggling at their own inability to walk a straight line. Emma spotted the broken car window about twenty feet away and began to run with her friend following behind. She flung open the back door and found Gracie just as the boys had left her, in a catatonic state, naked from the waist down.

"Gracie!" Emma shrieked, thinking she was dead.

Gracie's eyes moved to Emma's. "What happened, Gracie? Tell me who did this to you!"

Brianna ran to the other side of the car and opened the other back door. The two girls looked at each other, each searching for a sign from the other of what they should do. They both knew she'd been raped. "Bri, start the car. We have to find Sydney. We've got to get Gracie to a doctor."

Brianna nodded. Her beer buzz instantly replaced by adrenaline, she moved into the driver's seat and began to drive. They drove for just under an hour when they saw Syd sitting in the park with her street family. Emma rushed out of the car and ran to them. "Syd," she said, gasping for breath, "it's Gracie. She's been raped. I need to get her to a doctor. She's completely out of it."

Syd rose with urgency. "Oh fuck! Here's what you do. You have ID, right?"

"Yeah, I have a fake ID." Emma could feel her throat closing up on her. "But Gracie doesn't."

"Doesn't matter," Syd said, cutting her off. "Drive into the city and take her to CHOP."

"I have no idea what you're talking about, Syd. What's a CHOP?"

"Children's Hospital of Philadelphia, you know, the hospital," she explained. "Oh, come on, I'll go with you guys."

They ran back to the car, and within twenty minutes they were sitting outside of the emergency room. "Em, you take her in alone to make it seem more real. Tell them it's your little sister and your parents are on vacation. Don't put her clothes on. You want them to bring her right in, give them less time for questions. Because she's a kid they'll check her out quick. After you find out she's all right you take Gracie and beat it. Okay? You got that?" she persisted.

"Yeah, yeah, I got it," Emma responded, thinking how clever the girl was.

Emma practically had to carry Gracie into the depressing waiting room of the ER. The girl was still naked from the waist down, and just as Syd had told her, a woman and a security guard hurried over to them. The woman wrapped a blanket around Gracie's waist and sat her in a wheelchair as others looked on in horror.

Gracie was in bay 12 in the emergency room within minutes. A nurse strode in and began asking Emma questions. How old is she? What happened to her? Where did it happen? Where are your parents? How long has she been like this?

Emma answered the questions rapidly. She told the nurse that their parents were in Italy, but that she was twenty-one and could consent to treatment. Finally the nurse approached Gracie. "Hi, sweetie. You're going to be fine. In a couple of minutes a doctor is going to come in and check you out. You don't need to be afraid, you're safe now."

Gracie began to come out of her deep coma-like state and looked over at her sister. "You're fine," Emma assured her.

The doctor came in, his face tight, his eyebrows raised¬¬, and his forehead lined with concern for the young girl he'd heard about in bay 12. "Hello, Gracie. I'm Doctor Knoll. I'll be taking care of you. Can you tell me what happened?"

In a weak, almost inaudible voice, she said, "Three boys had sex with me."

Hearing Gracie utter those six words made Emma's stomach rise and drop, as if she was riding a roller coaster.

"Gracie, I know you've been through a great deal tonight. But I have to ask you some questions and then I'm going to take a look at you," Dr. Knoll explained in a kind voice.

"Are you related to this person that brought you in here tonight?" He motioned toward Emma.

"She's my sister."

"Good. Now, is there any chance you could be pregnant?" he asked gently.

Gracie looked at Emma with alarm. "She doesn't get her period yet," her sister responded for her.

"All right, that's fine. Now, Gracie, the boys stuck their penis in your vagina?"

Gracie nodded and turned her head away, embarrassed.

"Listen very closely, Gracie. It's not your fault," Dr. Knoll soothed. "Did they do anything else to you?"

Gracie shook her head.

Just then the nurse walked back into the bay. Addressing Emma she asked, "Do you have identification? We'll need to do a pelvic exam and I'll need you to sign a consent form."

Emma handed her the fake ID. The nurse wrote down the information from the card and handed the form to her. "Sign and date at the bottom."

Once Emma had signed the form the nurse opened a rape kit and methodically went through the procedure, capturing all of the evidence. She drew blood and sent the samples off to the lab, not knowing that the girls would never be around long enough to know the results. Once the nurse was finished, the doctor returned to bay 12 and looked at the scared young girl. "Gracie, I'm going to have to take a look at what they did to you. It may be a little uncomfortable, but it will only last a couple of minutes. I promise."

Emma stepped up to the bed and grabbed Gracie's hand. When the doctor was finished, he looked at the two sisters. "You're going to be fine. I can see that you're bruised, but it doesn't look like there is any internal damage that won't heal on its own. We're going to send in a social worker to talk to you about where you can get counseling. I'll come back in to see you after she is finished."

The nurse gave Gracie a pair of scrubs to put on since her clothes had been taken for evidence. Once she was dressed Emma said to her in a calm, firm voice, "Gracie, we are going to leave now that we know you're all right. If anyone asks, we say that you need to go to the bathroom. Are you ready?"

The two girls proceeded along the short corridor of the emergency room. Doctors and nurses rushed by them with a gunshot victim lying on a gurney. No one noticed as the sisters walked out of the emergency room doors. They found Brianna and Syd sitting in the car exactly where they said they'd be waiting.

The two girls looked on from the front seat in anticipation. "She'll be fine. The doctors said she's gonna be okay." Then Emma was silent as she considered what to do next. "We can't take her back to Kensington, it's too dangerous. We need to lay low for a couple of days where no one can bother us. Where the fuck can we go?"

Syd smiled. "I know the perfect place."

Chapter Twenty-Seven

S ydney led them to the Penn Tower across the street from the hospital. She explained that they could park the car in there and be a little safer. Emma decided they'd stay there for two or three days to give them time to figure out where they could go next. The parking garage was used mainly by medical staff and people visiting sick patients.

They parked on the roof where there were fewer cars because they were exposed to the elements. The next day they moved the car down two levels, just to be sure that no one became suspicious of them. Gracie woke seeming more herself. She told the girls what the boys had done to her and they reassured her that she would be fine. "Gracie, living on the streets is tough," Syd explained with her eleven-year-old wisdom, "but you have to be tougher than the pricks that want to bring you down. There are all kinds of assholes out there. You have to be more careful. You can't tell anyone where you're staying. What do these guys look like?"

"Two of them are tall and one is short and fat. They all have dark hair," she described vaguely.

"How old?" Emma pressed.

"I don't know. Maybe fifteen," Gracie offered.

Emma looked at Sydney for confirmation that she could make a connection, but the young girl just shook her head. "Okay," Syd blurted, "Brianna and I are gonna go find something to eat. You two stay here. You don't want to run into anyone from the emergency room."

Once on the street, Brianna and Sydney sat in front of a restaurant directly across the street from the hospital. It was a sandwich joint frequented mainly by hospital workers. Syd stood as two women in scrubs walked toward the entrance. "Excuse me, we're really hungry," she started innocently. "Do you think you could give us a couple of dollars to buy something to eat?" she asked, shuffling her feet from side to side.

The two women looked on, their hearts opening wide for the dirty young girls begging for a meal. "Sure, sweetheart. You stay here and we'll see you when we come out."

Ten minutes later the two women stopped to talk to Brianna and Sydney on their way back into the hospital. "Here, we brought you two hoagies. And wait." The other woman reached into a bag and came out with two bags of chips, two brownies, and two cold orange sodas.

The girls gathered up their food, thanked the women, and rushed back to the car. When they finished eating, Syd sat back against the front seat. "Listen, I'm gonna head out later today. I'll hop a train back to Kensington. My peeps are going to wonder where I'm at. Do you guys have money to get out of the garage?" she asked, willing to go beg for money before she left if they needed her to.

"Yeah, we have a little money left. We'll be fine," Emma told her. She liked the young girl. Sydney was the most resourceful person she'd ever met.

"When will we see you again?" Gracie asked, disappointed that Syd was leaving.

"Don't know. If you're ever back in Kensington just ask around and you'll find me," she told Gracie. Syd didn't get attached to people. She knew from her early years that people come and go from your life all the time. However, she liked the three girls more than she did most of the transient players in her life.

That night, after Syd left, the girls parked the car up on the roof of the garage, where it was open and they could see the sky. While they were sitting there it began to rain hard. The water slammed the car with such force it felt as if they were sitting inside a drum. Somehow, though, the rain made them feel protected. As if it was keeping predators away.

Emma was consumed with worry as she obsessed about how to get them off the streets. With the groceries they'd bought and the gas they had paid for, they were down to $148. They couldn't afford to stay in the garage longer than a couple of days.

She knew that the rest of their money would go in no time at all, and with winter looming, she was aware of the need to find a more permanent solution very soon. She was desperate enough to consider prostitution, but wanted to give herself a little more time to think of another option. She tucked the thought of selling sex into the far recesses of her mind, knowing it was there if they really needed the money.

Emma's thoughts were interrupted by the announcer on the radio. "Join us at Double Visions Go-Go Bar in Horsham for amateur night, every third Thursday, for a chance to win two hundred and fifty dollars," the announcer challenged. "You must be at least eighteen years old and have proof of ID to enter."

Emma sat up with a jerk. "Did you hear that?" she asked the others. "A chance to win money! Bri, I think we should go and try to win this thing."

Brianna laughed, assuming her friend was joking. "Seriously, Em," she chuckled, "how are we going to do that? I mean, we've never danced at a go-go before."

"That's why they call it amateur night, Bri. We have nothing to lose."

Gracie didn't really understand what it all meant. "What do you have to do?" she asked, confused. She was trying to mentally recover from the rape and the thought of Emma doing anything "sexual" scared the shit out of her.

Emma shrugged. "I don't know exactly, but it sounds like all you have to do is dance." Then she had an afterthought. "Do you think we'd have to get naked?" she asked Brianna.

"Don't know. Maybe," Brianna replied, unnerved at the idea of being naked in public. "I have an idea. The third Thursday is in two weeks. Why don't we go there this week and check it out to see what it's all about?"

Emma sat back again and smiled. "That would be perfect, Bri! We'll go there on Friday night and see for ourselves."

"If you have to do sex with anyone, you're not gonna go, right?" Gracie asked, wanting to be sure they wouldn't do anything stupid.

"Right," Brianna assured.

Emma preferred the idea of dancing to prostitution and was thankful for the fake IDs she and Brianna had bought. She relaxed into the car seat wondering what it would be like to go to a strip club. The thought of it made her both excited and anxious. What if the men thought she was ugly? Could she dance without clothes on in front of a bunch of men? These thoughts churned through her mind as she drifted off to sleep to the sound of the rain drumming a steady lullaby.

Chapter Twenty-Eight

They arrived at Double Visions around nine o'clock on Friday night. Emma was a little nervous about leaving Gracie in the car, which now sat in a well-lit area of the parking lot to discourage intruders from breaking in. They had, however, taken the precaution of making her lie down on the backseat and covering her with a sheet so that she wouldn't be visible to the club's patrons. Emma had also purchased a large knife, which Gracie now had in a strangle hold. There was quite a crowd at the bar and Emma had instructed her little sister that if anyone approached the car to run as fast as she could to the entrance, where no one would dare follow.

"I hate staying in the car alone," Gracie said flatly.

"We know, but we have to make some money. We won't be gone long, Gracie," she reassured her, leaning in for a long hug.

At the entrance of Doubles, the girls' IDs got them past the bouncer and they quickly settled into seats at the huge bar that occupied space in the center of the large room. Inside the bar were two stages, each with a pole in the middle. There were several bartenders, male and female.

A good-looking young bartender walked over to them. "What can I get you ladies to drink?" he inquired with a handsome smile, making them feel special.

"We'll take two of the cheapest beers you have," Emma told him.

The bartender gave them a small nod and came back with two drafts. The DJ played music while a girl performed on each stage. Emma and Brianna watched for a while. The girls were all topless, but not completely naked. Emma found that reassuring. Observing their moves carefully, she concluded there wasn't much to it. The strippers wiggled around and made sexy moves. They made eye contact with the men sitting around the bar, the I-want-to-fuck-you kind of eye contact. When the performers finished their set, they walked all around the bar, stopping in front of each person for a tip. They squeezed their boobs together so that the customer could tuck a dollar bill into their cleavage.

Alright, Emma thought, not so bad. When the first girl came up to them for a dollar, Emma shrugged. "Sorry, we don't have any money to spare. But you were really good," she offered.

The dancer gave them a knowing look and said, "Well, if you're looking for a place to make money without having to fuck anyone, you should come back for amateur night." Then she extended her hand.

"My name is Rana," she said. "I've been working here for about two months. That guy over there," she pointed to the far end of the bar, "that's Jay, the bar manager. He's a really cool guy and he treats us girls good."

"The thing is," Emma said hesitantly, "we've never done this before. I mean, we've danced at parties and nightclubs, but we've never danced for money."

"So what?" Rana said. "That doesn't matter. Take a look around. These guys could care less." Before moving on to collect her dollars from around the bar, she said, "Next Thursday night, you should try it."

The bartender approached them again. "You ladies know Rana? The guys here love her."

"No," Emma told him. "We just met her. We're thinking about coming back for amateur night next week."

The bartender smiled. "Good, can I get you another beer?"

"We wish," Brianna answered, "but it's not in our budget."

Minutes later, the bartender came back with two beers. "These are on me. Enjoy the show."

Emma and Brianna sat back and took in the atmosphere. They discussed coming back to the bar on Thursday night. Though a bit nervous about the idea, they both agreed they should try it. The second time Rana came out on stage, they watched her closely. This girl didn't just wiggle around. She could really dance. Emma and Brianna found themselves mesmerized by her performance.

When Rana came around the bar again, she asked, "Well? What'd ya decide?"

"I think we're going to give it a try. You can really dance," Emma added admiringly. "You're fun to watch."

Rana smiled. "Listen, let me find out if you can come downstairs to our dressing room. We can talk about it a little and I can fill you in on what to expect."

The girls eagerly agreed. After Rana finished doing her round of the bar, they saw her talking to Jay. She turned to them from across the room and waved them over. "This is Jay," she told the girls when they approached. "He manages the place. He said you could come downstairs with me."

Jay put out his hand to Emma, then to Brianna. "I understand you two might do amateur night," he said pleasantly. "That's great. Rana will show you the dressing room and fill you in on things. Hope to see you next Thursday."

His reassuring smile made Emma and Brianna feel safe somehow. They followed Rana cautiously and observed all the dancers bustling around the room practically naked and getting ready for their set.

Emma felt comfortable and could see herself easily fitting into this life. Looking around the dressing room, Emma sensed that the other dancers were similar to her. They went about doing what needed to be done, but something deep inside each of them had been stolen.

For the first time in her life, Emma felt as if she was where she belonged.

Chapter Twenty-Nine

I n the dressing room, Emma and Brianna took in every detail of their surroundings. There were about a dozen girls in the room; some were naked, others half-dressed. Rana pulled over two chairs and they all sat.

"First of all," she said, "Rana is my stage name. My real name is Alessa. That lady over there is Shiver. She helps Jay with all of us. She keeps things in order and helps the girls with whatever they need. She dances here too. They named her Shiver because the men say when she dances it makes them shiver from head to toe. Wait until you see her on stage, she's incredible!"

Emma liked Alessa instantly. She was about the same age as Emma and Brianna. Alessa had an innocence about her that was addictively appealing. Yet her eyes were old, as if she had been through a lot in life. Emma recognized that look; it was the same one she suspected other people saw in her.

"So, Alessa, how did you start dancing?" she asked. "I mean, what made you do it?"

"The same reason you're here, I guess," Alessa stated matter-of-factly. "I needed the money. I have a manager. His name is Harlin. He's my girlfriend's brother. I had some really bad shit happen to me a few months back. Now I pay for his protection."

"Is he your pimp?" Emma asked.

Alessa smiled. "No. He's not my pimp. I mean, technically, he probably is, but I'm not a hooker. I dance here and give him half of everything I earn. He drives me to and from work. I live in North Philly."

Emma knew from Alessa's tone of voice that there was more to the story than she was willing to share. She respected that and moved on to amateur night. "So what would we need to wear?" she asked. "Do we have to go topless?"

Alessa explained they needed a costume, but since it was amateur night, they could make their own. "You know, really short shorts and a bra," she elaborated. "You'll need some heels, though. The last amateur night, a couple of the girls didn't want to go topless and kept their bras on. Jay is fine with that, but don't expect to win then. The girls who do amateur night are seriously out to win. It's a quick two hundred and fifty bucks, ya know?"

A little embarrassed, Emma asked, "Do you think you could give us some pointers? I mean, you know, so that we might have a chance of winning?"

Happy to offer advice, Alessa quickly gave them the three most important tips. "One, make bedroom eye contact with the men around the bar," she began. "Two, the guys like it when you bend over and show them your ass; you know, touch your toes and sway your hips for a while. And three, you may not be comfortable with what you're doing, but pretend like crazy that you are or they'll know it. They need to think you're into them. Always remember: it's a stage and you're a performer."

Shiver joined them a minute later. "Alessa," she announced, "your next set is about to come up. You better get upstairs." Then she scrutinized the two girls and asked, "Who are your new friends?"

Alessa excitedly introduced them. "Emma and Brianna—they're thinking about coming back for amateur night and wanted some tips."

Shiver beamed. "Well, I'm sure our clients would love you two!" she exclaimed enthusiastically. She knew instinctively that the men would go wild over Emma's stunning beauty and sex appeal. She wasn't as convinced about Brianna, although the girl was cute and her tiny frame was just adorable. Brianna was the smallest, both in height and weight, of the girls that danced at Doubles. She would be something different Shiver decided.

About to leave the dressing room, Alessa called out to the girls. "Come on, I'll take you back upstairs." When they reached the bar, she said to them, "Well, nice to have met you," and moved toward the stage for her next performance.

It was at that moment that Emma noticed Alessa's "manager," Harlin, watching her. Although not a single word was exchanged between him and Alessa, it was clear to Emma from the way they glanced at each other that this was Alessa's "pimp" and she was afraid of him.

Harlin was looking at Alessa with pure contempt and Emma had to fight back her impulse to run over and rake her fingernails down his face. Alessa was a nice person and it made Emma's senses flare to see her being bullied by a thug like Harlin. She felt the blood rush to her head as her desire to protect Alessa nearly overtook her. Then she thought of Gracie and forced herself to calm down. This was no time for hate, she told herself, willing herself to get up and leave the bar.

As the two girls walked to Pam's car, Emma asked, "Why do you think people are mean? What makes someone prey on people who can't protect themselves?

"I don't know, Em. I guess they're just born that way. Maybe something bad happened to them and they just can't help themselves from being an asshole."

Emma wondered if that was what happened to her. She had killed her father and then Jake. Then she thought about what she did to her mother. "Bri, do you think someone who hurts people is evil if they do it to protect someone else?"

Her friend put her arm around waist. "No, those people are brave, Em. They risk their own ass to save someone they love," she assured her, knowing that Emma was feeling guilt over protecting Gracie.

When the two girls reached the car they found Gracie fast asleep.

"Well, what do you think?" Emma asked her friend.

"I think it's something I can do," Brianna replied. "Look, it's not like I haven't been exposed to this kind of stuff. My mom's a whore, remember? All we're doing is dancing; we won't have to have sex with anyone. Did you see all the dollar bills Alessa got when she walked around the bar? That was fucking awesome! I say we come back and see if we can win this contest. It's a one-time thing and no big deal. Besides, we need money and we need it now."

"Yep, I agree," Emma conceded. "It can't be any worse than being beat all the time. Let's do this!"

The girls stayed in the parking lot, talking until two in the morning, when the bar closed. They discussed the kind of costumes they could make out of the clothes they had with them.

Then Brianna came up with an idea. "Why don't we drive back and park somewhere close to my house so I can get us some slut clothes from my mom? We'll go one night this week, when she's out."

"Great idea, Bri!" Emma said excitedly. "You can get us some of her shoes too. We'll need to be careful, though. We're in and out, you got it?"

Brianna agreed. "I'm so tired," she said, yawning. "I can't wait to go to sleep. You know, since we're here, why don't we check out the area and see if there's somewhere we can park the car and crash for the night. I hate it in Kensington! It really freaks me out."

"Fine with me."

They drove about twenty minutes west of Double Visions to a little town called Ambler. They parked the car for the night on West Maple Avenue and slept peacefully, not knowing what waited for them in the small town.

Chapter Thirty

T he next morning, the girls woke up and checked out the area around them. They found themselves in another sketchy neighborhood similar to Chain Street, but still a whole lot better than Kensington.

When Gracie woke up, she started asking the girls a million questions. "How was it? Do you have to dance naked? What were the men like? Are you going to enter the contest?"

"Holy shit! Slow down, girl," Brianna joked.

Emma looked into the backseat. "It seemed reasonable. We met this very cool dancer and she showed us around and gave us some advice. We decided to go back for amateur night."

"Will you have to dance naked?" Gracie persisted.

"No. We don't even have to take our bras off if we don't want to," Emma assured her.

Gracie, now aware that they were no longer in Kensington, took in the neighborhood from the car. "Where are we?"

"We're not sure," Brianna giggled. "We drove around looking for somewhere different to stay last night. We didn't feel like going back to Kensington."

"Good," Gracie echoed. "I hate Kensington. Are we going to stay here then?"

"I don't see why not," Brianna said without conviction, hoping that Emma agreed.

"Yep, I think we should stay here," Emma pointed out. "Being back out in the 'burbs, we'll have more places to park overnight. We'll just have to be more careful during the day, because we risk standing out in the crowd."

At its center, Ambler was a quaint little town. Main Street was lined with small shops and restaurants. The town's east side, its better part, was primarily Italian. The west side, where the girls had parked, was a multi-cultural neighborhood. The only common factor that seemed to unite the people living there was their poverty.

It was Saturday and Emma and Brianna had four more days to go before amateur night at Double Visions. They had just enough money left to buy a few groceries and fill the car up with gas. That night, they drove over to Norristown. They parked on Main Street near Norristown Tattoo, a small local place known for its unique piercings and tattoos. Most of the locals went there and bikers came from all over the area to get their tattoos done by the parlor's talented artists.

Gracie was fidgeting in the back of the car once they parked. "Emma, I don't like being here. What if someone sees us and they try to make us go back and live with Mom?" she asked, remembering the shallow grave.

"Nothing is going to happen. Just relax. We'll be out of here in no time," her older sister assured her, prepared to do whatever she needed in order to keep Gracie out of harm's way.

Brianna went up to her house alone, leaving Emma and Gracie in the car. Twenty-five minutes later she was back, carrying a large tote and two grocery bags. She got back into the car and yelled, "Wahoo! I got each of us an outfit and shoes. And I picked up some groceries that my mom will never miss."

She pulled the outfits out of the tote. The first was a pair of denim cut-off shorts. From the size, Emma guessed they must have belonged to Brianna.

"They're mine," her friend said brightly. "I used to wear them about four years ago. I think they'll still fit, but they'll be really short for me, since I'm a little taller now."

"Yeah, like a half inch taller than you were before," Gracie joked as she laughed.

Brianna gave her a scornful look while Emma giggled along with her sister. Then for Emma, Brianna pulled out a black spandex miniskirt.

Emma laughed. "Oh, and I guess that's mine? This skirt is barely going to cover my ass. I'm a lot taller than your mom, ya know."

"That's exactly the point," Brianna shot back jovially. "Now, let's see. I got you a leopard-print bra and thong to go with your outfit and a pair of my mom's over-the-knee stiletto boots. I, on the other hand, have a red bra and thong. And these." From the bag, she pulled out a pair of four-inch heels covered in red glitter. "What do ya think?" she asked.

"I think you make a damn good shopper!" Emma told her with pride. She turned to the backseat to look at Gracie, who was slumped down and sulking. "What's wrong, Gracie?" she asked.

"Well, Brianna didn't bring me anything," she said, looking miserable. "So now you two have new stuff and I don't."

Brianna leaned over the backseat. "You didn't think I'd forget our little sister, did you?" she said in an appeasing tone. From the bottom of the bag, she pulled out a fleece jacket, a pair of jeans, and a tee shirt that had a smiley face with a bullet wound through the forehead. The caption read: "Shit Happens." She gave them to Gracie, who was delighted to have the second-hand clothes.

"Thanks, Brianna," Gracie said shyly, almost snatching the "new" garments out of her hands in her eagerness.

With all of them satisfied and a bit happier, Brianna drove back toward Ambler. On the way the girls stopped at McDonald's on Butler Avenue. Fast food was now a luxury they couldn't afford, but they all thought they deserved a hot meal. It had been a rough two weeks for them, and Emma figured if they were eventually going to starve to death, they might as well enjoy one good meal before they died.

Their tolerance of living in a car was weakening. Everything was much more difficult, and the cramped space tested the girls' nerves. Over time, the car that had once provided them their only shelter had become a prison. The interior now smelled like putrid meat with a hint of sweetness. Emma knew they all smelled as badly as the car itself. One time in a grocery store, waiting to buy a few things they'd picked up, a woman and her small child stood in line behind them. The woman watched them intently, her nose scrunched and her eyes unblinking. Finally Emma overheard the small child ask, "Mommy, what's that smell? Did someone go poop in their diaper? It stinks in here." It was clear to the girls how much they smelled. They all felt a little embarrassed as they paid for their groceries and quickly left the market.

They spent the next four nights moving from parking lots to street parking all over Ambler. On Thursday, the three of them snuck into the gym at Wissahickon High School and took showers. Again, they felt wonderful as days of living in a car washed off them and disappeared down the drain. The three of them had quickly learned that for people who didn't have a home or money, the two greatest things in the world were eating and showering. It was a lesson that none of them would soon forget.

That night, they drove back to Double Visions. As the older girls got out of the car, Gracie poked her head out from under the sheet. "Break a leg and make us some money. I really need more burgers," she teased.

Once inside the bar, they were escorted down to the dressing room. Alessa was there and greeted them warmly. "I'm so happy you two came back!" she exclaimed.

She stood talking to them as they got into their outfits, which would now be considered their "costumes." When they were done, she brought them over to her station and pulled up two extra chairs. She dumped out a large bag filled with makeup and hair products. "You guys can use whatever you want," she beamed, feeling good about helping them. When the time came for them to go on stage, Alessa walked them up to the bar. She herself was in costume under a silk robe that she planned to remove very slowly once she was up on stage. Jay had put Emma and Brianna on together at their request, and right before they went on stage, Alessa whispered to them, "If you two kiss up there, you'll get big points with the crowd."

"We can kiss, right?" Emma asked Brianna.

"Yeah, we can totally kiss. Just try not to give me too much tongue," she joked.

Emma and Brianna entered the bar, and each took one of the stages. When the music began playing, they swayed the way they recalled some of the other girls doing. Now sure that they definitely had the crowd's attention, Emma reached back and unhooked her bra. As she slid it off and her perfectly round breasts shot out, she rolled her head so that her beautiful long blond hair fanned across her face and finally settled down her back. The men erupted in a frenzy of yelling and hooting.

Brianna followed Emma's lead and did the same. To her delight, the reaction was similar, although not quite as enthusiastic as the response Emma's moves had gotten. Emma stepped down from the stage, walked over to Brianna, and took her hand. She pulled her friend down to her and they kissed. Emma was shocked that the kiss gave her such a wonderful feeling. Was it because she had, for the first time, kissed someone she actually loved? She did it again and liked it even better the second time.

Chapter Thirty-One

B y the time the music stopped, the girls were topless, their asses were hanging out, and they were completely electrified by the whole experience. They walked around the bar, squeezing their boobs together and collecting dollars from the men. From the way the crowd had cheered, they were both convinced they would win the contest. The girls didn't know that after all the contestants had performed, the winner would be determined by the strength of the applause their performances received. They didn't know either that every performer shrewdly brought along her own friends to cheer her so that the applause would tilt the verdict in her favor. In the end, it was a girl in her early twenties who was declared the winner. It seemed to Emma and Brianna that she was friends with half of the men in the bar. Clearly disappointed, the two girls started down the stairs to the dressing room to get changed before they left.

While they were on their way down, Shiver called out to them. "Girls! Hold up a minute, will you? Jay wants to talk to you."

Confused, they followed her into the manager's office.

"Soooo, did you guys have fun tonight?" he asked.

"It would have been a hell of a lot more fun if we had won," Emma responded, "but we did collect a decent amount in tips. So that's pretty cool."

"Well, you did a really good job. The guys really liked you. If you're interested, I can bring you on as a regular to dance. You work for tips. It's your call."

Brianna started to say something, but Emma cut her short. "Yes, we'd love to dance here," she said. "When can we start?"

Jay pulled out the schedule and put his glasses on. "Let's see...how about if we start you guys next Thursday?"

"No," Emma said firmly, "we need the money now. Can we start on Saturday?"

Jay laughed. "No, I can't give you Saturday until you get some experience. How about Sunday?"

"Sunday is fine," Emma declared. Then relaxing a bit, she added, "Thanks, Jay."

Back again in the dressing room, they walked over to Alessa, who was applying her makeup. She looked up at them with a smile. "Told you that kissing was good," she said.

Emma gave her a hug and kissed her on the cheek. "Thanks, Alessa," she said gratefully. "We owe you one."

"Now we need to try and get this makeup off our faces," Brianna reminded her.

"There's a shower down the hall," Alessa told them.

"Really?" Emma asked, elated that the two of them would now have a place to shower. Things were looking up. "Um, Alessa," she now asked, "how much money do you make here in a night?"

Alessa had started from scratch, like these two girls she had befriended. She knew they had no money.

"Well, I earn about fifteen hundred dollars a week," she told them. "I work six to seven nights a week, depending on how Jay schedules me. I asked him for as many nights as he can give me. If the guys like you, he'll give you what you want. That should be your goal—to make the guys like you. Once you make some money, you can buy different costumes. That way you're always changing your get-up. They like everything from the nerdy librarian look to the total-slut look."

Emma's head was still reeling from the figure Alessa had quoted. One thousand five hundred dollars a week! She was barely able to listen to the rest of her words. She didn't care what obstacles she had to overcome to achieve her goal; Emma was determined to make Jay love her—and Brianna. She and her friend would learn how to work the crowd, no matter what it took.

After the girls had finished talking to Alessa, they took turns showering. Two showers in one day was a dream come true for them. That night, as they drove back to Ambler, they both had reason to hope.

Chapter Thirty-Two

B y the time Sunday came around, they had already spent the money they made at Double Visions on food and gas. Back at Doubles that night, they made their way downstairs to the dressing room to put on the outfits they had worn on Thursday. While they were changing, Shiver approached.

"Hi, girls," she said. "Did you bring other outfits with you?"

"No," Emma told her, "these are the only ones we have right now."

Shiver felt sorry for them. "Well girls, they were good for amateur night," she explained, "but you're going to need to buy some other things to wear."

Alessa had overheard the conversation and came over. "Listen," she suggested, "I have two outfits I can share with you guys. But I can't let you keep them, because I don't have that many yet."

Shiver gave Alessa an understanding look and turned to the other girls in the dressing room. "Ladies," she announced, "we have some newcomers here and we all know how that goes. If you have any outfits you can spare for Emma and Brianna that would help them out."

The other dancers eyed up the two girls, but most of them were already put off by Emma's beauty, which triggered jealousy and competitiveness that worked against the two girls.

Shiver gave them a hard look. "Come on now," she said, her tone both stern and coaxing, "I know that some of you have old costumes you don't use anymore. Be nice. You never know when you'll need the favor returned."

One of the girls, Angelica, a very tall, tight, curvy brunette, walked over and handed Emma and Brianna a couple of costumes. "Here you go. These catty fucking bitches here don't ever want to help anyone but themselves. They're just jealous 'cause you're hot," she said, looking only at Emma.

"Thanks," Emma replied gratefully.

"Besides," Angelica said and lit a cigarette, "I figure if you bitches go out there before me, you can loosen up their pockets. Anyway, I have this ass shaking thing I do." She turned her back to them and wiggled her firm, round ass in their direction. "That makes me all the money I need. Good luck," she stated as she pulled a drag from her cigarette and walked back to her makeup table, bopping to the music that spilled into the dressing room from the floor above.

Angelica had given them two outfits: one, a very skimpy light-blue stewardess number that was made of spandex and had a matching cap; the other, a teeny-weeny maid outfit. Both were the type of costumes popular at adult Halloween parties with women who pretended to be prim and proper all year long before suddenly taking on the role of sexy vixens, using the pretext of Halloween to live out their secret fantasies without inviting raunchy criticism.

Brianna moved closer to Emma as they began to change into their chosen costumes. "I'm scared," she confessed. "What if we fuck up? I feel like a total freak on display. I don't know if I can do this, Em."

Emma was about to talk Brianna off the cliff she was on when Shiver approached. "Emma," she said, "you have the next set. So you need to head upstairs."

"What about me?" Brianna asked nervously. "I'm going to dance with Emma, right?"

"No, sweetie," Shiver told her, "that was fine for amateur night. But now that you're here as a regular, you won't always dance together. One of the girls here will be on the other stage when you're out there, but it won't always be Emma."

Realizing Brianna's fear was escalating to new heights, Emma pulled her aside and whispered, "Look, just chill the fuck out! It's no big deal. Just do what you did before. We need these jobs, Bri."

Brianna badly wanted to be as brave as Emma, but didn't share her boldness in this situation. She knew her friend was right. They did need the money. But for the first time since they had left Chain Street, the thought occurred to Brianna that she could actually go home. Unlike Emma, she wasn't running from anything. Pam clearly wasn't a great mother, but she gave her daughter the freedom she needed and didn't make her work.

Brianna loved Emma and Gracie, but her nerves in this moment made her question why she had run away with them. She had thought it would be an adventure, but was realizing over time how difficult it was to live on her own. She wasn't so sure any more about the choice she had made to leave home with her friends.

Emma could feel Brianna's fear. "Look, Bri," she said reassuringly, trying to talk her down from her rising panic, "it's going to be fine. It's just dancing, you know. It's not like you're selling your soul to the devil."

Brianna didn't respond. She only stared at Emma with watery eyes. Her heart was already racing and she was sweating profusely at the thought of stripping in front of a room full of men. Leaving Brianna panic-stricken and looking wretched in the dressing room, Emma went upstairs to dance her set

Alessa noticed and approached Brianna. "You know, it'll be all right," she stated soothingly, trying to make her feel at ease. "It's a little scary at first, but it'll get easier every time, I promise."

Brianna's tears spilled over and ran down her cheeks. "But I thought Emma and I would be dancing together," she mumbled. "I don't really want to dance without her."

Alessa tried her best to help Brianna calm down as she finished getting ready for her own set. A few minutes later, Shiver gave her the signal that it was time for her to head upstairs, leaving Brianna to manage on her own.

Emma was already on the second stage, and Alessa gave her a wide grin as she entered the bar area. Emma, having flung off her maid outfit and stripped down to her thong, continued to sway her hips, trying to swat away the feeling that she was an inferior dancer compared to Alessa.

A few minutes later, Alessa stepped off her own stage and up onto the stage where Emma was dancing. She positioned her body behind Emma's and leaned into her, placing her hands on her hips. As she swayed to the music, her movements forced Emma to follow the same rhythm. In less than a minute, the two girls were dancing in perfect harmony. Once Alessa felt that her new friend had the groove, she went back to her own stage and finished dancing to the song on her own.

While Emma went around the bar for her tips, Alessa moved to the second stage and noticed Brianna stepping onto the empty one. Brianna stood motionless as the music began to play with her arms crossed over her chest. Before Emma could react, Alessa started to move off her stage, but stopped short. Emma followed Alessa's fearful gaze to her sinister-looking manager, Harlin, who appeared ready to lunge at her. Alessa turned and continued to dance on her own stage, leaving Brianna on her own.

The men around the bar were all focused on Brianna now. At first, they cheered her on to dance, thinking her stage fright was an act. But when they realized she wasn't going to dance, they started yelling for her to leave the stage. Jay stepped into the bar at that crucial moment and helped Brianna down off the stage. Emma felt sorry for her, but finished collecting her tips nevertheless before going back downstairs to find her. She dreaded what was coming next.

Chapter Thirty-Three

In the dressing room, Emma found Brianna changing back into her regular clothes. She was crying and disheveled from having run her fingers through her hair countless times to calm her nerves, which had obviously gotten the better of her.

"What happened, Bri?" Emma asked, concerned. "Are you okay? I mean, you just froze out there!"

"Look, maybe you can do this, Em, but I can't!" Brianna retorted. "I feel like a freak. I just don't want to do it!"

Emma knew she would not be able to talk Brianna into dancing. The deal was done. "It's fine, Bri. Look at all the money I made for one dance!" she said, trying to infuse some hope into her friend and pushing the dollar bills toward her. "I can dance and make enough money for all three of us."

Brianna half-heartedly agreed, but knew that she couldn't stay in this new life they were creating. She now regretted leaving home for the first time since their adventure began. The thought continued to play in her mind that she did have a place to go back to. It didn't seem to matter so much that her mother was a prostitute. At least Brianna didn't have to degrade herself at home for the bare necessities of life, like having a meal or taking a shower. But she didn't want to let Emma down either. She deeply loved her and Gracie.

She nodded and said, "Okay, Em, that's fine. We'll work it out."

Emma was no stranger to lies. She knew that Brianna wouldn't be with them much longer and began to prepare herself for what was to come. She danced two more sets that night while her friend waited in the car with Gracie. When Emma finally slipped into the front seat next to Brianna, she smiled at her.

"I made three hundred and twenty dollars tonight," she told her. "See, we'll figure this out, I promise."

But Brianna had had plenty of time to reflect in solitude while she waited for Emma's performance to end. Her mind was made up; she would wait long enough for the siblings to get a real place to live and settle in. Then she would tell Emma she was moving back with her mother.

On the other hand, Gracie was beside herself at the news. "Three hundred and twenty dollars?! Holy shit! That's a lot of money, Em. It's so cool. Can we stop at one of those all-night diners and get pancakes?" she rambled with enthusiasm.

"Only if Bri is willing to drive us there," Emma bantered.

"Fuck yeah. I'll drive anywhere if you're buying pancakes. Good idea, Gracie," Brianna complimented.

Over the next three weeks, Emma saved $3,800 while dancing at Doubles. She had taken on the stage name of Amme, pronounced Amy, which was her real name spelled backward. It was Alessa who had come up with the idea and Emma loved the name.

The three girls had slowly become accustomed to Ambler's West Maple Avenue and had even formed a few friendships with some of the people who lived there. They felt at home here. One of them was a woman named Katie, whom Emma talked to every day. Katie had been beaten by her mother as a child. When she was seventeen, her stepfather had raped her and she became pregnant. Her mother had promptly thrown her six-months-pregnant daughter out on the streets claiming if her daughter wasn't such a slut it would never have happened.

While living on the streets, Katie had met a man named Bryce. Ten years older than her, he had taken a liking to the pregnant teen. Bryce had a thing for younger girls. Katie knew he cheated on her all the time, but she didn't care. He provided a roof over her head, which was all she really cared about. It wasn't as if she was madly in love with him. She had initially moved in with him because she didn't have a place to live and just never left after her daughter was born. Katie was now twenty-two years old with a five-year-old daughter that looked just like her.

A month after Emma started working at Doubles, and just a few weeks after meeting Katie, she announced to Brianna and Gracie that they were going apartment hunting. Katie had told her about an apartment for rent on Railroad Avenue. Katie knew the owner. He was the same guy that

Bryce rented their apartment from. He was a slum landlord, but he didn't ask too many questions.

The apartment turned out to be located inside a large three-story row home. Each apartment was on a separate floor. The outside of the building was covered in aged white stucco that had acquired, through years of neglect, the appearance of gray cement. They followed a cracked walkway to the rear of the house and into a small backyard that was littered with trash and a broken, rusted lawn mower. There, by the back entrance to the first-floor unit, they met the owner, a bald, stocky man who wobbled when he walked. He opened the door and told them to go in.

They entered through the kitchen. To the right was a small stainless-steel sink, smothered in grime. The faucet, suffering from a steady, nagging drip, was covered with mildew around the spout. To the left was a tiny stove that looked as though it belonged in a trailer home rather than in an apartment. Blackish-brown streaks ran down its sides from food that had once boiled over and never been cleaned. There were six cabinets with a few drawers along the longest wall, and the linoleum floor was two shades of brown, ugly and uglier. The white plastic tiles on the walls were yellowed and smeared with grease.

The open living room had unfinished wood flooring that had turned a dirty brown, and the white walls still sported scuff marks and crayon drawings from its previous tenants. The sole bedroom, with two windows, was situated in the corner of the apartment. The walls were orange and the wood floor had been painted black.

Emma thought the place was a complete dump. After they had finished looking it over, she asked, "How much is it?"

"It's four-fifty a month. I will need a five-hundred-dollar deposit and the first month's rent, if you want to take it today."

Emma turned to Gracie and Brianna. "Are we good?"

Both girls nodded.

"Great," Emma told the owner, "we'll take it."

She peeled off $950 from the wad of cash in her purse and handed it to him. From his back pocket, the owner pulled out a lease, which he had Emma fill in. She filled in the form, with mostly lies, signed it, and gave it back to him.

Handing her the keys, he said, "Make sure I get your rent check the first of every month. If you're late, you're out."

As he closed the door behind him, Emma said, "And fuck you too! Asshole!" She turned to Brianna and Gracie, who were both looking around the apartment.

"Gotta run," Katie said, leaning in to give Emma a hug before she left, "I'll catch you later."

The three girls walked from room to room, relishing all the space they now had to share. While the apartment was dark and depressing, in need of major repairs, they were all happy to have a place of their own. They had been living in the car for far too long.

"So," Brianna said, egging on her friends, "we need to get some furniture and stuff. What do ya say we drive over to the Salvation Army and see if they have anything?"

"Definitely," Emma said approvingly.

The girls made out well at the Salvation Army. They bought a used burgundy sofa that was in better condition than the one in the home Emma and Gracie had grown up in. They also bought a small television set, bath towels, and a mattress. When Gracie noticed the mattress in the far corner of the store, she dragged Emma by the hand over to it. Lying on top, she beamed up at her sister. "Now this is what I'm talking about. Ahhhhh! I can see myself sleeping like a baby on this beauty."

Emma laughed at her sister's theatrical performance. She liked seeing Gracie so happy and was, for the first time, grateful that they had left Norristown to find their own way.

Before they left the store, they scored various kitchen items and other essentials they needed. They drove to their apartment with enough things to get them started. It wasn't much, but it was the most they had since they left their home on Chain Street.

The three girls spent the rest of the day setting up their new apartment. By eight o'clock that night, they were high on the thrill of having a place to live but exhausted from all the work they'd done that day. Gracie and Brianna slept on the bare mattress, covered with the blankets they had used in the car. Emma lay down on the floor next to them.

She lay awake, filled with pride that they had come this far. Embracing the moment, she allowed herself to release the hatred she had stored within, a hatred that had always simmered just beneath the surface. She was now free of the bitterness, free to be happy. She didn't know that her newfound happiness would be so short lived.

Chapter Thirty-Four

A week later, when they were well settled into their apartment, Brianna broached the subject she had been meaning to discuss with Emma.

"Em, I want to talk to you," she announced somberly, interrupting her friend who was reading in the living room.

Emma looked up from her book. "What's up?"

"Em, now that you guys are all settled, I was thinking I would move back with my mom. I mean, I really want to finish high school, and this place is the perfect size for you and Gracie. It's not that I don't like living here with you, but I just can't see any future for me. You know what I mean?"

Emma had been anticipating this moment and had promised herself that when it did arrive, she wouldn't be selfish. "Come here, Bri," she said gently, pulling her friend onto the sofa and wrapping her arms around her. "I hate that you're leaving, but I get it. You're a good friend. Not many people would have stayed this long and put up with so much bullshit and uncertainty as you have when they had a place of their own to go back to. Besides, it's not like you'll never come back here to spend time with us, right?"

Brianna was relieved that Emma respected her decision. "Of course I'll be here all the time to see you guys!" she promised. "We're best friends and we always will be."

"So when are you going, Bri?"

"I was going to wait till morning so that I could tell Gracie myself. I don't want her to think I'm running out on you guys, ya know?"

The two girls stayed up most of the night, talking. They laughed about their experiences over the previous months, mocking themselves for the dirt balls they had been when they went a week or longer without showering. They talked about their mutual hatred for Jake and gloated over his untimely death. Just before daybreak, they fell asleep on the sofa.

Hardly a couple of hours passed before Gracie came out of the bedroom, banging around in the kitchen to get a bowl of cereal for herself. When she finished her breakfast, she joined the two older girls who were now awake in the living room. Brianna explained that she was moving back home. Gracie dissolved in tears at the news and cried for a long time. She was sad to see her go and worried they wouldn't see her ever again. With great effort, the two older girls managed to calm her down. Not long after, Brianna packed her clothes and drove back to Norristown.

The two sisters made dinner that night. As they were eating, Gracie asked, "Emma, am I going back to school at all? I'm just asking, because I really want to."

Emma thought about it for a moment. "Of course you are, Gracie. We're gonna get everything figured out."

Later, after Gracie had gone to sleep, Emma thought about getting her into school. She knew exactly what she had to do to make that happen.

The next morning, she made the dreaded phone call to her mother. The girls had left home without any real identification and Emma had no option but to call Valerie and tell her that she needed Gracie's ID so she could go back to school.

Valerie answered the phone on the third ring. "Hello?"

"It's me, Emma. I need to get Gracie into school. I want you to put her birth certificate and immunization records in an envelope and leave it under the cushion on the front porch sofa tonight. Someone will pick it up."

Valerie silently listened to her elder daughter. She knew from experience and from the reflection she saw every morning in the mirror of her disfigured face to what lengths Emma was capable of going to get what she needed.

"Emma," she managed to say, struggling in vain to keep her voice from breaking, "you've ruined my life. You destroyed my face and now everyone is afraid to come near me. Men used to think I was beautiful. Now people can't even look at me!"

"Good!" her daughter responded without a trace of remorse. "Now just do what I've told you. I'll need my birth certificate too. Just make sure you have everything out there before you go to bed."

"Aren't you even a bit sorry for what you've done to me, Emma?" Valerie persisted. "You've lost all compassion."

"You're right!" Emma shot back. "Not only have I lost all my compassion, I've also lost my innocence and my virginity that you allowed my father to rob from me. So don't give me any of your shit. If you had done something to protect us, things might have been very different today. Instead, you chose to beat us down just like they did. So now you can live with the consequences!"

Hearing the anger in her daughter's voice escalate, Valerie grew increasingly fearful. She didn't want to push her. Even though she played stupid all the time, she was secretly aware that she had participated in the brutal treatment of her two children by letting two men abuse them.

Realizing the girls were now older and could articulate enough to convince the police about their mother's culpability in all that had happened to them, she backed off. She feared that if the matter became public, its aftermath would be enough to keep her in prison for a very long time. She now wished that Emma had never found Gracie buried in the basement; since Emma had found her, Valerie's life had been ruined. Pepper was right after all, she should have aborted Gracie.

"Fine, Emma, the papers will be there," she said, wishing she could slap the shit out of her daughter.

Emma hung up the phone without saying good-bye.

Gracie had been sitting by Emma all through her phone conversation with Valerie. Now she covered her older sister's hand with her own. "I'm happy we don't live with her anymore. When Jake was beating me that night, before he buried me in the basement, she stood and watched him from the doorway. I begged her to make him stop and she just told me if I weren't such an annoying little bitch, Jake wouldn't have to punish me. I wished so hard for you to come home, and when you didn't, I wished that she was dead and Jake too. I hate her, Em," she said softly, looking for reassurance from her older sibling. "You're the one that has acted like my mom my whole life. We'll be okay. We'll always have each other, right?"

Emma scooped her up in her arms. "Of course we will. I'll love you till the end," she said warmly. "AND we're gonna be better than okay. We'll never have to deal with people hurting us again. Understand?"

Gracie nodded and relaxed in her sister's embrace. She knew how lucky she was to have Emma. She would do anything to stay with her, even if it meant lying, cheating, or stealing.

They found comfort in each other's embrace and felt fortunate, if for no other reason than to have been born sisters. They were encouraged at the new life they were beginning.

However, they were young, and while they were experts at dealing with what took place inside a home where evil dominated, they were naïve about the horrors outside of those walls of hell.

Chapter Thirty-Five

That night, Emma had Brianna pick up the papers that Valerie left on the front porch and deliver them to her in Ambler. Since she was scheduled for a shift at Double Visions the following night, Emma asked Brianna to come back again to the apartment to drive her to work.

"It's just a temporary arrangement, Bri," she explained, "until I can figure out how I'm going to get to work and back on my own. I'll talk to Katie tomorrow and see if she knows someone that will sell me a car."

"Who's gonna sell you a car, Emma?" Brianna asked, half-laughing.

"I don't know yet, but somebody will," she said confidently. "And I'll learn how to drive."

It was not in Emma's nature to worry about such minor details. Her primary concern was her sister's safety and her ability to earn a living so that they could remain in their apartment.

The next morning, Emma went to see Katie about a car. As it turned out, her friend knew a guy who sold stolen cars and was confident about being able to help work out a deal. Later that afternoon, the two girls went to meet the man. Not long after, they left in an old Chevy Cavalier for which Emma had paid $500 and an extra $50 to get a new out-of-state license plate, which too had been stolen. The crooked salesman had assured her that the plate would kill any suspicion about the vehicle being a stolen one.

"Besides," he pointed out, "the car won't be registered in your name anyway."

Katie drove the car and they chugged their way back to Railroad Avenue. By the time they got back to the apartment, it was almost dark. Gracie and Brianna came running out to see the car. It was a piece of shit, as cars went, but it would get Emma to work.

Brianna and Katie took turns teaching Emma how to drive, and a week later, she drove herself to Doubles for the first time. She left Gracie alone at home, sternly warning her never to open the door for anyone. She instructed her to call 911 if anything happened while she was at work.

It didn't take Emma long to settle into her job as a stripper. She didn't mind the work and she made a lot of money doing it. She had also become friends with Foster, the bartender she had met the first night at the go-go bar. Foster was almost six feet tall, had a stocky, muscular build, and wore his short brown hair spiked. He had a round, handsome face and his beard and mustache made him look older than his twenty-two years. He was friendly with everyone, but it was the way he cared about Emma that made him so special to her. At the end of her shift, she would sit at the bar and they would talk about their lives. Eventually she admitted to him that she had been beaten as a child. But that was as far as sharing secrets went. She neither revealed her age nor the fact that she had killed Pepper and Jake.

Emma also spent a lot of time talking with Alessa down in the dressing room. The two girls gelled perfectly and enjoyed being together. One night, as Emma was going up on stage, she noticed Alessa and Harlin standing in a corner of the room. It was obvious from the way Alessa shrank away from him that he was angry with her and that his fury frightened her.

Later that night, Emma overheard Alessa and Shiver talking about what happened. An hour later Emma was in the dressing room talking to Shiver when Alessa walked in and plopped down in a chair. As Alessa began to change back into her regular clothes Shiver approached her.

"What's going on?" Shiver inquired anxiously. "You still have another hour left on your shift. Has something happened? If one of our customers has been giving you a hard time, you just need to tell me who it is and he'll be out of here in a minute. Jay doesn't tolerate his dancers being harassed."

"No, it's nothing like that," Alessa explained. "One of the men asked me for a lap dance. I told him I didn't do them. Harlin overheard me and now he's really pissed. I've never seen him look so mad. He scared the shit out of me. I'm afraid of what he'll do to me once he gets me in the car."

Shiver had been curious all along about Harlin's relationship with Alessa. Now she had the chance to ask about it. "What is Harlin to you anyway?" she asked. "He's always around with those creepy friends of his, watching everything you do. Is he your boyfriend?"

"No, he's my best friend's brother. He lets me live at his house and I pay him for protection."

Shiver laughed. "Protection from what?"

Feeling stupid now, Alessa mumbled, "You know, if any of the men that come in here follow me home after my shift. Harlin makes sure I don't have to ride the bus to and from work. He looks out for my safety in North Philly too."

Shiver was visibly disgusted, "He sounds like an asshole to me."

But Shiver sensed the conversation was just making Alessa more nervous than ever. Worry and fear were plastered large on Alessa's face. She was having a hard time focusing on what Shiver was telling her. Poor kid, Shiver thought to herself. She herself knew a lot about being on the streets. It wasn't as if she had grown up in a perfect household and then decided to become a stripper. Shiver had begun dancing for survival. Now she danced because she enjoyed it and loved the money. It allowed her luxuries in life that she wouldn't be able to afford otherwise.

"Don't worry, Alessa," Shiver assured her now. "Everything will work out. I promise. In the meantime, tell the prick that I am going to teach you how to perform a lap dance. You get paid a lot of money for lap dances and they are easy, not as scary as you think. I will teach you everything you need to know. All right?"

Alessa reluctantly agreed, trusting Shiver not to make her do anything she wouldn't be comfortable with. She quickly changed and gave her a long hug.

"Thanks, Shiver," she said gratefully. "I don't know what I would do without you."

"I'm glad I can help," Shiver told her. "When I started out myself, someone was there to help me. We're a family here, remember?"

Alessa smiled and headed toward the door.

Over time, Emma began to observe more closely how Harlin treated her friend. She never failed to notice the look of fury on his face whenever he interacted with Alessa. Emma wanted to help her friend, but didn't know how. She began by asking Foster casual questions about the pair.

Foster didn't know much about Harlin, but clearly didn't like him either. He confided to Emma that he'd seen the guy roughly grip Alessa by the arm on several occasions and that he too shared Emma's conviction that Alessa was terrified of him. In the weeks that followed Harlin's outburst regarding Alessa giving lap dances, she became withdrawn, barely giving Emma a chance to talk to her.

During those weeks, Alessa performed more lap dances than any of the other girls at Doubles. At the end of each shift, she was utterly exhausted, and Emma suspected Harlin was forcing her to work beyond her capability.

One night, after Emma had witnessed this familiar pattern of events yet again, she confronted her friend.

"What's going on with you?" she asked, concerned. "You never have time to talk to anyone anymore. You do your set and then it's just one lap dance after another. Is everything all right with you? Is there something I can do to help? If you want to leave Harlin, I can help. You can come and stay with Gracie and me for a while."

Alessa wasn't going to share her painful secrets with anyone. "Listen, Emma," she replied, "I appreciate that you care about me and all, but you need to just stay out of it. Harlin is a very dangerous guy. So please, for your own sake, don't talk to anyone about me or him."

Emma reluctantly agreed, but couldn't help adding, "If this shit keeps up, Alessa, you're gonna have to tell someone. When you're ready and if you need a friend, you can talk to me. I'm not afraid of that asshole."

Alessa gave her a forced grin and thought to herself that if Emma knew what Harlin was capable of doing to people, she would know she couldn't help her.

The girls embraced in the same way that men shake hands when they come to an agreement. However, Emma knew that her friend would never ask for help and Alessa knew that Harlin was her problem and that she'd never cast him off on anyone. Emma contemplated how she could kill Harlin, but he always traveled with his gang and left no opportunity to catch him alone. While the thought of bumping off the hoodlum made Emma feel charged, she reminded herself that she had to keep Gracie safe. There was no telling what kind of revenge a gang would take on them if they found out who had killed their leader.

Only a few weeks later, Shiver came into the dressing room and gathered all the girls together. Then she told them that Alessa had been fired.

"Jay caught her having sex with one of our clients in the lap-dance room," she said solemnly. "I know we will all miss her very much, but this should be a lesson to everyone. Jay will not tolerate any of his girls selling sex in his bar."

Emma wished now that she had asked Alessa exactly where she lived in North Philadelphia. She knew how urgently her friend needed help at the moment, but resigned herself to the fact that there was nothing she could do for her. In the years to come, she would regret failing to intervene on Alessa's behalf.

Chapter Thirty-Six

A t the end of the evening, while Emma and Foster were still engaged in conversation centering on Jay firing Alessa, one of the dancers came up to the bar and asked for a shot of tequila. The moment Foster laid it on the bar in front of her, the girl, whose name was Jade, gulped it down quickly and ordered a second shot. Then she ordered another. And another. After chasing the tequila with a couple of beers, she was loaded and in no condition to drive. Emma offered to take her home. Half an hour later, she was driving a very drunk Jade to her home in Conshohocken.

Emma parked in the driveway in front of the girl's garage and, given her condition, decided to help her into the house. She found the dancer's living room well lit and cozy. It was certainly a nice place, considering that Jade was a single mom with two small kids.

"Do you own this house?" Emma asked with a twinge of envy.

"Nah, I rent it," Jade replied. "The landlord gave me a good deal, since I was willing to sign a five-year lease. I pay eleven hundred a month, but he takes care of the water bill. Not too bad, huh?"

"Not bad at all! Where's your babysitter?" Emma asked, looking around the living room.

"I don't have one," Jade said nonchalantly. "Once I get my kids to bed, they sleep all night."

"Oh, I thought your kids were young."

"They're six and eight, old enough to stay here on their own while I work," Jade said. She pulled two beers from the refrigerator, offering one to Emma, who declined.

"Six and eight? Aren't they kinda young to stay home alone all night?"

"What the fuck are you?" Jade retorted heatedly. "Some saint? They're fine! Besides, I fucking hate those kids. They ruined my fucking life. Before they were born, I used to be able to do whatever I wanted. Then their asshole father bailed when I got pregnant with the second one. I wish he had taken those two with him. But nooooo, I got stuck with them. It's so annoying being a mom and they're so fucking needy! Ya know what I mean?"

Emma felt as if she were talking to a female version of Pepper. She imagined her father having this kind of conversation with his drunken friends at the bar. She sensed that Jade really did hate her children, and that made Emma begin to dislike the bitch immediately. She wondered if it was the alcohol talking, but not even that would be a good excuse for hating her children.

Emma knew that if she ever had kids, which she wasn't so sure she would, they would be loved and nurtured. The way Mrs. Tisdale had cared for her and Gracie when they were younger.

"I just think you're a little drunk, Jade," she observed. "But I gotta tell ya what you're saying about your kids is pretty fucking lousy."

"Yeah, I know, but I can't help it," Jade admitted. "Maybe you're right. Maybe I am too drunk. I need to go to bed. You're welcome to stay overnight, if you want," she said, running her hand over Emma's ass. "I'm into chicks more than guys, if you know what I'm sayin'."

"Yeah, I know what you're saying, Jade," Emma told her. "But I have to go. See you at Doubles."

Once she was back in the car, she turned off the radio and drove in silence to Ambler. Dwelling on what Jade had said, she decided that she was a mean-spirited person who said whatever she wanted without using a filter. She wondered if her children knew their mother hated them, given how brutally honest she had been with Emma, whom she hardly knew. Emma decided she would get to know Jade better. She wanted to find out if her assumptions about her fellow dancer were true.

Chapter Thirty-Seven

O ver the next couple of weeks, Emma started to hang out with Jade outside work hours. She felt more like a stalker than a friend, but played her role convincingly. Jade, she realized with increasing disgust, never had a kind word to say about her kids, Claire and Mason. She also drank like a slob until she passed out. Night after night, Jade slept wherever her drunken body fell.

On a couple occasions Gracie went over to Jade's house and stayed with her children while Emma took their mother out, trying to understand the type of person she was. It was a warm summer night when Emma and Jade made plans to go to dinner. Emma didn't like what she'd already seen of her drunken acquaintance, but felt an overwhelming sense of responsibility to Claire and Mason, whom she was now getting to know better.

Gracie had offered to stay with the two children while they went out. When Emma and Gracie walked into the living room, they saw Mason sitting on the floor in the middle of the room. He was whimpering and Jade was leering over him. "Suck it up, you little sissy. All you do is whine, whine, whine!"

"But Mom, his arm hurts him. The doctor gave you painkillers, just give him one," Claire pleaded.

"You shut your dirty mouth, you little bitch. I'm the mother and I will do what I think needs to be done. He doesn't need painkillers; he needs a good kick in the ass!" Jade screamed.

"Jade, what's going on?" Emma asked with annoyance in her voice.

"Oh, sissy baby over here broke his fucking arm early this morning," she stated.

Mason turned to look at Emma. His face was red and puffy from crying. "It hurrrts so bad," the small boy offered, hoping Emma would convince his mother to give him a painkiller.

"Jade, give him a pill for the pain. What the fuck's wrong with you?" Emma shot at her.

While all of this chaos was taking place Gracie pulled Claire off to the kitchen. "Where did she put the pills?" she asked the small girl in a whisper.

"In her purse," Claire told her, "it's hanging on the banister of the stairs."

Gracie walked back out to the foot of the stairs, across the hall from the living room where Jade was still yelling at Mason. She and Emma met eyes and she pointed to the purse that hung next to her. Emma nodded as she engaged in irrational conversation with Jade to keep her from noticing what Gracie was doing. The stupid bitch is so easy to distract, Emma thought as she explained in a heated voice that when she was a kid and broke her arm it hurt like hell.

In the meantime, Gracie snatched the pill bottle from Jade's purse and dumped four of them in her hand. She replaced the bottle and shoved the pills into her pocket. "Listen," Gracie stated loudly, "this yelling is really getting under my skin. Just go, Em. You guys are supposed to go to dinner. We'll be fine."

Jade looked Gracie over. "Yeah, let's get the fuck out of here, I'm sick of these kids. They get on my nerves. Claire! Get sissy boy here an aspirin so he stops that blubbering!"

Emma nudged Jade. "Come on. Let's go."

Once they were out the door, Gracie quickly got a glass of water and gave Mason one of the pills his mother was hoarding. "Thank you, Gracie," he said, looking pitifully sad and defeated.

Meanwhile in the car, Emma was still giving Jade an earful for not giving the boy his pain medication. "Knock it off, Emma. I don't want to hear it," she deflected as she pulled the bottle out of her purse and choked one of the large, miraculous pills down her throat. She turned to Emma. "Want one?" she asked, extending the bottle of pills to her.

"Really, Jade? You don't want Mason to have them so that you can keep them for yourself?" Emma responded as she pushed Jade's hand away.

"Don't be such a party pooper. Every party has a pooper, that's why I invited you," Jade chanted, happy now that she would soon be feeling the effects of the drug.

"Fuck you, Jade," Emma responded as she continued to drive. "How did Mason break his arm anyway?"

"He's clumsy. Your typical six-year-old boy. Always hurting himself," she responded as she pulled down the visor to apply her lipstick.

Emma replayed her mother's voice telling the doctors, nurses, and teachers that she and Gracie were clumsy too. Her guts twisted as she remembered the feeling of being an isolated and fearful child who was consumed with worry that the next beating would kill her. The not-so-distant memories of the physical pain she endured sent icy shivers up her spine.

Then she let her thoughts wander to Mrs. Tisdale, and she realized that if the old woman had lived longer, she may have found a way to save her and Gracie from the torture they had endured. Emma wanted to rescue Jade's children from the prison sentence they had been given without committing any crime. She felt a protectiveness grow inside of her. The same feeling she had willed others to have so that someone would stop her parents. Everyone had failed her, and she wouldn't allow herself to fail Jade's children. Emma would give them what she had prayed for so many nights while she nursed her own bruises and attempted to comfort Gracie. She had a fierce desire to take Claire and Mason and raise them as her own. She knew she had to do something to help them escape the psychotic bitch with whom they shared the same DNA. She wouldn't stop until they were safe.

Chapter Thirty-Eight

A month later, Emma invited Jade and her two children to have dinner at their apartment. Her friend gladly accepted, but grumbled that she wished her stupid kids didn't have to tag along. Emma had assured her that Gracie would keep them occupied.

When she showed up at the apartment for dinner with her kids, all of Emma's silent questions were answered. Jade's son, Mason, was six years old, and the yellowed skin around his left eye was a sure sign of a black eye on the mend. His eight-year-old sister, Claire, had fresh finger marks on her forearm, as though an adult hand had clamped down on it painfully. Others might not have noticed these clues at all or, if they did, made light of them as typical injuries from the rough game's kids played. From having been part of a similar tragic story not so long ago, however, Emma's antenna was up. She recognized only too well all of the telltale signs of living with an abusive parent.

Emma and Gracie shared a look confirming that they both knew Mason and Claire were abused children. Wanting to keep the peace, the girls quickly welcomed everyone into their apartment.

From the moment they arrived Jade proceeded to drink and did not stop. During dinner, Gracie watched as Jade's intoxication turned her into an evil bitch. Then Gracie cleaned up after the meal while Emma took their guest into the living room. Jade continued to drink until she had passed out on their sofa. Though Emma was turned off by the girl's love of alcohol, she put on a show for Jade's children in an attempt to make them feel special.

Gracie had played with Claire and Mason the whole time. While they were playing Go Fish with a deck of cards that Emma had bought, Claire shimmied over the floor to sit closer to her. Gracie sweetly put her arm around the child. A bond had been formed and Gracie jumped at the opportunity. "Can I share a secret with you guys?"

Mason and Claire nodded their heads vigorously. They were starved for any adult interaction, even if that person was a young teen, and felt flattered that Gracie would confide in them. "Well, when Emma and I were young my father used to hit us really hard. He did awful things to us, especially my sister. It hurt, it hurt really bad. I don't know why he did it, but I wish I had told someone. A teacher, a friend, just anyone."

"What happened to your dad, Gracie?" Claire asked shyly.

"He died. He got really sick and died," she told them.

"Were you happy when he died?" six-year-old Mason asked with guilt.

"Yes, I was happy because he couldn't hurt us anymore. You know, when a mom or dad hits their kids all the time, it means that there's something wrong with them, not the kids."

Claire swallowed hard as her eyes welled with tears. "My mom beats me and my brother. She beats us really bad. She tells us that she wishes we were never born."

Mason moved over to his older sister and put his arms around her. Gracie was surprised by how mature he was for a six-year-old. He clearly wanted his sister to feel loved.

"My mommy is mean to us, Gracie," the young boy said. "She hits us all the time. See?" he ended, pulling up his shirt and revealing the bruises on his ribs and back.

Gracie cringed, remembering how those bruises hurt on the inside and outside. Being beaten stripped you of any inherent ability to see the good in yourself. She wrapped her arms around both of them. "What about your dad? Do you ever see him?"

"No, my mom won't let us see him. She says he left us after Mason was born, but he didn't. She made him move out. We talk to him on the phone when she's at work, but she doesn't know that. He says he really wants us to live with him and his girlfriend, but the police won't let us see him. My mom hates him just like she hates us," Claire revealed with desperation.

"Why won't the police let you see your dad?" Gracie asked gently.

"Because my mom told them that my dad did bad things to me and Mason. She told them that he touched us here," the girl stated, pointing to her crotch. "When the policeman asked me if my dad touched me there, I told them yes because my mom said she'd punish me and Mason real bad if I didn't. But I miss my daddy so much," she stated and began to cry.

Later that night, Emma brought the children into the bedroom and tucked them in for the night. Gracie sat on the side of the mattress with her sister and told her the stories that Mason and Claire had shared with her. Emma's heart twisted in her chest as she watched the small figures sleeping peacefully. That night, Gracie slept on the floor next to the mattress, in case they woke up during the night looking for someone to comfort them.

The next morning, Gracie woke early with Mason and Claire. She led them into the kitchen where she began toasting waffles for breakfast. Shortly after, Emma roamed into the room and poured herself a cup of coffee. She sat with her sister and the two children, chatting with them while they ate. Gracie opened the door for Emma. "Last night, Mason and Claire told me that their mom hits them. Just like our dad used to hit us."

"Hmmm," Emma pretended to ponder, "does she hit you every day?"

Claire timidly responded, "Yeah."

"Well, you know that no one should hit kids, right? You're doing nothing wrong. You're not making her hit you. Do you understand?"

The two children nodded in response, but didn't believe a word of what Emma had just told them. It was typical of children who are beaten to think they somehow provoke the violent behavior in their abuser. The self-blame is brought on by the abuser who never fails to blame the child while beating them.

Before Mason and Claire were finished eating breakfast, Jade woke with a full-blown hangover. She stumbled into the bathroom, from where the sound of her puking reached Emma and Gracie. Then she went out to the kitchen, where her children were sitting. When they saw her, both of them froze. Jade stared at them and immediately lit them up.

"If you two weren't such a pain in my fucking ass, I wouldn't have to drink!" she shrieked, spewing venom at them. "I drink so I can numb myself to the reality of being your mother. That stupid, fucking father of yours left me here to take care of you! I never asked for this!"

Gracie annoyed and feeling protective quickly moved to intervene. "Fuck, Jade, chill out. How can you blame them? They didn't do anything."

"Really? They were born, weren't they? Besides, who the fuck are you? Why don't you mind your own fuckin' business!" she yelled and moved toward Gracie in a threatening manner.

Emma quickly stood between Jade and Gracie, making it well known by her body language that she would defend her sister. It took every ounce of self-restraint for Emma not to bash Jade's head in. She knew she was seeing the other side of this reprehensible behavior. For some inexplicable reason, this mother of two had assumed that Emma and Gracie saw nothing wrong in the way she treated her children, not realizing that the sisters had more empathy for the children than most.

"Let's go!" Jade screamed, digging her nails into the underside of her daughter's arm.

Claire flinched from her mother's vicious grip, and Emma could see fear of the inevitable beating that lay ahead beginning to build in the two small children. She flashed back in time, feeling the helplessness and wishing beyond hope that either God or someone else would end their misery.

"Jade," she called out, "why don't you guys just stay here today? We can hang out for a while and—"

"No, I can't!" she snapped, cutting Emma off in mid-sentence. "I have to get these two brats' home."

Emma's temper flared. "What for, Jade?" she asked, turning sarcastic. "What's so important that you have to rush home?"

"I just can't today!" Jade shot back. Then she softened. "Look, Emma, I'm sorry. I just need to get them home. But how 'bout if we hang out later tonight?"

"Okay," Emma told her, her mind racing. "I'll pick you up around seven."

"Yeah, that'll work. I'll see you later," Jade said.

The children walked over to Gracie and took turns hugging her. Then they turned to Emma. Mason hugged her first, and when it was Claire's turn the small girl squeezed her as tight as she could and whispered, "Please help us."

Emma had no choice now. She couldn't stand by, knowing exactly what was happening to the children and still look at herself in the mirror. She had been officially called to duty.

Just before seven that evening, Emma parked on the street in front of Jade's house and knocked on the front door. Claire answered. She had a fresh black eye and a small scab was forming on her split lip.

"Are you all right?" Emma asked.

"Yeah," the child replied, averting her face shamefully.

Emma walked into the house. Jade's son had fresh bruises on his face and arms. Just then, his mother came down the stairs from the second floor.

"Hey," she called out to the children, "be in bed by nine o'clock and don't do anything stupid. You two hear me?"

The children stood in the foyer like two soldiers and nodded, not daring to utter a word in reply.

When they were outside, Emma suggested that Jade drive. She agreed and opened the garage door so they could get into her car.

"Oh, wait!" Emma said. "Pull over next to my car. I have to get something."

She got back into Jade's car with a bottle of Jack Daniels and a six-pack of beer. She smiled at her evil companion mischievously. "I was thinking we could do a little drinking before we go to the bar. It would save us some money."

Jade beamed. "Damn, you're my kind of woman!"

"I thought you'd like the idea. Let's go park down by the train station. No one will be there at this time," Emma suggested.

The two drove for a little over a mile and parked. In a replay of her last, fateful night with Jake, Emma poured the liquor for both of them and pretended to drink. A little more than halfway through the bottle of Jack Daniels and four beers later, Jade passed out on the car's front seat. After Emma had managed to get her into the passenger seat, she moved behind the wheel and drove back to Jade's house.

She parked the car in the garage and pulled Jade back over into the driver's seat. Then she put the automatic garage door control in the woman's hand and placed it on her lap. With the engine still running, Emma got out of the car and used the button on the wall to close the garage door behind her. Emma felt a surge of relief for Jade's children as she got into her Chevy Cavalier and started for home. By the time Emma entered Ambler, fifteen minutes had passed and Jade was dead from carbon monoxide poisoning.

At Double Visions the next evening, Emma pretended to be just as shocked as all the other dancers at Jade's misfortune.

"The police report said her alcohol level was well beyond what she could handle," Shiver explained to them. "Apparently, she passed out in the car with the engine still running, but she had already closed the garage door. She has two small children. I understand they placed the kids with Child Protective Services until they can investigate the father further. At one point, Jade told me the father had sexually abused them, but the older one, Claire, just told the police that her mother had forced her to lie about their father. I heard the kids were pretty banged up when they found them in the house alone and they told the police that Jade had been beating them. The whole situation is a nightmare. Jay is going to do a fundraiser for them to collect money for their college tuition. So we should all plan to help," she added.

Emma sat listening with a concerned look on her face, but inside, she was elated. She had done what no one was able to do for her and Gracie when their innocence was being beaten out of them.

It was her euphoria over Jade's death that made Emma acknowledge to herself that she had done the right thing. She considered what she had done to Pepper and Jake. And now Jade. She tried to feel a twinge of sadness as she focused on each of the three individually, but failed. She had no regrets at all. On the contrary, she actually felt immense satisfaction at having killed all of them. She had killed Jade because her children needed someone to rescue them from their life of pain. In Mason and Claire, she had seen her own miserable childhood and Gracie's. She had intervened, just as she had hoped in vain someone would when she herself had been a battered child.

She thought about Mrs. Tisdale. She had loved that old woman, and if there was still a shred of tenderness in her heart, it had been planted there by her warmth and affection. She loved Gracie and Brianna too, but she had to try very hard to love; it wasn't a natural feeling for her. Emma had been raised in a loveless home and her parents had no love to spare for their children. A cruel combination of being ignored and heaped with abuse had made her incapable of forming strong attachments to others. She was now almost seventeen years old, without ever having been in a romantic relationship with a boy. On one level, her lack of intimacy bothered her. On another, she had no interest in men at all—until the night she met Ethan Miller.

Chapter Thirty-Nine

It was two thirty in the morning and Emma had just arrived home from Doubles. Pulling up to the apartment, she noticed that all of the lights were on and immediately knew something was wrong. She rushed out of the car to find Gracie. Entering the apartment like a gladiator about to take on his opponent, she found her sister sitting on the sofa with a stranger.

"Who the fuck are you, and what are you doing in my apartment?" she demanded.

As the stranger looked on, Gracie ran to her sister and threw her arms around her. Finally the guy stood and extended his hand.

"I'm Ethan Miller," he said simply. "I was walking home when I heard Gracie here screaming. Some guys broke in through the bedroom window and, um, well, I think they kind of roughed her up."

"Gracie, what happened? What did they do to you?" Emma asked in a calm, firm voice. She held her sister at arm's length so she could examine her properly.

The side of Gracie's face was bruised and her shirt was torn. The girl just kept crying. Knowing that her little sister was too upset to speak she turned her attention to Ethan.

"So you busted through my door to save some kid you didn't even know?"

He nodded his head. "I was just trying to help. That's all. I've seen the two of you around the neighborhood and just wanted to make sure she was okay. I'm gonna roll out now," he said, heading for the door. Just before he left, he turned to the younger girl and said, "You take care of yourself, Gracie."

The moment she heard the door close behind him, Emma moved her sister over to the sofa. "Gracie, tell me everything," she said. "I need to know what the fuck happened here."

Gracie explained that two boys, older than her, had come in while she was sleeping on the sofa. She had woken up when one boy grabbed her breasts while the other began pulling her pajama bottoms off. She had fought back and her resistance had angered them. They had begun hitting her. Gracie pulled her shirt up and showed Emma the bruises down her right side.

"Did they have sex with you, Gracie?" her sister asked.

"One of the boys was holding me down and the other got my pants off, but that's when Ethan busted in and stopped them. They got scared and ran."

Emma was livid that these two boys had thought they could just waltz into her home and harm her sister. Her anger threatened to consume her until Gracie's sobs broke into her thoughts.

"Emma, please don't be mad at me!" the younger girl begged. "I didn't let them in. I did exactly what you told me. I even tried to get to the phone, but it was too late."

"I'm not mad at you, Gracie," Emma said gently. "I'm mad at myself for not protecting you. I don't want you to worry about this. I'll take care of everything and make sure you're safe. All right? It's all going to be fine."

She had to lie down beside her little sister and soothe Gracie with her comforting presence for a long time until she felt safe. And finally Emma was able to lull her to sleep. She made up her mind to go out in the morning and buy sturdy window and door locks. Leaving Gracie alone at home was a risk she had to take if she wanted to earn a living. So she would have to find the best way to arrange for her protection when she left her on her own in the apartment at night. Emma considered various options: maybe Gracie could stay with Katie when she was at work? Or would Katie and her daughter want to move into the apartment with Gracie and her? Maybe Brianna would consider coming back to live with them? Her thoughts ran around in endless circles, but finally, she concluded, it was up to Gracie and her to find a solution.

The next morning, the girls drove to Deck's Hardware Store in Ambler and bought brand new locks. Emma had just parked the car outside the apartment when they saw Ethan walking down the street toward them.

"Hey, Gracie," he called out, "how are you today?"

The young teen looked to her older sister for approval.

"She's fine," Emma said, speaking for her. "Can I help you with something?"

Ethan chuckled. "I just wanted to see how Gracie was doing. I didn't catch your name last night," he said to Emma.

"That's because I didn't give you my name. What does it matter anyway? Gracie is fine. Thanks for helping last night. Now just leave us alone."

"Whoa!" Ethan said, throwing his hands up in the air and taking a step backward. "I was just trying to be nice. You don't have to be so nasty. If you want me to go away, I will. No problem."

Having misunderstood his motive initially, Emma felt she'd been a little too harsh with him. Now she lightened up. "Yeah," she said. "Sorry. We just bought window and door locks. So I need to go. I want to get them installed today."

"Yep, good idea," Ethan told her. "Did you get the kind that screw into the wood? They're stronger. You can also drill holes through the sides of the window frame and put screws in."

Emma stopped and looked at him as if he had two heads. She hadn't thought about the kind of tools she would need to screw or drill locks in place. "I, um, I forgot about tools," she confessed. "We gotta go back to the store. Come on, Gracie."

"You don't have to," Ethan said. "I have tools. I just live a couple of blocks over. I'll go get a screwdriver and a drill. I can help you install the locks. If that's okay with you," he added, giving Emma a warm smile.

Still a little unsure as to whether she should trust him or not, she convinced herself that he seemed harmless enough. "Sure, Ethan, that would be great," she now said. "By the way, my name is Emma."

Chapter Forty

E than spent the afternoon helping the girls install their new locks. When they were done, Emma offered to cook him dinner, warning him that they were trying a new lasagna recipe, with no guarantee that it was going to be good. But Ethan was eager to stay anyway. He had made up his mind to tell them he loved the food even if it tasted like garbage.

Over dinner, he asked them many questions. Emma was a little uneasy about the way he was probing, but figured that's what people did when they were getting to know each other. Besides, she was prepared for such situations and had all the appropriate lies in place. She explained she was twenty-one and that Gracie was her younger sister. Their parents had died suddenly, leaving them orphaned with no other family.

"Wow! That's a lot of responsibility to take on," "So what do you do for a living?" Ethan responded, pretending to be impressed, but really only putting on an act so that Emma would trust him. Ethan couldn't care less about how hard their life had been. All he focused on now was getting into Emma's pants.

"I dance at Double Visions," Emma told him frankly and watched as his eyebrows rose in surprise.

"Double Visions? I've been in there a couple of times," he said. "How did you end up stripping?" He sounded more intrigued now than he had earlier.

"We needed the money. So I went to amateur night and have been dancing there ever since."

Ethan was beginning to like her more and more. First, she was fucking drop-dead gorgeous. Second, she was a stripper. And third, the two girls were living alone with no other family. He was pretty excited about the prospect of dating her and hoped that over time she would start to trust him. He knew that Emma would not be easy to break. She was strong-willed, and it would take a lot of work on his part to win her over and let him into her life.

When Ethan left that night, he promised Emma he would swing by the apartment to keep an eye on things. He picked up on her hesitation. "I won't go in, Emma," he reassured her. "I just mean I'll swing by and make sure nothing is going on outside the apartment."

Emma agreed, but cautioned Gracie before she left for work, "Don't let Ethan into the apartment while I'm gone. You get me?"

Gracie nodded. "Yes, Emma," she said, using exaggerated body language. "I get it, Mom!"

Emma laughed at her baby sister. She was relieved that Gracie wasn't freaking out about staying home alone, even though just a day had passed since those assholes had broken into their apartment. She wanted the girl to be fearless, just like her. While Gracie was much less fearful than most girls her age, she couldn't match her daring sister, who seemed incapable of fear. Experience had taught Emma to develop a kind of immunity in the face of danger. Given the aura of invincibility she exuded, Gracie was never afraid in her older sister's company.

At Doubles that night, Emma told Foster the details of the break-in at the apartment the previous night. By now, she and the bartender were good friends and she enjoyed his company.

He was alarmed, however, at the casual way she had narrated the story. "Emma, that's serious shit!" he exclaimed. "Aren't you scared?"

Emma giggled softly. "Look, Foster, when you've been through all that Gracie and I have been through, this seems like nothing. Of course I'm worried about my sister's safety, but I have to earn a living too. And anyway, the way I look at it, it's more dangerous for us to live on the streets in my piece-of-shit car than in an apartment. And for that, I have to keep working. Besides, I like working here. I never expected to like dancing, but I really do."

Foster couldn't really bring himself to share Emma's nonchalance about the break-in, but was too kind a person to pass judgment on her attitude. "Well, listen, Em," he offered, "if you and Gracie need to come and spend a couple of days at my condo, you're always welcome."

Emma leaned over the bar in a skimpy black lace bra that barely covered her breasts and hugged her friend. "Thanks, but we'll be fine."

As she left the bar area and made her way downstairs to the dressing room, Foster's gaze lingered on her. He had a serious crush on her, but she hadn't even noticed it. It surprised him to see how absorbed she was in her own world, failing to pick up on social cues. He tried to keep his feelings for her hidden, but even if he hadn't, he thought ruefully, she wouldn't have been affected by any of his love vibes. He had always been a ladies' man and the women usually fell at his feet. His charm had worked with all the girls he had dated in the past, but Emma seemed untouchable, a class apart.

Chapter Forty-One

As the weeks passed, Ethan spent longer periods of time with Emma and Gracie. He was extremely kind to them, and for the first time in her life, Emma began to feel the stirrings of attraction for a man. New to such feelings, she was confused and didn't know how to deal with them at first. But with the passage of time, she found herself accepting the idea of how attached she'd grown to him. He was certainly an attractive man with his broad shoulders and bulging arm muscles. His blond, curly hair, strong jaw, and wide smile, set off by a perpetual tan, gave him the look of a surfer who had just left the beach.

Six weeks after they had met, Ethan asked her out for a date.

"Em, I was thinking we could, um, go out for dinner before you go to work this Saturday night. What do ya think?"

"Sure, Ethan," she replied innocently, having failed to grasp that he had just asked her out for a real date. "As long as we don't go to a Mexican restaurant. Gracie doesn't like Mexican food."

Ethan leaned into her comfort zone. "I meant just the two of us, Emma. We've been friends for a while and the thing is I'm pretty into you. I thought you were into me too. Sooooo . . . I was thinking we'd go out on a date."

Emma had already acknowledged to herself that she liked Ethan a lot. In fact, she even had a tiny crush on him. "That sounds good," she said. "We'll just see how things go."

Gracie walked into the room at that moment, catching them in an embrace. She stopped short, her eyes wide with amazement.

"What's going on with you two?" she asked.

"Nothing, Gracie," Emma blurted out. "We, ah, we decided to go out on a date this Saturday night."

Gracie sized Ethan up for a moment. "Whatever," she said without enthusiasm.

Emma knew from her reaction that Gracie wasn't exactly thrilled with the idea of her sister dating Ethan. She also knew that her sister could be possessive about her and had always been a little jealous of her relationships with other people, including Brianna and Katie.

By the time Ethan went home that evening, Emma had begun thinking about him in a different way, in a "boyfriend" kind of way. He had been kind to them and was fun to be around. She decided to give the date a real chance and wait to see how the night turned out.

During the week that followed, Emma prepared for her dinner with Ethan. She was nervous about the date, and since it was her first, she wanted everything to be perfect. She had bought a new dress for the occasion that fit her perfectly, accentuating her tight curves and long, lean legs. It had made her feel so sexy when she tried it on in the store that she just had to buy it. As she got ready for their early dinner, her sister walked into the bedroom.

"So where are you two going to eat?" Gracie asked in a disinterested manner.

"Gracie, stop pouting." Emma said fondly. "It's one stupid date. I will never love anyone more than you. So stop worrying. We're going to eat at From The Boot. I'll be less than five minutes away."

"You're not going to have sex with him, are you?" Gracie suddenly asked, catching her sister off guard.

Emma laughed. "Well, I'm not planning on it, but you never know...now knock it off, before I whoop your butt."

Gracie grinned. "Oh my God, you're so gross!" she exclaimed. Then she hugged Emma and went back into the living room.

Ethan showed up shortly before four thirty, and Emma drove them the short distance to the restaurant.

From The Boot was located in the middle of town, which was bustling with people. Given that the only food they bought was from take-out restaurants, the night became instantly more special as she took in her surroundings. The couple was quickly seated at a table in the corner, and after they finished their beer, their meals came.

Emma didn't know if it was the excitement of the evening or her nerves, but everything she ate was bursting with flavor as her taste buds danced in her mouth. To her relief, the conversation between Ethan and her flowed easily, and he was as charming to be alone with as he was when Gracie was with them.

Ethan spoke of his mother and his sister, with whom he shared a small two-bedroom row house. "My mother cheated on my father when I was young and he moved away. We haven't seen him since. My mom sort of regretted it once he was gone, but she expected a lot out of me, still does. She thinks I should take over where my father left off, being the man of the house. It takes its toll. My sister, on the other hand, is a couple of years older than me and she's a total bitch. She's always trying to tell me what to do and how to act. They're both smothering. I've been thinking about getting a place of my own just so I can have my own space," he explained to Emma, hoping to pull at her heart strings.

Ethan talked about his job as a landscaper that he had taken up simply for the money it brought in. It wasn't the kind of work he was passionate about, he told Emma. He admitted that he had been in just one serious relationship earlier, but the girl had turned out to be a psycho. They had stopped seeing each other after her brother beat the hell out of Ethan.

"Why did her brother beat you up?" Emma asked, forever curious about the triggers that activated viciousness in humans.

"She told him a bunch of lies about how I was mean to her and he believed all of them. Whenever she didn't get her way, she would fly into a rage and pick a fight with me. I just couldn't take it anymore and finally told her it was over. But she didn't want to accept the truth and sent her brother after me," he explained convincingly.

Emma thought about what Ethan had just told her. He was such a nice guy and had been so attentive to Gracie and her since they'd met. She was truly tempted to confide in him and share what her own life had taught her: that a real monster could do unimaginably horrible things to the people he or she should love. But she thought better of it and held back. She wasn't ready to bare her heart to him in that way just yet. After all, she had already told him that both of her parents were dead and she didn't want to confess now that she had lied.

Two hours later Emma reminded Ethan that she had to return to the apartment and get ready for work.

"Of course," he agreed readily. "We wouldn't want your fans at Doubles to be kept waiting, would we?" he stated with a little sarcasm in his voice. His comment didn't go unnoticed by Emma, and strangely she found it flattering instead of odd.

Back at Emma's apartment, they stood at the door, looking at each other awkwardly for a moment. Finally Ethan leaned into her. His legs went weak as her lips parted and his own met hers in a passionate kiss. He was thrilled to be with such a beautiful creature and was determined to make her his own. Emma's hormones, too, were raging. Her body was alert, aroused. The kiss left her yearning for more. She had liked him a lot before the kiss, but now she felt irresistibly drawn to him.

"I was thinking," Ethan told her when they'd disengaged themselves from each other's embrace, "maybe I could come over here and cook us dinner tomorrow night, you know, for when you get home from work? I could come over in the afternoon and spend some time with Gracie, keep an eye on her while you're gone."

Emma considered the idea. "Well, I'm working the early shift at the bar tomorrow during the Eagles game. So I should be back by around nine." She added, "I'll let Gracie know you're coming over to cook."

Ethan pulled her toward him, kissing her again, and Emma could feel that he was aroused. He wanted all of her at that very moment, but knew he needed to go slow. Emma was a wary and guarded girl and would surely not be willing to rush into anything. He would bide his time and be patient with this one. She was exactly the kind of woman he wanted.

Up until then, Emma had no clue as to the kind of person Ethan really was.

Chapter Forty-Two

The next evening, when Emma returned from work and walked into her apartment, everything seemed perfect. The ambiance was serene. Yet anticipation filled the air. Gracie was already asleep in the bedroom. Ethan had the small kitchen table set for two, with lit candles and a bottle of wine.

"Welcome home," he said softly, gliding up to her and putting his hands around her waist. Then he kissed her. This time, the kiss lasted much longer than it had the first time, and when the two finally parted, they were both breathless.

"So, how was work? Did the other men love you?" he asked with the slightest hint of jealousy in his voice.

Emma was yet again secretly flattered at his anxiety about competition from other men, but rolled her eyes at him. "Oh, please!" she exclaimed. "Those men are harmless. They were all caught up in the Eagles game and not that interested in the girls. Although, since the Eagles were winning, I got some really good tips tonight," she gushed.

"Well, let's sit down and eat," Ethan suggested. "I made roasted chicken and potatoes. It's my mom's recipe, but I think I make it even better than she does."

"We'll see about that!" Emma teased.

After dinner, they took two fresh beers into the living room. They brought in the candles from the kitchen table and left the lights off, to prolong the romantic ambiance that they added to the evening.

"So what's it like when you dance?" Ethan asked suddenly. "I mean, I've been to strip clubs before and all, but what's it like to be desired by every man in the room?"

"Well, it's not like the way you're describing it," she told him. "I mean, yeah, the guys get turned on, but they're all cool. Once in a while a creeper comes in, but for the most part they're all pretty normal. I hardly think they all desire me. They just watch me perform and give me tips. Sometimes they want a lap dance. It's no big deal, really. For me, it's just a job."

Emma failed to notice how Ethan's jaw had tightened as she talked. He hated the idea of other guys looking at her or thinking about her in a sexual way. After all, in his mind, she already belonged to him. The only thing that Ethan liked about Emma being a stripper was the money she earned. The thing that pissed him off most about it was that he believed she was as much into the men at Doubles as they were into her. That made her nothing more than a lying, cheating bitch.

"Well," he said, "how about if you give me one of those lap dances?"

Emma stiffened. "Um, I don't think so," she said, her manner turning frosty. "Is that what this is all about? Do you think I'm some kind of whore or something?"

Ethan put his arm around her tense body to calm her down. "No, of course not! I was only joking, Em," he said, trying to convince her it was all in good fun. Be cool, he kept telling himself, just be cool.

Seemingly satisfied by his response, Emma relaxed and they began to kiss again. Ethan slowly put his hand up her shirt and softly slid his fingers under her bra to caress her breast. He opened his eyes and looked at her exquisite face while he stroked her firm breasts. She smiled and removed her shirt first; then she took off his. By the time they were lying on the sofa, they were both down to their underwear. With great anticipation, Ethan unsnapped her bra and practically drooled at the sight of her breasts. They were perfect, except for one small scar on her right nipple, where her father had burned her with a cigarette.

Emma was feeling dizzy and couldn't tell if it was from the beer or the passion she now shared with Ethan. She sat up for a moment.

"Ethan," she said, "I don't want to move too fast. I mean, you're the first guy I've ever dated. So I'd kind of like to enjoy it before we—you know."

Ethan gently laid her back down on the sofa. "It's fine, Em," he reassured her. "We don't have to have sex. I just feel really good right now."

He slipped his fingers between her legs and Emma was flush with a sensation so mysterious and powerful that she thought she was going to suffocate. They spent the next hour kissing and groping each other, but it didn't progress to sex. Emma loved every minute of it and was touched to see that he didn't push the issue about having her there and then. She was starting to believe he really did care about her. It was the first time in her life that a man had treated her gently and with consideration. That night, the defensive wall she had erected around herself began to come down, one brick at a time. And Emma made her first mistake by allowing Ethan into her heart.

Chapter Forty-Three

By the time Gracie got up for school the next day, Ethan was already gone. She leaned over Emma, who was sleeping on the sofa.

"Em," she said softly, "I need lunch money for school."

Emma gave her a tired smile. "I have cash in my purse."

Gracie walked over and opened the purse. It was easy to see that her sister had a really good night at the bar. There must have been at least four hundred dollars in one-dollar bills.

"Thanks, Emma," she said. "I need to get going. I'll see you when I get home."

"Bye, sweetie," Emma yawned. "See you later."

An hour later, there was a knock at the door. Still groggy from lack of sleep, Emma answered it. Ethan was standing there, with two cups of coffee and a bag of donuts. "Morning, beautiful," he beamed. "I thought we'd have some breakfast before I head off to work."

Emma put her arms around his neck and kissed him. "How thoughtful of you!" she teased.

Half an hour later, he was gone. Emma sat at the kitchen table, thinking about how good he had made her feel. She was definitely falling for Ethan. He was kind and smart and considerate, with a good sense of humor. She played the events out in her mind from the night before, and when she came back into the moment, she found herself longing for him to hold her again. She thought about him all day as she cleaned and shopped for groceries. And even when she showered to get ready for work, he was on her mind. She couldn't get him out of her head. The more she obsessed about him, the more her desire for him grew. Even when Katie stopped in after lunch, all Emma could talk about was Ethan.

"Well, look at you!" Katie teased. "I think you're falling in love, girl! I can't wait to meet this Ethan guy."

"I wouldn't go that far just yet, Katie," Emma told her. "Love is a pretty strong word in my world. But who knows? Maybe all the bad shit is behind me and I can actually be happy? That would be pretty cool. I'll take it."

That night, while Emma and Gracie were eating dinner, Ethan showed up at the apartment. The minute she laid eyes on him, Emma's heart started to race. This time he had come with a bouquet of flowers. He handed them to Emma and walked over to tousle Gracie's hair before handing her a Hershey's chocolate bar.

Gracie was less impressed with Ethan than her sister and pissed that he had only brought her a stupid candy bar. "Thanks," she said grudgingly, accepting the candy.

"Well, somebody's grumpy," he said to Gracie. "Look, I'll make it up to you. How about if I stay here with you tonight while Emma is working? We can make popcorn and watch a movie," he offered.

Gracie perked up at the unexpected attention. "That sounds great," she said. "I hate being here by myself at night anyway. Besides, the new episode of Vampire Diaries is on tonight."

"Well then, vampires it is!" Ethan cheered, which seemed genuine to the sisters.

Ethan looked to Emma for approval. She wasn't sure if it was such a good idea just yet. When it came to Gracie, she never threw caution to the wind.

Noticing the indecisive look on Emma's face, Gracie pleaded, "Please, Emma, please can he stay? I swear I'll go to bed right after the show. And this way I don't have to stay here by myself tonight. Pleeease?"

Emma pointed her finger at Gracie. "Okay," she conceded, "but you have to go to sleep right after the show. Promise?"

The younger girl nodded and ran off to the bedroom to get into her most comfortable pajamas.

Emma turned her attention to Ethan. "I'm not so sure about this," she said. "I mean, I like you and all, but Gracie is the only family I have and I get a little nervous about leaving her with other people."

Ethan walked over to her. "So now I'm just 'other people,' am I?" he asked mockingly. "I thought I was your boyfriend. Come on, Emma, relax! It'll be fine. At least she'll have me here to keep her company and I promise, scout's honor, that nothing will happen to her. Just go to work and I'll see you when you come home."

Emma was moved by his sweetness. Even the fact that he referred to himself as her boyfriend was exciting to her. In the end, she agreed. As she left for work, she reminded Gracie once more about going to bed as soon as her show was over.

Emma made a shit load of money at Doubles that night. Now that she was earning more money, she was able to buy some pretty dazzling costumes. The men liked costumes, and each time she went on stage, she took on a different persona, to match the costume she was wearing. She had even started working with one of the other dancers to learn how to do some tricks on the pole.

When Emma got home at two in the morning, she found Ethan sleeping on the sofa and Gracie in her bed. The apartment was quiet and everything seemed fine. She told herself she had been worrying needlessly. If she intended to be with Ethan in the future, and, she felt strongly she would be, it was time to begin trusting him.

Chapter Forty-Four

As time marched on Ethan continued to shower Emma with attention. Convinced that she was the woman who would give him everything he wanted, he was prepared to do anything in his power to make her fall in love with him. He knew her type: unloved as a child, bitter, beautiful, and naïve about relationships.

He brought her flowers all the time that he stole from people's houses where he did the landscaping and took her out to dinner at least one night a week. Ethan had even bought the two of them tickets for a live concert by Kid Rock, one of Emma's favorite singers. She had been pleasantly surprised by his gesture, which, he said, had been prompted by his desire to make her happy. But Ethan's only real motivation was to control her.

Emma felt safe with Ethan, as if with him around nothing horrible could ever happen again to either Gracie or her. He provided all that she had yearned for as a child: love, companionship, and a sense of security. Up until the time she'd met him, she had believed that she wasn't capable of loving a man. Emma had always felt insignificant, inferior, as though she were damaged goods from the way the boys in high school had treated her. It was stirring to finally have someone to rely on, someone who wanted to share her life.

In the beginning, she'd often wonder why she had been so lucky to have met Ethan. As the months passed, Ethan began spending even more time at the apartment. He was sleeping over four to five nights a week by now. He always slept on the sofa, while Emma and Gracie shared the only bed.

One morning, after Gracie had left for school, Ethan went into the bedroom and lay down next to Emma. He put his arms around her and she snuggled up to him.

"You know," he started in a calm voice, "the apartment on the second floor is for rent. It's a two-bedroom. I was thinking, maybe we could rent it and I could move in with you guys. You and I could share a bedroom and Gracie could have the other one to herself. What do ya think?"

Emma was taken aback, since they had never discussed moving in together. It had only been six months since she and Ethan began dating, although he spent so much time at their apartment, it almost felt as if he already lived with them.

"Wow! Well, good morning," she said jovially. Then her expression became serious. "I don't know, Ethan," she said. "I mean, I haven't thought about us actually living together."

Ethan kissed the tip of her nose, then her face, following up with soft kisses on her neck. Emma loved it when he kissed her neck.

"Well, Em, I've been thinking about it a lot, actually," he told her. "I love being with you guys and you like being with me, right?"

"Of course we like being with you! But we haven't even had sex yet," Emma reminded him.

"Yeah, about that," he said and moved on top of her. "We can just do it right now!" His tone was affectionate and teasing at the same time.

Emma gave him an incredulous look. "I don't think so, Ethan," she told him. "You're going to have to swoon all over me if you want to make love to me."

"I will swoon all you want! That's not a problem for a rugged man like me," he kidded. "Seriously, Em, what do ya think about it?"

The thought of him moving in with them excited Emma. Impulse urged her to say yes right away, but she wanted to talk to Gracie first. However, she didn't want Ethan to know her sister's opinion might influence her decision. She didn't want him turning against Gracie, in case she hated the idea.

"Give me a day to think about it, Ethan," she finally said. "I swear I'll give you an answer tomorrow."

Ethan was clearly disappointed and secretly frustrated that she hesitated. But he agreed to wait and began kissing her again. Later that morning, when Katie arrived for their daily coffee and neighborhood gossip session, Emma told her about Ethan's proposal.

"I like Ethan, Emma, I really do," Katie said gently. "But he still lives with his mother. Also, he only works in the summer, when he can do landscaping. Then he collects unemployment all winter. He's not what you would call super-motivated, if you know what I mean. He's nice enough, though. I just think you should take things a little slower. That's all."

Emma felt herself getting defensive about him. "I know, Katie," she agreed. "I get it. But I love him. I'm earning great money right now and he's been here for Gracie when I'm working. As far as I'm concerned, that kind of support can't be measured by how much money he makes. Besides, he treats us great and makes me laugh a lot. So maybe he isn't a millionaire, but let's face it: I don't think I'm going to be attracting any of those soon."

Katie reached across the table and clasped Emma's hand. "You can have any man you want, Emma," she told her earnestly. "You're an incredible person. You're smart and funny and great to be around. On top of all that, you're fucking gorgeous, with a kickass body. Don't settle for less just because someone is nice to you. That's all I'm saying. Have you slept with him yet?"

"No, I haven't slept with him," Emma admitted, a little embarrassed by the question.

"Oh great! So you're going to buy the fucking dress before you even try it on?" Katie said speculatively.

Emma laughed at her friend's analogy. "I know! I told him the same thing this morning. But ya know, it's only sex, Katie. How bad can it be?"

"Well, speaking from experience, it can suck pretty fucking bad or it can be great. Just depends on how they handle themselves," Katie responded, touting her wisdom.

Emma was naïve about love and consensual sex. Ethan was her first boyfriend and it would be the first time she had sex with someone she cared about. She was caught up in the excitement of adolescent emotions, and the sheer pleasure of being admired and flattered was hard to resist. She found herself longing to see Ethan every time they were apart. She wanted to be held in his arms. She wanted their passionate kisses to go on forever. Emma wanted to cling to the relationship they had built and believed Ethan's moving in with them would be the right thing for Gracie and her.

When her sister got home from school that afternoon, Emma sat with her at the kitchen table while she ate potato chips.

"This morning after you left for school," she began, "Ethan told me the apartment above ours is vacant. It's a two-bedroom apparently." Emma paused, waiting for Gracie to look at her. "He asked if we should rent it and move in together," she went on tentatively. "It's bigger than the one we live in right now and you wouldn't have to share. You would have your own bedroom."

"Did you say yes?" Gracie asked, feeling left out of Emma's life and ill at ease at the idea of Ethan living with them permanently.

"I told him I needed a day to think about it. I didn't want to agree to anything without talking to you first. So what do you think?" It was clear from her hopeful expression that Emma wanted Gracie to agree to the proposal.

Since he had appeared in their lives, Gracie had seen her older sister happier than she had ever been. She knew that Emma really liked Ethan. She, on the other hand, wasn't entirely sure that she did. There was something about him that made Gracie uneasy, but it wasn't anything specific that she could put her finger on. Now that the decision lay in her hands, she felt it would be selfish of her to stand in the way of Emma's happiness. She was the one person in Gracie's life who had always been consistent in her support and loyalty, always there for her. Besides, she knew that if things didn't work out, they could always throw him out.

"Well, I think Ethan is an okay guy and you get along good," she said. "If you want him to move in, that would be fine with me. You're sure I'll get my own room?"

"Yes, of course you'd get your own room! Always thinking of yourself—brat!" Emma teased, excited to tell Ethan that they could live together.

That evening, when Ethan arrived at the apartment to have dinner before Emma left for work, she practically ran to him as he walked through the door and flung her arms around him. He responded by pulling her body against his own and running his hand over her ass as he kissed her.

"I think that renting the apartment upstairs would be a good idea," she told him, feeling like the teenager she still was. "I think we should do this."

"Oh, baby, you have no idea how happy you've made me," he gushed. "This is going to be so fucking good for all of us!"

As Emma clung to him, he contemplated how great it would be living with someone like her. She was steaming hot and made a lot of money too. His dreams were all starting to come true.

When Gracie walked in on them, he went over to her and gave her a hug. "I think this is going to be great, Gracie. I think we're going to make a great family."

"Me too," she agreed listlessly, forced to utter the words as she noticed Emma watching them. "It'll be great."

But Gracie's instincts told her that something wasn't right.

Chapter Forty-Five

Two weeks later, the three of them moved to the apartment on the second floor. The rent was an affordable $850 a month, given the money Emma was now earning. Now that move-in day had arrived, Emma felt much better about the decision they had made to include Ethan permanently in their lives. She had taken Saturday and Sunday night off from Doubles for the move and worried about losing two whole nights of income, but Ethan assured her that everything would be fine.

On Monday night, when Emma was leaving for work, he asked her what time he could expect her home. A bit startled by the question, she gave him an odd look.

"Why?" she asked. "I'll be home when I get home."

Ethan's jaw tensed. "I just worry about you out so late at night, all alone."

Emma laughed. "I've been doing it for a long time, you know. I'll be fine. I'll catch you in the morning, before you go to work," she said, planting a kiss on his cheek and leaving him standing in the living room, watching her put on her coat and leave.

The next day, when Emma woke up and wandered into the kitchen to put on a pot of coffee and call Katie so she could come over, she was surprised to see Ethan sitting at the table.

"What are you doing home?" she asked. "Why aren't you at work?"

Ethan looked ragged. "I'm not feeling so good," he said. "I called out today. How about making me something to eat?"

"Sure, you want scrambled eggs?" Emma offered.

"Yeah, that's fine, but don't make them runny. I like my eggs cooked real good. So how much money did you make last night?" Ethan asked.

Emma cracked two eggs into a bowl and began to scramble them. "Around three hundred and fifty. Why?"

"I was just curious," was all he said.

They had been living together for two full days and Emma already disliked many of the things she'd observed about him: that he had called out sick from work, questioned when she'd come home, and wanted to know how much money she had made. She felt he was invading her privacy, but suppressed her annoyance, because she wanted it to work out between them. She told herself that these were the things couples discussed with each other when they lived together. The doubts that had surfaced in her mind were quickly forgotten, and by the time Ethan had finished eating his eggs and gone back into the bedroom to sleep, Emma had calmed down. See, you knucklehead, she told herself, he's just sick. That's all. He'll be back to normal when he feels better.

Over the next three weeks, Ethan called out of work eight more times. It was getting colder, and soon he would be laid off for the winter. Emma was worried that his inability to show up for work would get him fired and, come spring, he wouldn't have a job to go back to. She earned a good living, but they had made a deal to split the expenses. Emma expected him to keep his part of the bargain. She had already paid part of his share of the expenses because of the days he'd missed work.

They still hadn't made love. However, they'd engaged in oral sex, but Emma was holding him off for a special moment.

Katie pressured Emma to get on with it. "Have sex with him already, Em," she urged. "I mean, for fuck's sake, you've been living together for over three weeks! It's fucking weird!"

Emma knew her friend was right. She made it a point to plan something special for Ethan and her. She was off from work the following Wednesday night and arranged for Gracie to sleep over at Katie's so that she and Ethan could be alone. When he came home from work that night, she had a bath waiting for him. She met him at the door and kissed him softly. She peeled off his clothes slowly, one piece at a time. By the time they reached the bathroom, he was only wearing his socks.

Emma guided him into the warm bath and washed his back first, then his chest, as he lay back against the tub, his lower body submerged in the water, looking up at her with lust. She could see that he was aroused. Ethan stood and wrapped himself in a towel. Then taking Emma by the hand, he led her into their bedroom. He took off her shirt and unzipped her jeans, revealing her young, beautiful flesh. When she stood before him naked, he moved to the bed and told her to stand where she was. Lying down on the bed, he asked her to turn around. Feeling silly, she spun around quickly.

"No," he said, "slow down. I want you to turn slowly so that I can see every inch of you."

Emma turned slowly, just as he wanted her to, then walked over to the bed and got in next to him. Ethan ran his hands through her long, silky hair and began kissing her deeply. They were both panting and he explored her body, touching her very softly. It was almost as if his fingers were feathers as they glided over her breasts, down her abdomen, and to her inner thighs. His hands lingered a long time in the area between her legs, almost going inside of her, but stopping just short of giving her what she wanted and making her long for him more intensely. Finally, unable to hold back any longer, he entered her, and they moved in perfect harmony together. When they were done, she laid her head on his chest, deeply grateful that she had met him. Maybe Mrs. Tisdale sent him to me, she thought.

But it was more likely that Pepper had sent Ethan to her.

Chapter Forty-Six

B y the time November rolled around, the threesome had been living together for just over two months. With the winter season upon them, the cold weather had brought an end to Ethan's landscaping services. By mid-November, he had stopped working altogether. He stayed at the apartment and collected an unemployment check while focusing all of his energy on Emma and Gracie.

If there was one thing Emma didn't approve of, it was his habitual messiness. Now that he was home all day, the apartment seemed in constant disarray, as though she had just moved in or would be moving out soon. Just looking at the apartment, whenever she returned home from work made her feel strangely unsettled.

Emma had been raised with an iron fist and the only good she acknowledged that had come of it was her habit of keeping her apartment spotless and everything in impeccable order.

After several weeks of seeing dirty dishes pile up in the sink and complete disorder taking over the apartment, Emma finally lost her temper with her boyfriend.

"Ethan, I'm not your mother," she said, exasperated. "You're here all day. So I would appreciate it if you would take care of your mess."

Ethan was indignant at her tone. "You're right," he retorted, "you're not my mother. So quit nagging me, Em. While you're out all night, dancing for other men, I'm home taking care of Gracie."

Emma told him firmly, "Gracie is fourteen years old, Ethan. It's a stretch to claim that you're 'taking care' of her. She's perfectly capable of taking care of herself. As for 'dancing for other men,' you probably need to be reminded that I'm out making money that way. And if it weren't for the money I earned, we wouldn't be able to afford living here. Your unemployment check certainly can't pay all the bills."

His ego in tatters, Ethan grew more incensed by the minute. Finally he strode to the sink, where Emma was washing the dirty dishes he had left the night before, and shoved her aside.

"Fine, Emma!" he snapped in a show of temper. "I can wash my own dishes."

Stunned that Ethan had pushed her aside so roughly, Emma left the kitchen and went into their bedroom for some much-needed sleep. When she woke up late in the afternoon, she found that he had cleaned the whole apartment. She recalled how mean she had been to him and guilt overwhelmed her. She went to look for him and found him sitting at the kitchen table alone while Gracie sat on the sofa watching television.

"I'm sorry, Ethan," she said remorsefully, "it's just that I'm working long hours and I'm exhausted when I come home. I shouldn't have gotten mad at you that way, but I want our home to look nice and be taken care of."

Ethan pretended as if she hadn't said a word, even refusing to acknowledge her presence with a glance.

"So are you just going to pretend that I'm not talking to you?" Emma persisted.

Gracie had a feeling of impending doom as the atmosphere of silent tension finally exploded in an argument. She got up and left the living room, taking refuge in her bedroom so that Emma and Ethan could say what they wanted to each other without her being a part of the argument.

Gracie had been praying that Emma would stop wanting Ethan to live with them and she was hoping that her prayers were being answered now. In fact, she had started hating her sister's boyfriend within the first month of his moving into their apartment. She desperately wanted him to move out and was momentarily elated when Emma took exception to his sloppy ways. Although she hated the slob that Ethan had turned out to be as much as her sister did, when it came to doing something constructive about it, she had fallen back on her old habit of leaving Emma to do battle. From the temporary sanctuary of her bedroom, Gracie could hear the two of them fighting. She sat on her bed, tense with anticipation, willing Emma to tell Ethan to move out of the apartment.

Meanwhile, in the living room, tempers flared as the argument raged between them and the couple flung words at each other that were loaded with venom. After a while, Emma retreated into a cold silence, refusing to engage with him. Ethan watched her moving around the kitchen making dinner for herself before getting ready to go to work.

Realizing that she wouldn't play his game, he walked over to her and said contritely, "I'm sorry, Em. You know how much I love you, right?" Then he nuzzled her, hoping to soften her stance.

At first, Emma refused to respond to his attempt to make up, her anger making her rigid in his embrace. But as the moments passed, she allowed herself to be appeased somewhat and leaned back against him, relaxing in his arms. Deep down, though, she was still annoyed, and the feeling persisted even as she left for work that night and drove down to Doubles. Her mind lingered on the issue that had triggered her first serious spat with Ethan and she now questioned her decision of allowing him to move in with them. Did I make a mistake by agreeing to live with him, she asked herself. She wondered if she really loved him as much as she had imagined and if it was time for him to move out.

When she got home from work early the next morning, however, Ethan was waiting for her.

"Well, it's about time you got home. I worry about you, Em," he said, giving her a tender hug.

Exhausted, she ignored his comment and headed for the bedroom. Ethan followed. When she was taking off her work clothes to get into her pajamas, he came up behind her and wrapped his arms around her.

"I've missed you so much," he crooned in her ear.

As he began to touch her body, she pulled away from him.

"Come on, Ethan," she said impatiently. "Not now. I'm so tired."

"Fine!" he grunted, pushing her away from him and toward the bed. "I sit and worry about you all night. And then when you finally come home, you just blow me off."

Too numb from exhaustion to get into another argument, Emma pulled him down on the bed next to her and slowly began to seduce him. When they made love that morning, Ethan wasn't too concerned about satisfying her. It was all about him. When they were fully undressed, he entered her swiftly, blew his load, turned away from her, and went to sleep.

You selfish little prick, she thought, lying awake for a long time before sleep took over and she fell into a dreamless state.

By the time she woke up, Gracie and Ethan were both out. Emma wondered where he had gone. Maybe he was at the grocery store. She looked out the window and saw that he had taken her car. Deciding to count her earnings from the previous night, she reached for her purse. The wad of money she'd stuffed inside was missing. Panicking, she dumped the contents of her purse on the kitchen table. Yes, the money was gone. Fuck, fuck, fuck, she thought, someone ripped me off before I left Doubles! She sat down with a thump, anger and despair taking hold of her.

At that moment, Ethan came home. "What's wrong with you?" he asked, looking at her shattered expression.

"I put my fucking tips in my purse and they're missing!"

"Oh, I took them," he told her casually. "I thought it was risky for you to be carrying all that money around."

"Give it back to me!" she screamed in a rage, striding forward with her hand extended. "Don't you ever take money from me!"

Ethan reached into his pocket and gave her back the money. His mind was churning with possibilities as he considered how he could better control this living arrangement he had chosen for himself. He realized that Emma was a strong woman and couldn't be manipulated as easily as his last girlfriend. Deliberately softening his tone, he tried to free himself from the awkward position he had landed in.

"I took the money to protect you," he began. "I don't want you carrying all that money around. You're an easy target. In fact, I was thinking that I could start driving you back and forth to work. I don't like this shit, where you're out late at night by yourself. I'm just worried that something will happen to you."

Emma was still angry at him, but she looked at Ethan with a little more sympathy now. She never had anyone actually worry about her before and the thought that he was concerned softened her heart. While she didn't like the fact that he had opened her purse without her knowledge and taken her hard-earned money, she decided that his intention had been sincere and that she should overlook his mistake.

Ethan followed her into the bedroom and they made love. When it was over, Emma lay on her back, staring up at the ceiling. She was still conflicted about living with him. One week, she thought. She would give herself one week to decide if she would tell him to move out.

Chapter Forty-Seven

The next evening, Emma made the mistake of allowing Ethan to drive her to Doubles.

"I'll be waiting out here at two-fifteen to pick you up," he reminded her.

As if she could possibly forget. Emma didn't feel right about him driving her to work and back every evening, but thought if he saw for himself that it was no big deal and she wasn't in harm's way, he would chill out and stop wanting to chauffeur her back and forth.

Once in the bar, she said hello to Foster. He could tell by her body language that something was bothering her, but ignored his instinct to ask her any questions. Emma shared what she wanted to, but for the most part, she was guarded about her private life.

As she went on stage to dance that night, Emma released all of her pent-up emotions from the past twenty-four hours. Then she noticed a new face in the crowd, a man who seemed content simply watching every move she made, never once looking over to the beautiful Asian woman on the stage next to hers.

He had been looking at her all night, and he found her long blond hair almost as lovely as her long, lean body. He liked everything about her. When she came around the bar to collect her tips, he looked into her sparkling green eyes and was bowled over by her exquisite beauty.

Emma had been taking in the stranger's appearance without making it obvious. He was tall, with dark-brown hair and eyes the color of honey. His olive skin revealed his Italian heritage. The stranger beamed as she bent over to collect his dollar. After he had slipped his tip between her breasts, Emma took it out and saw that it was a twenty-dollar bill.

"How about a lap dance?" he asked.

"Sure," she said. "Let me finish going around the bar and I'll take you back."

After she was done, Emma went over to the stranger again. When he stood up to follow her, she did not fail to notice his perfectly tailored suit and knew his tip for the performance to come would be more than generous. She led the stranger back to the lap-dance room.

As she climbed onto his lap, he thought he would lose his mind. To look at her was a pleasurable experience, but to share the same space and be touched by her aroused incredibly erotic feelings within him. He had seen and been with many beautiful women, but this girl they called Amme was magnificent. More beautiful than any other woman he'd ever seen. He was utterly captivated by her.

When the song ended and she got off his lap, he sat with his eyes closed for a long time.

"You all right?" she asked without much concern.

"Yeah, I'm fine," he replied, trying to get a grip on his hormones. "By the way, my name is Salvatore," he said, extending his hand to her.

She shook his hand firmly. "I'm Amme. Nice to meet you, Salvatore."

Emma stood looking down at him. He realized she was waiting for a tip. He reached into his pocket and handed her a hundred-dollar bill. Emma was pleasantly surprised, and knowing immediately that she didn't want to lose him as a customer, she hurried to make small talk.

"I've never seen you in here before. You on a business trip?" she said, trying to engage him in conversation.

Salvatore laughed. "No, I live in Philly and have been meaning to come and check this place out. I finally made it out here tonight. I'm glad I did."

"Good. Then I'll see you here again?" Emma asked, eagerly thinking of the hundred-dollar bill she had tucked away in her palm.

"You can bet on it!" he told her.

At two in the morning, she put her street clothes back on to go outside, where Ethan was waiting for her. She put her tips into her purse, except for the hundred-dollar bill, which she tucked inside her shoe. She was wary of Ethan prying into her purse again and taking her money. As she got into the car, she could tell by his bad-tempered greeting that he was in a foul mood.

"I've been watching these assholes come out of the bar," he said sullenly. "It bothers me that they are all getting to look at you while you're practically naked. I want you to promise me that you'll never cheat on me."

"Oh, Ethan, of course I won't cheat on you!" Emma reassured him. "I love you. By the way, these 'assholes' you're talking about are completely harmless. It's just business." She leaned over to kiss him.

At first he responded to her kiss, but then he bit into her lower lip.

"Ouch!" Emma yelled, reacting to the pain. "What the fuck!? Ethan, that hurt!" she could taste the blood from the split in her lip.

"Fuck, Emma!" he yelled. "It just makes me crazy to think about you dancing for these guys. I feel like I'm sharing you with other men and I don't like it one fucking bit."

"Well, you're not sharing me with other men," Emma said firmly. "And by thinking this way, you're making everything difficult. You knew I was a stripper before you moved in with us. Now all of a sudden it's an issue. I'm beginning to think that maybe our decision to move in together wasn't such a good idea after all!"

Ethan was shocked into silence. He didn't want to lose his golden goose. For the first time in his adult life, he had found a way of doing what he wanted without having to work for it. He liked hanging out during the day. He enjoyed his new lifestyle and was sure that he would eventually transform Emma into the woman he wanted her to be.

"I know, I know," he soothed, trying to pacify her. "You're right, Em. I'm acting like an asshole. I want us to make a life together. Maybe even get married someday and have kids. Please don't give up on me so easily. It's just that you are so beautiful and I worry that you'll find someone else."

Emma almost felt sorry for him again, but then thought better of it. If Ethan wanted to live with her and Gracie, he would have to accept things the way they were. She wasn't going to change for him or for anyone else.

She finally said, "Okay, Ethan, but you need to pull yourself together. If we're going to make this work, I can't have you acting like a jealous boyfriend. I'm not going to cheat on you. So stop worrying. Deal?"

"Deal," he agreed, without meaning it.

His jealousy would always get the better of him. It probably had a lot to do with the insecurity that had been a part of his nature since his father had left them after catching his whore mother cheating on him. Because of what his mother had done to his father, Ethan put very little value on women.

For the rest of the ride home, Ethan talked about how much he wanted his own landscaping business. While he yammered, Emma daydreamed about the new guy, Salvatore. He was so handsome and obviously rich too. He had been very nice to her and she liked the way he had told her how beautiful she was, because she knew he truly meant it. Ethan often complimented her on her looks too, but his words of praise were invariably twisted with jealous, out-of-context references about how desirable her customers at Doubles must find her.

When they got home, they made love and Emma fell asleep in Ethan's arms. He held her and stayed awake for hours, consumed by his twisted imaginary thoughts, which turned into a jealous rage of her cheating on him. As he watched her sleeping peacefully, he had the overwhelming urge to beat her silly, but he knew that stupid sister of hers would come rushing in.

In the morning, Gracie crept into their room quietly and woke Emma.

"What is it?" Emma whispered, concerned to see her sister looking so terrified, and slipped out from under the covers.

"I'm bleeding," Gracie told her.

"What? Where?" Emma asked, frantically looking her over.

"No, Em, I got my period," Gracie explained, a bit embarrassed.

Emma smiled. "I guess we need to have that talk about the birds and the bees now," she teased her.

"Knock it off, Em. I need you to show me how to use those things," Gracie whispered, not wanting the evildoer to wake up and butt into her personal business.

Explaining to her sister how to use a tampon wasn't a moment Emma had prepared herself for. When she was done, she left Gracie in the bathroom to take care of her business in private.

Gracie reappeared in the kitchen ten minutes later and the two sisters sat down to breakfast. Ethan came into the kitchen while they were eating. He was showered and dressed.

"Where are you off to?" Emma asked, surprised that he was going out.

"I have some errands to run," he replied, then reached into her purse and took her car keys and a handful of the money she'd earned the previous night. "Ethan!" Emma yelled, outraged, when she saw him take her money. But thinking better of it, she fell silent. She didn't want to start another big fight in front of Gracie. She knew her sister had heard them arguing over the last several weeks and wanted to spare her the ordeal of watching them bicker again.

"Never mind," she told Ethan when he turned to her inquiringly.

After Gracie had left for school, Emma went into the bedroom closet where she kept a couple pairs of new shoes in their boxes. She pulled a pair of boots out of a box, slid the hundred-dollar bill, along with some of her other earnings, into the toe of one boot, and placed it back in the box. She felt better knowing it would be there if she needed it. She planned to talk to Ethan when he returned home about him taking her money again. She didn't like this habit of his. She worked hard for her money and it was meant exclusively for her use and Gracie's. No one was going to take it from her.

When Ethan walked into the apartment a couple of hours later, Emma practically pounced on him. He was carrying two bags. One contained a pair of expensive sneakers he had bought for himself. The other held a sexy corset and thong for her.

Ethan seemed irritated by her onslaught of questions about the money he'd taken out of her purse.

"Em, really," he said, unfazed, "you need to stop it. We're living together now, making a life together. The money you earn is for both of us. Besides, I bought you a present."

His dismissive way of handling her and the money issue infuriated Emma, but once again she felt her anger ebb when he mentioned the present he'd bought for her. When he pulled out the corset and thong, she stared at them in surprise.

"Are these for Doubles?" she asked.

"No, they're not for fucking Doubles!" Ethan snapped. "What the fuck, Emma! These are for you to wear for me. I'm so sick of this shit!"

In an attempt to calm him, she said, "I made a mistake. I just didn't know, that's all."

Suddenly he lunged forward, grasped her around the waist, and kissed her. Then he lifted her shirt and put his mouth over her breast. He led her into the bedroom and handed her the gift he'd bought her. Emma began to undress, but before she could put on the corset and thong, Ethan told her to go to the bathroom to change so that she could surprise him. She thought it was a weird request, but didn't refuse him, touched as she was that he had thought to buy her a present, even if it was with her own money, and it wasn't lost on her that it was a gift for him rather than for her. All the time she was gone, Ethan sat stewing on her question about the lingerie being for her use at Doubles.

When Emma came back into the bedroom and Ethan saw how hot she looked, lust surged through him. Silently he motioned her onto the bed. She inched closer and bent down to kiss him. He yanked her down on the bed and began touching her intrusively. Taken off guard by his aggression, she took a moment to respond. In those few seconds of hesitation on her part, his arousal was fueled further by anger. He reached down with one hand and ripped her thong off. Before she could react, he had jammed his fingers inside of her with unexpected force. She arched back from the pain and tried to push him away. In retaliation, he pinned her arms down on the bed, pushed himself inside of her, and slammed into her over and over again until he came.

He looked at her afterward. "What the fuck is your problem?" he demanded. "Why were you lying there like a dead fish? You got a problem? I buy you nice things and then you treat me like shit!"

Emma was angry. "I wasn't lying there like a dead fish, Ethan!" she retorted. "I was surprised at how aggressive you were. What the hell is going on with you?"

"What's going on with me? What's going on with ME? I'm sick of your fucking bullshit! That's what's going on with me!" he howled.

"Look, Ethan, I'm not going to put up with this," she told him firmly. "You're acting like a crazy person!"

Ethan got up and left the bedroom. Emma sat on the edge of the bed, bewildered by what was happening between them. She loved him and didn't want to hurt him. Her thoughts wandered back to the moment when they had first met and she felt wistful recalling his kindness toward Gracie and her. Maybe he was just going through a rough time, she tried to reason. She wasn't afraid of change. She knew she could live without him. The only glimmer of doubt Emma had was the thought of losing the only man she'd ever loved.

Chapter Forty-Eight

As the Fourth of July approached, Ethan told Emma that he wanted to throw a party at the apartment. Not wanting to have another scene on her hands, Emma declared it was a great idea. Having consented to it, she intended to enjoy it. Planning everything for the party together with her sister, she and Gracie set out to make it a great holiday. They even bought new dresses for the occasion: a short red sun dress for Gracie, a long white cotton dress for Emma.

On the day of the party, the girls were brimming with excitement because they were getting to spend some time with Brianna, who they hadn't seen much since Ethan had moved in with them. Emma was the perfect hostess, eager to make everything just right for their guests. They had spent most of the day in the small backyard, eating hotdogs and hamburgers. Ethan had bought a keg of beer, and the tenants from the other two apartments in the building had joined the festivities as well.

In the late afternoon, most of the guests had moved inside, along with the keg of beer. Emma was standing in the kitchen, catching up on girl talk with Katie and Brianna. Her childhood friend had just finished a funny story about a creepy guy she had gone on a date with a couple of weeks earlier and, being Brianna, had made fun of the guy's appearance, making all of them laugh hard.

Their hearty laughter reached Ethan who was in the living room with his friend, Pete Somers. The two young men automatically glanced through the kitchen doorway and Pete's gaze was drawn to Emma. It was clear to Ethan that his friend couldn't tear his eyes away from her. He followed Pete's gaze as it took in the silhouette of Emma's long legs through the flowing material of her white dress, which had turned transparent in the waning sunlight streaming through the kitchen window.

Turning to Ethan, Pete couldn't help exclaiming, "God, man! Emma is fucking gorgeous! How did an ugly fuck like you land something like that?"

His tone was playful and Ethan smiled mechanically in response, but fury surged through him. As Emma looked over at him, the two of them locked eyes. His hateful stare pierced through her. She knew at once that something had pissed him off and she wondered nervously what could have gone wrong. She did her best to bury her anxiety and played the perfect hostess until everyone left.

Finally, after Gracie had left to sleep over at a friend's house, Emma sought out Ethan. He was sitting alone in their bedroom, perched on the edge of the bed.

"Ethan? Is everything okay? It was a great party, wasn't it?" she asked, testing to see if he was still angry while wishing the prick would move the fuck out of her apartment.

He stood and walked up to her. "I bet it was a great party for you, Em!" he snapped.

"Why?" she asked, irritated. "What's wrong?"

"I saw how you and Pete were looking at each other," Ethan snarled. "What the fuck is going on here? Are you fucking him? Don't make me lose my head!"

Before he had even finished uttering those ominous words, he shoved Emma into the closet door. She struggled to keep her footing, but he was on top of her in an instant, his left hand grasping her throat in a vise-like grip. She fought him hard, kicking and wiggling to get out from under him, until he brought his free hand up and pinched her nostrils shut. Realizing she couldn't breathe, Emma fought harder to free herself. Just as she passed out, he released his hold on her.

When she came to, she realized she was lying in the same spot where he'd left her. Confused at first, she began to replay what had happened right before she blacked out. Emma rose gingerly to her feet and made her way into the bathroom. She looked at herself in the mirror and was horrified by what she saw: the bruises on her neck and a glimpse of the abused child she had once been. She sat on the edge of the tub and cried. Then, exhausted, she crawled into bed and fell into a deep sleep.

Hours later, not knowing what time it was, she woke up to find Ethan having sex with her. She didn't fight him, because she knew that would only lead to another, more serious brawl. Rather, she lay there like a lifeless doll, letting him do whatever he wanted. But a slow, grinding anger was building up within her and she welcomed it this time, letting it course through her veins and reach her heart, its flames red-hot, obliterating, and turning to ashes any love she might have once felt for him.

Chapter Forty-Nine

While Emma's relationship with Ethan had turned rotten, her closeness with Salvatore ripened. He had been at Doubles almost every night since he first met Emma. Within a couple of weeks, they had fallen into a routine. She would give him a lap dance and he would reward her with a hundred-dollar tip. Over time, Salvatore and Emma became friends. After she performed her lap dance, they would sit and chat at the bar. He was a kind man. Yet he commanded respect from everyone who talked to him. She was turned on by the aura of power and authority he exuded and couldn't quite understand where its source lay. All she knew was that when Salvatore talked, people wanted to hear what he had to say. He always came to the bar alone and showered all of his attention on Emma, a fact that made her feel flattered and reassured her that she had something that made her stand out from the others.

Eventually Emma confided in Salvatore about her past. She told him how she had been beaten as a young child by her father, pointing out the scar on her right breast from the cigarette burn and that the slash marks on her lower back were a permanent reminder of her father's relentless beatings. It was as if God never wanted her to forget the pain that abuse can cause. She told him about Jake and all that he had done to Gracie and her. Salvatore felt his anger flare at the injustices she had suffered and wished Pepper and Jake were still alive so that he could kill them with his bare hands. Yet his anger was dimmed by his fascination with the courage and resilience that this seemingly innocent young girl had shown to survive such horrors in her life.

Emma told him about some of the ways in which Ethan treated her, but was too mortified to share all of her stories or go into detail. She did tell him that whenever her boyfriend was aiming to launch into a jealous tirade against her, he would create an opportunity for himself by yelling, "Don't make me lose my head!" as though she had provoked him in some way and was, therefore, responsible for his loss of temper.

"Ethan has been taking my money. Just last night he was angry with me and he well..." She stopped, noticing his clenched jaw.

"He what?" Salvatore demanded.

"He choked me until I passed out. Then while I was out cold, he started having sex with me. With all the arguing and jealousy, he's become a real pain in the ass," she shared nervously.

Enraged by Ethan's violent behavior, Salvatore suggested giving the dickhead a much-needed visit, but Emma urged him to stay out of it and mind his own business.

"No, I can deal with it," she stated confidently, assuring Salvatore that she wasn't afraid to fight back in self-defense.

Emma and Salvatore enjoyed a rapport she hadn't shared with anyone. He was full of wisdom and never seemed bothered by anything. He listened to her stories patiently and never once accused her of any wrongdoing. On the contrary, he became more protective about her, something she began to sense over time. He rarely spoke about himself, giving his full attention to her every time they were together.

That same night, while Emma sat at the bar with one of the other dancers, Foster came over with two beers.

"These are from Salvatore," he told them.

The girls lifted their beers to toast him from across the bar and he lifted his shot of grappa, toasting them back.

"Em, he also wanted me to give you this," Foster said, sounding concerned.

Emma took the paper from his hand. It had a phone number written on it. "What's wrong with you, Foster? It's just a fucking phone number," Emma said mockingly.

"Yeah, well, Salvatore doesn't give his phone number to just anyone," Foster replied. "You get me?"

"Not really." Emma looked at him, puzzled. "Why are you being so mysterious, Foster? Can you just speak English, please?"

"You've been dancing for him for months. Giving him lap dances almost every night. And the two of you have been talking for a long time. You do know who Salvatore is, right?"

"No, I don't," Emma shot back. "He's just a nice guy who comes in and wants to spend time with me. What the fuck, Foster! Tell me what you know!"

"Shit! His name is Salvatore Morano. Ring any bells?" Foster asked.

"No, it doesn't ring any bells. What's the big deal?" Emma persisted, beginning to lose patience with him.

"Salvatore's father is Johnny Morano. He's the head of the Mafia family here in Philly. You know, his dad is the Godfather. I'm sure you've seen the movie. Now do you get it?"

"Oh my God! Oh my God! I didn't know!" Emma said, more to herself than to Foster.

Anxiety suddenly overwhelmed her. She had told Salvatore so much about Gracie and her. He knew just about everything there was to know about her life, including where she lived.

When Emma got up from the bar to leave for the night, Salvatore stopped her.

"That number the bartender just gave you is my cell number. If you ever need me, call me. Understand?" he said, planting a small kiss on her forehead.

"Yeah, Salvatore, I understand." Emma turned to walk away, but stopped abruptly. "Thanks," she said and kissed Salvatore on the cheek.

On the drive back to her apartment that night, as Ethan rambled on about the Eagles losing another football game, Emma was submerged in her own thoughts. The evening's events, the time she spent with Salvatore, lulling her into a false state of security.

Chapter Fifty

The next day, Emma went to see Katie. As the two women chatted over coffee and Emma poured herself another cup, she handed her friend the piece of paper with Salvatore's cell phone number.

"I need you to put this number in your cell phone," she told Katie. "Ethan checks my cell phone all the time. He keeps worrying that I'm cheating on him, the moron! Anyway, put it under the name Sal M., all right?"

"Sure, but what's going on?" Katie asked, intrigued and a little excited by her friend's need to keep the number a secret from Ethan. "Who's Sal M.?" Was Emma about to dump Ethan for a new boyfriend, she wondered, hoping that she would.

"He's one of the regulars at the bar," Emma confided. "A powerful guy. I want to keep his number, just in case I ever need it. Don't tell anyone."

"You know I won't, Em," Katie promised. "So what's up with you and Ethan? He's been a bit of an asshole lately, hasn't he?"

"What do you mean an asshole?" Emma asked, wanting her friend to validate her decision that he was no good.

"No, nothing, really," Katie replied. "I've just been getting a bad feeling about him. He just isn't the nice guy he used to be when the two of you met. And why the fuck isn't he working anymore? He's taking advantage of you, Emma."

"I know. I'm going to tell him he has to move out," Emma assured her.

However, there was something in Katie's tone that caused Emma's stomach to turn. "Are you sure there isn't anything else going on?" she asked her friend. "You know you can tell me. Right, Katie?"

"There's nothing wrong, Em," she reassured her, not wanting to reveal that she got a bad feeling every time she watched Ethan when Gracie was around. It was almost as if he was jealous of the young teen.

Over the next couple of days, Ethan's jealous rages grew completely out of control. He yelled at her for trivial things, such as spending too much money on food at the grocery store. The morning she was going to tell him to move out, things between them deteriorated to an all-time low.

Ethan entered the bathroom while she was showering and ripped back the shower curtain. "What the fuck is this?" he demanded.

Standing in the shower, wet, naked, and unprepared for yet another argument, Emma felt vulnerable. She focused on allowing her suddenly accelerated heart rate to slow down.

"I don't know what you have in your hand, Ethan," she said calmly. "Let me get done here and then we can talk."

"Don't make me lose my head!" Ethan warned. "I'm holding a bill for birth control pills. Ninety fucking dollars! Are you taking them so that none of the guys you're fucking at the bar get you pregnant?"

His expression was ugly as he shoved the bill at her. Then he pushed her face against the wall of the shower with brute force.

"Fuck you, Ethan! You know I'm on birth control. That's what we agreed on right from the start, remember? You know what? It doesn't matter anymore. I want you out of here!" Emma demanded.

Without a word, Ethan slammed her into the tile wall again. As Emma collapsed in the tub, nose bleeding, he yanked her up by the hair. "You're a worthless piece of shit!" he snarled. "I don't know what the fuck I see in you! Look at you, laying there like a wet animal!"

Then as Ethan dragged her out of the tub, her defense mechanism kicked in and she rammed her elbow into his gut.

"Get the fuck off me!" she yelled, her voice filled with malice. As he doubled over in pain, she stood before him, naked and wet. "Ethan," she now said evenly, "I will kill you."

While Ethan had no clue as to what Emma was capable of doing to him, the way she had attacked him and announced with chilling calmness that if he didn't back off she would kill him, he suspected that she was dead serious. But he still hadn't gotten the message that he was being thrown out. He had underestimated Emma's unwillingness to be controlled. In deep denial of the truth, he left the apartment a few minutes later to drink beer with his friend Pete and then go buy steaks so that he could cook her a special dinner. On his way to the market he thought to himself that she was one tough bitch who needed to be tamed.

When Gracie came home from school hours later, she found Emma huddled on the sofa, drinking a cup of tea.

"Are you feeling okay?" she asked. "You look sick."

"I'm fine," Emma lied. "I just feel a little tired."

"Em, I know that you and Ethan aren't getting along that good. I've heard him say some pretty mean things to you lately. He's been a real dick to me too when you're not around. I don't understand why you're still letting him stay here," Gracie confided.

"I know. You're right. I told him today that he has to move out," she explained.

Gracie smiled with enthusiasm and hugged her sister. "Good! I was starting to worry that you were never gonna get rid of him. It's going to be so much better without him here, like it was before he moved in with us. He's such a dick!" she announced with great relief.

When Ethan arrived home with his special steak dinner, he found the apartment empty. Emma and Gracie had purposely gone out so that they weren't there when he came home. Annoyed that Emma had made a fool out of him, he threw the steaks in the sink and went into their bedroom and slept. That night, to avoid another fight, Emma slept in Gracie's room.

The next morning, after Gracie had left the apartment, she found Ethan. "Listen, Ethan. I wasn't kidding. You need to pack your shit and get out of here...today!"

Ethan smiled at her mockingly. "Oh, I'll move out, but I warn you that you'll need to keep a close eye on your precious little sister. You think you're clever, Em. But you can't be with her every minute of every day. I will find the right time and I will crush that little pathetic bitch," he threatened.

Emma thought about his threats, and realizing that he might be capable of hurting Gracie, she gave in and allowed him to stay, but just long enough for her to figure out how to get rid of him for good.

Ethan smiled, thinking he had finally won.

Chapter Fifty-One

The following day Emma began contemplating how she could get rid of Ethan. She decided there were only two options: either she could leave him and hope he wouldn't bother her again or she would have to kill him. She wouldn't be held prisoner by him. She was now older and more resourceful and believed herself to be a true asshole for putting up with him for so long. Just imagining the various ways she could kill him made her feel powerful.

Shortly after Ethan threatened to hurt Gracie, Emma came across an article in the local newspaper. It was about a man who killed his wife by slipping antifreeze into her drinks. This was one way she could do it. Or she could use rat poison on him the way she had with Pepper. There was one problem with those two methods: his pesky mother and sister were always calling him for something. He would surely whine about feeling sick once the poison started to affect him. She needed something that would act much quicker.

Knowing she needed a cleverer way to kill Ethan, she made her way out into the living room and sat on the sofa next to Gracie. Her younger sister was maturing by the minute. She looked at the teen who had turned fifteen just three months prior. Gracie looked back at her sister, and having churned for days, she finally got up the nerve to tell Emma about her problem. The timing was the best she could have hoped for as it was rare for Ethan not to be in the apartment with them. His mother had awakened him early and asked him over to her house before the rain started that day to fix a fallen gutter.

"Emma? I need to talk to you," she said in a strained voice.

Emma read the urgency in her tone and expression and knew she was about to learn something significant. "Sure, what's up?"

"Em, I'm...I'm pregnant," Gracie blurted out, tears rolling down her cheeks.

Emma wasn't prepared for this at all. "Gracie, are you sure?" she asked anxiously. "How do you know you're pregnant?"

"I took a pregnancy test. My girlfriend stole one from her mom. It was positive," Gracie whimpered.

Emma stood up and put her arms around her little sister. "Who got you pregnant?"

"Remember that boy on the football team that me and my friends always talk about? The one who wears braces?" Gracie asked.

Emma nodded.

"Him!" Gracie sobbed.

"Okay," Emma said, trying to arrange her thoughts rationally. "Well, calm down," she told her weeping sibling. "We need to think about this. We should talk to Katie too. She might know what to do."

Emma felt out of her league. She had never thought of putting Gracie on birth control. She was only fifteen years old, for God's sake!

When the girls went over to Katie's apartment and told her what had happened, their friend gasped at the news, making it worse for Gracie. "I'm sorry," she said seeing the girl's troubled expression. "I just wasn't prepared for this. Then she said briskly, "I think we should go to the clinic and make sure you're really pregnant. Sometimes those tests can be misleading. They say you're pregnant when you're not."

"Oh my God!" Gracie exclaimed. "I hope you're right. Please be right. I don't want to be pregnant."

Emma felt the same way, but was less optimistic about it. She thought back over the last several weeks and remembered Gracie laying around the apartment a lot and not wanting to eat certain foods that she normally liked. She recalled her sister saying how the smell of bananas, a fruit she had always loved, made her nauseous. Emma had assumed their living situation was making Gracie extremely moody, but now it was all starting to make sense.

Katie drove them to the clinic. An hour later, the doctor who had examined Gracie confirmed she was pregnant. She appeared to be about two months along in her pregnancy, but there was no way of knowing for sure without an ultrasound.

The three of them were unusually quiet when they left the clinic, each one trying to come to terms with the reality of a pregnancy. With

Gracie being so young, Emma knew they were in for a hard time. The thought of raising a baby seemed a monumental task quite beyond what the two of them were capable of doing. Gracie stewed in the deep regret that overwhelmed her, feeling ashamed of what she had done. She was overwhelmed with guilt and hated herself, scared that one day soon her sister would hate her as well.

Chapter Fifty-Two

Later that day, Emma told Ethan about Gracie's pregnancy. She hadn't given any more thought to how she would get rid of him, being distracted with her sister's news, but his reaction reinforced the need to think of ways for him to go.

Ethan was livid. "How the fuck did you let this happen?" he snapped at Emma.

"I didn't let anything happen, Ethan," she spat back at him. "I didn't even know she was having sex."

"You're the one who strips for other men. Maybe she learned how to be a slut from you," he accused.

Emma got away from him and ran into the kitchen. Ethan followed. Gracie stood in the doorway as he began shoving her sister into the wall and cabinets.

"Stop it!" Gracie screamed. "This is not Emma's fault. Just stop it!"

Ethan turned abruptly to Gracie. "You're getting an abortion. Do you hear me?"

"No, I'm not!" she yelled back. "You're not my father and you can't tell me what to do!"

Ethan started moving threateningly toward her, enraged at the way she had yelled at him. Just then, Emma pulled a knife from the butcher block on the counter.

"Leave her the fuck alone, Ethan!" she told him, holding the knife out in front of her. "Get out of here! You're just making everything worse. Just go."

Ethan eyed her. The resolve with which she gripped the knife was apparent and he was sure she would actually use it against him. In a bid for self-preservation, he decided quickly that he would leave the apartment for the night and come back the next morning, when everyone had settled down. But he would not forgive Emma for what she had just done. No one, especially not some tramp like her, could threaten him with a knife and expect to get away with it.

With Ethan gone for the night, the two sisters sat on the sofa together and talked about the baby.

"Emma, do you think I should have an abortion?" Gracie asked.

Her older sister sat for a moment in silence, "I don't know sweetie. I mean, I definitely didn't want you to get pregnant right now, that's for sure. But you have to be the one to decide. I'll be there for you no matter what you choose."

"Well, I was thinking that we don't have much family. Actually, there's only you and me. I don't want to be pregnant at fifteen either. I just don't know if I can go through with an abortion," Gracie considered out loud.

But hours later, they agreed that Gracie would keep the baby and Emma would help her raise it. They didn't know yet how they would work out the details. For instance, someone would need to be there to look after the baby while Gracie was at school. Realizing it was just too soon to worry about such details, the siblings stayed up most of the night, discussing different names for the baby.

Emma worried about how much everything was going to cost. She had hoarded a lot of money from her tips at Doubles and hidden it away so Ethan couldn't get at it. Now she was grateful for having kept the stash secret. Neither of them could even begin to imagine how hard it was going to be to raise a child. While they had missed out on the carefree pleasures of childhood, they were still children themselves. But they agreed to stick together and make it work.

The next morning, Ethan came back to the apartment and stood just inside the kitchen, watching Emma.

She looked him over and finally said, "Why are you here?"

"About last night," Ethan began. "I left because I couldn't stand the sight of you for another second. But I want you to know that this changes nothing. In fact, it makes it even better. If you force my hand, I will kill that little cunt and her unborn kid. You got me?"

As if he had punched her in the face, the reality of her abusive relationship with Ethan crashed in on her. She felt foolish and annoyed with herself that she hadn't really recognized it before this moment. How had she momentarily forgotten all the pain she had suffered at the hands of her father?

Chapter Fifty-Three

In a few short months, Gracie's belly had grown, making her pregnancy obvious and eliciting nasty stares from perfect strangers, the kind of stares that reminded her, over and over again, that she was no more than a dirty young slut of fifteen who had brought this condition on herself. Emma kept reminding her that the opinions of others didn't matter one bit and that Gracie should ignore them, but it wasn't easy. This didn't keep the sisters from being excited about the baby. Emma had tried her best to prepare for her new niece or nephew.

Ethan wasn't happy at all that she was spending money on things for the baby. Soon after Emma had made a trip to the Salvation Army and bought a crib for fifty dollars, Ethan freaked out on her.

"Who the fuck do you think you are, just going out and buying shit?" he yelled. "Did we ever talk about you spending fifty fucking bucks?" Then he added irrationally, "I bet you bought presents for your boyfriends at the bar too!"

By now he had backed her into the corner of the living room. Emma had her arms up to protect her face and her mind reeled, trying to think of what she could use as a weapon against him.

Stalling to give herself some time, she mumbled, "The baby needs somewhere to sleep and the crib was only fifty dollars."

"How am I supposed to keep us on a budget when you go out and spend money whenever you want? What are you, an idiot? Are you that stupid?" he ground out through clenched teeth.

Emma's ability to control her temper was waning. If she had a knife in her hands, she would slit his throat with it. The very thought of his blood gushing out of his body delighted her and she yelled back at him, trying to cut him down to size and show him up for the lowlife he was.

"How about you move the fuck out and leave us all alone?" she hurled at him. "How about that, huh? I earn all the money and I have a right to spend it any way I like!"

Emma left him standing in the room screaming at her. When she came back she stood very close to him, holding a hammer from his toolbox. He stared at her in disbelief.

"I want you out of here today," Emma told him in a calm, serious voice. "I'm not kidding, Ethan. You have an hour to be out of here. There is nothing I'd like better than to plunge this hammer into your skull. So you better get moving, before it's too late."

Gracie was eavesdropping from the other side of the door. Her insides were bursting with glee and she secretly wished her older sister would bash Ethan's filthy brains in with the hammer. Finally, she thought, finally, the asshole will get out of the apartment for good and leave us to ourselves.

Ethan was both intimidated and infuriated by the resolve with which Emma stood her ground. He had finally worked himself into her life and now she was throwing him out on the streets, not even worried about his threats to harm Gracie anymore.

She faced him squarely. "This is no joke, Ethan," she said. "I'm dead serious. You need to get your shit out quick or you'll find everything scattered on the sidewalk. I have put up with more from you than I ever should have, which probably makes me an asshole. But it's over now. Get out, and trust me, motherfucker, if you even have a thought about touching Gracie, I will kill you."

Ethan knew he'd lost her for now. He had threatened to kill Gracie, thinking that Emma would never have the balls to stand up against him with that threat looming over her head. He moved around the bedroom, packing his clothes. Fifteen minutes later, he walked into his mother's house, bitching about Emma for throwing him out of the apartment for no good reason.

"I know, honey," his mother cooed, "I always knew there was something wrong with that girl. But you don't have to worry about that girl anymore, you're home now."

Ethan took no comfort from his mother. In fact, he found the whore bitch even more annoying than before he moved out. He decided he'd wait it out for a while before trying to lure Emma back to him.

Chapter Fifty-Four

For as long as Gracie could remember, she had a hard time expressing her feelings to people. Even with Emma, she couldn't bare her heart. She was the polar opposite of her sister, who talked to everyone and told people exactly what she thought. Not even Gracie's closest friends knew how she felt about things most of the time. In fact, her friends were a lot like her—introverts. With nothing but time on her hands, she had taken to writing in the journal Emma had given her the previous year.

Gracie yearned to talk about her pregnancy, how it had happened, but couldn't bring herself to do so. The first time she felt it move inside her, she wrote in her journal:

> **I just felt my baby move in my belly. It feels like there's an alien inside me. I've never felt so ashamed of myself. I want to love my baby, but am afraid of loving anyone but Emma. What if my baby ends up hating me? What if Emma hates me after the baby is born?**

Gracie was too young to understand all that was happening to her, and though Emma was there for her all the time, she knew just as much about babies as her younger sister did, which was absolutely nothing. Gracie worried about what would happen after the baby's birth. Would she go back to being a teenager? Would she need to quit school and get a job? These questions ran through her mind all the time, but she never dared ask them out loud. All she could do was suffer as they continued to plague her.

One week from her due date, Gracie's water broke while she was helping Emma make breakfast. The girls looked at each other in panic as the water pooled on the kitchen floor. Gracie hurried to get the small duffle bag of clothes she had prepared for her stay in the hospital. Emma snatched up her car keys and called Katie.

Twenty-two hours later, Gracie gave birth to a girl. Her older sister had picked the name, Isabella, for the baby. Emma's joy over the birth of her niece was far more intense than she had expected and she fell to dreaming about how the three of them would make a close-knit, happy family.

Before she left the hospital that day, Emma held Gracie in her arms for one long moment. Then she leaned down and whispered in her ear, "She's beautiful, Gracie. Isabella is just perfect."

Chapter Fifty-Five

A few days after Isabella was born, Emma brought in pictures of the baby to show the girls at Doubles. When Salvatore saw the pictures, he smiled fondly and said, "Izzy—that's what I'll call her. I love that name. She's beautiful, Amme." Then he teased, "Are you sure she isn't your kid?"

"Izzy..." Emma said, feeling the name on her lips. "I love that, Salvatore. She's such a gorgeous baby. Everyone says she looks like me, but I just don't see it."

Emma was still blind to the impact her good looks had on others.

"That's because you don't always see what others see," Salvatore told her. "Your view of things isn't always the right one, you know."

Uneasy with where their conversation was heading, Emma asked light-heartedly, "So do you want to give me therapy or do you want a lap dance?"

Salvatore lightened up immediately. "Well," he drawled, "I was thinking I could give you therapy while you were dancing for me."

They both laughed and made their way to the lap-dance room.

Salvatore was more captivated by Emma now than he had been the first night he'd met her at Doubles. If anything, she seemed to become more charming with time, both in appearance and in personality. It was during such moments that he wanted to take her in his arms and make passionate love to her, to reassure her of her worth. But he knew that if he so much as hinted at his feelings for her, she would conclude that sex was all he had ever wanted from her. Salvatore knew that where Emma was concerned, he wanted much, much more.

Chapter Fifty-Six

The first two years with Izzy were wonderful. A cheerful toddler, she charmed everyone she met. More precocious than most children her age, she knew exactly how to get what she wanted. And it was easier to manipulate a mother and an aunt who were both too young to be raising a child on their own. A few days shy of seventeen, Gracie struggled to do justice to her role as a teen mom, but with Emma's help, she managed to make it work.

They enjoyed being together as a family. Lying in Gracie's bed with Izzy between them, the girls would talk about what they would wear to each other's weddings. They speculated about Izzy's future and how she would meet a prince and get married someday. Unlike their own childhood, they wanted Izzy's life to be a fairytale, filled with love, hope, and dreams.

Gracie had never told Emma about the hateful things Ethan had said to her. She knew it would only result in yet another of their vicious fights that caused her sister so much anguish.

Amidst the negativity generated in her heart by thoughts of Ethan, there was one thing that did make Gracie very happy: Izzy's beauty; the baby looked just like Emma and bore no resemblance at all to her mother. She also shared the same strong personality as her aunt. Gracie felt honored that her own child was so much like her older sister.

On a Saturday night in December, Emma left the apartment for her usual shift at Doubles. Gracie was going out with friends and Katie was babysitting Izzy. Emma had already danced two sets when she froze on stage. Ethan was standing at the bar. She stared at him, wondering why he was there. She hadn't seen him in a very long time and had no interest in ever seeing him again. She watched intently as Ethan talked to Foster and the bar manager. Then Jay waved her over.

"Emma, go get dressed," he told her, his voice tense with concern. "Your little sister has been in a car accident. Ethan's going to drive you to the hospital."

Emma turned pale with shock. Then she raced down to the dressing room and changed, coming back upstairs in less than ten minutes, ready to leave for the hospital. Ethan put his arm around her and escorted her out of the bar. Salvatore watched the scene from across the room. When he found out from Jay what had happened, he couldn't help being concerned for Emma as she left the bar with that little weasel.

Fifteen minutes later, she and Ethan were at Chestnut Hill Hospital. Emma rushed through the emergency room doors and went up to the first nurse she could find.

"I'm looking for my sister," she said breathlessly. "Her name's Grace Murphy.

The nurse looked her over, her expression disapproving as she took in Emma's tight jeans, a tee shirt with a plunging neckline, and knee-high stiletto boots. She was still in full makeup from her dance performances, and the nurse assumed she was a hooker.

"She's in surgery right now," the nurse announced harshly. "Take a seat in the waiting room. A doctor will come out and talk to you shortly."

"What happened?" Emma persisted, not to be brushed off so easily.

The nurse softened a little when she caught the look of anguish and bewilderment on the girl's face. "Your sister was in a car accident," she explained. "From what we've heard, a drunk driver slammed into the car she was in. He was driving an Expedition at top speed and the impact of the collision pulverized the car your sister was in. Grace has internal bleeding and the doctors are trying to help her. They are doing everything they can, honey."

Emma felt out of body. She said nothing as Ethan took her by the arm and led her to a chair in the waiting room. She shed silent tears and prayed for her baby sister, too emotionally spent to protest, even when he held her. After all she had been through in life, she wasn't prepared to lose Gracie. She willed her to be all right and kept telling herself the doctors would save her.

Ethan said encouraging things to keep her hopes alive and she was grateful he was there to see her through this period of unspeakable torment. He was gentle with her, the gentlest he'd ever been, almost as if he feared that if he raised his voice even a little, she would break in two.

He spoke to her in a confident, calming voice, trying to coax her out of her despondency as the hours wore on. He managed to get a blanket from a nurse to cover Emma with and brought her a cup of tea from the vending machine.

"It's gonna be okay, Em," he reassured her gently. "She'll be fine, babe."

Four hours later, the doctor came into the waiting room to speak to them. He introduced himself and explained that Gracie had come out of surgery. They hadn't been able to stop the bleeding, however. The injuries were too extensive.

Emma was on her feet at once. "Well, will she be all right?" she asked, coming straight to the point.

This was the moment all doctors dreaded. "It took the rescue workers over an hour to get her out of the car," he explained somberly. "Based on what we know, more than two hours passed between the time of the accident and her arrival here in the ER. In addition to other serious injuries, Grace's pelvic bones were broken and the blood vessels along them torn."

Emma couldn't understand a word of what he was telling her. All she wanted to know was if her baby sister would live. "What does that mean?" she shrieked.

The doctor gave Ethan a solemn look. "We've done everything we could. We'll reassess her condition in a few hours to see what else we can do for her. Your sister is critical at the moment."

Large tears streamed down Emma's cheeks. "What about Gracie's friend, the girl who was driving?" she asked softly. "Where is she?"

The doctor bowed his head. "She was killed instantly. I'm sorry."

Despite all the horrors Emma had been through in her pathetic life, there was no darker or more frightening moment than the one she faced as she stood on the threshold of the room where Gracie lay motionless. The only sound in its eerie stillness was the rhythm of the machines that monitored her vital signs and kept her alive.

Chapter Fifty-Seven

E mma stepped into the room and paused. She could not bring herself to go over to the bed. What if Gracie died? She forced herself to move forward, covering the distance between the door and the bed step by step, as if it were the longest distance she had ever traveled. She stopped by the bed and willed herself to look down at the still figure. There was a hard wedge of icy fear where her heart had been and her tears seemed thick, making the skin on her face tighten. She wished she could rant and scream and release her pent-up feelings in a downpour of weeping. Maybe then it wouldn't hurt so much.

Oh God, Gracie! Emma thought. Please, please don't leave me!

She took her sister's limp hand in her own and thought about all they had been through together. Many of their experiences had left them with emotional scars and dark memories, but they always had each other to fall back on. Emma had spent her whole life protecting Gracie. Even when she had failed to keep her from harm, they had always found a way back to each other.

Watching Gracie lie utterly still made Emma's heart ache. An indescribable sorrow overwhelmed her. If only she were in her baby sister's place! The girls were united by a bond most siblings didn't share, the bond of loyalty that came from shared experience of how terribly cruel life could be to helpless children. But the Murphy girls had made the harrowing journey together, always knowing that they were loved by at least one other person in the world: their sibling and partner in pain.

Emma couldn't imagine going on without Gracie. As she sat next to her bed, her chest finally began to heave with grief, and she prayed: Dear God, please let Gracie live. I've never asked you for a fucking thing! My baby sister has had so much undeserved sadness in her life. Please, God, she has a daughter! Please, God, save her! Please!

Ethan held Emma, watching her reactions closely. He comforted her and assured her that everything was going to work out, but she seemed deaf to his words. Only when Gracie opened her eyes would everything be all right again, she told herself.

Emma sat next to the bed holding Gracie's hand. She was giving her the will to survive, reminding her of all that they had accomplished, "Gracie, we've beat so much bad shit in our lives. This is just another thing that we'll get through together. We're doing a good job with Izzy and we're really happy." She rambled on like this for hours, believing it would give her sister the strength to pull through and fight on.

Finally Gracie opened her eyes and looked up at Emma. In a weak voice she said, "Stay with me, Emma. I'm scared. I don't want to go. You won't leave me, right?"

"Of course I won't leave you, sweetie. I'm right here. I'll stay here until you're better," Emma promised, suddenly reenergized now that Gracie had spoken to her.

At daybreak, Emma was still sitting in the chair, holding onto Gracie's hand. As she woke, she looked around the room and saw Ethan sleeping in a chair in the corner. Emma watched her sister sleeping peacefully; she studied her chest as it rose and fell with each precious breath she took. Things were going to be normal again, she told herself, Gracie made it through the night and from here on she would just get stronger.

In the light of day, Emma could clearly see the damage caused by the car wreck. Gracie's body had been severely battered and broken. She had wires and tubes attached to her that looked like an endless ball of string and seemed to have no beginning or end.

"Good morning, Gracie," she whispered. "You have to wake up so that the doctors can help you get better. You've been through worse than this, so come on now and open your eyes. Please, Gracie, for me," she begged.

A few seconds later, Emma's anguish turned to hope when Gracie opened her eyes and looked at her. Her bloodless lips curved in a faint smile. Emma moved closer to her.

"Oh, thank God you're awake!" she exclaimed. "I love you, Gracie. You know I love you. You're going to get better and we're gonna take you home soon. Everything will be fine. I'm here and I won't leave you. I'm so happy you're awake!"

There was the suggestion of a nod from Gracie, as if to acknowledge that she understood what her sister had just told her.

The gesture made Emma's hopes soar and she just knew that Gracie was going to recover.

Then Gracie parted her lips and said, "Izzy..."

Emma clung to the word and knew she needed to focus on Izzy. That's who would give Gracie the strength to fight. Emma silently thanked God for giving them a break. In the next moment, a continuous high-pitched screeching came from the heart monitor. Gracie was gone.

Chapter Fifty-Eight

A doctor and two nurses rushed into the room. They tried in vain to revive Gracie, but it was too late. She had sustained too much damage. It took great effort for the doctor to convince Emma that her sister was gone. She refused to acknowledge that Gracie would never be back.

"I promised Gracie I wouldn't leave her," she argued. "I have to stay with her so that she knows she isn't alone. Gracie hates to be alone, it scares her," she wailed.

"You can stay with her as long as you'd like," the doctor told her with profound sadness at Emma's desperation.

Emma climbed onto the bed with Gracie and wrapped her arms around her sister's lifeless body. She lay there for almost two hours; stroking her sister, weeping and wondering how she would move on from that moment. Her new reality was the most pain she ever had to suffer in her life. She felt as if God had reached his mighty hand down from the heavens and snatched away the one person who gave Emma the courage to go on. Her grief was so raw that even the nurses were weepy and talked in low voices outside of the hospital room. One nurse said, "I don't know how this girl is going to recover. Her friends told me that Gracie is her world, she was the only family she had."

"Poor girl. This is all so sad. I hope she has a good support network," another nurse chimed in. "She won't make it through this alone."

Finally, after an hour of coaxing, Ethan managed to pry Emma loose from Gracie with his soothing words and urged her to accept that it was time to go. Before leaving Gracie's bedside, Emma leaned over her sister and kissed her softly on her cheek. "I love you, baby," she whispered.

When they walked into the hall, Brianna and Katie were waiting for them. Emma threw herself into Brianna's arms. They gripped each other tightly and shed tears of deep, unrelenting grief.

Finally Brianna managed to say, "Oh, Em, I'm so sorry."

Emma turned to Katie, who held Izzy in her arms. Young as she was, even the child knew something wasn't quite right and looked at her aunt in bewilderment. As the two women embraced, Emma took Izzy from her friend and held on tight to her niece. She shed more tears thinking of the motherless child then remembered how Gracie had died with her daughter's name on her lips.

From that day on, Izzy would belong to Emma. She would love her more than she had loved anyone in her life and vowed to not only keep her safe, but to do whatever was needed to give her a good life. She resolved to tell Izzy about Gracie when she got older and let her know how much her mother had loved her.

Ethan put his arm around Emma, jolting her back into the present. "Come on, Em," he said in a soothing tone. "Let's take our family home."

Brianna and Katie locked eyes at Ethan's statement. They wanted to argue with him and tell him to go away and leave Emma and Izzy alone. They knew he didn't belong there and that he wasn't good for Emma. But their friend had just lost the person she'd loved the most in her life and they didn't want to cause her any more hardship.

Over the next three days, while funeral arrangements were made, the apartment filled with visitors. Many of the girls from Doubles came. So did Jay and Shiver. Ethan's friends came over as well, although Katie suspected it was more for the free beer and food than to express their condolences to Emma. Even some of the neighbors stopped in with a cake or a casserole. The apartment was crowded with people from morning until night, but Emma felt completely isolated, utterly alone. She tried to fake interest in her visitors, but her conversation was half-hearted. The desire to live seemed to have vanished. She was merely going through the motions. It was an effort for her to even breathe.

The day of the funeral dawned, the worst in Emma's life. It seemed as if the sun had not been allowed to rise that day. The sky was sullen and dark and the clouds looked ominous as they hung motionless like a gray shroud over the earth, making her feel the depth of her emptiness. The rain was relentless, never stopping even once as Emma walked to the plot in the cemetery where she would be leaving Gracie forever.

When it was over and the time to leave arrived, Emma dropped to her knees in the muddied grass and bawled until there were no tears left, her chest rising and falling in dry, gasping heaves. Her fists were clenched on the grass around the hole where Gracie's coffin hung, suspended in midair.

"Nooooo," Emma whimpered, "I can't leave her here. Oh God, why?" she shouted, looking to the heavens for an answer.

Then her shoulders slumped as she cupped her face with her hands and let out a moan that came from the center of her belly, a sound of pure sorrow. She felt as if she were a lost soul forced to walk among the living.

Ethan and Brianna stepped in and took charge. They helped Emma to her feet and led her back to the car, against her will. Sitting in the passenger seat in front with the cold penetrating her bones, she had the sudden urge to run back to where Gracie lay. She could not imagine leaving her there alone and dreaded facing life without her.

Once Gracie's funeral was over, the crowds of people visiting the apartment dwindled to nothing. Only Brianna and Katie continued to check on Emma every single day. They were amazed at how Ethan had taken on the role of caregiver. He had been staying at the apartment since the night Gracie died and seemed totally transformed. He was so gentle and loving with Emma that it was hard to believe he had been such a bastard to her in the past. He had once again become the man Emma had fallen in love with. Their hesitation over Ethan being with Emma was dismissed.

Since Emma had taken time off from Doubles, the other strippers decided to put together a fundraiser to help compensate for the income she would be losing during her absence. While performing on stage, the girls asked their clients to be generous with their tips, which they planned to hand over to their friend.

"It's for Amme," they explained. "She's hurting real bad and needs our help. So dig down deep."

That night, Salvatore found Jay and said he needed to talk. The bar manager was quick to respond. "Sure, Salvatore," he said, "what do you need?"

"How is she? Is she holding up?" Salvatore's voice was soft with sympathy.

Jay was surprised by the man's genuine concern for Emma. It was so out of character for a man like him.

"She's doing the best she can," he replied. "Her little sister was the only family she had, and from what I hear, she'd been taking care of her since she was a child. Shiver told me she's been talking to Emma's friend, Brianna, a girl who worked here before. Amme is apparently pretty depressed. I'll be surprised if she comes back here anytime soon."

Salvatore reached into his suit pocket and pulled out a large envelope of twenty-dollar bills. "Here's five grand," he said. "See that she gets this money, will you? Just say it's part of what the girls raised for her."

Jay was less impressed by Salvatore's generosity than by the apparent depth of his feelings for Emma. He had no idea the girl had developed such a strong bond with the powerful man who was feared by so many.

"Sure, Salvatore," he said. "Whatever you want. I'll give the money to Shiver as an anonymous donation."

"Good. I like that. Remember that if there is anything Amme needs, anything at all, I want to know about it."

Salvatore left the bar. On his way back to Philadelphia, he thought about Emma. He was worried about her, especially after he learned from Jay that Ethan was staying at the apartment with her. Then he let his thoughts drift to her niece, Izzy, whom Emma had talked about all the time when Gracie was alive. It was sad for all of them. Emma no longer had a sister and Izzy had no mother. Salvatore knew that this woman he loved would do everything she could to make it right for Izzy. But he couldn't help worrying about the price she'd be willing to pay for her niece's happiness.

Chapter Fifty-Nine

Weeks turned into months, but the darkness inside Emma would not leave her. Consumed by thoughts of Gracie's untimely death, she spent little time with Izzy, whom Ethan was now taking care of. He had moved back into the apartment and settled them into a routine. He helped Emma shower every day; he practically forced her to eat; and he sat with her for hours, sometimes yammering about nothing and at other times just sitting with her in comforting silence.

Observing the way he was taking care of her and the child, Emma had looked deep into his eyes and said, "Thank you, Ethan. Thank you for taking care of Izzy and me. I love you so much."

Many months after Gracie died Ethan broached the subject of Emma going back to work. They had been living on food stamps and welfare checks, something he himself had arranged so that she could get some financial support while she wasn't working. Ethan had burned through the money received from the fundraiser at Double Visions in record time, spending it on new accessories for his car and clothes for himself. The money they received from welfare just wasn't enough to keep them going and Ethan had no intention of working some menial job when Emma could make a substantial income by dancing.

Emma wearily contemplated the prospect of going back to Doubles. She knew that she would have to return to work sooner rather than later. The decision was practically forced on her on Izzy's third birthday, when Emma snapped out of her funk. She was lying in bed, silently staring at the wall, when for the first time in a long while she heard Ethan raise his voice.

"I said eat!" he yelled at the child.

Those words were followed by the sound of a slap. There was a momentary silence. Then Izzy burst out crying.

Emma sprang out of bed and ran into the kitchen. "What happened just now?" she asked, dreading the answer.

"She's a fucking little brat!" Ethan snapped at her. "That's what happened!"

"Ethan, she's only a baby!" Emma said incredulously. "Did you hit her?"

"I gave her a little slap. Don't make a big thing out of it," he said righteously.

"Well, it's a big deal to me," she retorted, looking Izzy over quickly until her gaze stopped on the bright red mark on the child's arm.

Izzy gave her a bewildered look and said in a hurt voice, "Eatin hit me."

When Emma lifted her out of her chair, Izzy clung to her so tightly her aunt could sense her terror. It was a telling reminder of how Ethan had treated Emma herself before being thrown out of the apartment. Now he had dared strike her baby niece. People rarely changed, she told herself, realizing that the brute within Ethan was still very much alive.

Emma felt furious and ashamed of herself. She had been so absorbed in her own grief that she had neglected Gracie's child, the most precious thing in the world, whom she had vowed to take care of as if she were her own. She had received the wakeup call she needed in order to get her shit together and move on with her life. She owed that much to Izzy. She didn't want her niece living through the ordeal that she and Gracie had endured as children.

She walked out of the kitchen holding Izzy in her arms and declared to Ethan, "I'm calling Jay today. I'm going back to work."

She understood that the only way for her to give Izzy the life she deserved was to make money. That was what Gracie would have expected of her. She remembered her sister murmuring her daughter's name with her dying breath. It was a plea to Emma to take care of her baby. And she was determined to do that, even if she had to do it alone. She was grateful to Ethan for all that he had done for her over the past six months, but now his cruel hot temper came creeping back into her life. Emma decided she would overlook Ethan's behavior with Izzy for now. She would wait to get back on her feet, which she knew wouldn't take long. She did pledge to herself, however, that until she was back on her feet financially, if he ever touched Izzy again, she would make him regret he had ever been born.

Emma called Jay that afternoon, and he assured her she could go back to work in three days. She called Katie to update her on the most recent developments, and Katie agreed to watch Izzy while Emma worked at night. Emma knew it would make little difference to Ethan; he would be happier having his nights free to hang out with his friend Pete.

However, while Ethan would enjoy not having to babysit anymore, he wasn't happy about Emma finding her independence again. He vowed to himself he wouldn't lose her a second time no matter what it took to keep her.

Chapter Sixty

The first night back at Doubles, most of the dancers made a huge fuss over Emma. She had lost a great deal of weight since they'd seen her last and many of them whispered behind her back that she didn't look good. Her eyes had all but lost their luster and were ringed with dark circles. Her hair was longer now, because she hadn't cut it since Gracie died, and it looked dull and lifeless. Some of the dancers, the catty bitch ones, were secretly happy that she looked bad. They hadn't missed her beauty at the club, which had earned her a lot of the tips they believed were rightly theirs.

Foster gave Emma a quick hug and a warm hello as she entered the bar area to get on stage. The moment she stepped onto the first stage to dance that night, there was warm, welcoming applause from the clients in the bar. The unexpected surge of emotion that welled up inside took her breath away. After all the months of misery and emptiness, she was overwhelmed by the response.

After the performance, she made her way around the bar to collect her tips and was deeply touched by the words of encouragement many of the guys had for her. Then she found herself standing in front of Salvatore. Having heard from Jay she was coming back that night, he had made sure he would be there.

He reached out and grasped her hand as she approached him. "I've missed you," he confessed. "How's Izzy doing?"

Hearing him ask with genuine concern in his voice, she was moved to tears.

"None of that now," he told her with almost paternal affection. "How about a private dance?"

Emma wiped away her tears and walked him back to the lap-dance room.

As she was about to start performing, Salvatore pulled her onto his lap. "No dancing tonight," he whispered. "I want to know that you're doing all right. You've lost a lot of weight and you look tired. Tell me how you've been."

"Oh, Salvatore, it's been unbearable. At first, I had to work on breathing. Even now there are moments when I feel like absolute shit. I miss her so much. I always thought we would be together, you know? I'm doing the best I can with Izzy, but I just can't shake this feeling of darkness," she confided.

Salvatore began to run his warm, soft hand up and down her arm, as if he was trying to ward off the cold.

"Since Gracie died nothing is the same. I see life so differently now. I keep wondering if I will ever feel happiness again. She and I had been through so much together as kids and we had finally found a way to make it work out for the three of us. I wish it would have been me instead of her, Salvatore. I wish I had died in her place," she told him tearfully.

Salvatore listened to her intently for a long time, understanding her better than he had before. She was a good person whom life had dealt a bitter hand. He wasn't the type of person who felt much for other people, but Emma was the exception. There was something tantalizing about her courage that made him want to be close to her. She didn't fear him like others did. She had endured far too much pain in her life to be intimidated by a man just because he belonged to the Mafia. In fact, she felt better whenever she was in Salvatore's company. That made her all the more special to him.

While Emma was on stage again, doing another set, Salvatore made his way to the bar, his mind on the kind of things he could do to make her life easier. As a member of the Mafia, his own life was extremely complicated. Being a part of the underworld had its ups and downs. There was always plenty of money at his disposal, but it came at the cost of his freedom. There were so many people who wanted him dead that he had to be careful about the places he visited and the company he kept. He had to watch his every move. The smallest error of judgment on his part could prove fatal, both for him and for those close to him.

Salvatore decided he would wait and observe Emma's progress. If she needed him, he would instinctively know it and would be there to help her. He watched adoringly as she did her last dance of the evening. Emma still had no clue that Salvatore had fallen in love with her. She didn't know that while she was away, he had missed her so much. But now that she was back, he wasn't willing to let her go again so easily.

Chapter Sixty-One

I sabella became the guiding star of Emma's life and she found new energy in providing her with a good life. She vowed to stop living in the past and focus on the present. The first step in that direction involved going through Gracie's room, getting rid of her sister's belongings and making it a special place just for Izzy. Brianna and Katie immediately agreed to help. Partly because they figured there would be a lot of things to sort through, a formidable task for one person to accomplish, but mainly because they anticipated how stressful it would be for Emma to go through and dispose of her sister's possessions.

The three girls began working early in the morning, and by dinnertime, they had removed all of Gracie's belongings, except for a few things that Emma either kept for herself or left in the room as a loving reminder to Izzy of the young girl who had given birth to her and whose last thought had been for her baby. They decided to move the bed against the far wall so that Emma could get a bedrail and Izzy could sleep there on her own.

It was while lifting the mattress that Brianna found Gracie's journal. She and Katie exchanged a startled look and set out to talk to Emma in the kitchen.

"Em," Brianna said, trying to sound casual, "we found this under Gracie's mattress."

At the very sight of the journal, tears sprang to Emma's eyes. "Thanks," she said in a broken voice, reaching for it.

This time Katie spoke. "Emma, I think it might be a little too much for you to read right now. Do you want me to hang onto it until you're ready?"

"You're right," Emma said gratefully, "I won't read it just yet." With those words, she tossed the journal into the bottom of the duffle bag in which she carried her dance costumes.

The moment her friends had left, Emma went right back to her bedroom holding the journal. Leafing through its pages, she discovered that Gracie had written a lot about her. It was mostly about how much she loved her older sister and how she'd felt responsible for ruining Emma's life when they had to flee their home years ago. Emma smiled as she read through the private reflections of a very typical young teenager. Several of Gracie's entries indicated that she wasn't very fond of Ethan, but this came as no surprise to Emma. They had discussed Gracie's aversion to him.

Emma found herself engrossed in the concerns that had plagued Gracie during the span of her short life. The guilt and anxiety caused by their troubled childhood had weighed heavily on her. It was shocking for Emma to discover how often Gracie had relived the nightmarish experience of being buried in the basement by Jake. She felt guilty for not having coaxed her sister into sharing her trauma with her. The burden of failing to perceive how much Gracie had actually suffered and her inability to ease her pain would always remain with Emma. She'd imagined that Gracie had put her past behind her and moved on, but as she read on, Emma realized how seriously she had been mistaken in her assumption and how much lingering anguish her sister had lived with over the years. Crushed as she was by Gracie's revelations, it was more heartening for Emma to read of her sister's many fond remembrances. She was especially touched by the number of times Gracie repeated her faith in the depth of Emma's love for her. Emma found herself smiling, laughing out loud, and weeping in turn. Then she came upon an entry made by Gracie just a couple of months after her fifteenth birthday:

Tonight, the worst thing happened to me. Ethan came home shit-faced drunk, while Emma was at work. He tried to kiss me and when I ran into my room, he followed. He hit me and forced me to have sex with him. It hurt so much when he put his dick in me. I hate myself for what happened! If Emma ever found out, she'd hate me too. What kind of person am I to have sex with my sister's boyfriend?

Emma's blood ran cold. She read the entry again and again, desperately hoping she had misread or misinterpreted the words. She flipped forward to the next entry:

Ethan came into my room again tonight, after Emma left for work. He threatened to tell Emma I had come onto him if I didn't give him a blow job. She wouldn't believe him over me, right? I hate Ethan! I hope he dies.

Just then, Emma heard the apartment door open and close. Ethan was home. She put the journal into the bottom of the duffle bag and went out to the living room. She would get justice for Gracie. Ethan was now no different from Pepper and Jake in Emma's eyes and she felt as much hatred and contempt for him as she had for the other two men.

"Hey, babe!" he called out when he saw her approach. "What's for dinner?"

Emma shot him a loving glance while an inferno burned inside her. "I made meatloaf and mashed potatoes," she told him. "It'll be ready in about half an hour."

He moved up close and rubbed up against her, sliding his arm over her shoulders. Then he turned her to face him and pulled her in to make her feel his erection. She battled the urge to run into the kitchen and grab the butcher knife so she could cut his dick off. He had committed the ultimate crime, for which there could be no pardon. He'd raped her sister. A huge mistake, she thought to herself.

That night at work, Emma used every free minute to read the remaining segments of Gracie's journal. She turned down requests for lap dances on the pretext that she suspected she was coming down with something and didn't want to risk passing on the bug. She even refused Salvatore's request that night, leaving him deeply disappointed.

As Emma went back to reading her sister's journal, it became increasingly clear to her that Ethan had been forcing himself on Gracie almost daily. Then two months after it had started, it seemed to stop suddenly. Emma was barely able to get through the next, devastating entry:

Oh God, no! I'm pregnant! Now what the fuck am I supposed to do? I just know that this is Ethan's baby. I told him I had taken a pregnancy test and it was positive and that he was the father. He called me a liar and then kicked the shit out of me—literally. He kicked me so hard in the gut that I shit my pants. He said I was just

saying that to avoid giving him sex again. He threatened that if I told Emma, he would kill me—and the baby. What am I gonna do? Emma is going to hate me for doing this to her. I hate myself! I wish I were dead.

Emma had barely finished reading the words when she stumbled to her feet, ran to the bathroom, and threw up.

One of the strippers passing by said, "Yeah, you probably do have that fucking flu. Don't get near me."

Emma needed time to think. She needed a plan of action. Much as she wanted to, she couldn't give in to her rage and rush impulsively into just anything. She had Isabella to think of. She would be of no use to her niece if she ended up in prison. When her desperation got the better of her, she considered confiding in Salvatore, but then decided to keep him out of it. She didn't want to owe anybody anything.

Shiver came in to tell Emma that she was up for her next set, but when she saw her hugging the toilet bowl, she said sympathetically, "Never mind. I'll get someone to fill in for you, sweetie."

"Thanks, Shiver," Emma replied weakly.

"No problem. Do you want me to call your boyfriend to come and pick you up early?" she offered.

"NO!" The word burst from Emma. "I'm still feeling really nauseous. I'll stay in the bathroom until I think I can make the trip home."

"Okay, sugar. I'll check in on you later."

After Shiver left, Emma went into the dressing room and picked up Gracie's journal from where she had dropped it. She locked herself in one of the bathroom stalls, sat on the toilet, and continued to read.

I told Emma about being pregnant and they took me to a clinic to make sure. It's definite now. Ethan's mad that I told Emma about the baby. He said I could only live here until the bastard was born. Then I would have to get out. He forced me to give him another blow job tonight. I tried to refuse him, but he flung me down on the ground and started kicking me all over my body. He even kicked me on the head. I was afraid that if I didn't suck him off, he would kick me in the stomach

and kill the baby. After I had done it, he left. Then a couple of hours later, he came back into my room. He was reeking of alcohol and he told me to whack him off. He made me get naked and stood over me while I pulled it. He came in my face and said that's what happens to filthy whores like Emma and me. I've never kept a secret from Emma before. I feel really bad about lying to her and not telling her that Ethan is the father. But I feel worse to tell her that I had sex with her boyfriend, not that I wanted to, but what if Ethan is right and I did something to make him have sex with me? I hate Ethan! Please, God, make this stop happening to me!

Emma read up to the point where she had thrown Ethan out of their apartment. A profound sadness for Gracie washed over her. She had left her in the care of a man who had sexually tortured her. Throughout it all, Gracie had been consumed with guilt for something she wasn't responsible for.

The entries after Ethan's exit expressed relief that he was finally gone from their lives. This time Emma broke down in tears not because Gracie was dead, but because she had failed her sister so abysmally. She hadn't been able to protect her from Ethan and was devastated by the knowledge that Gracie had lived and died with the misconception that she had betrayed Emma. So much made sense to Emma now, little things that she had shrugged off as normal teenage behavior. And Ethan? He was still there, she thought, nonchalant and guilt-free. Emma's mind was filled with sinful ideas about how she would make him pay for what he had done to her sister. But first she had to put enough distance between the two of them so that no one would ever suspect her of any wrongdoing.

Chapter Sixty–Two

E mma's whole persona changed after reading her sister's journal. She
found the energy to go on with her life and to get rid of Ethan once
and for all. He was a pedophile and a bully, just like Pepper had been; the
only difference was Ethan was sneaky about his abuse of Gracie.

A few days later, Ethan confronted her aggressively. "You've been acting
fucking weird lately," he accused belligerently. "You got something to say
to me?"

"No. I've been working hard and I'm tired. Just leave me alone!" Emma
couldn't help the hatred she had stored within blazing forth in her tone
and attitude.

Ethan seized her by the shoulders and flung her against the refrigerator.
"Who the fuck do you think you're talking to like that, you piece of trash?
I will fuckin' destroy you! Do you understand me?"

Emma had become immune to his vicious threats. She despised him and
the very air he breathed. She was revolted by the smell of his breath and the
touch of his fingers gripping her shoulders. Ethan was nose to nose with
her, screaming at the top of his lungs. But Emma was now deaf and blind
to his abuse.

Seeing that he wasn't getting through to her, he unzipped his pants,
pushed her to the kitchen floor, and held out his penis for her. Her instinct
was to bite it off and she had to tell herself: Hold on! All in good time.
But she did refuse to give him oral sex. Beginning to feel the loss of his
power over her, Ethan seized her by the hair, dragged her to the bed, flung
her down on it, and forced himself on her. After it was over, she lay there,
motionless. She hadn't shed a single tear, emitted a single cry of protest, or
blinked the entire time he was on top of her. She just stared at the ceiling,
thinking that this was exactly what he had done to Gracie. He was a vile,

corrupt pervert—nothing more and nothing less—and she wanted to get away from him as quickly as possible.

Ethan lay next to her, catching his breath after his attack on her.

Still staring at the ceiling, Emma said in a voice devoid of feeling, "Ethan, I'm leaving. I don't want to be with you anymore."

Ethan silently got out of bed and went into the living room. When he came back, he had a gun in his hand pointed at her head. Emma's pulse raced as he approached her, spewing aggression.

"You're leaving, are you?" he snarled. "No, you're not. You're staying right here with me, so I can teach you how to be a good girl!" He pressed the barrel of the gun into her cheek. "Are we crystal?" he asked.

Emma hadn't known he owned a gun. She struggled for the right words, and when none came, she said in a shaky voice, trying to call his bluff, "I know what you did to Gracie, Ethan. I know that you raped her and I swear I'll tell the police about it."

Ethan was livid. How had she found out? Had Gracie told her? He hadn't thought she'd dare. He was sure he had convinced the little bitch that whatever they had done together was entirely her fault and Emma would hate her if she found out.

Feeling cornered, he unleashed his anger. "I didn't rape her!" he shouted. "That little slut wanted me. She begged me to give it to her. You have it all wrong, and if you try to leave now, I will kill you—and that rotten kid."

Recognizing the terror in Emma's eyes, he knew he had her. Yeah, he thought, this bitch will do anything to keep the kid safe. Turning away from her, he moved toward Izzy's room, where she was sleeping.

Emma ran after him, but wasn't quick enough to stop him from pulling the child out of bed.

"No, Ethan, no!" she screamed.

Awakened abruptly, Izzy cried out in alarm and reached for Emma, but Ethan kept her clutched in his vicious grip. Then he placed the gun against the toddler's head.

"Are you going to behave now?" he challenged Emma.

Emma took a step toward him. He retaliated by kicking her in the hip.

"Okay, bitch," he said grimly, "I see that you're not hearing me, Emma!" With that, he pulled the trigger on the revolver.

Chapter Sixty-Three

In the split second when Emma heard the click inside the barrel her breath stopped as she braced herself for the inevitable. But nothing happened. The gun wasn't loaded.

Ethan burst out laughing. "The next time you dare to disobey me," he said with an evil smirk, "the gun will have bullets in it. I can go get them now, if you want me to. Do you?"

Emma bowed her head in defeat. "No," she said in a low voice, "I will do whatever you want me to. Just leave Izzy alone. Give her to me."

Tossing the frightened toddler into her arms as though she were a sack of potatoes, Ethan whacked Emma hard on the back of her head.

"Go get that kid back to sleep," he ordered. "It's time for make-up sex, darlin'."

The next day, when Ethan had left the apartment to go over to his mother's, Emma quickly packed clothes for Izzy and herself and got into the car. She set out with a trunk full of clothes, a couple of hundred dollars, a three-year-old kid and no idea whatsoever as to where she was headed. She forced herself to focus on the road as she drove in the general direction of Philadelphia, calling Doubles to inform Jay that she'd be out for a while but would stay in touch. Emma's plan was to find a safe place for Izzy, where she would be cared for. Thinking of where she could go without him finding them, she hit upon the perfect idea. She had lived in a car for a couple of months with Gracie and Brianna. It had been a hard time for all of them, but they had managed. Now she and the baby would do the same.

Arriving in West Philadelphia, Emma continued driving until she was at Fifty-Second and Market Streets, a seedy area overrun with people who looked eager to find trouble. By the look of the place and its residents, she could tell drugs were a part of life here. This is it, she told herself, knowing instinctively that this was one place where Ethan would never search for her. In a town like Ambler, he could come across as a mean hard ass, but here, in the streets of West Philadelphia, he would never risk it, because he knew he would be eaten alive. Besides, she thought, Ethan only picked on women and kids. He would never be man enough to challenge those who were clearly capable of fighting back. Then a feeling of contentment washed over Emma as she realized that he had completely underestimated her.

"Fucking asshole!" she muttered to herself.

Emma found a parking spot on a side street, got Izzy out of the car, and started walking down Market Street. They stopped at a restaurant, where she ordered chicken fingers for Isabella and a sandwich for herself. As they walked back to the car slowly, Emma became uncomfortably aware that they stood out. The community here was predominantly black, Asian, and Latino. Not that she was afraid—not for herself, anyway. But the way the men eyed her made her feel uneasy. She tended to forget that with her five-foot-eight-inch height and long blond hair, she would attract attention anywhere. Now confronted by these hungry male stares, her awareness of the impact her beauty made on others came back to her in a rush. She felt like a complete white honkus screaming: "Look at me, look at me!"

Once darkness fell, Emma began to feel more vulnerable as the streets came alive with still more disreputable-looking characters. Around ten o'clock that night, she and Izzy had just fallen asleep in the car's backseat when there was a loud thump on the window. Startled awake, she sat up to find their car surrounded by a gang of young twenty-something's hollering for her to open the door.

One tall Asian boy yelled, "Open the fucking door! If we have to break the windows, you'll get worse!"

Emma had been holding Izzy down under the sheet, but as she moved to grasp the knife she kept in her purse for self-defense, the child's head popped up and she started howling. When the gang saw her, they started kicking the car violently.

"Go to sleep, you little idiot!" one of the boys yelled, banging his fists on the roof.

Several of them began rocking the car from side to side. This terrified Izzy, who screamed louder still.

"Leave us the fuck alone!" Emma yelled at the tall Asian boy. "We're not bothering anyone!"

The gang was into getting some action from the pretty blonde, but had no desire for any of that kid shit.

The Asian boy signaled to his friends. "Let's go," he said. "This bitch is probably all torn up from having that stupid kid anyway."

As they walked away, Emma's heartbeat returned to normal. Once the boys were out of sight, she started the car and drove around until she had found a small street in a middle-class neighborhood. She parked and heaved a sigh of relief. She was annoyed with herself for being so stupid. She'd learned all about street living years ago and now she would have to dig into her arsenal and pull out all that she knew to keep her and Izzy safe and alive. But Emma didn't know the creatures of the night that waited to find their pleasure through her pain.

Chapter Sixty-Four

During the day, Emma spent time in different areas of West Philadelphia. At night, she was careful to park in residential neighborhoods. However, that came with a risk too, since most of the area where she stayed was riddled with crime. A couple of days later, while driving around, she found herself on Fairhill Street. The neighborhood was a mix of families, thugs, and abandoned buildings. At nightfall, she found a spot on North Fairhill and got into the backseat of the car with Izzy to sleep.

Emma woke up at two in the morning. She had to pee. Leaving Izzy sleeping, she climbed out, ducking into the alley, from where she could keep an eye on the car. Just as she squatted, the sound of men talking at the tops of their voices reached her. Their rowdy behavior left her in no doubt that they were either drunk or high. Emma held her breath, hoping the shouting wouldn't wake up Izzy. She knew it was important to keep their presence hidden from these strangers and worried that if her niece woke up, she would begin crying and blow their cover.

Emma heard their voices draw closer. Deciding it was time to act, she ran toward the car. That's when they saw her from the far end of the alley. They chased her fleeing figure, and before she knew it, they were upon her. One of the men grabbed her by the hair and yanked her away from the car door. She reeled back and landed on the sidewalk.

"Well, now," an unkempt, long-haired man said, eyeing her up, "what do we have here?"

The three other men with him all stepped up to get a closer look, and one of the younger ones spoke first.

"Goddamn, this bitch is fine!" he exclaimed. "What are you doing out here all by yourself, beautiful? You looking to give us a good time?"

Terror seized Emma. She knew she was no match for four men, and her voice quivered as she replied, "No, I'm not a hooker. I don't do that."

The men laughed. "Oh, she don't do that!" one of them mocked.

"How about this?" another man suggested. "You suck our dicks and we'll let you go without bashing your fucking brains in."

Emma would have done anything to keep them away from the car where Izzy was sleeping. She gave in to their proposal, and the long-haired man unzipped his pants and commanded her to get on her knees. Emma was about to give him what he wanted when Izzy began crying. The men looked at the car.

"You gotta be fucking kidding!" the long-haired man said to Emma. "You have a fucking kid in that car? You must be totally brainless!" Then he turned back to her, ignoring the toddler's whimpers. "Let's go, now! Get on with it!" he said, pushing his pelvis toward her.

From the way he stank, Emma could tell he hadn't showered in a long time. His dick smelled like he had shoved it up his own ass. She nearly gagged from the odor, annoying him so intensely that he punched her on top of the head. This seemed to fuel his anger still more, for he proceeded to kick her. The others joined in on the fun until Emma lay unconscious. Then they took turns raping her.

Just before dawn, Emma woke up. She was lying in the same place where they had attacked and beaten her. She was naked from the waist down and badly bruised. Her clothes had been flung off to the side and there was dried blood on her face and between her legs. She got up and hobbled over to the car. Izzy lay inside, perfectly still. Emma yanked open the back door in panic. Izzy's eyes flew open, and she breathed a sigh of relief.

From the blood on her inner thighs and the soreness between her legs, Emma suspected that the gang had raped her while she was unconscious. She was convinced at last that she couldn't go on like this. It hadn't even been a week since they'd started living in the car and she had already put Izzy in harm's way more than once. She had to find a different solution.

Emma decided to go to Clark Park, where she had heard homeless people hung out. Maybe someone would be able to tell her where they could go, or at least where she could stay for a while. She figured it was worth a shot. Once she got there, she was pleasantly surprised by the variety of people who frequented the place—college students, homeless people, couples, and families. She strolled around the park, searching for someone who might be willing to talk to her. Then she heard a woman call her name. She turned to see Alessa standing nearby with a handsome man and a young girl. She ran up and threw her arms around Emma.

"Oh my God! Emma! How have you been?" Alessa asked, genuinely pleased to see her.

Distraught over all that had happened to her the night before, she held onto Alessa and dissolved in tears. Ashamed that she had broken down in public and was crying so helplessly, she could only blubber, "I'm sorry, Alessa, I had some bad shit happen to me last night."

Alessa took a closer look at Emma and noticed the bruises and cuts on her face and arms. "What the fuck happened to you?" she asked, alarmed.

"Four guys beat the shit out of me last night," Emma said, feeling worn out and defeated.

Alessa hugged her tight. "It's all right, Emma," she consoled her. "I understand. Believe me, I do. I've been where you are right now. But you have to believe that things will get better." Then she turned to the man and the young girl Emma had seen her with. "This is my husband, Remo, and our daughter, Lucy," Alessa said, introducing her small family.

Emma looked down at Izzy, who was staring at all of them. "This is Izzy," she said. "Isabella. She's my sister's kid. Gracie died two and a half years ago."

For a moment Alessa didn't know how to respond. Just then Lucy stepped forward, put her hands on her knees, and leaned over so that her face was level with Izzy's.

"Hi, Izzy, I'm Lucy," she said cheerfully. "Want to blow bubbles?" She held out the bottle of bubbles Remo had bought her.

Emma looked a bit uncertain, but Alessa assured her, "She'll be fine with Lucy. Most of the people here in the park know her. Besides, Remo will be with them."

As Lucy led Izzy away, Remo trailed behind the two children.

Emma turned back to Alessa. "How come I never knew you had a kid? Aren't you a little young to have a kid her age?"

"Well, after being fired from Doubles, I was homeless for a while," Alessa explained. "Then I met Lucy, who was homeless too. We've been together ever since. She's the most amazing thirteen-year-old I've ever known." She turned to Emma and gave her a sharp, discerning look. "What about you, Emma? What happened to your sister?"

"She was killed in a car accident. Now I'm raising Izzy." It was difficult for her to utter the words. The pain of losing Gracie seemed never-ending.

"I'm looking for a place where Izzy and I can stay for a while. I'm sure my ex is trying to hunt us down. I just need time away from him, time for myself to think."

Alessa's expression was regretful. "The three of us actually run a refuge for homeless people," she explained, "but we don't have any free beds right now."

"I understand," Emma told her. "We're living in my car right now. I'm just trying to find safe places to park at night. It's not a big deal. It'll all work out. No worries," Emma offered.

But she was far from feeling as confident and optimistic as she tried to sound. Emma was bitterly disappointed and felt once again as if there was nowhere to turn.

Chapter Sixty-Five

A lessa felt miserable about not being able to help Emma, who was obviously in a bad place, but there were many others in the city, even less fortunate than her, who had to be turned down as well. She offered Emma the only option she was able to.

"How about if you and Izzy came back to our place?" she suggested. "We live in the apartment on the top floor. You guys can get showers and sleep over tonight. How's that sound?"

When you are living on your own and trying everything you can to make it work out, a simple offer like Alessa's can seem a godsend. It gave Emma some hope.

"That would be great!" she said gratefully. "Oh man, I really appreciate it!" Impulsively, she gave Alessa a tight hug.

On the walk back to the Outside Inn, a house for homeless teens that Alessa and her family ran, the girls caught up on small talk. Finally Emma asked the question that had been on her mind for a long time.

"So you finally got rid of that asshole, Harlin?" she asked. "Man, when the other dancers found out what he was making you do, they couldn't believe it. How did you manage to get away from him?"

Alessa acknowledged the truth with a silent nod. The ghost of the past still haunted her whenever she thought about Harlin.

"You know, it wasn't easy," she admitted. "I ran from him. I started in a shelter for women, where I met my best friend, Ebby. She's a psychologist. But within a couple of weeks, I had to run again and was living on the streets. That's where I met Lucy. I stripped at some shit-holes for a while to keep us going. I got lucky and met someone who helped me get back on my feet. Eventually I met Remo. After that, we started dating, fell in love, got married, and opened the Outside Inn to help other homeless people."

Emma listened to her; awestruck at the way she had overcome the obstacles in her life since they'd last seen each other. The story made her believe that better things could be lying ahead for her as well. Emma wanted to be happy, the way Alessa was now.

Back in Alessa's apartment, the two young women sat on the sofa together while Lucy took Izzy into her bedroom to play a board game. Remo excused himself to make the three of them coffee and get dinner started. As the night wore on, the two friends settled on the sofa with blankets.

Finally Alessa asked her, "What's your story, Emma? Do you have any family who could help you out?"

As memories of Mrs. Tisdale popped into her head, Emma was overwhelmed with sadness. "No," she replied truthfully. "Once I lost Gracie that was it. My father died when I was a teenager. The bastard beat me for as long as I could remember."

"What about your mom?"

Emma shook her head. "Useless. A stupid woman. I wouldn't spit on her if she were on fire."

Alessa laughed out loud at her friend's comment about her mother.

"I know that sounds cruel, but I hate my parents," Emma said honestly.

Alessa leaned back into the sofa. "You don't have to make excuses to me, Em. When I was a kid, I didn't have anyone who had my back either. My father died a couple of years ago, but I wasn't close to him. As for my mom, she's a self-centered bitch I don't talk to anymore."

"Why?" Emma asked.

"Why what?"

"Why is your mom a self-centered bitch? I mean, my mother tore my ass up with verbal assaults, let my father beat me, and never once did anything about it. She never cared about what happened to me and Gracie. What did your mom do to make you hate her so much?" Emma asked, craving reassurance that she wasn't the only person on earth whose parents didn't love her.

"My mom allowed my uncle to rape me when I was seven years old," Alessa said calmly. "It wasn't until I was sixteen that I managed to run away. When I was old enough, I finally got up the nerve to tell her what he had been doing to me, but she practically ripped my head off. She sacrificed me so that she could continue to live without having to work, I guess. I'm not sure I'll ever know the real reasons. Maybe she's just fucking crazy."

The composure with which Alessa talked about her mother made it clear to Emma that her friend had found a way to come to terms with the traumas of her childhood. She had learned to get over the fact that her mother had neglected to protect her. Alessa had moved on, and the peace and serenity Emma now saw in her friend were things she wanted for herself. It was comforting to discover that she wasn't the only one with fucked-up parents or a rotten childhood.

The girls stayed up talking until two in the morning. Just before Alessa went into her bedroom, she turned back and said, "Hey, I know some people who manage restaurants in the city. They donate leftover food to the people who live in this building. If you're interested, I can make a couple of calls tomorrow and see if I can get someone to talk to you about a job."

Emma smiled, grateful that she had run into Alessa that afternoon. "That would be great! Thanks for everything."

As she lay on the sofa waiting to fall asleep, Emma let her hope soar that she and Izzy could have a normal life. She desperately wanted a life that was free of violence and hatred.

But fate had other plans for Emma.

Chapter Sixty-Six

E mma was excited that a job interview had been set up for her that afternoon at two the next day. It was with a friend of Alessa's, a manager at Bar 210 in Rittenhouse Square.

Camouflaging the bruises on her face with makeup, Emma walked into the restaurant, Izzy in tow, optimistic about beginning her life over. She asked to talk to the manager and looked around her as she waited. The place was upscale and trendy, the customers elegantly dressed in the latest styles. The women were well groomed and wore expensive perfume. The men were handsome and polished. It made Emma hopeful that she could earn decent tips here.

Eileen, the manager, looked Emma over as she came out to greet her. She immediately noticed the girl's shabby clothes, but decided it hardly mattered. While working, this new employee would be wearing the required attire—black pants and a white shirt. She considered Emma's stunning beauty as an asset and believed she would fit in just fine with their patrons. After a ten-minute conversation, Eileen decided that she liked Emma. She might be rough around the edges, but what she lacked in poise, she made up in sweetness and charm, qualities Emma had acquired from her years of working at Doubles.

"Are you a single mom?" Eileen asked now, glancing at Izzy and wondering if Emma's kid could be a problem. She needed someone dependable, free of baggage.

"I am, but don't worry about Isabella," Emma replied, gesturing toward the child. "We call her Izzy. I have lots of friends who are willing to babysit her while I'm working."

Suspecting the reason behind Eileen's question, Emma had no qualms about lying. She really needed the job.

"Well, hello, Izzy. How are you?" Eileen said with a bright smile. "You sure do look like your mom."

"My mommy died," Izzy pouted.

Eileen was shocked. "Oh? I'm sorry to hear that." She gave Emma a confused look.

"This is my niece," Emma explained. "My sister died and I'm raising her."

"Oh, I see. Well, you're a very devoted aunt. I'm sorry to hear about your sister. Was she sick?" Eileen was genuinely moved.

"No, she died in a car accident," Emma replied before quickly changing the subject. "So do you have something for me?" she went on. "I can start right away. Well, tomorrow, so that I can get Izzy taken care of."

"Tomorrow would be great," Eileen told her. "I'll start you on the lunch shift, and if it goes well, I can get you on the dinner shift. The wait staff makes much better tips at night."

Eileen handed Emma a clipboard with a job application attached. "Just fill this out and leave it with the bartender. See you tomorrow at eleven."

When Emma finished filling out the application providing information that was mostly fabricated, she handed it to the bartender, who gave her a welcoming smile.

"Glad to have you here," he said, hoping that she was single.

Emma smiled noncommittally. She had recognized that look, the I-want-to-get-in-your-pants stare, from her days of working at Doubles. She wanted nothing more to do with men.

With a job to start the next morning, she headed back to Alessa's apartment to thank her. "Listen," Alessa said, "you and Izzy are welcome to stay here for a couple of days, until you find a place of your own. Izzy can share Lucy's room and you can sleep on the sofa."

Emma was grateful to have Alessa as a friend. But she needed to find a place quickly and knew that it would be difficult with the couple of hundred dollars she had.

While the two young women were chatting, Izzy came into the living room.

"Aunt Emma, I'm hungry. And I want pizza," she declared.

Twenty minutes later, Emma was parking the car on Chestnut Street, not far from where Alessa lived. She and Izzy walked up to Giovani's Pizza.

Izzy let out a piercing squeal. "I love pizza!" she yelled, jumping with joy on the sidewalk and clapping her hands together.

Emma ordered two slices and took Izzy over to an open table. A few booths away, a group of unruly teenagers sat at a table. Emma had noticed them right away and gauged from the state of their clothes and their lack of hygiene that they were either homeless or came from very poor families. Their bragging about the amount of money they had made from begging that morning merely confirmed her suspicions. Then Emma overheard two of the teens yammering over their success in stealing a woman's purse that morning when she had set it on the sidewalk to look at a shirt from a street vendor. She immediately began feeling a little nervous about Izzy's safety around the teens. She hardly needed any more trouble. She held her breath as the disruptive group walked past to leave, each of them eyeing her up then staring at the child.

One of the girls who had been watching Emma without her being aware of it stopped abruptly at their table.

"Hey, is your name Emma?" she asked as if she knew her.

"Who the fuck are you?" Emma shot back, feeling defensive.

"You are Emma, aren't you?" the teen asked. "It's me! Sydney!"

Emma stared at her in disbelief, her mind racing back in time remembering Syd. The eleven-year-old who had once saved her life. Now here she was, all these years later, standing before her. Sydney was beautiful. Emma felt a tiny spark of joy light up within her once reality set in.

"Oh my God!" she exclaimed. "Syd! Look at you, all grown up! You're fucking gorgeous!"

Sydney snickered. "Well, I'm fifteen now. Anyway, I would have recognized you anywhere. Those green eyes are a dead giveaway and your daughter looks exactly like you."

"I'm Izzy," the child volunteered proudly.

The teen gave her a big smile. "Hi, Izzy. I'm Sydney."

The rest of the group came back to see who Sydney was talking to, and Izzy moved a little closer to Emma.

"Where are Brianna and Gracie? Are they here too?" Sydney asked excitedly.

Sadly, Emma explained, "No, I'm on my own now. Brianna moved back home and Gracie died in a car accident. Izzy is her daughter."

"Fuck, man! I'm sorry to hear that. So do you live around here now?" Syd wanted to know.

Emma blushed with embarrassment. "No, Syd. Izzy and I needed to get away from some asshole. I was living in my car for a while. Now I'm at a friend's place, but I need to get out in a couple of days and find a place of my own. We'll probably go back to living in the car until I can save enough money to rent an apartment."

"No shit, that sucks! I know what it's like," Sydney said with genuine understanding. "Did the guy you're running from fuck up your face?"

Emma wanted to blurt out the truth, to tell Syd everything that had happened to her. She was just so relieved to see a face from the past, from the time Gracie had still been alive.

"No," she replied truthfully, "I got jacked up two nights ago by a gang when I was trying to take a piss in an alley. Izzy was in the car, but luckily they didn't bother her."

A thought suddenly struck Sydney. Telling Emma she'd be right back, she went and joined her group of friends, who were waiting a few feet away. She seemed to be discussing something with them. Then she walked back to Emma excitedly.

"My herd just agreed that you and Izzy could stay with us for a while, if you want to," she announced. "We rent a house in Kensington. It ain't much and the neighborhood blows, but it's better than being on the streets. It's a four-bedroom row home and thirteen of us share it. Rent is only six hundred a month. It's cheap enough. If you want to stay, we'll only charge you for one person, not the kid. It would cost you forty-three bucks a month, plus around five bucks for electricity, but we only use that at night and for cooking. What do ya think?"

Emma thought it was the best offer—the only offer—she had. At least there would be other people around and it would be less dangerous for Izzy than living in the car.

"Well, what if the other six people say no?" Emma asked, referring to the herd's absent housemates and curious as to how a few of them could make a decision on behalf of everyone who lived in the house.

"The herd votes on everything and the majority rules," Sydney explained. "So we're cool. The other six won't care, anyway. The less rent we each have to pay, the better off we all are."

By now Emma had heard the word used often enough and couldn't contain her curiosity. "The herd? What the hell is the herd?" she asked, amused.

"Oh, well. We call ourselves the herd," Sydney explained, laughing. "It's really a reference to a herd of misfits. That's what we are. We all came from shitty backgrounds and met on the streets."

Emma smiled at the explanation, understanding what it was like to feel like a misfit. "Well, I think it's a great idea," Emma said approvingly. "I don't have much money, but I just found a job that I start tomorrow."

Sydney turned to the group and gestured a thumbs up. They sauntered over to take turns introducing themselves. Emma and Izzy quickly finished their pizza and headed back out to the street with the herd.

"Let's all pile into your car and you can drive us back to Kensington," Sydney suggested. "We can show you where we live."

As Emma drove off, the teens gabbed with excitement about having a housemate with a car. That could save them from sneaking onto the train or paying bus fare to get to Center City. Sydney explained that some of the kids had legitimate jobs and had to work in the city.

"There ain't no jobs in Kensington," she told Emma. "We only live there because we can rent our house for cheap and the landlord doesn't give us any shit."

They all seemed nice and took an immediate liking to Izzy, who was talking up a storm with them. She was busy telling them about the doll she had brought with her, explaining that it was her baby. As Emma drove into Kensington and looked around, she noted that nothing had changed in the four years she had been gone. The streets were still crawling with hookers, drug addicts, and pimps. As depressing as her surroundings were, Emma smiled to herself.

A little while later, she parked in front of their new home and looked at it. The initial impression was far from promising. The wooden siding, once white, was chipped and rotting. The sidewalk was nothing more than chunks of old cement that opened up to a wide set of stairs leading up to the house. There was a small landing in front of two doors. The entire block of row homes looked as if they had been abandoned, like a scene from the Twilight Zone. They were two-story homes, with large eaves and roofs that peaked at various places. Emma sensed that at one time the homes had been beautiful, built for upper-class families rather than the poverty-stricken tenants who now occupied them.

I'm getting another chance, she thought hopefully.

Chapter Sixty-Seven

E mma drove back to Alessa's to tell her about the day's events. From the pep in her step, Alessa could guess from where she sat on the porch that something good had happened.

"Guess what?" Emma gushed. "I ran into a girl I used to know and she offered Izzy and me a place to live with them."

"Them?" Alessa asked, happy for her friend but a little concerned that Emma had hooked up with a gang. Alessa was no stranger to the evil of being associated with a gang. She didn't want to see the two of them get sucked into that kind of life.

"There are thirteen of them renting a house together," Emma explained. "Rent is going to be less than fifty bucks a month. It's a place where we can stay until I save enough money to get my own apartment. I'm so stoked!"

Relieved that they weren't going to live with a gang, Alessa gave her a hug and they went upstairs to the apartment. "Remo is making us dinner," she announced. "He's a pretty decent cook. Way better than me!"

After dinner, Emma grabbed the few bags she had brought up from the car and gave Alessa a big good-bye hug.

"We're gonna head out," she said and called for Izzy.

The child came running out with Lucy following her.

"Izzy is so smart!" Lucy said. "Aren't you, Izzy?"

The little girl smiled up at her. "Yeah," she affirmed, "I'm smart!"

Emma knew how smart Izzy was. She was also incurably talkative and utterly adorable. As the friends said their good-byes, they promised to keep in touch. Lucy gave Izzy a prolonged embrace.

"You be good to your Aunt Emma, Izzy!" the thirteen-year-old instructed.

As Emma drove back to Kensington, she hoped this new opportunity would turn out to be exactly what they both needed. About ten minutes into their ride The Beatles started blaring on the radio. Emma started singing along with "Let It Be," and seconds later, Izzy joined in. As young as the child was, she knew the words to many of the songs that streamed over the radio in their apartment. Emma and Izzy both loved music. They were happy and they were alive. For the first time in a long while, Emma felt young and carefree.

Sydney was waiting for them when they arrived and flung open the front door to let them inside. The only light in the once-formal sitting room came from a few small lamps, and Emma imagined how beautiful it must have been. The large front windows now stood ghostly and bare, with half-burnt stubs of old candles still standing twisted on the windowsills. The room was spacious, with a high ceiling and ornate angels carved into the wood tucked into the corners of the high ceiling. The small angel heads looked demonic and gave Emma the willies. The wallpaper was nothing more than scraps of color in random places, except for a wall that the herd had painted black.

"This is where we all hang out," Sydney announced excitedly, then led them up the stairs.

They followed her down the hallway to the last room on the right. Sydney opened the door.

"This is where I sleep," she explained. "Izzy and you will sleep in here with me and two of the other girls."

There was one single mattress tucked away in the corner of the room, which Sydney had found discarded on a side street in Kensington. She had dragged it back to the house alone and made it her very own bed. The other three "beds" were rolled-up sleeping bags and pillows.

"Do you have any sleeping bags or blankets with you?" Sydney asked hopefully.

"Yeah, I have some blankets in the trunk of my car," Emma told her.

As they went to fetch Emma's meager belongings they discussed where their lives had taken them since they had last seen each other as homeless kids. That night, as they all settled down to sleep, Izzy got out from under the covers and went over to Sydney, who gave her a big smile.

"Hey there, beautiful," she said to the child, "it's time to go sleep."

Izzy smiled back. "I want to sleep with you," she said boldly.

Sydney laughed. "Okay, then. Whatever you say, but no kicking," she teased, moving over to make room for the child.

Emma smiled at them from where she lay. Sydney was easy to like. She was so sweet and generous with the little she owned. Emma was glad they had run into her. Because of her, they had a place to sleep, with the safety that came from having lots of people around them.

Emma was excited about starting her new job the next morning. She didn't care that she wouldn't be earning anywhere near the income she had at Doubles. It was a first step in the right direction, she thought. She knew Gracie would be proud of her for leaving Ethan and moving on with Izzy to start over. She knew that things were about to change.

Chapter Sixty-Eight

Back in Ambler, two weeks had passed, and Ethan was still searching for Emma. He was pissed off that she had the nerve to run from him. He had threatened her that she would never get away from him, and he intended to make good on his claim. Ethan sat on the sofa, trying to figure out where to look for them next.

As his temper boiled over, he got up and kicked at a blanket that had been thrown in the corner of the room. It flew off, revealing the duffle bag Emma had used for work. In a rage now, he snatched it up and emptied out its contents on the floor, looking for a clue that might give him a hint of where the bitch had gone. The last thing to fall out of the bag was Gracie's journal.

Ethan picked it up and looked it over as if it were a foreign object. Then he began leafing through the pages. Initially, there was nothing but a bunch of little-girl bullshit, but further on, he came upon Gracie's entry, recording the events of the first night he had raped her. Slowly he realized why Emma had turned against him.

That fucking bitch read this shit, he thought.

He kept reading, unable to stop himself, until he got to the part where Gracie had confronted him about her pregnancy.

"Fucking stupid little whore!" he cursed aloud.

Ethan blamed his break-up with Emma on Gracie. He had been furious when she decided to keep the baby. A kid had never figured into his plans, and when he found out Gracie was pregnant, he had kept beating her in the hope that she would miscarry.

Ethan called Pete. "Yo! I need to find Emma," he said. "She ain't getting away from me this easy. You have any luck?"

"No," Pete told him. "Nothing yet. I'll keep you posted, though. All the guys at the bar are keeping an eye out for her. Don't worry, she'll turn up. And if she doesn't, you can find another girl."

"Fuck you, Pete! I don't want another girl. I want her. That bitch belongs to me. Do you understand? She needs to come home and get her ass back to Doubles. I had to borrow money from my stupid-ass mother this month to pay the fucking rent on this dump. Just keep looking!"

"God, dude, okay! Don't worry. We'll find her. Chill the fuck out," Pete shot back.

Ethan hung up the phone, pulled out one of Emma's costumes, and ripped it to shreds.

"You fucking whore!" he screamed to the empty apartment. "When I get my hands on you, I'm going to tear your ass up!"

Chapter Sixty-Nine

E mma fell into the pattern of her new life quickly. She was fond of almost all the other tenants she shared the house with except for one doper named Jamie. He was stoned all the time and she didn't like his raunchy sense of humor or sarcasm. However, she loved having so many people around her all the time. They worked together to make the house run well and keep each other safe. Most of the housemates were wonderful with Izzy. When Sydney wasn't available to keep an eye on the child while Emma worked, the others took turns watching her. She couldn't have asked for a better situation than the present one and was grateful for all that had happened to them recently.

Emma's only concern was that some of the housemates liked to party excessively. They drank and smoked pot, although they avoided the hard-core stuff. She discussed the issue with them and they came to an agreement that they wouldn't smoke dope in front of Izzy. Emma also made sure that she never left the child with any of the pot smokers or heavy drinkers when she went to work. She always worried they might in some way harm her niece, who was now like a daughter to her.

Izzy, however, was clearly happy in that house. When Emma was at work, the child spent a lot of her time hanging out with Sydney. The two had forged a special bond, and the teenager felt an overwhelming sense of responsibility for Izzy, perhaps because she derived some kind of emotional fulfillment from caring for someone the way she herself had longed to be cared for as a child. Whatever the reason, the two were inseparable.

Sydney was smart and pretty. She had large brown eyes and light brown hair. Because of her petite frame, she looked good in whatever she wore, even though it was always second-hand. Emma was happy to see that she had survived the streets and never forgot how she had helped Brianna, Gracie, and her when they had just left home.

Having grown up on the streets, Sydney was quick to snap when anyone got in her face. She was not easily intimidated and never backed down if you did her wrong. Emma implicitly trusted her and felt that Izzy was safe with her.

In the mornings, when Emma was sleeping, Sydney would take Izzy into Center City, where they begged for money and visited the different historical sites Philadelphia had to offer. Emma wasn't exactly thrilled at the idea of Izzy begging with Sydney, but she knew some compromise was unavoidable if she wanted Izzy to be looked after.

Things had worked out well for Emma at Bar 210. Within two weeks of her starting her new job, Eileen had given her the dinner shift. Emma was a responsible employee, and it wasn't just the men among the customers who liked her; the women did too, for she was sweet and kind and attentive to their needs.

When Emma hung out with Izzy and Sydney, they chatted and played games for hours. Izzy had become fascinated with board games from the short day and a half she had spent with Lucy.

"Aunt Emma, I want to play games like the ones Lucy played with me. Can you buy me some games?" she asked one night when the three girls were hanging out talking and watching Izzy color.

Emma couldn't resist the opportunity to tease Izzy. "How about if I give you and Sydney money, and tomorrow, when I'm at work, you go out and buy a game? But that's only if Sydney agrees to take you."

Sydney smiled mischievously at Izzy. "Well, I don't know," she drawled. "I might have some important things to do tomorrow. I guess if Izzy gave me lots of hugs and kisses, I might be able to find the time."

The little girl scrambled to her feet from the floor, where she had been sitting next to Emma, and flung herself into Sydney's outstretched arms, planting kisses on her face and nearly strangling her with a tight hug.

Sydney burst out laughing. "Okay, Okay!" she exclaimed, conceding defeat. "We'll go to the store tomorrow and buy you a game. You win!"

"This is going to be so great!" Izzy announced. "I'm gonna be the best game player ever!" She looked at Sydney. "Guess what, Syd?" she said suddenly. "I'm gonna be a lawyer when I grow up."

"I'm sure you will, little woman," Sydney responded with conviction, assured in her belief that Izzy would be whatever she wanted to be. "I think you'll make a great lawyer. You're definitely smart enough and you're bossy too, for a three-year-old."

"I'm almost four!" Izzy protested, but a satisfied smile played on her lips. Not only was she getting to buy a game, she could also be a lawyer when she grew up. Then a thought struck her. "Sydney? What do you want to be when you grow up? Maybe you can help me be a lawyer?"

Sydney and Emma chuckled at the child's willingness to allow her friend to be something that could help her in the long run.

"How about if you figure out what game you want to buy first, before you plan out your whole life and mine?" Sydney suggested, running her hand fondly through Izzy's hair.

"I already know what game I want, Syd," the little girl replied indignantly. "I want Chutes and Ladders. That's my favorite one, because that's the one Lucy played with me."

"Oh, all righty then, I see you already know what you want," Syd remarked.

"Aunt Em? When can we go see Lucy again?"

"Soon, baby, real soon," Emma said soothingly. "Right now I'm busy working, but in a couple of weeks, we can go to the park where you first met Lucy. Remember that park?"

Izzy rolled her eyes dramatically. "Of course I remember, Aunt Em!" she exclaimed with a touch of exasperation, as though her aunt had just questioned the obvious. "I love that park! It's my favorite one ever!"

"Hmm, well that's interesting, since it's the only park you've ever been to," Emma said wryly, then leaned over and tickled her niece until she begged her to stop.

Before Emma knew it fall had faded into winter. Two days before Thanksgiving, on a bitterly cold night, the group decided to celebrate the holiday by preparing a sumptuous dinner. No one in the herd, apart from Sydney, who had some knowledge of Emma's past, was aware of her consummate culinary skills. Few could have guessed that she had honed those skills while cooking meals for her family from a tender age. As Emma roamed around the kitchen with her friend, planning their grocery-shopping list, Sydney felt the time had come to ask her some of the questions that had been playing in her mind since they'd arrived to live in the house.

"Em?" she now asked hesitantly. "What was Ethan like? You said when you first met him that he was really nice. Then after a while he started treating you like shit. What did he actually do to you?"

"Well, Syd, he's a total asshole," Emma replied. Then her voice dropped to a whisper. "I found out that he'd raped Gracie. He's Izzy's father."

Sydney gaped at her. Every time Emma disclosed a fact, she was left wondering how, after living through such terrible ordeals, she could still be so resilient. Sydney knew that Emma had been beaten as a child, that she had lost her parents, and that her sister had died. And she had just learned that Gracie had not only been raped, but borne her rapist a child—Izzy.

"Well, I mean, what did he do to you, Em?" she persisted.

Emma put down the pen she was writing with and wondered if she should tell her friend the whole truth. Her gut told her to share every detail of her sordid experiences with Sydney. Maybe someday it would save her from a similar fate.

"He hit me," she said. "He berated and insulted me and accused me all the time of being stupid. He called me a whore and a slut for working at Doubles. But the worst he put me through, when I refused to obey him, was to put a gun to Izzy's head and pull the trigger. The gun wasn't loaded, but I didn't know that then. Then he threatened me that the next time it would be loaded."

Sydney gasped. "Fuck, Em! He's a crazy prick." She sprang to her feet and came to stand next to Emma. "He won't ever see Izzy again," she said with conviction. "We'll protect her."

Emma reflected on what her life had been like with Ethan. She had not only lost her sister, but a great deal of herself during that time. She hoped that Sydney was right about them never having to see Ethan again. If she did ever see him, Emma promised herself, it would only be as a God-given opportunity to kill him. Dead was the only way she ever wanted to see him again.

Chapter Seventy

I zzy woke up excited on Thanksgiving Day. The house was buzzing with conversation as everyone discussed the big dinner Emma was planning. The little girl had helped her aunt make pumpkin pies the night before. Emma had even let her mix the pie batter.

Izzy ran down the stairs and into the kitchen. "Aunt Em, Syd! Happy Thanksgiving!"

The two looked up from their work and gave the child a hug. Sydney was cutting pieces of bread to use for the stuffing.

"Syd, can I help you cut the bread?" Izzy asked.

Sydney hoisted her up on the chair next to where she stood and let her rip the bread into small pieces. As they worked and chatted, Earl, a herd member, came into the kitchen.

"Man, it sure smells good in here!" he remarked.

"Well, you don't smell very good!" Izzy commented disapprovingly. "You better go take a shower or you're not going to get to eat with us."

Earl walked over to the little girl and gave her a big, affectionate hug. "What do you mean I smell?" he said, pretending to sound offended. "Boy, you sure are bossy!"

"EWWWW!" Izzy shrieked, pulling away from him. "Get off me!"

The teenager laughed and went off to take a shower. On his way there, he wondered if the others thought he smelled too. He didn't have a steady job, and while he showered fairly regularly, he was losing the incentive to wash his clothes as often as he should.

"That wasn't a very nice thing to say to Earl, was it?" Sydney asked Izzy. "He doesn't have a lot of money to spend on clothes," she explained. "We should always be nice to everyone who lives in the house, ya know."

Izzy was defiant, shaking her head from side to side. "Well, Syd," she retorted, "he stinks. You can't stink on Thanksgiving."

Emma butted in. "Izzy, there was a time when I used to stink too. So did your mom. We didn't have anywhere to live and we couldn't take showers."

Izzy looked perplexed. "You used to smell?"

"Yeah. We didn't want to smell, but couldn't help it, because we couldn't take a shower."

"Well, Earl can take a shower," Izzy stated.

Emma gave her an exasperated look. "You know, I think you'll make a great lawyer!"

Izzy had a magnetic personality and was the kind of kid people wanted to be around. She could be both sassy and compassionate. She was straightforward and able to see things clearly, like most children her age. For Izzy, truth had no boundaries. Emma hoped that her niece would always be able to see the world as clearly and that nothing would ever happen to cloud her vision.

After a wonderful Thanksgiving dinner, Sydney and Emma settled in their bedroom. Sydney wasn't done with their earlier conversation, however. She really wanted to know Emma better, even if it meant prying. She idolized her and considered her the ultimate role model.

"Dinner was delicious!" she began, then quickly broached the topic that had been on her mind. "You know, I don't really understand, Em. You're such a strong person and you were so close to Gracie. Why do you think she didn't tell you Ethan had raped her?"

Emma pondered the question for a long time. Then the answer came to her.

"Because she thought that I would hate her for having sex with Ethan. He fucked with her mind and I think he convinced her that it was all her fault. You have no idea how much I wish she had told me what was happening. I feel like I let her down. She put up with all kinds of crazy shit from him. It really bothers me, Syd," she confessed.

Sydney listened to her in silence, thinking about her own life on the streets since she was eleven and comparing it to the horrors Emma and Gracie had been through. Suddenly her own situation didn't seem quite so bad. At least she had always been able to love and care for people, she reasoned.

"Well, I think you're wonderful, Em," Sydney told her.

"Thanks, Syd," Emma said gratefully. "I appreciate that. And by the way, I think you're pretty great too. Now I need to go to sleep. Tomorrow is Black Friday. I volunteered to work a double shift for lunch and dinner. I need to make some extra money, if Santa is going to visit Izzy this year."

They both glanced at the child, fast asleep on Sydney's mattress. From the look of it, Izzy was in a Thanksgiving dinner coma. Her arms and legs lay sprawled across the bed as if she owned it. The two friends laughed at the sight, then settled into sleeping bags for the night.

Chapter Seventy-One

On "Black Friday," Sydney took Izzy into downtown Kensington. Since people would be out shopping in that area, there was a better chance of them making a little more money from begging. As the two of them sat on a busy street corner, Rock, the drug dealer friend of Syd's father, approached them. People called him Rock because he specialized in the sale of crack cocaine, or "cookie," as the drug was known on the streets. He looked every bit the picture of a man involved in a shady business. He wore his black hair long, combing it back with a greasy hair-care product, and kept a full beard and a mustache. Even in the heat of summer, he never went without a leather jacket. He patrolled Kensington Avenue regularly, keeping a close eye on his street dealers and "whores," as he referred to the prostitutes working for him, and was always on the lookout for young people to make money for him.

"Hey, Syd! You get hotter every time I see you. You know, if you're tired of making nothing begging I can offer you some work. All you'd have to do is sell a little dope for me. I bet you'd be pretty good at it, like your father was until he decided to fuck everything up," he suggested and eyed her up in a way that made her uncomfortable.

"No, man, I'm not interested." Sydney told him, knowing the troubles that come with dealing dope. "I don't want to sell your drugs."

"You're an awfully beautiful little girl," he murmured, redirecting his attention to Izzy.

Izzy shrank back and hid her face behind Sydney. Cold as it was, Sydney began to perspire in sheer terror as Rock looked Izzy over in a way that made her skin crawl.

"Leave her alone, Rock," she said, trying to keep her voice from trembling. "She's a kid and you're scaring her."

"Ohhh, I didn't mean to scare this beautiful creature!" he wheezed, bending down to Izzy's level and extending his hand with its long fingernails toward her.

Sydney pushed his hand away. "Stop it! Leave her alone."

Rock let out a sinister laugh. "Well," he smirked, "if she ever needs a home, my old lady and I would be happy to take her in. Would you like to come and live with Rock, sweetheart?" he asked Izzy.

"NO! I want to go home, Syd," the child said, beginning to cry. "I don't like it here!"

Sydney jumped to her feet, clasped Izzy's fingers in a tight grip, turned quickly, and started down the street back to their home. It was a stupid idea to come here in the first place, she thought to herself. She should never have taken Izzy into Kensington. She should have known better. Over the last year, every time she ran into Rock, he tried unfailingly to convince her to join his gang of dope peddlers. He had even suggested that she could make a lot of money prostituting, promising her protection from other men on the streets. She had grown increasingly worried about seeing him. As a child she had looked out for her, but now that she was older he wanted nothing more than to exploit her for his own good.

Rock was infamous for arm-twisting people into doing what he wanted. Since he controlled most of the drug pushers and prostitutes in the area, he had any number of people at his beck and call. His reach was endless. If he wanted to get to Sydney and Izzy, he could do so easily.

When they got back home, Sydney quickly locked the front door and sat in the common room with Izzy on her lap. Although some of the other herd members were there, they were already too drunk to take much notice of the girls still clinging to each other out of fear. Sydney wasn't afraid for herself; she had lived on the streets for years and was used to Rock and his slimy ways. She was frightened that she had exposed Izzy to a person like him.

Fuck, Sydney now said to herself, holding the child tighter, I'm such a fucking idiot!

She resolved never to hang out with Izzy in Kensington again. From now on, they'd take the bus into Center City, Philadelphia. She brooded for hours over their encounter with Rock and decided not to tell Emma about it and hoped that Isabella wouldn't either.

Chapter Seventy-Two

As Christmas quickly approached, Emma worked as many hours as she humanly could to earn enough to buy presents for Izzy and something special for Sydney. She hadn't talked to Brianna or Katie since she fled Ambler. It was just too risky for her to have any contact with anyone from her past. She knew that Ethan wouldn't give up on hunting them down.

Izzy's excitement over Santa's imminent arrival mounted and she could barely contain her enthusiasm on Christmas Eve when Emma put her to bed.

"Santa's coming tonight, right?" she asked her aunt for the hundredth time that evening.

"Yep, he's coming," Emma assured her.

After Izzy had fallen asleep, Emma snuck downstairs and put up the used tinsel tree she had bought at a yard sale. She hung a string of twenty-five lights on its silver branches and half a dozen shiny balls she had picked up at the dollar store. Then she carefully laid out a winter coat with gloves and a hat, a new pair of jeans, a generic Barbie doll, and a Monopoly Junior set. Emma knew it wasn't much, but it was what she had been able to afford; it would have to do. She had bought Sydney a new sweater that she'd gotten cheap from a local street vendor.

Izzy woke early on Christmas morning and nudged Emma in her sleeping bag. "Do you think Santa came?" she asked, bursting with anticipation.

Emma rubbed the sleep out of her eyes. "I guess there's only one way to find out."

After waking Sydney, the three of them went down to the common room to find the small lit tree and the presents laid out underneath.

"He came! He came!" Izzy yelped gleefully.

She ran over and touched each of her presents several times. Having so many gifts at once was a new experience for her and beyond exciting. Emma looked on, her heart melting at the sight. She hoped she could give Izzy the kind of life that she and Gracie had been denied. Emma took the newspaper-wrapped sweater out of a nearby closet and gave it to Sydney.

"Merry Christmas, Syd," she said. "This is from Iz and me."

Sydney sat in silence for several minutes, holding the package in her lap, staring at it as if she didn't know what to do with it. She turned it over and over in her hands as the tears slid down her cheeks.

"What's wrong?" Emma asked in alarm.

"Nothing," Sydney said quietly. "It's just that this is the first present anyone ever gave me in as long as I can remember. My father was always too fucked up on dope to remember to buy anything for me." She opened the present slowly, savoring every moment of the experience, then looked up at her friend. "The sweater's beautiful! Thank you so much, Emma."

"Hey! What about me?" Izzy yelled with her small hand firmly poised on her hip.

"Oh, I'm sorry!" Sydney exclaimed. "Of course! Thank you, Izzy." Then she looked back at Emma. "I'm sorry. I didn't have any extra money. So I couldn't buy you anything. But Izzy made you a gift."

Isabella ran up to the bedroom where they had hidden Emma's gift. Then she came charging back down the stairs, breathless.

"Merry Christmas, Aunt Emma!" she puffed.

In Izzy's hand was a necklace made of macaroni. Emma put the necklace over her head and arranged it around her neck. Then she gushed that it was the most wonderful gift anyone had ever given her. The child was glowing, believing that she had done something really special for her aunt.

Later, as they sat on the floor in the common room playing Monopoly Junior together, Emma was overwhelmed by a sense of being surrounded by family. Christmas had never been a good time for her, but now, in the company of two people she loved, it felt like a whole new beginning, as they sang along with Frosty the Snowman on the small transistor radio.

Chapter Seventy-Three

By spring the following year, Emma had nearly stopped thinking about Ethan. She had a few offers from her co-workers and her customers at the restaurant to go on dates, but she had always turned them down. Scarred by her past experience, she wasn't ready to risk getting back into another relationship that might turn out to be abusive. She had decided that being single might be the only way for her to remain unharmed. Besides, everything she did now was for Izzy. She had been saving as much money as she could from the tips she earned waiting tables and was hopeful that in a couple of months she would be able to rent a small apartment somewhere in the city. She was planning on taking Sydney along with them.

A little before five thirty, she went to look for Sydney and Izzy. She found them down in the common area, watching Nickelodeon. Emma leaned over and squeezed her niece.

"Where are you going, Aunt Em?" the child asked innocently.

"I have to go to work, sweetie," she replied, "but Syd is going to take care of you while I'm gone." She turned to Sydney and handed her ten dollars. "Here," she said, "for dinner. Buy a pizza for yourselves."

A whole pizza was a luxury in their home. "Really?" Sydney said, pleased. "Wow! Thanks, Em."

Emma laughed. "Well, a pizza to babysit for eight hours is a good deal for me."

Sydney smiled mischievously. "Yeah, well, I don't have high expectations. That way, I'm never disappointed."

Emma smiled back, but deep down she felt sad, aware that beneath the bantering tone, Sydney was serious. Growing up the way they had, not having expectations was the only way to cope in the wild jungle they had been thrown into. Each of them had learned how to take it one day at a time, to be grateful for all the good things, no matter how insignificant, and to run as fast as they could from the things that kept them down. It was a sad way to live, but it was the attitude needed to get by.

Bar 210 was overcrowded that night. Emma was already three hours into her shift and didn't notice Pete entering the restaurant with a couple of friends who had talked him into spending a night in the city. One of them had visited Bar 210 the previous week and had joked with Pete that it was a place where you could meet girls who weren't on welfare.

Pete was pleased to see all the well-dressed women sitting at the bar. It was while he was taking a seat next to a pretty blonde that he saw Emma walk across the room. He stared hard, intent on making sure he hadn't made a mistake. No, it really was her. Pete was too far away for her to notice him, but he wouldn't have missed that silky hair from a mile away. In fact, that was what had initially caught his eye. He waited impatiently until she had gone back in the kitchen then he raced outside to call Ethan.

On the other end of the phone, Ethan felt powerful as he wrote down the name of the bar. "I'll be there in forty-five minutes," he told his friend. "Whatever you do, don't let that cunt out of your sight!"

When Ethan arrived at Bar 210, he found Pete waiting outside the restaurant. He had warned his friend not to go back inside. He didn't want Emma to recognize him. The two men sat in their car down the block and waited for her to leave after work.

At two-fifteen that morning, Ethan saw her come out with a couple of other people who worked there. Wishing them goodnight, she walked in the opposite direction toward her car. The men sat absolutely still in their car until she got into hers. Then they followed her back to Kensington, keeping back far enough that she wouldn't get suspicious. The moment she parked the car, Ethan moved briskly. As she got out, opened the car's rear door, and reached into the backseat for her purse, she felt the cold blade of his knife against her throat.

"I told you I would never let you go," he whispered. "Now get back in the fucking car! We need to talk."

As Emma complied, she focused on breathing evenly and remaining calm. She knew that if she betrayed any sign of weakness or fear, Ethan would take further advantage of her. She hadn't expected him to find her. But here he was and she had to deal with the inevitable.

"Look, Ethan," she began, trying to sound reasonable, "I don't want to be with you anymore. I'm making my own life now and you're free to move on with yours."

"So is this the shit-hole where you're keeping my daughter?" he asked as though he hadn't heard a word she'd said.

"Leave us alone," she said dully.

"We both know I'm her father, Emma," he told her. "In fact, while you were milking your sister's death for all it was worth, I had a paternity test done. You never know who else that little scumbag sister of yours was fucking when she was fucking me! I have the papers, Em. I have a right to my child."

Emma froze. Then deep regret set in as she realized that in her rush to leave the apartment with Izzy, she had forgotten to take her most precious possession: Gracie's journal. She wondered how she could ever have forgotten it. Stupid, stupid mistake!

"What do you want from us, Ethan?" she asked, already knowing the answer.

"I want my kid, Emma. You have a choice: you can either come back to me with her oooorrrr she can come back with me on her own. You know how impatient I can get. You don't want her coming back with me alone, right?"

Emma's breathing quickened. She faced the prospect of the only decision with a helplessness she hadn't felt in a long while. But she couldn't give up without a fight.

"Ethan, she's just a kid," she said. "How about if we leave her here and I come back with you?"

Ethan cackled. "Do you think I'm stupid like you? Nah, she's coming home to Daddy. Now let's go inside and get my little girl. And I'm warning you: if you do anything stupid, I will call the police, show them the paternity test results, and you will never see Izzy again. You got me?"

As they left the car and headed up the front steps to the house, he reminded her once more, just in case she'd forgotten, "Don't make me lose my head, Emma."

Chapter Seventy-Four

As soon as Izzy set eyes on Ethan, she started to cry. Young as she was, the child instinctively knew that being in his presence was a bad thing for them. Emma rushed over and picked her up.

"Sydney," she said to her friend, her voice betraying no emotion, "this is Ethan. Izzy and I are going to pack our things and go back with him."

Stunned into silence, Syd didn't know what she could do to help. Knowing of the rotten things that Ethan had done to Emma and Gracie, she grimaced as she locked eyes with him and willed him to die in the doorway. Street smart and wise beyond her years, Sydney detested slimy little pricks like him. She followed Emma up to the bedroom.

"Christ, Emma!" she protested. "Have you lost your mind? What the hell do you think you're doing? You know what he's capable of! Why are you going back to him?"

Emma's voice was fraught with tension as she replied, "He threatened that if I didn't, he would come back with the police and take Izzy away from me. He said he had a paternity test done right after Gracie died. And it's true that he's Izzy's father. Fuck, I can't believe this is happening all over again!"

Sydney put her arms around Emma and the two friends hugged. Izzy went up to the pair and wiggled her way in between them. Then she held up her arms and said, "Me too."

The three of them stood in the middle of the room and said their good-byes. When they came back downstairs, Ethan was standing in the same spot where they had left him.

"Come, baby, come to Daddy," he cooed to Izzy in a successful attempt to torment Emma.

"Noooooo!" Izzy started to whine, clinging to Sydney. "I don't want to go with you. I want Sydney. I want to stay with Sydney!"

Sydney looked down at the child, then glared at Ethan.

He noticed her hostile expression and said belligerently, "What? You got something to say to me, you filthy little pig? Go take a fucking shower, you disgusting bitch! Get away from my kid before she catches something from you! Let's go, Emma. NOW!" He was bellowing and his words echoed throughout the house.

Ethan walked over to Sydney and began prying Izzy from her arms.

The child refused to let go and held on as tight as she could. "I want to stay with Sydney!" she cried.

Ethan gripped her small arm in his large hand and squeezed it like a vise.

"Owww! Stop it! You're hurting me!" Izzy screamed.

Emma came up quickly behind him. "Leave her alone," she said with authority. She held out her arms and Izzy went to her and wrapped herself around the only mother she had ever known.

"Aunt Em, I don't want to go anywhere! I want to stay here!" Izzy sobbed.

"I know, sweetie," Emma soothed. "It'll be okay, I promise."

She looked back helplessly at Sydney and then at the other people she had lived with so peacefully. All the housemates felt terrible about what was happening to the duo they now considered family members, a part of their herd.

Once he had managed to get aunt and niece into the car, Ethan slapped Emma across the face for the scene she had caused. "If you ever embarrass me like that again, I will destroy you. You better get it clear in that empty skull of yours that what I say goes."

He screamed at her and showered abuse on her during the entire drive back to Ambler. Emotionally exhausted by the ugly scenes she had witnessed, Izzy cried herself to sleep within fifteen minutes, despite all the white noise Ethan was making.

When they reached the apartment, Emma carried Izzy in from the car, kissed her cheek softly when they reached the bedroom, laid her on the bed, and pulled the covers over her. Then she went out to the living room to face the devil.

"You think you're something else, running off like that?" Ethan hurled the moment she appeared. "You're nothing, do you hear me? Nothing! Things are going to be a lot different around here now. For starters, you have no driving privileges. You're gonna call Doubles in the morning and make sure you get your job back. And you're gonna give me every penny you make. I had to borrow goddamn money from my mother to keep our apartment! Do you know how embarrassing that was for me? Do you?"

"Maybe you should have gotten a job," Emma stated, her tone judgmental.

"I see, you bitch! So this is the way you want to start things off! Fine with me!" Ethan fumed.

Ethan took off his belt, grasped her arm in a tight grip, and dragged her into the bedroom. "Take your clothes off," he ordered.

"No, Ethan, I won't take my clothes off," Emma told him firmly. "And you're right. Things are going to change around here. I'm not your kid. You can't control me anymore."

Emma didn't see the first punch coming, and it threw her off balance.

"Well, Miss Mouthy," Ethan said in an ominous tone, "somebody is getting a beating for leaving. You can take your clothes off and accept what's coming to you, or I'll give Izzy the beating that is meant for you." Then he turned and started for the bedroom where the child was sleeping.

"I hate you!" Emma said with all the venom she could muster as she began removing her clothes one by one.

Ethan flayed her with his belt until the welts on her back and legs were so swollen they started to bleed. To have her at his mercy again was a real turn-on for him. It made him feel powerful and in control once more. When he was done, he was so aroused by the punishment he had given Emma that he climbed up behind her, his penis erect, and entered her fast and furiously.

In the morning, when Ethan had left to meet his friends, Emma somehow limped into the kitchen, followed by a still sleepy Izzy who had just woken up, and took out the jar of honey and a cloth.

"Izzy?" she said softly. "Sweetie, I need you to put this honey on my scratches, okay?"

Izzy examined the "scratches" with a critical eye. "They look like pretty bad scratches, Aunt Em. How did you get them?"

"I don't want to talk about that now, baby. Just put some honey on them, will you?"

"All right, Aunt Em."

Izzy gently applied the honey to the wounds, muttering all the while about how ugly they were. "Aunt Em," she added, "don't forget that when

I grow up, I wanna be a lawyer so that I can tell the judge to send people to jail."

Emma smiled in spite of her agony. "You can be anything you want to be, sweetheart," she told her.

Izzy's voice rose in excitement. "Me and Sydney watch lawyers on TV all the time! Lawyers tell judges that people should go to jail because they do bad things. That's what I'm gonna do, tell the judge to send Ethan to jail because he's mean to us."

Emma's voice caught in her throat. She didn't want her niece exposed to this kind of life, never wanted her to imagine that it was acceptable.

"That's great," she responded, trying to match the little girl's enthusiasm. "I hope that someday you do become a lawyer. Another thing, Izzy. I want you to understand that when Ethan does mean things, he's wrong. He should not be doing them."

"Then why don't you stop him?" the child retorted with the logic of a savvy forty-year-old, startling and shaming Emma. "If it's wrong, he shouldn't be allowed to do it. That's what you always tell me."

"You're right, Izzy, you're so right."

"Aunt Em," the child said suddenly, moving off on a tangent, "I miss Sydney."

"Me too, baby," Emma agreed.

Still lying on her belly, she stretched out an arm and Izzy snuggled into her.

All Emma could think about was how to end this once and for all.

Chapter Seventy-Five

When Emma finally felt able to walk without limping, she made it to the phone and called Katie.

"Oh my God!" her friend exclaimed. "Where have you been? Ethan has been like a lunatic, looking for you."

"I'm back at the apartment now," Emma said tiredly. "We spent some time in Philadelphia. I was hoping Ethan wouldn't find me, but he did."

"You don't sound good. Did he hurt you? What did he do to you?" Katie asked, dreading the answer.

"He beat the hell out of me with his belt," Emma replied, the fury in her voice barely suppressed, "but I'll survive. Ethan is a little boy who thinks that if he can control me, he will magically become a big man."

"I'm coming over," Katie said, and without waiting for Emma to reply, she hung up the phone.

Fifteen minutes later, Katie knocked at the door. When she saw Izzy, she rushed over to her. "There you are!" she said. "I've missed you, Iz."

Isabella vaguely remembered Katie, who seemed so excited to see her. She looked to her aunt for reassurance that this woman who was now hugging her was safe to be with. Emma casually nodded and Izzy relaxed. The two friends talked for hours. Emma filled Katie in on all that she had gone through since her departure from Ambler.

Katie listened to the story, and while she was sad that Ethan had found her friend, she was selfishly happy that she was back in her life again. She had been lonely while Emma was in Philly.

A week after she returned to Ambler, Emma was back working at Double Visions. Informed about her comeback, Salvatore was at the bar, waiting. When he saw her come out on stage, he was barely able to contain himself. He badly wanted to talk to her, to find out where she had been all these months. When she went around the bar to collect her tips, he was waiting at the end.

He gave her a warm embrace. "Where the hell have you been?" he asked. "I've been worried."

"I had to get away from him, Salvatore," Emma told him frankly. "I took Izzy and ran to Kensington. For a while, everything was going fine, but then the prick found us. I'm back at the apartment, but I don't plan on being there for long."

"You don't have to stay there for another minute if you don't want to," he told her. "I can help you."

This time, Salvatore's offer seemed nearly irresistible to Emma. But the very thought that letting him help her meant she would become dependent on yet another man who might not treat her right made her hold back. Not that Salvatore was anything like Ethan. But that was where the problem lay. Salvatore had real power at his fingertips. And if he turned out to be anything like Ethan in temperament, Emma would never be able to escape the situation.

Alone in the lap-dance room, Emma sat on Salvatore's lap. She took a deep breath before she spoke. "Ethan raped Gracie. Isabella is his daughter," she said and quickly added, "He threatened to take Izzy from me if I didn't move back in with him."

Salvatore said nothing. He sat and thought about what Emma had just revealed to him. Driving home that night, he had to fight back the urge to drive over to Ambler and shove his gun into Ethan's mouth. He wanted Ethan to beg for mercy, until he finally pulled the trigger so that he could watch the blood drain from his skull. No, he thought to himself, that wouldn't make Ethan suffer enough. Maybe, he considered, he would cut off his fingers one at a time and then his hands to prolong the agony. As the underboss of the Morano family he rarely got his hands dirty anymore. But this time it was different. This time it was much more personal.

It was unlike Salvatore to sit by idly for so long and let an arrogant jerk-off like Ethan get away with hurting the woman who he had come to love. It was in his DNA to set things right, and his rage had now taken control over his will to stand by and do nothing.

Salvatore had been exposed to violence his whole life. He was now reminded of how the Mafia had begun centuries before he was born. His father told him of the story of a French soldier who raped a Palermo girl, only fourteen years old at the time, on her wedding day in 1282.

When the raped girl's mother found her she ran through the streets crying and screaming "ma fia, ma fia," or "my daughter, my daughter." Sicily's citizens banded together and revolted against the French. On Easter Monday, at the church of the Holy Spirit, outside of Palermo, a bloodbath ensued as the Sicilians slaughtered thousands of French residents.

This beginning made Salvatore and his family feel righteous in their actions. They decidedly ignored the fact that over time they had become nothing more than ruthless business people who killed anyone who stood between them and what they desired.

Salvatore's mind drifted back over the years, remembering a time when he was twenty years old and one of his father's soldiers, Francesco, killed a man from another mob family because he had sex with his girlfriend. Francesco stabbed the guy forty-eight times, his anger uncontained as he thought about him with "his girl." Later that evening, he went to his girlfriend's apartment and beat her to death with the butt of an ax. After she was dead he planted the blade of the ax in her crotch, splitting her in half up to her hips. Francesco had been seen entering the murdered man's apartment and the other mob family threatened revenge on the Morano family. But Salvatore's father took matters into his own hands.

Salvatore and two other men were ordered to take Francesco to an abandoned house in North Philadelphia that was owned by the family. The three men told Francesco that they needed to keep him hidden until things cooled off between the two crime families, but the three mobsters tortured Francesco for days. They stripped him and tied him to a metal chair where they beat him with a bat, cut his arms and legs with dull knives, and three days later killed him by wrapping his entire head in plastic wrap, watching as he suffocated to death. His long punishment and slow death were meant to be a message to everyone in the Morano family that no one sought retribution without the permission of the mob boss. The other mob family sent members into the house to look at the mutilated Francesco to ensure that they had taken care of him properly.

Still annoyed about Ethan, Salvatore parked his car in front of his house in South Philly. He vowed to himself that he would take care of things the way they should have been taken care of a long time ago—even if it meant that Emma ended up hating him. At least then he would feel like a man of honor. He was more concerned about her being unharmed than winning her approval so that one day he could make her his.

Emma had been back with Ethan for a month. Yet it felt like years to her as she endured his fits of anger. He constantly threatened to harm Isabella, and his cruelty seemed to have escalated since her return. There was no sign of humanity in him anymore. Emma was stifled by his very presence. She wasn't even allowed out of the apartment unless he accompanied her. The only time Emma could spend away from him was at Doubles.

Though he had used his paternity test results as a blackmailing tactic to keep Emma in line, Ethan treated Izzy as if she didn't exist. The only time he seemed to acknowledge her existence was when Emma resisted his orders. Then he would ensure her compliance by threatening the child.

Darkness had descended on Emma's life all over again. As with her father, she obsessed about killing Ethan by poisoning him, but knew it was too risky; too many people were aware of the situation between the two of them. If he died, the first finger of suspicion would be pointed at her. And if she landed in prison, Izzy would be on her own and helpless, orphaned in the true sense of the term.

One Friday night Emma was home with Izzy, and Katie came over for a beer. Ethan had gone to the bar with Pete, and the two young women were happy to have an evening to themselves without the ogre lurking in the background. They were having a good time together, drinking and talking about different people in the neighborhood when Katie forced Emma to confront the most crucial issue in her life.

"Em," she began, "what are you going to do about Ethan? We both know how important it is for you to get away from him. And he's certainly no good for Isabella either."

Emma wasn't surprised by Katie's undisguised antagonism toward Ethan. She was well aware that her friend considered him a miserable piece of shit who wanted to be in complete control of Emma and Izzy's life. The young women had shared a lot over time.

"I don't know, Katie," she said frankly. "Ethan's been a fucking bastard all through, but he's worse now, if that's possible, than he was before I left him. I know he's out of control and things can only get worse. I'm just keeping things together for now, until I come up with a plan so we can get away from him for good."

Katie slid over on the sofa until she was sitting closer to Emma. "I don't care if you have to live on the street or back in the car again, Em," she said. "You can't live like this! It's madness! You deserve better than this. Whatever you decide, you need to do it soon."

"I know, Katie. I agree with you. Things are going to change very soon. Trust me," Emma assured her.

At ten forty-five that night, when Katie was getting ready to leave, Izzy woke up. Katie went to check on her, and when she came out of the bedroom, she picked up her keys off the kitchen table.

"Izzy wants juice and you don't have any more in the fridge," she informed Emma. "I need to stop by the grocery store for coffee before I go home anyway. I'm gonna run over to the store and swing by with it. I won't be long."

Five minutes after Katie's departure, Ethan came busting through the door with Pete in tow. The two of them were cackling like schoolboys. Emma, who had been stretched out on the sofa, sat up abruptly. From their noisy exchanges, she could tell they were both very drunk and stood up quickly to retreat to the sanctuary of the bedroom. Ethan's laughter died when he caught Emma in the act of escaping to the other room. He had been fixated on her for days. He had a overpowering desire to hurt her for not wanting the two of them to be together. As Ethan glared at Emma from across the room he was reminded of his mother, who had destroyed their family by being a dirty, rotten slut.

"Where the fuck are you going, Emma?" he growled. "Don't you see we have a guest? You have to be the rudest whore on earth."

Emma stopped in her tracks before turning toward the kitchen, assuming that if she offered them a beer, it would appease the anger she saw in Ethan's expression. It was tough resisting her natural urge to charge at him, regardless of his friend's presence, and rip him to shreds with her bare hands. Just be nice, she told herself. Try not to kill him right now. It will ruin everything.

"I was just going to get you two a beer," she said lamely, trying to pacify Ethan.

"Well now, that's a good girl. Come on, Pete. Let's follow Em here so she can get us a beer," Ethan said mockingly.

As she opened the refrigerator, Ethan stepped up beside her and stared down into her face.

"Pete here wants a little lovin'," he leered. "He's always telling me how hot you are, and I agreed that he could taste some of that ass. This way, you can get that slut inside out of your system. And at least I'll know who it is you're fucking. I promised him you'd give him what he wants tonight. Besides, I know you've always wanted to screw him."

Emma started to shake. "No fucking way, Ethan," she said. "I won't do it."

"I never asked you if you would do it," he sneered. "Now take him to our room and show him a good time. You do it all the time at that whore job of yours."

"No, Ethan, stop it! I'm not going to fuck your friend. I don't want him. It's just your delusional mind that assumes I want every man I see. So take your drunken asses out of here and leave me alone!" she warned him in a steely voice.

Ethan pounced on her and seized her by the shoulders. Then he pushed her roughly toward the kitchen table. His face twisted with drunken anger as he issued the familiar, ominous warning: "Don't make me lose my head!"

He snatched the worn tablecloth off the table and ripped it in half. Then he pushed Emma, face down, onto the table. As she lay on her belly, he pulled her right arm up and pinned it behind her back. Pain shot through her shoulder and elbow, keeping her locked in place on the table. She kicked him in an effort to free herself, but Ethan told Pete to hold her down. In a hurry, his friend held tight to the arm behind her back while Ethan yanked her legs apart to stop her from kicking, tying them one at a time to the legs of the table. Then he moved to her arms, roughly pulling each one and tying them each by the wrist to the table's legs at the other end. When he was satisfied that she was securely held down by her bindings, he pushed up her nightshirt. He took out a pair of scissors from a drawer in the kitchen and sliced through her underwear, flinging the lacy bits and pieces into the air with complete disregard for what he was about to do.

Turning to Pete, he said, "I told you she was a no-good bitch. Maybe a good, hard fuck will do her some good. Go for it, bro!"

Pete eyed Emma with lust as she begged them to untie her. He had wanted her from the very first time he had seen her. Now, as she lay tied to the table, he knew he finally had his chance to nail her. It was a stroke of sheer luck that Ethan wanted him to have sex with her. Pete watched, his desire flaring, as Emma fought in vain to loosen her bonds. Her magnificent hair shimmered in the soft moonlight, her lean muscles flexing as she attempted to free herself. The harder she fought, the more her struggles turned Pete on. He turned to his friend once more for approval.

"Go, man!" Ethan egged him on, slurring the words. "Fuck her hard! Fuck some sense into her!"

Pete needed no further encouragement. He walked over to where Emma lay, dropped his pants, and straddled her. Then he entered her with brute force. The alcohol in him made it hard for him to come and he kept slamming himself into her until he finally exploded and collapsed on top of her.

All through this act of rape, Ethan had been studying the expression on Emma's face, his fury growing steadily as the minutes passed. He could not contain his rage that Emma had actually fucked another man. He had always known that she was a compulsive liar who cheated on him. No matter how much she protested to the contrary, his twisted mind convinced him that she enjoyed fucking other guys and had been doing so the whole time she was with him. Ethan's twisted view of reality finally won out over any common sense that the nitwit had been born with.

Minutes after Pete had finished, Ethan offered him a beer and the two stood in the kitchen laughing at Emma as she lay tied to the kitchen table, exposed and humiliated. But even as he doubled over in laughter, Ethan kept glancing over at her, hating her for her participation in a sex act with a man other than him.

Shortly afterward, Pete left the apartment, telling Ethan he'd be waiting for him in the car. Once alone, Ethan came back into the kitchen and stared at a sobbing Emma who couldn't bring herself to accept what she had just been put through. She couldn't reconcile herself to the fact that Ethan had not only urged his friend to rape her, but had masterminded the whole sick scene.

Ethan leaned down and gazed into her eyes. "You fucking little whore!" he cursed. "You bitch whore! Who the fuck do you think you are, cheating on me?"

"Fuck you, Ethan!" Emma cried out. "You did this to me deliberately! I hate you! And believe me, you'll pay for this! How could you do this to me?"

"How could I?" he rasped. "How could I? It was clear that you wanted it all along. I watched you the whole time while it was happening and I could tell you enjoyed it. You got exactly what you asked for! You're a fucking embarrassment! Pete will tell all of my other friends that I'm living with a no-good slut who fucked him while I stood here and watched."

Ethan's own words seemed to inflame him. He swung around, picked up the wooden rolling pin Emma used to make the occasional pie, and slammed it down on her body with as much force as he could muster. He continued hitting her and reveled in the sight of the welts and bruises that instantly sprang to the surface of her skin. The blows he landed on her carried the full impact of his raw strength, and while the pain was indescribable and tore harsh screams from deep within her, it was the sound and searing sensation of her bones breaking that Emma's mind seemed to focus on.

Infuriated by the shrill screams that grated on his nerves, Ethan yanked the dish towel from the sink, wrapped it around her neck, and twisted it tight. Emma's eyes began to bulge as she tried to suck in fresh air. Ethan let go of the towel only after she fell unconscious. Satisfied and feeling like a new man, he left the apartment to meet Pete. On his way to the car, he assured himself that he was finally the man of the house. Emma would now submit to him the way he'd always wanted her to. Besides, he promised himself, it would be a very long time before he forgave her for cheating on him with Pete.

Chapter Seventy-Six

S hortly after Ethan left, Katie came back to drop off the juice she had gone to buy. Unsuspecting, she walked into the apartment and found a naked and battered Emma strapped to the table. Her gorge rose and vomit splashed all over the kitchen floor. She grabbed a butcher's knife from the block on the counter and looked around quickly to ensure she was alone. In a panic, she checked for Emma's pulse the way she'd seen people do on TV. To her relief, her friend was still alive. Bloodied and beaten, but still alive. She watched Emma closely, knowing that her friend had just lived through some kind of horrible nightmare most people couldn't even imagine. Chills ran up her spine and she had to struggle not to flee the apartment, still stinking of the malice that had prompted the sadistic brutality whose results were there for her to see.

Snap out of it, Katie told herself as she rushed toward the screams coming from Izzy's room. She found the child sitting in the middle of her bed, scared and crying. Relieved that she was unharmed and had not witnessed the horrific scene in the kitchen, Katie pulled out her cell phone and looked for a particular number. She scrolled until she had found the right name and pressed "send."

Salvatore answered on the second ring, irritated that someone was calling him so late at night. "Yeah?" he huffed into the phone.

"Um, hi, this is Katie, Emma's friend," Katie said in a rush.

"Who?" His voice was impatient.

"Katie. I'm Emma's friend. She works at Double Visions. You know her by her stage name, Amme," she explained.

Salvatore was instantly on alert. "Yes, Katie," he said. "Emma has told me a lot about you. Is everything all right?"

He realized it was a foolish question. If everything were okay, she wouldn't be calling him.

"No," Katie started, then burst into tears. "Ethan has hurt her really bad!" she blubbered. "Really, really bad! Please help!"

"Where is she?" he demanded with authority.

"We're at her apartment," Katie responded.

"I'll be right there," he said, hanging up the phone.

Katie put the phone in her pocket and rushed back to Emma. She began to hyperventilate as she looked at her friend's broken body. She didn't dare untie her for fear of causing more injuries. Instead, she bent down and gently stroked the back of Emma's head.

"I'm here," she whispered. "And Salvatore is on his way. Everything is going to be fine," Katie comforted.

Salvatore knocked at the door thirty minutes later. With him were three of his men. The state in which he found Emma, beaten, exposed and unconscious, made the blood in his veins run cold. Without a word, he strode over to the kitchen table and gently untied her bonds. He motioned to the three men who had accompanied him and they gingerly carried her to the sofa and laid her on it. He gave Katie two precise instructions: she was to go get something for Emma to wear and pack enough clothes for Izzy and her.

"Do it quickly," he commanded with an air of power.

In less than thirty minutes of his arrival, Salvatore had Emma in the car and they were being driven to his apartment in the city. He called the family doctor on the way there.

"We'll be there in thirty minutes," he said crisply. "Get over to my place as fast as you can. Hear?"

With Izzy asleep in her arms, Katie sat in the back of the sedan with Salvatore. Emma lay between them, still unconscious. He reached across and touched Katie's hand in a gesture of reassurance.

"This will all work out," he murmured. "She'll be fine. Just relax."

He uttered the words with such certitude that Katie allowed herself to let go of her fear and laid her trust in this man she'd never met and didn't know.

The "family" doctor was already waiting for them when they arrived at Salvatore's apartment. The men carried Emma in and placed her in the bedroom their boss indicated. Katie followed; the beauty of Salvatore's plush, immaculately done-up home was completely lost on her. Her mind and heart were focused entirely on Emma.

When the doctor finally emerged from the bedroom to give them an update, Katie's heart lurched. But as he launched into a description of her friend's condition, she found herself breathing again. The doctor explained that Emma had four broken ribs, a collapsed lung, and a lot of tears and bruising.

"This guy fucked her up real good, Sal," he said grimly. "If he had beaten her anymore, he might have killed her. She got lucky."

Salvatore's pulse quickened at the words and his impulse to avenge what had happened to Emma began to play in his mind again. He was annoyed with himself for not taking care of the rotten motherfucker sooner.

"What do we need to do for her now?" he asked, anxious to make Emma as comfortable as he possibly could.

"She'll need to stay off her feet for about a week so those bones can start to heal," the doctor said. "Other than that, give her the painkillers I left on the dresser every four hours and keep an eye on her. If there is any change in her condition, call me right away. And I'll be checking in on her tomorrow." Then the doctor pulled Salvatore into the bedroom, "Sal, you know who did this to her?"

Salvatore nodded.

"Well, I know she must mean something to you. That fucking bastard tore the shit out of her. She should be dead right now, Sal. You understand what I'm saying?" the doctor asked to imply that the guy who did this should have to pay the price.

"Yeah, yeah, I understand. I'll take care of it," Salvatore confirmed.

Salvatore went into the other bedroom to check on Izzy, who was still sleeping. Gazing at the expression of complete trust and peace on her face, he was comforted. His thoughts returned to Emma, and he blamed himself for not having taken care of the problem called Ethan long ago. Then he walked back into his living room and called one of the men who worked for him. It was a call he should have made a long time ago, he told himself grimly.

Chapter Seventy-Seven

E mma regained consciousness the next morning. Not remembering
what had happened to her and not knowing where she was, she tried
to get out of bed. The excruciating pain that shot through her broken ribs
jolted her into awareness. She looked around the room. It was beautiful
and tastefully decorated. She wondered if she was dreaming. Then her eyes
wandered to a chair in the corner where a man she recognized sat sleeping.

"Salvatore?" she managed weakly.

He woke instantly and sprang to his feet. Then he came over to her and
knelt by the bed.

"Hush, Bella," he said. "You've been badly hurt. The doctor said you
can't get out of bed for a while."

"Bella?" she asked, confused.

A tender smile played around the edges of his lips. "Yes, Bella. It means
beautiful," he told her adoringly, grateful that she was alive.

Emma played through the fragmented recollections of what had recently
happened to her.

"Where's Izzy?" she asked.

Salvatore continued to smile at her. "She's safe in the other bedroom,
sleeping. Don't worry. Ethan didn't touch her. Do you remember what he
did to you last night?"

It took her several minutes and many tearful pauses, but Emma was
finally able to tell him all that had occurred the previous night.

"This friend of Ethan's," Salvatore asked, "what's his name?"

"That doesn't matter, Salvatore," Emma said. "He was drunk. And all
that really matters is that Ethan was the one who planned it. He is the one
who did this to me. He let it happen. When I get better, I will even the
score. Trust me."

Salvatore stroked her hair and handed her two tablets and a glass of water. "Here, take these," he urged. "It's important that you rest. These will take the pain away and help you sleep."

Emma took the pills and waited for them to work. Right before she dozed off, she put her hand over Salvatore's.

"Don't let Izzy out of your sight," she murmured sleepily. "I don't know what Ethan is capable of doing to her."

"Izzy is safe with me," Salvatore assured her. "You have nothing to worry about. Now sleep, Bella."

Later that night, Ethan arrived back at his apartment still nursing a hangover from the night before. He walked into the kitchen and turned on the lights, expecting to feast his eyes on a naked and injured Emma. The sight of the bare table threw him into a rant and he started screaming her name. He ran into Izzy's room. She was gone too. He noticed that the other bedroom door was closed. He figured Emma had locked herself in, along with that little brat. No matter, he told himself, he would break down the door if he needed to. No one would stop him from brawling with the raunchy bitch for cheating on him with his friend, Pete.

Chapter Seventy-Eight

When Ethan twisted the doorknob to the bedroom, however, the door swung open, and he turned on the light switch. Two men were standing just inside the room.

"Who the fuck are you?" he spewed at them, fear and anger working at cross purposes within him.

Neither of the men uttered a word. Tony, the larger of the two, walked up to Ethan silently and punched him in the face, knocking him to the floor. Then his partner, Vincent, bent down and strapped Ethan's wrists behind his back, jammed a rag inside his mouth, and covered it with electrical tape. Tony dragged Ethan out to the kitchen by his hair and sat him on one of the chairs. Ethan was so terrified by now he could barely draw in a breath.

"Our boss sent us to pay ya a visit," Tony began. "Our boss, he's, well, let's just say he runs a lot of businesses around here. Italian businesses, you understand me? Do you know who Salvatore Morano is?" Tony asked him.

Ethan understood that Tony was talking about the Mafia and nodded vigorously. He felt a little calmer now, assuming they had the wrong guy. He had no connection with the mob, and all he had to do was explain it was a big mistake; after all, he definitely didn't know anyone named Salvatore Morano.

"No, now see, I think you do know him, sorta," Tony tormented. "He's a pretty powerful guy, if ya know what I mean."

Ethan shook his head and tried to talk through the gag and tape over his mouth.

"Yeah, it ain't your turn to talk yet, you get what I'm tellin' ya," Tony told him coldly. "So like I was sayin' 'fore you rudely interrupted me, Salvatore Morano, well, he's a very, very good friend of the woman who lives here wit' cha," Tony stated and stood back to wait for Ethan's reaction.

Panic surged up in Ethan's chest, constricting his breathing. He had never been more terrified in his life. His eyes grew wide and sweat beaded up on his forehead.

"Yeah, there it is. That's what we been waitin' for. Yeah, that look, right there. Ya see it, Vincent? You know- the 'I'm so fucked right now' look. Yeah, priceless, ain't it, Vincent?" Tony asked, nudging his partner. "See, Salvatore sent us to see ya,. He said we should tell ya that he found Emma tied to this here table last night. Sounds like ya let your buddy have a little party wit' her."

Then in a monotone voice that hid all of his emotion, Tony concluded, "Ya know, we don't like guys like you that do shit like that to women."

Quickly, Tony picked Ethan up by the back of his shirt and slammed him, face down, on the kitchen table. Vincent walked over and casually put a gun to his head while Tony cut the binding on his hands. Slowly and deliberately, Tony tied Ethan's wrists and ankles to the legs of the table, mimicking what Ethan himself had done to Emma the night before. When he was done, Tony went behind him with a razor blade and sliced his pants from the waist to the cuff of the pant legs on either side. Then he cut away his boxers. When he was done, Ethan lay with all his limbs tightly bound and naked from the waist down.

Then Vincent walked a few steps, taking each one deliberately slow, and opened the kitchen closet. He took out a broom and walked around the table to show it to Ethan, who immediately burst into tears and mumbled for forgiveness through his gag. The men looked at him and even pretended to consider his pleas, but it was obvious that they were simply amused.

"So it was all right for you to do this to your girlfriend, but it ain't all right for you. Huh?" Vincent asked.

Ethan shook his head vigorously.

Vincent looked at the broomstick. "You know," he seethed, "what I'd like to do is split your fuckin' head open with this, but if I did that, you wouldn't be awake for all the fun you're about to have. Now would ya?"

Ethan tried to scream for help through the gag and tape that covered his mouth. Vincent walked slowly around the table and looked at his partner, who gave a quick nod of approval. The broomstick entered Ethan with such force he thought it had broken through his rectum and into his stomach. Then the man withdrew the broom just as abruptly and did it again. And again. And again. Dropping the broom to the floor, he made his way around to look Ethan in the face.

"Ain't too nice, is it?" Vincent tormented.

Tony cut Ethan loose and tied his hands behind his back again. They led him out to the sedan in the dark, still half-naked, and placed him in the trunk. No one noticed them coming or going. No one heard Ethan's screams through the gag that covered his mouth. As they drove away from the apartment, the two men sat in silence. They lived for these moments. There was nothing more enjoyable than killing for justice.

Chapter Seventy-Nine

F our days later, Emma woke just as the sun was going down. She had drifted in and out of slumber since the attack, partly because of the severity of her injuries and partly owing to the effect of the narcotics she was being administered for pain every time she opened her eyes. When she awoke this time, Salvatore and Izzy were sitting nearby, watching the television in her bedroom. As Emma gently stretched her limbs, feeling the tenderness of her broken ribs, Izzy slid off the large sofa on the other side of the room and ran to her bedside.

"Aunt Em, we're watching Barney," she said in her endearingly squeaky voice. "Salvatore said he looks like an ugly purple monster. Can you tell him that Barney isn't ugly?"

Emma chuckled as she pointed her finger at Salvatore. "Knock it off!" she told him. "Barney is our friend."

"Yes, of course he is!" Salvatore responded pleasantly, then turned to the child. "Well, Izzy, aren't you a little tattletale!" he teased.

Izzy giggled and climbed onto the bed next to Emma, who leaned in the best she could, given her injuries, to give her niece a kiss.

"I'm starving!" Emma announced to them both.

"Good," Salvatore said, getting up from the sofa, "because I have a wonderful dinner planned for us tonight. Now how about if you go and take a long, hot shower while I have dinner set up in the dining room?"

After she had showered and struggled into clean pajamas, Emma walked unsteadily out into the living room. She was overwhelmed by the size and beauty of Salvatore's apartment. She had known he had money, but hadn't imagined him to be this wealthy. There were plush green sofas and oversized chairs arranged around the vast living room. The floors were black and white marble, and contemporary artwork was perfectly mounted on the walls. The talking point of the formal dining room was a steel chandelier in an abstract design that incorporated stems pointing in different directions and metal figures of men holding the light bulbs that cast a glow on the table.

Emma seated herself next to Izzy, who was already waiting for her dinner.

"Salvatore made me macaroni and cheese," the child piped up, letting her aunt know she was special.

Just then Salvatore walked into the room carrying Izzy's food and placed it in front of her. A moment later, he returned with a large platter filled with blackened swordfish and penne pasta in vodka sauce. Emma's senses whirled in the delicious aromas that wafted up her nostrils and she gobbled down the food as though she had never eaten before.

"So did you cook all of this yourself?" she finally asked, sitting back in her chair, full, and rubbing her belly with satisfaction.

Salvatore smiled like a delighted young boy. "Let's just say I helped."

"Helped how?" Emma teased.

"My boy, Tony, in the kitchen," he motioned toward the door, "did the actual cooking, but I told him what I wanted him to make."

Tony popped his head into the dining room. "Yeah," he said, "he wishes he could cook like I do."

Emma laughed, but was a little startled to realize that there were other people in the apartment whom she didn't know about.

"How many other people are here in the apartment with us?" she asked in a low voice, curious and more than a little embarrassed that they all knew what Ethan and Pete had done to her.

"Oh, just Tony and Vincent are here," Salvatore replied. "You can always find them here around dinnertime. That's what they do best—EAT!" he said, yelling the words loud enough for his friends to hear. They responded by yelling something back in Italian that Emma didn't understand. Salvatore laughed at the words and turned his attention back to her.

"How are you feeling?" he asked. "You were in pretty bad shape when we found you in your apartment."

Emma felt the blood rush to her face. "I'm feeling much better," she said in a low voice, suddenly overcome by shyness. "I'm still sore, but at least I can breathe now without feeling excruciating pain."

"Good, Bella, good," he replied, patting the top of her hand.

"In a couple of days I should feel well enough to go back to my own apartment," she assured him. "But first I have to figure out how I'm going to deal with Ethan." She looked down at her plate as she spoke. "I think you'll understand this, so I'll just say it: his days are numbered. I won't let him get away with this. The situation could have been a lot worse. They could've hurt Izzy. I can't risk that anymore."

Salvatore smiled at her. "I completely understand," he said. "In my business, we deal with the things that need to be dealt with." He turned to Izzy. "Come, sweetheart, let's get you ready for bed."

He took her by the hand and led her into a bedroom across the hall from her aunt's. Emma hobbled behind them, slow to catch up. Then Salvatore flung the bedroom door open and she nearly gasped. This was perfection itself. Done up in shades of pink and purple, the room was based on a princess theme. It had been decorated for Salvatore's niece when his sister came to visit from New York. But in an effort to make Izzy feel completely at home, while her aunt lay unconscious in the other room, he had told Isabella that the room was decorated especially for her.

"Wow, Izzy!" her aunt said. "This is the greatest room ever!"

"I know!" the child responded, bubbling with excitement. "Salvatore said it's going to be my room while we're sleeping over here. Look, Aunt Em, I have my own TV too!"

Emma sat on the chair in the corner while Salvatore helped Izzy out of her clothes and into her nightgown. Once he had tucked her in bed, he helped Emma across the room so that she could give the child a kiss.

"Goodnight, sweetie," Emma whispered to her precious niece.

Then Salvatore led Emma out into the living room. He sat her on the sofa, gave her a warm blanket to cover herself with and a glass of wine to help her relax.

"We need to talk," he said.

His tone was so serious Emma suspected he was withholding bad news that involved either Izzy or her.

He picked up a newspaper and sat down beside her. He was nervous, unsure of how she would react to the news. The last thing Salvatore wanted was to lose her after waiting for so long.

"What you said about Ethan a little while ago," he began tentatively. "Well, I have some news for you. Something happened a couple of days ago."

Salvatore said no more. He leaned over and put the newspaper in her lap. Emma read the headline.

LOCAL MAN'S BODY FOUND

Investigating a complaint from neighbors of a foul smell emanating from an abandoned row house in Norristown on Monday morning, police discovered an unidentified naked, limbless torso in an advanced stage of decomposition. On Tuesday morning, a man's head was found on the banks of the Schuylkill River near Boat House Row by a group of University of Pennsylvania students. DNA tests subsequently carried out confirmed that both the head and the torso, found in separate locations, belong to a West Ambler resident Ethan Miller, 28. Police have no leads so far. According to investigators, no eyewitnesses have come forward with information that can help the investigation. Nor has any motive been found for this "particularly gruesome murder," a police source told our reporter. Local police are assisting state investigators, but were not forthcoming with any further details on the case, claiming it would be premature to make a comment.

Emma looked up from the newspaper and stared at Salvatore.

"It appears to me that Ethan finally lost his head. Such a shame," was all he said. He looked at her anxiously, waiting for a reaction, the smallest sign that she was relieved to know the news.

Slowly she began to smile. "Well, I guess Ethan must have pissed someone off really bad to make them do that to him, you're right, that is a shame," she said and lifted her wine glass in the air to Salvatore.

"Salute," he said, tapping her glass with his own. Emma understood that Salvatore would never admit to her that he had Ethan killed. Hell, she thought, he may have even done it himself. She preferred that he didn't admit killing him because if his involvement in the murder remained unspoken, it kept her from owing him anything in return. She beamed at Salvatore, quite impressed not only with the way he had handled it already, but with the symbolic way in which he did it. In the end, he had made Ethan regret the words he'd used so often to threaten her.

Chapter Eighty

As the weeks passed, Emma and Izzy remained at the apartment with Salvatore, primarily because of his insistence that they weren't ready to go back home. Besides, as she was quick to admit to herself, Emma had never lived in such luxury, and having given her a small taste of this lifestyle, it was easy for Salvatore to convince her to stay.

Tony and Vincent also enjoyed having Emma and Isabella at the apartment. They were a lively diversion to the work they performed everyday as gangsters. On one occasion, after eating spaghetti and meatballs, Izzy sat at the kitchen table coloring. Tony nudged his friend and they shared a smile. "Hey, Iz," Tony began, "don't cha have to color inside the lines?"

She looked up at him with indignation. "Yes, you do, and I am."

"Nah, look, see here where your crayon isn't in the line?" he teased.

"Yeah, I see dat too, Tony," Vincent confirmed, chiming in on the fun.

Isabella hopped off the chair and planted her feet firmly on the floor. With her hands swinging in the air above her head she ranted, "You two don't know what you're talking about. I'm coloring in the lines. See?" she glowered and pointed to the coloring book. "Besides, I bet you can't even color. You probably don't know how to, and I'm gonna tell Aunt Em that you're acting mean to me," she raved, stomping off into the living room to find her aunt.

Ten minutes later she came back in the kitchen with her homework. "What happened, Iz? I thought you were gonna tell on us," Vincent reminded her, the grown men getting their kicks out of teasing her.

"I did tell on you, but Aunt Em said I have to do my homework." She opened up her binder and looked at the simple addition and subtraction problems. She cleverly turned to them. "Can you help me with my math homework?" she inquired innocently.

Vincent looked over at Tony. "I ain't no good in math, you're gonna have to help her."

"Me?" Tony argued. "I don't know nothing 'bout math. What do I look like, an accountant?"

Isabella began to giggle at them and they quickly realized she was getting back at them for teasing her. "You think you're real smart, do ya?" Tony said, playfully lifting her into the air over his head.

"Smarter than you two," she giggled. "I gotcha!"

Salvatore, Emma, and Isabella loved being together. Each of them with their unique personalities made it a fun and relaxing place to live. They watched movies and ate dinner together at least three or four nights a week. On the nights that Salvatore had to be away, he explained that he had business to take care of. Then he would be gone all night, only reappearing the next morning. Emma never questioned him about these absences, because she knew it was none of her business. They weren't romantically involved and she considered her time at his apartment a gift from him to Izzy and her.

Salvatore's feelings for Emma had become more intense. Now that he had her so close to him, he found his love for her growing. He worked hard at keeping his feelings to himself, but could not help dropping subtle hints that he was attracted to her. His gaze would linger a little longer when he looked at her, and when he accidentally touched or bumped into her, the two of them would giggle like school children. He suspected that she was drawn to him as well, but neither would admit it in so many words.

Salvatore was captivated by her beauty and resilience. Emma was in awe of his power, fearlessness, and luxurious lifestyle. An impartial observer would have known, looking at them, that the two shared a special bond, the kind between a man and a woman who wanted each other desperately. Their physical attraction for each other ran deep. Yet they kept their distance from each other, not wanting to make the other feel self-conscious or uncomfortable, reluctant to ruin the friendship they had forged so painstakingly, but most of all, working to prolong indefinitely the initial stage of their relationship that drew its sustenance from banter and flirtation and meaningful smiles.

It was finally Salvatore who made the first move. It was a Friday night and they had just finished watching The Little Mermaid with Izzy. Having put the child to bed, Emma joined Salvatore in the living room for wine. As he handed her the glass, their fingertips brushed. The sensation was like electricity zapping their bodies. He sat close to her on the sofa, closer than he usually did. That made her both nervous and excited.

"Em," he began, "I would like to take you out on a real date. You know just you and me, spending a romantic evening together." He stared at her steadily, unblinking, waiting for her response.

"Um, sure," she said, her heart fluttering. "That's fine. But when you say 'romantic,' do you mean going out as a couple?"

"Yeah," he smiled, "as a couple."

He leaned in and kissed her softly on the cheek. She blushed as desire for him flared within her. It had been so long since Ethan had made love to her. It wasn't sex she missed, but the kind of tenderness they had shared when she first started dating him. She longed for Salvatore to kiss her now, passionately, but he didn't.

All he did was brush her hair back from her face and say, "I'll take that as a yes. Next Saturday night. All right?"

She nodded, her eyes screaming with the desire she felt for him. Hard as it was for him to resist her in that moment, he forced himself to say goodnight and leave the room. He wanted to keep that desire unquenched until neither of them could endure it anymore. It gave him something to look forward to and made him come alive with feelings he hadn't experienced in a long, long time.

While living at the apartment, Emma had observed how men were always coming and going. They would follow Salvatore into his office and emerge smoking cigars and shaking hands with him. Tony and Vincent, his two main men, were at the apartment every day. Always present at dinnertime, they taught Emma how to cook different Italian dishes after she had sufficiently healed. Salvatore, Emma, and Izzy ate their evening meal in the dining room, while Tony and Vincent almost always had theirs in the kitchen, where they preferred to eat.

Emma never needed to go out, even after she had completely healed, because everything was taken care of for her. Groceries were delivered to the apartment, a stylist from Nordstrom was sent over to fit her for clothes, and anything else she needed was taken care of by Salvatore, who made sure it was delivered to her. In fact, Emma looked forward to her date with him, not merely because she was drawn to him, but also for the opportunity to get out of the apartment. It struck her one day that she didn't even know which part of the city she was staying in. She had been so wrapped up in her fantasy life that everything else seemed to have come to a standstill.

The following Saturday afternoon, Emma was sitting in the living room reading to Izzy when there was a knock at the door. Five minutes later, Tony came back with a young woman in her early thirties.

"Hey, Em," Tony announced. "Macie here is my kid sister. She's gonna babysit Izzy for ya tonight while you two go out. She came early to meet the kid."

Emma looked up at Macie and smiled. "Hi, Macie, I'm Emma and this is Izzy," she said. "I hadn't really thought about who was going to watch Izzy tonight. Kind of stupid of me, I guess."

A plain woman who seemed to teeter on the edge of homely looking, Macie wore black pants and a baggy gray sweater.

"It's fine," she told Emma. "Salvatore wanted me to come over so Isabella could get to know me a little." She approached Izzy and got down on her knees so that her head was level with the little girl's. "Hi, Isabella, I'm Macie," she said with ease. "You and I are going to hang out tonight. We can play some games or watch movies. How does that sound?"

Izzy eyed her warily then looked at Emma, who gave her a nod of reassurance.

"Yay," she yelled excitedly and taking Macie by the hand. "Do you want to come and see my room? It's a princess room and Salvatore made it just for me. Come on!"

Emma heard Izzy chattering away to Macie in her high voice as she led her down the long hallway to her bedroom. She smiled to herself, thinking of the evening ahead. Salvatore had refused to tell her where they were going. He wanted it to be a surprise and had only disclosed that it was a wonderful restaurant and she would need her stylist to get her a cocktail dress. Emma felt as if she were living in a dream, but a seed of apprehension continued to gnaw at her gut. Is he everything he seems to be, she wondered, or will he turn out to be just like the other men in my life? If he turned out to be a tyrant and a sadist like the others, the type of man who would end up abusing her, getting rid of him would be far, far more difficult. These fears continued to fester inside her, but at five o'clock, Emma put them aside and went to get ready for her date.

Chapter Eighty-One

A t six thirty there was a knock at Emma's bedroom door. When she opened it and peeked out, Macie was standing there.

"Salvatore wanted me to find out if you were ready," she told her shyly. "Your reservations are for seven o'clock and he's particular about being punctual."

Macie's formal ways made Emma a little uneasy, but she considered that given Salvatore's identity and stature within his circle, this was the way people acted around him. She didn't know that it was Macie's strict upbringing that made her so formal, unlike her brother Tony, who had always felt he belonged to the "family." After all, Salvatore, Vincent, and Tony had gone to school together since the first grade. They knew each other better than their own parents knew them.

"Tell him I'll be out in a minute," she told Macie.

Emma approached her full-length mirror and gave herself a quick once-over. Satisfied that she had chosen the right outfit for the occasion, she walked out into the living room to meet Salvatore.

Seated in his favorite chair, he was sipping a glass of wine when she entered. His eyes followed her into the room and traveled from the top of her head to the tips of her toes as she approached. He had to admit to himself that he had never experienced such pleasure in looking at a woman as he did now, a sensation so intense that it bordered on pain. He could not decide if it was his overactive hormones or Emma's stunning beauty that prompted his response. Nor did he care. He thought she was the most magnificent woman he'd ever laid eyes on.

She stood before him in a knee-length figure-hugging red dress with a plunging round neckline that showed off the upper curves of her beautiful, perky breasts. The red silk tulle overlay gave it just the right touch of sophistication. Her long blond hair fell past her shoulders and her green eyes sparkled with desire as they met his gaze. Observing the eagerness with which his eyes took in every detail of her appearance, her lips parted in a tiny smile. Emma enjoyed the hunger in his gaze, his yearning for her, his desire to be near her.

Salvatore stood slowly, unable to take his eyes off her.

"You look incredible," he murmured. "I mean, you always look great, but tonight, you are more beautiful than I could have ever imagined." He moved toward her and gently took her hand. "Are you ready to go?" he asked.

Basking in his adoring gaze, Emma felt beautiful. She knelt to kiss Izzy, who had come in to say goodnight and was star-struck enough to claim that her aunt looked like the "prettiest princess ever." Then Emma turned back to Salvatore. She linked her arm through his and instructed Macie to put Izzy to bed by eight thirty.

"Of course," Macie responded sweetly.

Going down in the elevator, Salvatore leaned over and kissed her softly on the neck. She felt for his hand and firmly laced her fingers through his. Out on the street, Emma was awakened from her trance by all of the people strolling on the sidewalk, many of them turning to admire the handsome couple as they made their way into the black sedan waiting at the curb for them.

Driving through the Italian Market, Emma watched the vendors hurriedly putting their goods away for the evening. Not long after, the car pulled up in front of a restaurant called Dante & Luigi's.

As they entered, the maître d' came forward to greet them personally and extended his hand. "Mr. Salvatore," he said, "how wonderful that you are joining us this evening! We have a special table for you in the back, where you will be assured greater privacy. I saved it especially for the two of you."

Salvatore shook the man's hand and murmured a polite "Grazie." Then he and Emma followed him to the table reserved for them. A small bouquet of roses, arranged in a cut-crystal vase, stood in the center. As they were seated, Emma noticed that the ambiance of the place was old-world Italian. Soft music played in the background. The restaurant buzzed with happy conversation and the occasional anticipatory "Ahhhh...," as plates of food with wonderful aromas and colors were served. Emma found the place charming. She felt as if she had stepped into another place and time.

While she took in her surroundings, Salvatore ordered a bottle of Brunello di Montalcino and watched his companion for a moment.

"This is one of the oldest Italian restaurants in the country," he told her. "The very first place my great-great-grandfather came to when he arrived in Philadelphia from Italy. Someone had written down the name of the restaurant on a piece of paper for him. He got himself a job here as a waiter and lived upstairs. This place is known for helping Italian immigrants find their way in America."

"It's wonderful, Salvatore," Emma told him. "I really envy you for knowing so much about your heritage. You're really proud of being Italian, aren't you?"

"Yes, that's true," he admitted. "I love everything about my heritage—the food, the culture, the traditions, but it doesn't mean that I don't love other things that aren't Italian." He lifted her hand and kissed it gently, gazing into her eyes all the while.

Emma laughed, feeling both flattered and happy. He was so serious at times that it made her feel as if she were older than her twenty-one years. She couldn't decide if she liked that or not. She wanted to be independent and didn't want to feel as though she were aging before her time. She loved being young and reckless. She missed working at Doubles, and while she was definitely attracted to Salvatore, she still couldn't decide if she was ready for a serious relationship.

During the first half hour, as they sat sipping their wine, several men came over to them and shook Salvatore's hand. They told him how good it was to see him and asked about his father.

Finally he waved over the maître d' and told him firmly, "Please see to it that there are no more interruptions."

The man nodded respectfully and withdrew. Emma watched him whisper instructions to the group of waiters on his way back to the podium where he stood to greet guests. After that, it was just the two of them, Emma and Salvatore. They talked about Izzy and what a wonderfully lively and endearing child she was.

Then Emma asked, "So what's Macie's story?"

Salvatore explained, "She never married, probably because she doesn't even know how to talk to a man or behave in his presence. Her parents were very strict with her and she never really had a social life beyond family circles. Anyway, Macie loves children. Since she has none of her own, she likes to babysit other people's kids. Tony and I have been friends since we were six-years old. He's very protective of his sister and she only babysits for people he can trust. I've known her for years. Don't worry, Izzy is safe with her. She's a little odd with adults, but great with kids. Her parents didn't let her do anything when she was a kid. She never got to experience much of life."

"I'm not worried, just curious. In fact, there are a lot of things about you that make me curious. Why, for instance, does everyone rush to greet you as though you're some kind of celebrity? What's up with that?" she asked casually.

Salvatore answered carefully, "It's a respect thing. People show their respect by acknowledging my presence. It's respect for my father and me. Respect for my whole family, really."

It was on the tip of Emma's tongue to ask him if this respect came from the awe in which everyone held his father, the head of the Italian Mafia, but she already knew the answer. Salvatore himself had never mentioned the Mafia in his conversations and instinct told her to tread carefully in this area.

However, a few days prior her suspicions had been confirmed when Emma overheard Tony and Vincent talking to Salvatore in his office. They hadn't shut the door completely and she couldn't help but eavesdrop on their conversation. "Yeah," Tony had stated in an excited voice, "the kid did real good, Sal. He took it nice and slow just like ya wanted him to do. First, he broke his fuckin' kneecaps wit da hammer then he smashed his knuckles to bits wit the butt of his gun. Then to top it off he cut his lousy, snitching tongue out and strangled the motherfucker to death wit' his bare hands. It was beautiful, Sal, you woulda been real proud of 'im."

Although she wanted Salvatore to admit to her that he helped run the Mafia by pursuing this line of conversation, she knew that she risked unleashing his wrath. But she was eager to know everything there was to know about his mysterious life and resolved to find out more over time. She let the thought drift out of her mind and enjoyed the distinctive flavors of the dishes he had ordered for them.

The cheeses were creamy and sharp, the meat tender and juicy, and the pasta was cooked to perfection. They had just finished dessert when Salvatore placed his arm along the back of her chair and leaned close to her ear.

"I have a surprise waiting outside for you," he whispered.

"Oh really?" Emma teased, unable to imagine what more he could possibly do to impress her.

"Yes, really," he said.

As they stood to leave, she felt the gentle pressure of his hand on the small of her back guiding her out of the restaurant, which sent an exhilarating thrill through her body.

Waiting at the curb outside was a horse-drawn buggy. For a fleeting moment, Emma felt like Cinderella climbing into her carriage. Once they were seated, the driver slowly started moving through the city. Emma leaned back against the soft leather seat and closed her eyes, imagining how great it would be to have a whole lifetime as perfect as this night. As they made their way slowly through the city, she began hoping that she and Isabella would never have to leave.

Chapter Eighty-Two

B y the time they returned to the apartment, Macie had the fireplace blazing for them.

"Did you two have a good time?" she asked with a touch of envy.

Macie had loved Salvatore since she was a teenager, but her feelings had neither been articulated nor reciprocated. For Salvatore, she was nothing more than Tony's sister.

"We had a wonderful time, Macie. Thanks for coming over," he told her, leaning over to give her a quick peck on the cheek.

Watching the woman blush, Emma instinctively knew that Macie had a crush on him. She felt sorry for the woman, because she knew how it felt to yearn for someone's love when that person didn't love you back. On an impulse, Emma went over to Macie and embraced her.

"Thank you so much for taking care of Izzy," she said gently. "I really appreciate it."

Macie was surprised by the warm gesture from a woman as beautiful as Emma. She wished she could, just for one day, be as beautiful as the blond creature who stood before her. If she had been born with Emma's looks, she consoled herself, maybe Salvatore would have loved her instead. It was hard for her to dislike this lovely young woman, however. She was kind and polite and her niece was a wonderful kid, as smart as they came.

Before Macie left for the night, Salvatore went into the kitchen, leaving the two women in the living room. Moments later, Tony and Vincent emerged from the kitchen with three very large men in tow, a fact that did not escape Emma's notice.

"Goodnight, Emma," Tony said, giving her a wink. "See you tomorrow."

Salvatore led her over to the sofa in front of the fireplace. He made her sit down and handed her a glass of cognac. Emma took one sip and started coughing.

"Yuck!" she grimaced. "What is this?"

Laughing, he explained, "It's cognac, an after-dinner drink. It's an acquired taste. It's meant to be sipped slowly and enjoyed thoroughly."

Emma shook her head. "Well, I'm gonna need some cheap alcohol, then. That shit is like drinking gasoline."

Laughing at her refreshing honesty, Salvatore walked over to the bar and poured her a glass of wine. It was her third glass that evening and she was starting to feel a little tipsy. She told herself to drink the wine slowly. The last thing she wanted to do was barf in the middle of this perfect night.

He slipped onto the sofa next to her and put his strong arm around her shoulder. "So tell me who Emma really is. I know a lot about you, but I want to know everything about you."

Emma considered his request for a moment. She had already told him about her childhood with Pepper and how Jake had treated Gracie and her. Should she tell him the whole truth about her past? Would that turn him off or make him love her more? Would telling him that she had murdered three people be too much for him to handle? Being a Mafioso, he was no stranger to violence. But he might feel differently about murder committed by a woman. She was pretty sure that in his world, women didn't do the killing; they did the cooking.

"Well, what do you want to know?" she now asked. "I've told you about my childhood. You know how awful that was." She was trying to gauge what he wanted to hear.

"Yes, I know," Salvatore said gently. "I want to know how you got away from your father and Jake. How did you end up at Double Visions? You needed the money, I know, but what drove you from your home? You told me Jake had died. So why did you feel the need to run?"

"Well, I knew it was just a matter of time before my mother found another man," Emma replied, her quick mind helping her to present a logical explanation. "I didn't want to take any more chances. So I fixed her up real good, loaded Gracie into a car, and split. We spent some time living in a car. I heard about Doubles on the radio, went to amateur night there, met Ethan, met you, and here I am!" It had all come out in one breath and she hoped it would stop him probing further. Then she quickly changed the subject. "You know, the truth is that you know a lot about me and I know practically nothing about you."

Up until that moment, she had known about him being a member of the Mafia, but they had never openly talked about it. She hoped he would now. She had so many questions.

"Well, my family runs a big business," Salvatore told her. "I'm the fourth generation running it. My great-great-grandfather, whom I told you about earlier, started the business when he came to America at the age of twenty-three. We've been very successful, and I consider myself a lucky man to be a part of it all." His casual manner made it all sound very legitimate.

Emma stared at him in wonder, then took the plunge. "Your father is the boss of the Mafia in Philadelphia, right?"

Salvatore choked on his cognac. "Well, Bella, we don't talk about such things," he managed, recovering quickly from the initial shock. "I'm sure you can understand why. But I do admit that my family is influential and has a lot of power. We have many businesses throughout the city."

She tilted her head to one side. "So you don't run the Mafia?" she persisted.

Salvatore thought quickly. Those who were a part of the Mafia never admitted it to anyone, not even their spouses, and he had never been blatantly asked the question before now. However, he wanted her to be careful since people had seen them together and would know that she was an interest of his. He had to be mindful about not putting Emma in harm's way. At the same time he had to ensure that if things didn't work out between the two of them, the interests of the family to which he belonged were not put at risk and by its very nature putting her at risk as well. The Mafia never left loose ends. Balancing both with the women he had been involved with was an art he had mastered over the years.

"As I said," he repeated, "we have many successful businesses throughout the city. That's all there is to it."

Emma felt agitated at his avoidance of the truth and the way he had eluded answering her question. After all, he knew almost everything there was to know about Izzy and her. While she stewed silently, he leaned over, plucked the glass from her hand, and placed it on the table. Then he leaned in closer and kissed her neck. With every subsequent kiss he planted on her neck, her annoyance dissolved, flaring into passion. He kissed the top of her breasts, peeping over the deep neckline of her dress. Then he slowly raised his head and looked into her face. Emma leaned in and kissed him softly on the lips.

Salvatore stood, pulled her up to him, and turned her around. He started to kiss the back of her neck while his fingers slowly unzipped her dress. As it fell to the floor, she stepped out of it and turned to face him. She was wearing the most exquisite undergarments—a black lace bra and thong and fishnet stockings with a matching garter belt—that showed off her figure to perfection. She stood before him, young, beautiful, and confident. Salvatore stepped into her and kissed her lips softly, parting them with his tongue. Emma experienced a shock of pleasure as their tongues brushed and their kiss deepened. They wanted each other desperately, and now nothing stood between them.

Salvatore laid her down on the fur rug, but before he could join her, Emma had reached up and unzipped his pants, letting them drop to the ground. When he lay down beside her, she tore his shirt open, popping the buttons off one at a time. With desire overpowering him now, his fingers were clumsy as he removed her bra and put his mouth over one of her breasts. He had wanted to have her for so long it seemed almost unreal to him that she should now lie there beside him, ready to love him back. They touched each other, carrying out their explorations with a sense of wonder, until finally he slipped his fingers inside her. She gazed up at him, her eyes wide and imploring, as if begging him for more, and unable to hold back any longer, he gently eased himself inside her. They made love with a frenzy neither had felt before that moment, until each of them exploded at the peak of their own ecstasy. Afterward, they lay naked, staring at the fire. Engrossed in their thoughts, they contemplated their feelings for each other and reflected on the wonderful experience they had just shared.

Both hoped their love affair would never end.

Chapter Eighty-Three

T he next morning, Izzy was confused when she found them both in the same bed. "Aunt Emma, why are you in Salvatore's bed?" she inquired with innocent concern. "How come you didn't sleep in your room? Were you scared? Did you have a bad dream?"

Emma reached out and pulled her up onto the bed. "No, it's just that, sometimes, big people sleep together because they like each other," she explained simply. "Remember how Ethan and I used to sleep in the same room?"

Izzy scrunched up her face. "Yeah, but you didn't like Ethan. He was mean. Remember? He used to yell all the time and, sometimes he would grab my arm and squeeze it real hard and that would hurt too. Or sometimes he would yell at me with his nose touching mine. I didn't like him."

Emma gathered her niece in her arms and she wiggled her way under the covers between the two adults.

Izzy continued to chatter. "Well, I like Salvatore and I would sleep in here too, except I can't, because I really like my princess room."

Salvatore gave her a gentle squeeze. "Yep," he said, "we wouldn't want you to give up the princess room."

"Ewww, your breath stinks!" Izzy said with disconcerting candor. "You should go brush your teeth."

Salvatore laughed, shuffling out of bed and making his way to the bathroom.

"Are you and Salvatore going to get married?" the child asked Emma bluntly.

Emma was shocked that Izzy even knew about the concept of marriage. "No, we're not planning on it right now, Little Miss Thing! We just really like each other. Now stop asking so many questions so we can go make pancakes for breakfast! Hurry up! Then we can surprise Salvatore!"

Izzy jumped over her aunt before she could sit up and ran to the kitchen at full speed. "Don't come in the kitchen, Salvatore!" she sang. "Me and Aunt Emma are surprising you, okay?"

With a mouth full of toothpaste, Salvatore yelled back, "Ohray!"

When he came out of the bathroom, Emma was sitting on the side of the bed, staring at him.

"Well, good morning, gorgeous," he said, striding across the room, laying her back on the bed, and giving her a long kiss.

"Good morning," she managed to respond when they came up for air. "Let's not forget we have Little Missy Nosey in the other room. You never know when she'll come running in here demanding to know what we're doing. So unless you're prepared to explain to her why you have your tongue in my mouth," she added mischievously, running her hand over his ass, "we better get moving!"

"Oh, really?" Salvatore teased, looking sexy as hell. "You're going to tell me to get moving and then touch me like that and expect me to just go?"

"Yesss!" she hissed, but what she really wanted to do was pull him back under the covers and make love to him again. "Now move it!" she added with gusto.

He stood and pulled her to her feet. "You know, I'm used to doing the bossing, not getting bossed. I like it, though, when you're bossy. It turns me on."

"Oh God! Whatever, Salvatore. You're so weird!" Emma teased.

In the kitchen, they came upon an amusing little scene. Izzy was insisting that Tony and Vincent leave so that she and her aunt could prepare a surprise breakfast for everyone. The two men were busy teasing her, declaring she was too little to cook. Hands firmly on her hips, Izzy glowered up at the two men, who towered over her, and demanded they do what they were told without further argument.

"Hey, Miss Bossy!" Emma called out. "Maybe if you say 'please' they'll listen to you."

"But Aunt Em," Izzy complained, "they said I didn't know how to cook, that I'm too little! Tell them that I can cook. They're really making me mad!"

Salvatore looked at his two childhood friends. "You two better be careful before Izzy really gives it to you!" he quipped. "If I were you, I'd be scared silly. Besides, Izzy knows how to cook. So why don't we go in the living room while the ladies prepare breakfast for us."

"Fine," Tony said in a teasing manner, "but only if I get a lot of bacon, crispy bacon."

Vincent joined in on the fun. "And I want potatoes, well done. Make sure they're nice and brown, will ya?"

With the men out of the kitchen, the girls started to cook breakfast. For the first time, Emma felt as if she and Izzy were in a place where they belonged.

After breakfast, Tony pulled Emma aside. "Hey, Em, I need your help."

"Sure, what's up?" she responded, wondering what he could possibly need from her but happy she could return all the kindness he had showered on Izzy and her.

Tony didn't mince words when he spoke. "My sister Macie, well, she needs a little help. Ya see how ugly she makes herself look. I'm scared if she don't do somethin' 'bout that appearance of hers, she'll end up an old spinster. Listen, between you and me, she's thirty-one years old and I don't think she's ever been laid. I was thinkin' you could take her out and pick some nice outfits for her. Maybe get her hair done up real nice and teach her how to use some makeup so she don't look dead all the time. Hey, you could take her to get paint on her nails. Ya know, spruce her up so maybe a man will come along and want to marry her or somethin'. I need ya to make her womanly. Could you do that for me?"

Emma was amused at his description of all the fixing up he believed his sister needed and touched that he loved her enough to ask someone to help her. "Of course I'll do that for you, Tony. We can make it a special day together, just her and me. How about tomorrow? Can you be here with Izzy?"

"Yeah, sure, tomorrow. That's real good. I like that. I don't know how much I like babysitting, but hey, how bad can it be, right?" he asked, looking for Emma to tell him it wasn't a big deal to watch Izzy. But instead she laughed at him and left the room to call Macie.

Emma told Macie that she was tired of being stuck in the apartment and needed some "girl time," which made Macie chuckle out loud. "So I was thinking we could go shopping, get our hair done, and, you know, just hang out and do things that girls like to do."

Flattered and excited at the thought of spending time with Emma, she agreed quickly.

Salvatore called an acquaintance of his at Nordstrom to let them know that Emma and Macie were coming in. "Make sure they get treated real good. I want them to be taken care of and get all the attention they need. It's your job to send them home happy. Understand?" he told the man who managed the store, who assured him that everything would be perfect.

When the two girls arrived at the store they were immediately escorted into a private area. Emma quietly told the salesladies to focus on Macie. Once out of the old lady garb that Macie normally wore, Emma noted that she had a nice figure. She hosted a healthy round ass, hourglass curves, and perky breasts. Macie was elated as she watched her own transformation. After they had bought nearly a dozen outfits for Macie they were taken to another room where they were greeted by a hair and makeup stylist. By the time they were finished, the girls were high on excitement. It had been a fun day, and while Macie didn't say too much the whole time, the perpetual smile on her lips told Emma she had done a good thing.

As they walked through the apartment door they were greeted by Isabella. "Macie! You look beautiful. What did you do?" she blurted.

"Your Aunt Emma took me out to buy some clothes and get my hair done. Do you like it?" she asked, feeling a little self-conscious about how different she looked.

"I love it!" Izzy told her.

Just then Tony and Vincent entered the foyer. "Well now, look at you," Tony said to his sister. "You clean up real good," he went on in an attempt to flatter her.

"Thanks," his sister replied bashfully.

Vincent was watching Macie from a distance. When he was back in the kitchen with Tony cooking linguini and clams, he looked at his friend hard. "What the fuck are you lookin' at, Vin?"

"Listen, Tony. Macie was lookin' real nice when she came home. I was wunderin'...I was just thinkin' maybe I'd ask her out on a date. Who knew she looked like that under all that grandma shit she's always wearin'? How 'bout it? You think that'd be okay?" Vincent finished.

"Oh yeah? So now ya wanna take my sister on a date, huh? Yeah, well, I guess that'll be all right. But you need to ask her yourself. And I want ya to be real nice about it too. She ain't never been out on a date before so don't go acting like an asshole," he ordered.

"Who me? When did ya ever know me to be an asshole, Tone?" Vincent mocked, pretending to punch his friend in the stomach.

"You're always an asshole, Vin. Just don't be one to my sister or I'll lace your fuckin' pasta with laxatives so you can't leave the bathroom for a week," he joked.

Later that day, after Macie had gone home, Tony found Emma sitting on one of the large sofas reading. "Em, thanks for what ya did for Macie today. She was real happy. Vincent thought she looked good too. He's gonna ask her out on a date."

Emma got off the sofa and stood on tiptoe to give Tony a kiss on his cheek. "No problem, Tony. It was a lot of fun actually."

"Well, if ya ever need a favor, just let me know." he offered.

"Hmmm, now that you mention it, I do want you to show me how to make that lasagna you cooked the other night," she told him.

"Consider it done. I'll show ya how to make it tomorrow. That sound good?" he asked.

"Sure, Tony. Tomorrow is good," Emma responded, excited at the prospect of learning a new recipe that Salvatore would enjoy.

As he left her standing in the room by herself it became clear to her that every day with Salvatore was good. She was good. Izzy was good. Salvatore was good. Everything just seemed too good to be true.

Chapter Eighty-Four

Four months later, the three were still enjoying a blissful existence. Emma talked every week with Katie. After everything had happened that night with Ethan and Pete, Katie had put all of their belongings in a storage unit that Salvatore had rented for her. Emma had also been in touch with Brianna, who had met a guy from the US Air Force. She was planning to move in two weeks to Germany, where he was stationed.

"Bri, you're out of your fucking mind!" Emma had exclaimed. "Why are you moving across the fucking globe? You haven't even known him that long!"

Brianna had felt deeply insulted. "You know what, Em?" she had shot back. "You're also living with some guy you barely know. Fuck, he didn't even ask you to move in! You just went there and never left. Stop being such a bitch! I need you to be happy for me. Now do you want us to get together before I head out or what?"

Emma had felt guilty about upsetting the friend who had once sacrificed everything for Gracie and her. "Of course we're going to get together!" she had assured Brianna. "Hey, I'll see if Salvatore can hook us up with something special to do in the city. You can come for the weekend and we'll make it a two-day party! How's that sound?"

"That sounds like the Em I know and love!" Brianna had said, mollified. "Let's plan on next weekend. I can't wait to see Izzy either!" she added excitedly before hanging up the phone.

As it turned out, Salvatore was preoccupied with work the following weekend. He worked every other weekend, which meant Emma and Izzy were alone in the apartment, except for the presence of Tony and Vincent, who came in to cook or check on them. Emma missed Salvatore when he was gone all weekend, but he had insisted that he needed to do his part for the family business. She understood and didn't ride him about it, but missed him nonetheless. Brianna's decision to spend the weekend with her was therefore a cause for celebration. Salvatore made the necessary arrangements at the restaurant and impossible-to-get-into nightclubs. He also arranged for Macie to stay with Izzy.

When Brianna arrived at the apartment, she couldn't believe the style in which Emma lived.

"Fuck, man!" she said, wide-eyed. "If I met a guy who could let me live like this, I'd never leave either. Girl, you hit the fucking jackpot with this one!" In the very next moment, she grew serious. "Does he hit you, Em?" she asked in a whisper. "Is he mean to you?"

"No, Bri, he doesn't. I know that's hard to believe, considering that every other man in my life abused the shit out of me. But no, he never has. He's gentle and loving with me. He never raises his voice and we get along so well. We started out with this great friendship and now it has turned into this thing that's so fuckin' awesome. We eat at great restaurants and he buys me stuff all the time," Emma explained.

"Does he talk about getting married and having kids?" Brianna asked, her tone envious.

"Nah, we don't talk about that shit," Emma said nonchalantly. "I don't really care. I never really saw myself getting married. So I don't think about it. As far as kids go, I don't want to have any. I have Izzy and that's enough."

"Well, whatever works for you guys," Brianna said.

At the end of the weekend, when it was time for her to leave for the airport, the two stood in the foyer and embraced for a long time. Emma was sad to see her friend moving so far away and silently wondered if this would be the last time they'd ever see each other. The idea of never seeing Bri again dampened her spirit, even though she knew that both of them had found a better life for themselves, and this gave her some comfort.

"I'll see ya when I see ya!" Brianna yelled from the elevator.

"Yeah, take care of yourself and call me!" Emma shouted back.

As Emma shut the door, tears began to run down her cheeks. Even though the two girls hadn't seen each other in a long time, they still shared a special bond, reinforced by their shared memories of Gracie. Emma knew she would miss her friend and wondered if she could convince Salvatore to visit Brianna and her boyfriend in Germany someday. He'd never denied her anything, and she would ask him when the time was right.

For now, she thought, it was time to consider what she should do next with her own life. Sure, living this life was wonderful, but she needed something that was all her own. Something she could do to earn a living. She missed having her own money. Salvatore always made sure she had plenty of cash in her wallet, but she had no right to it. Emma liked the feeling of holding cash she herself had earned.

Chapter Eighty-Five

Just two weeks after Brianna left for Germany, Emma was in the kitchen making pork sauce from a recipe she had picked up from the boys. Salvatore stood by, watching her.

"You need to add more salt to the sauce. You have to be generous with the salt. It makes the flavor pop," he told her, creeping up behind her and putting an arm gently around her waist.

She poured more salt into the palm of her hand as he nuzzled her.

"I have a surprise for you," he said, plunging his face into her thick, soft hair and taking a long breath, as if he were taking a drink of her. "You smell delicious," he murmured, licking her earlobe gently.

"Thanks, but in case you haven't noticed, I'm cooking," Emma teased.

Salvatore turned down the flame on the stove and led her into their bedroom. She kissed him passionately once the door was closed and locked so that Izzy couldn't burst in on them. Slowly Emma removed his clothes. When he stood before her, fully naked, she couldn't control her urge to have him. He tore at her clothing, and soon they were entangled between the sheets on the bed. The sex between them was indescribably intense and dripped with passion.

Emma would tease him with her mouth. Kissing him on the neck and working her way down his body. She would glide her tongue slowly over his erect penis, waiting to give him exactly what he wanted, until she knew that his desire for her was piqued. Salvatore would feel as if he was standing on the edge of a cliff with a parachute, waiting, anticipating with excitement the explosive pleasure she gave him. Only then would she give him the satisfaction he so desired and fully take him into her mouth until he came.

In turn, Salvatore's gentle hands and mouth made Emma's body ache for more of him. She was like a drug addict who needed her next hit of cocaine, she found him so addicting. He would kiss her everywhere; there wasn't an inch of her body that his tongue didn't know. She felt blissful when he was inside of her, moving in a slow, steady rhythm, stopping at perfectly timed intervals to run his tongue between her legs until her excitement swelled beyond her ability to control it and she exploded with the pleasurable sensation that only an orgasm can bring.

When they had finished, they lay in the bed, holding each other.

Finally Salvatore spoke. "Now, about that surprise..."

"Oh yeah, I forgot," she said, rolling onto her side to look at him.

"We're taking a little trip," he said mysteriously.

"A trip, huh? And where are we going?" Her voice was full of anticipation.

"I'm taking you to Saint Thomas for a long weekend," Salvatore told her, feeling like a knight in shining armor. "My family owns a condo on the beach. It's a wonderful place and I know you'll love it. I've arranged for us to go next weekend."

Emma was thrilled. She had never been anywhere exotic. Hell, she thought to herself, the farthest she'd ever been was that shit-hole Kensington!

"What about Izzy?" she asked. "We're taking her with us, right?" she asked, a little nervous to leave her behind.

"Yes, of course Izzy is coming. Macie will come with us too. She can keep an eye on her so that we can have some time alone."

Emma hugged him and jumped out of bed, her naked body so beautiful and perfect that Salvatore wanted to pull her back and make love to her again.

She noticed how he was looking at her and said in a bantering tone, "Hey, knock it off! We have to go tell Izzy. She's going to be so excited."

They found Isabella sitting at the small desk in her room, drawing. She looked up at them as they entered.

"Look what I did! I drew a princess, and see?" she said, pointing to the tiny picture. "My princess has wings and a halo!"

"Oh, so you drew an angel princess! Is that supposed to be you?" Emma asked.

"Of course it's me! It looks exactly like me, doesn't it, Salvatore?" She looked to him for confirmation.

"Yes, Iz, it looks just like you. Our little angel!" he said affectionately.

As Izzy leapt from her chair and hugged Salvatore, Emma experienced a moment of terror. He had referred to her niece as "our little angel." That scared her. She didn't want Izzy building up false hopes of any kind. Things had been perfect between the three of them so far, but Emma was concerned that the child would become too comfortable with what might turn out to be a temporary phase of their lives. Emma was fine with the way things were, but hearing him murmur words to her niece that offered a promise of a future together gave her reason to pause.

Ever on the alert, Salvatore had noticed instantly that something he'd said had disturbed Emma. He took her hand in his own. "Do you want to tell Izzy about the surprise or do you want me to tell her?" he asked, hoping to bring back that happy moment they had just shared while discussing the trip.

"Oh yeah," Emma said. "I'll tell her. I have great news, Iz," she now announced, turning to her niece. "Salvatore's bought us a surprise. He's going to take us to Saint Thomas for a vacation."

"What's Saint Thomas?" Izzy asked, clearly unenthusiastic.

Salvatore bent down on one knee so that his face was level with Izzy's. "We're going to the beach, sweetheart."

"YAY!" she screamed and ran to her bookshelf. She pulled out a book and flung it at Salvatore. "Like the beach in this book?" she asked, beside herself with excitement. "Curious George Goes To The Beach, right?"

"Yes, that's right. Just like Curious George," he said enthusiastically, trying to feed her excitement.

Izzy turned her attention to her aunt. "I don't have a bathing suit," she complained suddenly.

"I don't either," Emma told her with a shrug. "I guess we'll both have to go to the store and buy one before we go."

Izzy started bubbling over with excited chatter about all the things they were going to do at the beach. She told Salvatore that he would have to help her build a castle in the sand and informed him that she didn't know how to swim. So he would have to hold onto her when she was in the water. Her mind raced with thoughts of how much fun they would all have together. She was an imaginative child and a receptive one, and the fact that Macie had spent a great deal of time reading to her over the months had stimulated her creativity further.

That night, as Emma and Salvatore lay in bed, she thanked him for everything he was doing for them. She told herself this man owed them nothing. He was kind and generous with both of them. The trip was just one more way to make her love this lifestyle. His comment to Izzy earlier had given her something to think about. As she drifted off to sleep that night, she wondered for the first time if she would, someday, marry him.

Chapter Eighty-Six

A week later, their plane landed at the airport in Saint Thomas. He had flown them first class, of course, and Izzy hadn't wanted to leave the plane because of all the attention she'd received from the flight crew. After Salvatore picked up his rental car, he drove them down to Redhook on the east end of the island. As they pulled into a gated community called Cowpet Bay West, Emma took in the beauty of the place and caught glimpses of the ocean between the buildings as Salvatore drove down to his condo.

The condo turned out to be as tastefully decorated as his apartment in the city, with explosions of Caribbean color on the walls that gave it the feel of a resort straight out of Luxury Travel magazine, the latest issue of which Salvatore had bought for her to look at once he'd shared his plans about the trip.

After they settled in, Salvatore accompanied Emma and Izzy down to the beach while Macie decided to stay at the condo. Isabella immediately ran off with her bucket and shovel to play in the sand, while he and Emma settled themselves at the bar on the beach. As day faded into night, they enjoyed the feel of the warm, silky breeze against their skin. From the moment they arrived, everything seemed to be moving in slow motion. Emma felt that people here were more relaxed. Strangers talked to each other with ease, eager to share their contentment at being on the island. The wonder of finding herself in so special a place cast a rosy glow on everything and everyone, making them all appear perfect.

After dinner that night, Emma and Salvatore took a stroll on the beach. The waves from the ocean, sun-warmed all day, lapped over the tops of their bare feet. He pulled her to him and kissed her gently. Then they found a private spot on the beach and sat together.

"This is the way we live, Em," he murmured. "You could be a part of this life with me forever, if that's what you wanted."

Emma didn't quite understand what he meant. Was he asking her to marry him?

"I don't know what that means," she confessed. "We're together now and I don't have any plans on leaving."

"Well, that's all I meant," Salvatore whispered softly. "I want you to stay. I promise you will always be taken care of and have the best things money can buy."

Emma was surprised at the depth of her disappointment that he hadn't asked her to marry him. First, marriage wasn't something she'd ever wanted, not after seeing what had happened between her own parents. Why, then, had she nurtured such expectations in the first place? Since when had she gotten so soft, so vulnerable? Second, what had possessed her to even imagine he would want to marry someone like her? Salvatore was, after all, a powerful man who belonged to one of Philadelphia's first families. Why would he ever marry some nonentity from Norristown? What had made her harbor such absurd notions? Had she had too much to drink?

Emma sat next to him in silence, wondering why she was being so emotionally needy, when she had taught herself to harden her heart against such meaningless things. Salvatore leaned over and kissed her. Slowly they undressed each other and made love on the beach. The whisper of the surf was background music as the waves rolled up the sand and crashed gently just short of where they lay.

The next morning, Salvatore drove Emma, Izzy, and Macie over to Megan's Bay on the other side of the island. With a beach that ran a mile long, it was a beautiful place. Izzy played with Salvatore in the water and they built the sandcastle he'd promised her.

Macie studied Emma secretly trying to understand what it was about her, aside from her obvious beauty that made her so appealing to Salvatore. After their day of shopping, Macie had come to like her more, finding her almost intoxicating. But Salvatore was a strong and powerful man. What was it, she wondered, that made him so infatuated with Emma?

After much thought, she decided it was Emma's confidence that had lured him to her. She was so sure of herself; she didn't seem to care about the opinion's others might have of her. She said what she wanted to say when she wanted to say it. Salvatore seemed, in fact, to adore this quality of hers. It wasn't a quality Macie had ever been allowed to nurture or develop in her life.

Over the long weekend, she was coming to understand that Emma was, without doubt, a woman of substance. She wasn't well-educated or well-read. She didn't use big, complicated words when she spoke. In fact, some of the things she said might have embarrassed men other than Salvatore. Her remarks, for instance, about everything being so expensive or when she openly admitted to the waiter in a fancy restaurant that it was her first time eating lobster might have turned off many. Most men who belonged to Salvatore's circle would have regarded Emma as white trash and dismissed her as nothing more than some cheap piece of ass. But now, spending so much time with her, Macie could see where Emma's attraction lay. For all that she lacked in experience and social graces she made up for in charm and confidence. There was, in fact, something close to intimidating in Emma, if you got to know her well: the fact that she feared nothing. She reminded Macie of a female version of Salvatore.

On their last evening on the island, Salvatore took Emma out to dinner at the Old Stone Farmhouse. She admired how the stone steps descended into an open-air courtyard where small tables were set with expensive white linens. Along the main building's stone walls, tucked away under arched alcoves built of stone, were plush sofas, where people sat eating and drinking heavily.

Salvatore led her to the front entrance of the farmhouse and they were ushered to a table that sat underneath an open window. The ambiance of the old but immaculately maintained building and the warm breeze wafting through the open windows made Emma feel as if she'd stepped into an altered reality, another universe altogether. The staff people bustled around them as if they were royalty, the most special individuals on earth. The manager invited them to the kitchen to meet the chef, and as they walked through the farmhouse and into the lower level of the building, the tantalizing aromas of food greeted them. Salvatore stopped Emma on their way down to the kitchen so that they could sign their names on the wall in the long hallway, a tradition both the restaurant owner and his patrons found enchanting.

Once they were back at their table, Salvatore ordered them a delicious meal of steak and lobster. When they had finished their main courses, they moved out to the open stone terrace to have dessert.

Their waitress, Autumn, approached them with big grin. "How was your meal?" she asked.

Emma gushed, "It was wonderful! This is the nicest place I've ever eaten." Instantly curious about the waitress who was around her own age, she asked, "Did you grow up here?"

"No, actually I was born and raised in Maine," Autumn replied, pleasantly surprised that a customer was taking an interest in her. "I just moved here a couple of months ago. I was offered a job on a boat that does snorkeling excursions and I couldn't resist. So this is a part-time job for me, you know, until business picks up. Right now, we live on the boat." She seemed a little embarrassed by her own situation.

Emma was amazed by the courage and spirit of this girl who had set out on her own to make a life for herself. She wondered if things would have been different had she taken Gracie far away from home. Maybe she would still be alive today. She felt guilt-stricken for not having thought things through before leaving home and seeking refuge in the streets.

Salvatore saw a shroud of sadness cloud Emma's eyes. "What is it, Bella?" he asked, concerned.

"Nothing," she replied wistfully. "I was just thinking that if I'd made different choices, maybe Gracie would still be alive today. I still miss her so much."

He reached over and took her hand. "I'm sure you did everything you could to protect her," he soothed. "Sometimes things just happen. I learned when I was very young that you can't live with regret. She knew you loved her."

Emma simply nodded as a single tear rolled down her cheek.

When they'd finished their dessert and the bill came, Emma leaned into Salvatore.

"Please give Autumn a good tip," she urged. "I know where she is in her life and it's a tough place. She needs the money."

"Of course, an extra special tip just from you then," Salvatore promised, placing an extra $200 with the bill.

The Old Stone Farmhouse would remain for Emma a cherished memory for years to come. In the silence of occasional bouts of loneliness, she would remember that night and the girl she'd met, the one who had made a very different choice from her own.

Chapter Eighty-Seven

B ack in Philadelphia, life returned to normal for Emma. Men were always coming and going in Salvatore's apartment and she started feeling more and more like his wife instead of his live-in girlfriend. However, although they'd been living together for almost a year, he had never taken her to meet his father. She often wondered if he was ashamed of her in some way or afraid that if his family asked about her history, there would be mayhem when she revealed the sordid details of her background as a stripper. The thought kept playing in her mind, and eventually she decided she would put the question to him bluntly.

They had just returned home from dinner and were in their bedroom getting undressed when Emma blurted out, "Salvatore, when am I going to meet your mom and dad?"

Her candor and directness never ceased to amaze him. He had noticed how she never attempted to ease her way into a discussion by beating about the bush before coming to the point, but boldly broached the topic, however difficult it might be.

"Well, that's a good question," he responded. "I don't know. Why do you want to meet them?"

Given their relationship and the fact that they had lived together for so long, she found his counter-question odd and a bit disconcerting.

"I don't know what to say to that," she replied. "I thought we were a couple. Are you ashamed of me?" she demanded in a defiant tone.

"Whoa, hold on a minute!" he said, shocked. "Aren't you being oversensitive? Em, one of the things I love about you is that you aren't needy. You don't require constant reassurances. As for the reason for not introducing you to my family, you're reading something into the matter that isn't there. I haven't thought to introduce you because I haven't told them about you yet."

"What!"

"Listen, Emma," Salvatore said with seriousness, "there are good reasons for everything I do. My family is very private and they like to keep it that way. My parents aren't open to meeting new people. You have to understand that they are very different from normal parents. In my family, you don't just waltz people in to meet them. There are rules that must be followed. It's not possible to explain everything to you because there are things, I just can't tell you."

Emma was exasperated by his vagueness. "Fine then!" she sulked. "I don't need to meet them. I can just go on being your dirty little secret!"

He walked over and wrapped her in his strong embrace. "You are even more beautiful when you're angry. Do you know that?" he said softly, trying to lighten the mood.

She shrugged within his arms. "Whatever."

"Whatever?" he asked, gingerly raising her chin with a finger to look into her face. "What we have is real, and it's between the two of us. Meeting my parents doesn't confirm my love for you in any way. I love you the way you are. I love your spirit and your courage. I even love your nastiness when you don't like what I'm telling you. It turns me on."

Emma was aggravated and refused to look into his eyes. He continued to stare at her until she finally lifted her eyes and met his gaze.

"Whatever," she mumbled. "Fine. At least I know you're a good lay. I have that to hang on to," she joked.

"What do you mean 'a good lay'? I'm a great lay! Hell, girl, I'm the best fucking lay you've ever had!" he said, slipping off her thong and rubbing his hand gently between her legs.

He was a great lover, always making sure that she was satisfied. He was never greedy about sex, and it aroused him just to see her turned on. A soft moan escaped her and she found his lips and began to kiss him with a fiery passion. Then she unbuttoned his shirt and worked her way down his body. When they made love that night, it was more intense than usual. They were both aroused, but it was Emma's slow, simmering anger over certain words he had uttered that fueled her passion. She knew he belonged to her, even if he wasn't willing to let her meet his parents. But a red flag had now been waved in front of her. There was a reason he hadn't told his family about her, and she was disgusted with herself for being so dependent on him. It was time for her to find a way to support Izzy and herself.

The next morning, when Salvatore came back from the Italian Market with olives, bread, and cheese, Emma was waiting for him in the kitchen.

"Salvatore," she began, "it's time I went out and made my own money again. I was thinking about going back to Doubles."

He turned quickly and looked at her. "No! I don't want you doing that anymore," he said without mincing words. "I give you everything you need."

She looked at him with confidence. "I know you do, but I need to be independent. Which means I have to be able to support Izzy and myself."

"So why not get a job waitressing?" he suggested. "You worked in a restaurant for a while. You-you can do that again..."

He was stammering, grasping at straws. Salvatore adored Emma and wanted to keep her to himself. He couldn't bear the thought of other men looking at her now that she belonged to him. He wanted to be the only man on earth whom she paid attention to.

"Listen," he said thoughtfully, "I'll talk to a friend of mine who owns a small café in the Italian Market. I'm sure he could use you there. You could work lunches. This way, you could be home for Izzy in the morning and when she gets back from school."

Isabella attended the Christopher Columbus Charter School; a school Salvatore had insisted was right for her.

The following afternoon, Salvatore told Emma about Sabrina's Café on Christian Street. "The owner will be waiting for you. He needs a dependable waitress during lunch," he explained. Emma wasn't thrilled that Salvatore had arranged a job for her, but was still willing to check it out and see if it was a place where she wanted to work. Later that day, she met the owner, a short, stocky Italian man who was very nice to her but left her feeling uneasy. She wondered why and realized, in retrospect, that he had seemed nervous and too anxious to please her. He had seemed to be trying too hard. Emma didn't know that Salvatore had convinced the café owner that hiring her would be a favor to him. The café owner was more than eager to please the Mafia boss's son and, having met Emma, deduced correctly that this beautiful woman was more to Salvatore than a mere acquaintance. He introduced her to the other employees and asked her to return the next day.

"So how did your meeting go?" Salvatore asked when she returned.

"It was fine," she told him. "He's kind of a nervous little guy, though. Is there something wrong with him?" she pressed, wanting to know more and surmising accurately that the café owner was nervous because of her status as Salvatore's girlfriend. "Did you tell him I was your girlfriend?"

"Of course I didn't tell him that!" he retorted. "I wanted you to get the job on your own merit."

The skeptical look remained on her face. "Well, that's funny, because he didn't even ask me if I had experience," she remarked. She turned to Tony, who was enjoying a cup of hot espresso. "Could you please drive me to Ambler tomorrow so that I can pick up my car?" she asked. "I want to be able to drive myself around. It's time things got back to normal."

Tony nodded. "Sure. Whatever you want," he said, looking over at Salvatore, who seemed unfazed by her request.

Emma entered the bedroom and sat down on the chair next to the bed. She was tired, but her mind still toyed with the idea of going back to Doubles. She knew she could make so much more money there but was conflicted because of Salvatore's objections. She didn't want to hurt him, but she didn't want him making decisions for her either. She decided to give her job at the café a week and see how it went. If she didn't like it, she would again broach the topic of going back to Doubles.

Chapter Eighty-Eight

When Tony drove Emma past her old apartment in Ambler the next day, her stomach lurched. Katie had moved her car from its usual place and parked it in front of her own apartment. The moment they pulled up to Katie's place she came running outside and the two young women excitedly greeted each other.

Katie whispered, "I've missed you so much, Em!"

Emma gave her an affectionate squeeze. "I know, Katie. I've missed you too! Everything is so different now, but all in a good way. Izzy is doing great. She's really happy, and Salvatore treats us well."

"I'm happy for you, Em," her friend replied, smiling at her. "You deserve to be happy. Come inside. I have some cold beers waiting for us."

Emma turned and waved good-bye to Tony, who had remained in the car. As he drove off, his gaze lingered protectively on her reflection in his rearview mirror; he had to make sure she was all right. He wanted Emma to be safe and not just because Salvatore would literally kill him if her life was endangered in any way. Tony cared just as much for her well-being, because over the past year he had really come to like her.

Inside her apartment, where the two women made themselves comfortable, Katie cracked open a Budweiser and handed it to her friend.

"So what the fuck's up? Tell me everything!" she begged.

"Oh my God, there's so much to tell!" Emma replied. "Salvatore is a great guy and we have incredible sex. He's hot, he's powerful, and he's rich! What more is there?" She gave her friend a teasing glance. Then she turned serious. "I love him, Katie," she confessed. "The thing is, he hasn't taken me to meet his parents, and I get the feeling he isn't ready for it yet. He's already admitted that he hasn't told them about me. He's trying to keep our relationship a secret from them. I did bring up the subject with him, but don't want to nag him about it and make him feel like I'm some freak who is all needy and shit. I told him I wanted to go back to work at Doubles and he got upset. He said he didn't want me stripping anymore. So he hooked me up with a waitressing job at a café. Some place his friend owns."

Katie looked at her with concern. "So are you happy?"

Emma leaned back in her chair. "I've never been happier," she said. "He makes me smile all the time. But dragging his feet about taking me to meet his family really bothers me. It's like he's ashamed of me. What terrifies me most is that I'm so comfortable with him. If the time ever came for me to move on, away from his life, how would I ever know?"

Katie shook her head. "When smiles fade, girl, that's when you know it's time to move on. Until that time, you need to focus on how happy you are with him. Izzy is doing well and he clearly adores you."

Emma reached over and clasped her friend's hand. "When smiles fade," she repeated. "Thanks, Katie." Emma raised her beer. "Here's to good friends with great tits!" she exclaimed.

They knocked their beer bottles together and laughed.

As Emma drove back to Philly, she reminded herself how simple life could be sometimes. As long as she and Izzy were happy, she didn't have a reason to be bummed out. She felt so much better after talking to Katie. She realized how much she had missed having other women to talk to. At Salvatore's apartment, she was always surrounded by men. She had tried chatting with Macie on several occasions, but had found her to be a strange bird, a girl who was strung too tight. Emma resolved to make a serious effort to spend more time with Katie.

The next few weeks flew by. Her new job wasn't the most exciting career option, if you could call it that, but at least it gave her a chance to go out of the apartment every day. At the café, she was able to talk to other people and she enjoyed listening to their stories. There were, she was beginning to realize, many colorful people who lived in South Philly, tough on the outside, but all heart on the inside.

Emma loved the Italian Market and the culture there. It was a Tuesday afternoon. The lunch crowd was gone and Emma had stayed a bit longer to help prep for the dinner crowd. When she was finally done, she left the café and stopped at the butcher to pick up steak for a special dinner she planned to prepare for Salvatore. Her conversation with Katie had put her relationship with him in perspective and she was in a good mood, grateful now for what they shared.

She had just stepped out of the butcher store and was walking down the pavement when Emma heard one of the store owners yell out half a block from where she stood:

"Salvatore, you forgot your salami!"

A wide smile of recognition spread across her face as she saw Salvatore turn and walk back the way he had come. Emma quickened her pace to catch up with him.

Then a child's voice rang out happily. "Daddy! Daddy!"

Emma looked up and paused in mid-stride. A little boy was running toward Salvatore, who had stopped and was waiting for him with outstretched arms. The moment the boy reached him, he bent down and hoisted him up in his arms. It was only then that Emma noticed the third person, a tall, dark-haired woman who had caught up with them. Salvatore leaned down and kissed her. Emma heard the little boy speak again.

"Mommy," he asked in his endearingly squeaky voice, "if Daddy says yes, can we go to the zoo this weekend?"

"Sure, son," the woman replied, winking at Salvatore.

As the three of them turned to walk away, Salvatore reached out and pulled his wife to him. Then some kind of sixth sense made him glance over his shoulder. Maybe it was the morbid hatred that Emma suddenly felt for him or that she was glaring at him so hard that she had broken some invisible barrier to let her into his head. When their eyes met, his own were filled with remorse. His wife sensed the change in his body language and followed his stare. The moment she noticed the stunningly beautiful blonde behind them looking back at her husband with an expression of dismay and anger, she knew what to do. Entwining her arm with her husband's, she pulled him forward firmly, as though Emma was invisible. Mrs. Morano wasn't naïve enough to be unaware of Salvatore's other women, but she had told herself that there was no reason why she had to acknowledge their existence. Denying his many infidelities was the most effective way of keeping their marriage strong and healthy, she reasoned.

Emma swiveled around and ran in the opposite direction toward her car. She got in, laid her head on the steering wheel, and cried like a baby. Minutes passed before she started to bang her hands on the wheel, unleashing all of the anger, disillusionment, and sense of loss that overwhelmed her. No, she told herself, this can't be happening. She desperately wanted to pretend that she hadn't noticed him standing there with another woman and child. She had put so much hope and love into her relationship with Salvatore that she now felt petrified of living without him. Her chest heaved as grief washed over her. I have lost him, she told herself. Pain stung her heart and sank deep into her bones. As she had when Gracie had died, Emma felt utterly alone once again.

Chapter Eighty-Nine

Once Emma's sobs subsided, she started the car and slowly drove back to the apartment. There was no choice for her now, she thought; the decision had already been taken out of her hands. She felt the old ghosts of loss and sorrow creep in and wrap their long, bony fingers around her soul.

She thought of Katie's words: "When smiles fade, girl, you'll know it's time to move on." Those words had seemed so meaningful to her at the time they were uttered. They had convinced her about the importance of loving Salvatore unconditionally, without harboring expectations, and learning to cherish the life they had together. Now those very words had come back to haunt her, helping her sever all ties with him and turn her back on all they had shared.

Emma was honest enough to acknowledge to herself that she had never experienced a moment of peace until she became a part of Salvatore's life. Living with him had been such a blissful time in her life that she had stopped worrying and agonizing about her past. She had even been able to release the anger that would occasionally gnaw at the pit of her stomach, especially when she thought about her parents and the cruelties they had heaped on Gracie and her.

When Salvatore returned to the apartment an hour later, he found Emma in the bedroom, packing her clothes.

"Emma, wait," he said urgently, "we have to talk about this. It's not what you think."

She stared at him dully, her eyes loveless. "You're a married man with a son," she said, her voice devoid of expression. "You've lied to me and kept me here like your little whore. I want nothing more to do with you. Go back to your family."

Anger at her words flared within him and he moved suddenly in her direction, his attitude almost threatening. Emma stood her ground without flinching. His stance made the tiny hairs on her arms rise. But, as she stared back at him, she thought to herself, who the fuck does he think he is, coming at me like that? Big Mafia man!

Emma's refusal to be intimidated wasn't lost on Salvatore. He smiled inwardly, marveling at her strength and courage. They were what he admired about her most. When he was within touching distance, he paused and took a deep breath.

"Look, Emma," he said earnestly, "I love you. I was only twenty-two when I married the woman who is now my wife. She has been a good Italian wife and mother. She fulfills all my family's expectations. But I don't love her in the same way that I love you. I'm married to her, but you are my soul mate, the woman I was meant to live my life with."

Emma turned away from him, her sense of loss threatening to make her throw herself into his arms, to fill the empty space in her chest where her heart had thrived. Instead, she continued packing her belongings. Salvatore stared at her with deep regret. He knew he had lost the only woman he'd ever loved. Unable to come to terms with this devastating reality, he sank into the chair in the bedroom as she moved about silently, emotionless, arranging her possessions in suitcases.

"Where will you go?" he managed to ask.

"Salvatore," she said, not even trying to conceal her frustration, "go home to your wife and kid."

He stood and went over to her, putting his arms around her, but she stiffened in his embrace. Reluctantly he released her, lifting her chin with a finger so that she was looking directly into his face.

"All right, Bella. I understand," he said gently. "I want you to know that I love you. If you need anything, anything at all, you know how to get in touch with me."

She wanted to scream that all she ever needed from him was his love and honesty. As much as she wanted to stay there with him, she felt she'd be no better than her own mother, who would have done anything to keep her man. She softened for just a quick moment. "Thank you for everything you've done for us. I wish I could stay here and be fine with this, but I can't. If I ever need you, I will call."

Then she turned her back to him and continued packing. After he'd left the room, she felt drained and empty inside. After all these years, she had become, once again, the nonentity Pepper had reduced her to. Her tears were spent now. No internal conflict tormented her. All she felt was the urge to leave this place as quickly as possible.

A few hours later Emma and Izzy stood in the foyer. Tony and Vincent had come out of the kitchen to say good-bye. "Now listen," Tony told her, giving her a hug, "ya know how to get a hold of us if you need to."

Vincent hugged her next and the two men knelt down and focused on Izzy. "Ya keep bein' bossy like you are, okay? When ya grow up you're gonna be a real good lawyer. Ya take care of your Aunt Emma, ya hear?" Tony instructed the child.

Moments later Salvatore was standing with them at the front door, and after Izzy had said a bewildered good-bye to him, Emma loaded their possessions into her car and left.

"Where are we going, Aunt Em?" Izzy asked uncertainly.

"To Katie's," Emma replied in a reassuring voice.

"Can we go back home to Salvatore afterward?" Isabella wondered aloud.

"No, Izzy. That's not our home anymore. You and I are going on an adventure to find a new home," Emma replied, trying to make it sound exciting.

Izzy slumped against the car door, tightly clutching the stuffed giraffe Salvatore had given her on her birthday. "I don't want a new home," she sulked. "I want to go back to my room."

Emma drove back to Ambler in silence. By the time they reached Katie's apartment, Izzy had fallen asleep. Emma carried her in and Katie put the child on the sofa and covered her with a blanket. Then she joined her friend in the kitchen.

"What the hell, Em?" she asked in a low voice so as not to awaken Izzy.

Teary-eyed and emotional, Emma began explaining what had happened that afternoon. Katie listened intently, trying hard to support her friend's stance, although she genuinely believed that Emma had found a better life with Salvatore and didn't want her to give it up on a mere whim. But as Emma finished recounting her story, even Katie couldn't argue against her decision to leave Salvatore. The man was not just someone's husband, he was a father too, and it would be wrong to try and convince Emma to return to him. There was no future there for her. Besides, Katie knew how resolute her friend could be. There was no way she would ever be able to change her mind.

"So now what, Em?" she asked sadly. "What's your plan?"

"I don't know," Emma replied, sounding helpless and unsure. "I haven't had time to think. Could I stay here for a couple of days? Do you think Bryce would mind?"

"I'm sure it will be fine with him," Katie lied smoothly, knowing quite well that her boyfriend would be furious at the prospect of Emma and Izzy staying with them and crowding an apartment they themselves had outgrown. Then she decided to be upfront. "Em, I should tell you," she said. "Bryce was offered a job. A really good job as a realtor in Nevada, and we're moving out there in three weeks."

Emma looked up from the coffee her friend had made her. "That's great, Katie," she said without enthusiasm.

Her disappointment at the news was obvious. She had been counting on staying with Katie until she could get her shit together and go back to Doubles. Going back to dancing wouldn't be that difficult, but without someone who could babysit Izzy for her at night, it would be impossible.

Emma realized with a pang that of her only two friends, one was already far away and the other would soon be gone. Brianna was in Germany and now Katie would be leaving for Nevada. All she could think to do was to sleep on it. As she lay on the floor next to Izzy that night, she considered doing something different. Maybe the moment had come for her to move far away? She considered going to Saint Thomas, like the waitress she'd met there. But what would she do for work? She hadn't seen any strip clubs there during their stay. Besides, she would still need someone to babysit Izzy. That option seemed just too complicated with a small child. And she knew that no matter what decision she made, Izzy would have to be her first priority.

Chapter Ninety

The next morning when Bryce came into the kitchen where the two women were having coffee, Emma could tell from his expression that he wasn't happy about having guests in the apartment. Fucking asshole, she thought. She had woken up knowing there was only one option open to her.

"Katie," she now said, "we're going to head out today. I can tell Bryce is pissed that we're here."

Katie was torn between disappointment and relief. Bryce had, in fact, torn into her because she had allowed them to stay even for one night.

"I pay the fucking bills here!" he had barked. "I don't want your freeloading friend and her ankle-biting kid hanging around eating my food and sucking up my electricity."

Although Katie had been livid with him, she could say little in Emma's defense. Bryce was, after all, the breadwinner and financially ran their home. She knew that any argument about the need to help others would sound lame coming from her.

"I'm sorry, Emma. Where will you go?" Katie asked feeling like a piece of shit.

"I have one place left I can try," Emma answered. "If that doesn't work, I'll figure something else out. Don't worry about us. You know we'll be fine. I've been through worse. By the way, I'll need the key to my storage locker where you've kept all of our shit—my furniture and things—from the apartment."

Katie opened a kitchen drawer and handed her the small key she'd kept inside.

"I packed everything as best I could," she told her, "but since I had to get your shit out quick, I didn't do too good a job."

After lunch, Emma carried Izzy out to the car, "I probably won't get to see you before you leave for Nevada," she said sadly. "Let me know once you're settled in."

Katie assured her they would stay in touch and remain friends forever. She really meant it. But well-intentioned as the promise was, Emma knew it was one they were both incapable of keeping. She started the car and pulled away as Katie continued to wave at them from the curb until they were out of sight.

Emma headed for the only place she knew where she might get shelter. Half an hour later, she parked in Kensington in front of the house where she had lived with Sydney and the herd. As they walked up the broken steps, Izzy chattered in happy anticipation of seeing Sydney again. Emma was pleasantly surprised that her niece remembered her friend and took some comfort in the child's excitement. Emma knocked on the front door and the pair stood, perfectly still, waiting anxiously for someone to answer.

Jamie, one of the housemates they had known, answered the door. Just as when they had lived there before, he was stoned out of his mind, and Emma had to introduce herself three times before he even began making the connection.

"Yeah!" he finally said. "I remember you, Emma! You're the chick who cooked us Thanksgiving dinner one year, right?"

"Yeah, that's me," she answered dryly, annoyed at his pathetic state. He was swaying in the doorway and his eyes were barely open. She remembered how much she had disliked him when they lived there the last time. He was trashed day and night.

Izzy's hand tightened on Emma's when the boy leaned down a little too close to her and said, "Yeah, I remember you too. You sure look just like your mom!"

"Right," Emma said curtly. "Is Sydney here or what?"

"Yeah, man," the boy replied, standing back to let them enter. "She's upstairs with some dude. You can go up, though, if you want to."

As the two of them climbed the stairs to their old room, Emma was afraid of what sights she might come across in the bedroom. She knocked on the door softly.

She heard her friend yell, "Come in! It's open!" and pushed the door open.

When Sydney saw them standing in the doorway, she jumped to her feet. Still naked, she came running up to them.

"Oh my God!" she exclaimed, both excited and moved. "I can't believe you guys are here! Where the hell have you been?" She dropped to her knees and opened her arms. Izzy slid gently into them and snuggled against her. "Hey, little woman!" she said to the child. "How are you? Look how tall you've gotten! I can't believe it! You remember me, right?"

Izzy giggled. "Yeah, Syd, I remember you. Not that good, though. I just remember that you used to play games with me. Now I like to read a lot. I brought all of my books with me. So we can read together. But you should put some clothes on first," she added disapprovingly.

They moved into the bedroom and closed the door. Wrapping herself in an old robe, Syd looked over at her friend who was lying on the mattress in his boxers.

"Dude," she said, "put some clothes on, will ya?"

He laughed and pulled on a pair of dirty jeans.

Sydney explained, "This is a friend of mine. Well, you know," winking at Emma, "a friend with bennies."

Emma looked over at Sydney's friend with disgust. The intensity of her stern green gaze boring into him, willing him to leave, was intimidating. Taking in all of the not-so-subtle signals she sent him, he announced that he was leaving.

"Your friend is kind of a bitch!" he whispered in Syd's ear as he kissed her good-bye.

Emma hadn't said much while he was there. The moment he left, she dropped onto Sydney's mattress and let herself relax.

"Syd, I'm in a jam," she told her friend. "I got away from Ethan and we were living with this guy. Everything was fucking perfect, then I found out he was married, with a kid. We don't have anywhere to go and I thought maybe we could come back here."

Izzy looked up at her pleadingly. "Can we stay here, Syd?" she implored. "Please, please! We don't have anywhere to live," she finished, her eyes brimming with tears.

Syd looked at Emma. "You know how this works," she said. "I need to talk it over with the herd. We have four new people living with us who weren't here when you were, but a lot of the herd will remember you guys."

Sydney left them for a moment to go downstairs and see if there were enough members of the herd home to take a vote. To her delight, bringing Emma and Izzy back into the fold proved to be no problem at all. She ran back upstairs with the good news.

On her way out to the car to get their clothes, Emma relaxed, knowing that at least they had a roof over their heads, even if it did leak.

The first couple of nights took some adjustment for Izzy. She had grown accustomed to having her own room and was now forced to share a room with five other people. Even though she was only six years old, the young girl wasn't able to adapt as quickly to her changed circumstances as Emma had hoped. In the first two weeks of living in Kensington, she told her aunt every day that she wanted to go home and back to her school. Over time, however, Izzy began to come to terms with her new surroundings. But she did occasionally cry herself to sleep. For she sorely missed Salvatore, the only father she had ever known and loved.

Chapter Ninety-One

Over the first couple of days, Emma filled Sydney in about everything that had happened with Ethan and Pete and how she had ended up living with Salvatore. She explained about Salvatore's wife and son and her decision to leave his home.

"You must feel like shit!" Syd observed. "I mean, it sounds like you had everything and you just walked away from it all."

Emma shrugged. "Yeah, it was great to live that way, but I couldn't be his dirty little secret. I mean, he wasn't going to leave his wife. He wanted me to just accept the situation."

"I'm sorry that happened to you, Em. Do you miss him?" Syd asked curiously.

"Yes, I miss him," Emma admitted without shame, "but it's better this way. It would have bothered me to stay. He made me believe he spent every other weekend away from the apartment so that he could take care of business, but now I know the truth. If I had stayed, I would have wondered what he was doing with his wife when he went back home. It's all too much. I wish it hadn't turned out this way. But it did."

As Sydney listened intently, she thought that if she herself had been raped, then fell in love only to discover that the one guy she ever wanted to be with was married, she would have been devastated, but she wouldn't have left Salvatore. She would have stayed with him and lived in his home forever. Who cared if he was married? Syd couldn't understand why Emma was so freaked out about the man being married. She could have had a nice place to live in and plenty of money too. Had Syd known Emma well enough, she would have understood that within her friend burned a fierce desire for independence and a determination to never compromise on anything ever again.

Emma put Salvatore behind her as best she could and focused on taking her life back. She was looking forward to going back to Doubles and getting Izzy into another school. One week after Emma and Izzy arrived, she informed the herd about the furniture she had in storage and made them an offer: if they helped move it to the house, she would put some of her things in the living room for everyone to use.

The next day, Emma rented a small truck and drove out to the storage locker with some of the housemates. They came home with two beds, one for her and Izzy to share and the other for Sydney. All of the other items were arranged in the common areas, replacing makeshift furniture like milk crates that they had collected by picking over trash. For everyone in the house, it was a welcome luxury to have some relatively new furniture, including a kitchen table and chairs.

The rest of Emma and Izzy's belongings remained packed in three cardboard boxes. Emma put them in the corner of the bedroom, promising herself that she would go through them in the next day or two. In the meantime, she contacted Jay at Doubles and was asked to come in for an "interview," which really meant that he wanted to make sure she hadn't lost her figure since she left. She had also talked Syd into babysitting Izzy at night for five dollars an hour while she was at work. It was the first regular, paying job Sydney had ever held. Earning somewhere around $140 a week was quite beyond her imagination.

Following her "interview" at Doubles, which required her to stand in front of Shiver and Jay wearing only a thong, Emma went back to work the next evening. Although many new dancers had joined Doubles since she worked there last, there were still some that Emma knew. The new girls weren't pleased to face the kind of competition she brought to the club. Emma was smoking hot and experienced. Of course, the regulars who frequented the bar remembered her and were all happy to see her back.

The first night Emma got back on stage boosted her confidence and her sense of power. Dancing to the music, she derived immense pleasure from watching the men go wild over her every move. She gazed at each of them, her demeanor reeking of sensuality, and none of the men could tell that her heart had turned to stone and she would never love another man again.

It was obvious to Emma that many of the other dancers were standoffish with her. With Brianna and Katie so far away she'd hope to fire up some female friendships at the club. But jealous women made for catty times, and her guard was up when she went into work every night. Other than

Shiver and Foster, it seemed the only people who really wanted to spend any time with her were the men that frequented the bar.

Emma had been back at Doubles for a month when Maggie, a new dancer who had joined a few days before, approached her with an idea. "Hey, Emma, I was thinking that we could team up and put on a show. You know, some kissing, undressing each other, that kinda shit. I think we could make a lot of money."

Maggie was a stunning girl, just as beautiful as Emma but in a different way: she had a long, lean body with black hair and light blue eyes that under the black lights of the go-go club appeared to have an iridescent glow. She had full, plump lips, and her facial structure couldn't have been more perfect. She was a sweet person and Emma enjoyed her company.

When they put their talents together on stage, they were entwined in a mass of silky hair, flesh, and muscle. It was the kind of show men fantasized about. With these two dazzling creatures touching each other, the clients went wild, and as a result their tips were generous. After their first performance together, they sat down at the bar for drinks and to get to know each other better.

"So how did you end up at Doubles?" Emma asked Maggie.

"Well, the money is really good, and my pimp thought this would be an easy way to supplement our income. I do some hooking on the side. Rock, that's my pimp, sets me up with guys and I meet them at different places," Maggie explained, as if it were nothing.

"You're okay with hooking?" Emma pushed.

"Let me tell you, it can be a hell of a lot worse. My family sort of lost me when I was a kid. I ended up living in pure hell. Lots of horny adults out there, if you know what I mean. So dancing here and turning some tricks during the week is a hell of a lot easier than when I was a kid," Maggie explained with an odd sense of distance.

Emma's interested was peaked and she had to know Maggie's story.

Maggie had a dark, tragic life that began when she was eight years old. She had been a victim of sex-trafficking. She gave Emma a small glimpse into her past, and the two girls became friends quickly, having shared a traumatic childhood. Each of them had a tainted view of the world based on all they had endured.

Emma felt sorry for the girl. They were about the same age, but Maggie seemed trapped in a world of sex. She couldn't imagine having to live her friend's life. It was in these moments of pure clarity that Emma realized how lucky she was compared to some of the others. Emma was intent on making sure that Maggie remained a friend forever. They didn't have much in common; their childhood stories veered in two different directions. But they shared the same emptiness, the feeling in the pit of their stomachs when they lay alone in their beds at night waiting and hoping for sleep to rescue them from the loneliness.

As time passed, Emma and Maggie began lap dancing together, earning a lot of money with each act they performed. Emma thrived on the sense of independence her earnings gave her and looked with satisfaction at the other dancers who had cast her aside. Watch out girls, Emma thought, this bitch is back, and she intended to use everything in her arsenal to make as much money as possible!

Chapter Ninety-Two

B ack at home, Sydney spent her evenings with Izzy. They read and played games together. At nine o'clock sharp, she would put Isabella to bed and spend the rest of the time hanging out with her friends in the common area. It was easy work and she felt fortunate to be earning such a large amount of money just to hang out with the kid. She often treated the others to beer and once in a while scored a bag of weed.

One evening soon after Emma had left the house for her shift at Doubles, Sydney gave in to peer pressure and went off to buy weed, setting out with a couple of the girls to find one of the many dealers who hung out on Kensington Avenue. The group had planned to be gone only for an hour, but once the girls got to Kensington Avenue, they were sidetracked by one of the local prostitutes who accused them of hooking in her spot, a common occurrence in their filthy slice of the world.

"You fucking bitches need to get the fuck out of here!" the woman screamed. "This here is my spot and I'll fuck you up if you even think about trying to make money on my turf!"

Syd and the other two girls were used to this kind of bullshit. Besides, they were experiencing a high, a sense of power, that night.

"Shut the fuck up, you whore!" one of the girls yelled back at the prostitute.

In an instant, the two of them were snarled in a fist fight. Syd and the other girl kept egging their friend on. Down the side of a building came another girl, running toward them with a knife in her hand. Noticing her approach, Sydney snatched up a discarded beer bottle from the street and flung it at her. The bottle hit the other hooker in the face. She went down on her knees, her hands clutching the gash on her forehead in an attempt to hold back the blood that was gushing from the large slash.

Meanwhile Syd had run over to help her friend kick the shit out of the other hooker. Sydney was a fighter who had lived on the streets of Kensington for a long time and had honed her combat skills after having her ass whipped several times.

Ten minutes after the fight broke out, the police arrived and nabbed all of the teens. They were questioned individually, handcuffed, and shoved into police cars, one at a time. Syd was in a panic because she had left Izzy at the house with some of the other teens.

When Emma got home at eleven thirty at night, she heard a voice yelling upstairs. Recognizing it as Jamie's, she took the stairs two at a time.

"You're a fucking pain in the ass!" she heard him scream. "Just shut the fuck up and go to sleep! I don't know where Syd is and I'm sick and tired of hearing you bawl!"

Then she heard Izzy's thin, scared voice yell back, "I want my Aunt Em! Leave me alone!"

Emma burst open the door. There stood Jamie, reeking of alcohol and unsteady on his feet. Glancing at Izzy, she noticed that her face was red and streaked with tears and her eyes bulged from crying. She stared the boy down, then strode up to him and stood facing him almost nose to nose. If she could have swallowed that motherfucker alive, she would have gladly done it at that moment.

"Who the fuck do you think you are talking to her like that?" she demanded.

"That fucking little brat over there!" he said, pointing to Izzy with a shaking finger. "That bitch, Sydney, went out to score some weed and left her here. Everyone else split and I got stuck with her. I'm nobody's babysitter. You understand?"

"Oh, I understand perfectly," Emma said, her calm, even voice laden with sarcasm. "Now get out! Go and crawl back into the hole you came out of. And don't you ever mess with my kid again!"

Grumbling under his breath, Jamie slunk off. It wasn't that he didn't like Emma or her kid; on the contrary, he had volunteered to stay with Isabella when the others decided to go out. Jamie thought she was a beautiful little girl, so beautiful that he saw womanlike qualities in her. So he was very annoyed when she started crying for her aunt.

Alone in the room with a sniffling Izzy, Emma asked gently, "What happened, Iz? Where's Syd?"

"I don't know, Aunt Em," she answered in a trembling voice between hiccups, "she went out, saying she'd be back in an hour, and left me with some of the kids. Then they left me here with Jamie. But Syd never came home. And Jamie was mean to me the whole time. He told me to sit in the living room and not say a word. When I asked him if I could read, he said I was too stupid to read. Then he grabbed me by my arm and dragged me up here and yelled at me. I didn't do anything wrong. I swear! I was being good."

Emma sat down on the bed next to her and put her arms around her. Her heart went out to Izzy who had been left alone and defenseless against the teenage asshole. From her own experience, Emma knew exactly how that felt. She stroked Izzy's hair and sat with her quietly, until she felt her begin to relax.

"It's all right, sweetie," Emma soothed her, "I know you're a good girl. I'm sure you didn't do anything wrong. So stop worrying about it. Let's go find out what happened to Sydney."

She picked up her purse, reached into it for her cell phone, and noticed that she had missed a call from a number that was unfamiliar to her. Mystified, she dialed it.

"Kensington Police Department," a voice at the other end announced.

"Hi, my name is Emma Murphy," she said. "I missed a call from this number."

She was confused as to why the police would be calling her. Then a shiver of alarm went through her as she figured it might have something to do with Sydney.

A couple of minutes later, the officer came back on the line. "We have a Sydney Cooper in custody," he stated. "She asked if you could come and make bail."

"Why is she there?"

"She was arrested for disorderly conduct. A few girls got into a fight. Are you coming down or not?" he snapped, his patience worn thin.

"How much is the bail?" Emma wanted to know. She was beginning to lose her own patience with him because of his lack of providing the details.

"Five hundred," he told her and went silent.

"I'll be there. Tell her I'm on my way."

Hanging up the phone, Emma heaved a sigh of relief. The charges could have been far more serious and the bail so steep that she might not have been in a position to pay it. So little Syd had got herself into a brawl on

Kensington Avenue, she mused. While Emma was furious with Sydney for having left Izzy with some of the kids and ultimately someone as irresponsible and intolerant as Jamie, she was also secretly proud of her for not being afraid to fight when the situation called for it. Knowing Syd, Emma assumed that she hadn't started the fight, but had exchanged blows in an effort to defend either herself or her friends.

She took Izzy by the hand and urged, "Come on, we need to go get Sydney."

"Where is she?" her niece asked with a child's curiosity.

"She's in jail," Emma replied, then amended, "I mean she's with the police. They're keeping her safe until we get there."

Izzy ran to find her shoes and slipped into them. "I've never been to a police station before!" she exclaimed excitedly.

Her aunt, however, was feeling quite the opposite. The last place Emma wanted to see was the inside of a police station.

Chapter Ninety-Three

As Sydney got into the car with Emma, she was apprehensive of her reaction. How much did Emma know? Had anyone told her they had gone out to score weed?

"Thanks for coming to get me, Em," she said tentatively, trying to gauge her friend's mood. "I'm sorry about all of this. We were minding our own business until this hooker came up and accused us of muscling in on her turf. She thought we were prostitutes and wanted to steal her business. Her friend pulled a knife and I flung a beer bottle at her—I nailed that chick right in the forehead!" she snickered.

Emma listened patiently until Syd had finished.

"Shit happens, Syd," she said quietly. "The same thing happened to Bri, Gracie, and me when we were living out of our car. That's not the problem, as far as I'm concerned. The problem is that you left Izzy at the house so that you could go out and buy pot. I came home and found Jamie screaming at her. Why would you do that, leave her there with the others?"

"It was stupid," Sydney admitted remorsefully. "I swear it'll never happen again. Fuck, Em, this is the best job I've ever had! I didn't even think we'd be gone an hour. I'm truly sorry."

"You're right," Emma responded, her voice like steel. "You won't do it again, because if you do, I'll kick your fucking ass. I love you, Syd, but Iz will always come first. Are we clear?" Her tone made it obvious that she wasn't joking.

"Yeah, we're clear. Trust me, it won't happen again. I'll never leave her. Are we cool?" Sydney asked, hopeful that they could put this behind them.

"Yeah, we're cool."

"I'm cool too," Izzy chimed in from the backseat of the car. "Can we read when we get home?"

Syd turned to face her. "Yeah, little woman, we can read. I'll read as much as you want tonight."

When Emma tucked Izzy into bed that night, she lingered for a few minutes.

"I love you very much," she said gently. "You know that. Right, Iz?"

"Yeah, I know. And guess what? Everyone is scared of you, but I'm not, 'cause you're my aunt and you protect me," she said.

But the uncertainty in her eyes told Emma that she was looking for confirmation of this assumption. Isabella was still a little worried that her aunt might be angry with her over her confrontation with Jamie. Having observed how coldly Emma had treated the boy and how scared he had been of her, Izzy wanted to be sure she had remained in her good graces.

"That's right, Iz," her aunt now reassured her. "I will always protect you."

"Even if I did something really bad?" the child pressed and started to cry.

"What's wrong, Iz? What did you do that was really bad?"

"Jamie was really mean to me tonight. Not just the usual stuff, like calling me an idiot or stupid. Last night, when I was in the kitchen, he started barking at me like a dog. I tried to get away from him, but he just kept coming at me and shouting, 'Woof! Woof! Woof!' Then he put his teeth together real hard and growled at me. I started crying and told him to stop, but he wouldn't. When I tried to leave the kitchen, he just kept pushing me back into the corner, so I couldn't get out. He pushed me really hard! See?" she said, pulling up her shirt so her aunt could examine the small bruise on her hip.

Izzy hesitated and shrank back from her. "What is it, Iz?" Emma asked. "What else happened? I promise I won't get mad at you," she assured her, wanting to know what else Jamie had done to her.

"After he barked at me, he dragged me up here. And," she looked down at her hands, instinctively knowing that what she'd done was wrong, "he pulled his pants down and told me to pull his weenie."

Emma's eyes grew to the size of silver dollars. Oh fuck me," she thought, he's a fucking dead man. She took a deep breath and held Izzy closer. "What did you do?"

"I told him I wouldn't do it and he locked me in the closet. Then he said I had to stay in there until I was ready to do what he wanted. I got really scared and I was crying really hard and I felt like I couldn't breathe. So I...I told him I would do it. He made me pull on it until mayonnaise came out and then he told me to go to bed. I started crying, and that's when he was yelling at me when you came home," she finished, hoping her aunt would still love her, knowing that she shouldn't have touched a boy's weenie.

"Did he touch you down there?" Emma asked, pointing to Izzy's crotch.

Izzy shook her head and lowered her head in shame. "Listen to me, Iz. You didn't do anything wrong. Jamie never should have done that to you. Understand?"

Emma leaned over and kissed Isabella on the forehead. "I want you to go to sleep now. Don't worry about Jamie. He'll never bother you again. All right?"

Izzy nodded vigorously, feeling safe in the arms of her protector.

Once Izzy had fallen asleep, Emma focused her thoughts on taking care of unfinished business with Jamie. For the briefest moment Emma's body flushed with heat as she began to regret her decision not to stay with Salvatore. At least with him, she knew that this tragic event never would have happened to Isabella. She pushed aside the thought and went downstairs to find Jamie. He was down in the living room, sprawled full-length on her sofa. Reaching down, she pulled his legs up by the knees and flung them away toward the floor.

"Hey, what the fuck!" he protested.

Emma resisted the urge to clobber him to death on the spot. She had a vision of him forcing Izzy to whack him off and she couldn't forget the sight of him screaming at her niece, veins pulsing on his forehead. She knew what a deranged person he was and there was no way he would get away with it. Emma simply couldn't allow it.

She sat down next to Jamie, her stance rigid at first as she set out to manipulate him.

Ignoring her, he picked up a bottle of cheap whiskey off the floor, where he had put it down earlier, and took a long swig.

"Don't you think you've had enough of that shit?" she asked. "You're already wasted."

Emma considered talking him into drinking more so he might drink himself to death. All she had to do was sit there and encourage him to be a sloppy drunk and he would guzzle on command. She contemplated the idea for several minutes, but decided that a death in the house would be an unwelcome event. The herd didn't need the cops coming in, poking around and scrutinizing their living conditions. Several of the tenants were just teenagers, well under the age of eighteen.

While Jamie continued to drink from his bottle of booze, like a baby suckling its mother's breast, Emma watched him. He was a booze-hungry beast. He'd always partied, but now he was a drunken slob from morning till night. She knew she had to get him to trust her, just as she had with Jake years before.

"So, Jamie, how old are you anyway?" Emma now asked, fluttering her emerald greens at him in a flirtatious manner.

"I'm twenty. I mean I'll be twenty-one in a couple of months, I think," Jamie told her.

"Oh. How old were you when you left home?" Emma asked, pretending to be interested in his answer.

"I don't know. Around seventeen or eighteen, I guess."

"Yeah," Emma said. "I left home when I was sixteen. My father was a total asshole. He used to smack me around and my mother was a selfish fucking bitch. I had to get away from them. So I split and landed in Kensington. What about you? I mean, were your parents fucked up too?"

Jamie leaned forward on the sofa. "Nah!" he scoffed. "My parents were fucking saints! My dad is a big shot lawyer. My mom always took care of the family. They're great parents. They would always take us on cool vacations and buy us whatever we needed. I was just so fucking bored living like that! They were always up my ass about going to college and shit. You know, like they thought they knew what was good for me. Like I didn't have a mind of my own. Just because I drank a little, they accused me of wasting my life. Finally I got sick of hearing it and split. Eventually I met one of the people from the herd and came here," Jamie explained righteously.

Emma made a mental note of how lucid he was for someone who had seemed dead drunk just a minute ago. That gave her an inkling of how much alcohol it took for him to get wasted. She felt the blood rush to her head as she listened to the spoiled jerk-off rattling on about how his life at home with his parents and siblings had been so nice he couldn't stand it anymore and had taken to the streets before joining the herd. Jamie was the first person Emma had met who didn't have a legitimate reason for choosing his current vagabond lifestyle. This made her think even less of him, if that were possible.

"I can't believe you actually left home because your parents wanted you to go to college and have a normal life," Emma said cynically, watching him squirm beside her. "That's what the rest of us here have always longed for but were denied. Seems kind of fucked up, doesn't it?"

"Yeah, well, you don't know, if you've never lived through it," Jamie said defensively, pushing his whiskey toward her. "Want a swig?"

Oh yes, Emma thought to herself, *I certainly do want a swig.* She took the bottle, tilted it, and threw back her head, taking a mouthful of the brown liquid that made her tongue feel as if she had just stuck a lit match on it. Having swallowed it, she let a low howling sound escape from her throat.

Jamie bounced back on the sofa, laughing. "Good shit, ain't it, Emma?"

"That's the grossest fucking stuff I've ever put in my mouth!" she told him. "How the hell do you drink that? If you're gonna guzzle booze every day, you could at least find one that tastes decent. This one's just plain nasty."

Over the next couple of days Emma called out sick from work, claiming to have the flu. She wasn't going to leave Izzy alone for one moment. In fact, Emma made a point of spending more time with Jamie after she put Izzy to sleep. She knew exactly how to handle the situation and called upon what she had learned years before to execute her plan.

Chapter Ninety-Four

A few days later, Emma asked Sydney to take Izzy to the movie theater in downtown Philly to see the movie, Annie. They would ride the bus into the city, and Emma had offered them cab fare for the journey back home. Izzy was particularly excited about the ten dollars her aunt had handed her to buy a treat of her choice from the snack bar.

"I'm getting a big bucket of popcorn!" Izzy had told her, ecstatic.

After they left, Emma went up to her room pretending to read. She had placed the bait on the hook the day before, flirting with Jamie like a young teenage girl. Now all she had to do was wait for him to take a bite. As she had anticipated, there was a rap on the bedroom door, and a moment later Jamie stepped inside. Emma was sprawled out on the bed in a tee shirt and a pair of daisy dukes, her long legs crossed at the ankles. Jamie eyed her with sexual hunger and she allowed him to be intoxicated by her sensuality. "I saw Syd and Izzy leave. I was going to head down to a bar on Kensington Avenue," he told her. "You wanna come?"

"You know, I'm at bars all the time," Emma explained. "How about if we just have a couple of drinks downstairs?"

"Yeah, okay, I guess," he agreed grudgingly. "But we ain't got that much liquor in the house."

"Well, if we run out," Emma said, licking her lips suggestively and flashing him a provocative smile, "we can go out and get some more, can't we? It's not like there aren't a million fucking places to buy booze around here."

When they went downstairs, Emma found the place empty. All of the other housemates were gone, which, being that it was a Saturday night, wasn't unusual.

"Where is everyone?" she asked, already knowing the answer but wanting confirmation that they were the only two in the house.

"Ah, a lot of them had to work tonight," Jamie told her. "The rest of 'em went over to Fairmount Park for some free concert or benefit or some shit like that."

They settled on the sofa and Jamie began to drink. Emma pretended to join him, but every so often she told him she was going to the bathroom or the kitchen and poured her drink down the drain. Jamie became progressively more intoxicated. He pulled out a joint, lit it, and took a long, hard drag. Then he offered it to Emma.

"No thanks," she said casually. "I don't like pot."

He smiled. "Fine, more for me then."

An hour and a half later, Jamie had gone through eight beers and a pint of whiskey. When he looked at Emma, he was practically cross-eyed. "We need to go get some more shit to drink," he slurred.

He and Emma left the house and headed for downtown Kensington. She had chosen a route along the back streets to avoid being seen together by the hookers and drug dealers on the main drag. At the liquor store, Emma waited in the alley next to the store while Jamie went in and made his purchases with his fake ID. On the twenty-minute walk back to the house, he stopped and led Emma off the street into a grassy area that edged a park. They sat on the grass and he continued to consume more liquor. Finally he leaned over and kissed her.

She played along, leading him on, allowing him to think that the attraction was mutual. She rose to her feet, pulling him up with her, and he drew her to him and slid his hands into the back pockets of her jeans. She almost threw up on him, so repulsed by this slithering snake groping her, this young man who thought he could get away with molesting and terrorizing her niece.

"Come on! Let's go back home where it's more comfortable," she whispered.

On their way back they walked along the same dark, lonely street, lined with more open lots than buildings. It was a part of town that pedestrians generally avoided for fear of encountering the ruthless gangs that often hung there. Emma spotted the place that she had scoped out the day before. She stopped abruptly at a twelve-foot-high chain-link fence. Jamie staggered back, one hand in hers and the other holding his coveted bottle of brown syrup. Emma peered in and scrutinized the area the fence protected.

She grasped Jamie by the arm. "I heard about them having a shitload of copper in there," she whispered. "If you go in and snatch some, you can throw it over the fence to me. We can cash it in and buy enough booze to keep ourselves drunk for a month."

Jamie was so drunk and intent on getting into Emma's pants he would have done anything to please her. He wanted to have sex with her more than he wanted booze, and he always craved alcohol. Girls who looked like her didn't fuck guys who looked like him and he wanted to make that score. Jamie handed her the bottle and slowly climbed up the twelve-foot-tall fence, losing his footing every few seconds and managing to get a hold again after a struggle.

When he reached the other side, he stood unsteadily, then leaned into the chain link fence and said, "Give me a kiss for luck."

Emma took a step back from the fence and looked past him. A grim smile formed on her lips that instantly haunted him. He swiveled around to see what was behind him just as a low growl reached his ears. Three pit bulls stood facing him. His instinct told him to climb back over the fence to safety, but with all the alcohol he'd consumed, his motor skills were impaired, his gait was wobbly, and sheer terror had frozen his feet in place. Before Jamie could put his fingers through the chain-link fence to get the grip he needed to begin his climb, the dogs were on top of him. They gnawed at the flesh of his calves as if they were eating chicken wings served at a Super Bowl party.

Emma flashed him a sinister smile as he screamed and begged her for help.

"Oh, Jamie," she said, her tone malicious, "I thought you liked dogs. At least that's what Izzy told me. Woof! Woof! Woof! You big dick! She told me what you made her do, you fucking perverted prick!"

Jamie's eyes bulged out of their sockets. He realized too late that she had set him up. Terror devoured him as the dogs chomped through his flesh and began to rip him to pieces.

Before walking away, Emma paused a moment longer to read the large sign that Jamie had missed on their way to the liquor store. It read: WARNING: ATTACK DOGS ON PREMISES. NO TRESPASSING. She glanced back once more to witness Jamie's dying moments. He was screaming and thrashing at the dogs, but they had overpowered him and toppled him over. As she moved away, Emma heard the slushy wet sound of canine teeth penetrating human flesh. A moment later, unbeknownst to her, one of the dogs chomped into Jamie's neck and severed his carotid artery. In less than two minutes he was dead.

On her way back home, Emma's adrenaline was pumping and she felt as if she had been injected with a fulfilling serum of retaliation. It was a feeling she hadn't experienced in a long time, not since Pepper and Jake had died. She thought about Gracie and looked up at the night sky.

"Don't you worry, baby sister," she whispered. "I'll take care of your girl, Izzy. I won't let anyone hurt her."

Chapter Ninety–Five

The next morning Emma was awakened by a commotion downstairs. She opened her eyes to find Izzy standing over her.

"What's going on, Iz?" she asked. "Why is everyone making such a racket?"

"I don't know," the child replied, rubbing the sleep from her eyes. "They woke me up too."

"Well, let's go see what all the noise is about," Emma said decisively, pulling on a pair of shorts.

Down in the living room, the girls were crying and consoling each other. The boys stood around, shaking their heads and muttering, "What the fuck!"

Emma managed to find Sydney in all the chaos. "What happened?" she asked.

Sydney's eyes were red from crying. "A couple of the guys went out to buy smokes this morning," she began. "There were a bunch of cops and an ambulance on North Lee Street. The boys heard some guy had got bitten to death by pit bulls last night. They went over to check it out and saw it was Jamie!" The tears welled up in Sydney's eyes again and her voice broke. "Oh God, Em!" she whimpered. "The boys came back and told us the dogs had torn him apart. The worst part is that we can't even claim him, 'cause then the cops will know about all of us and some of the kids here aren't even eighteen."

With that, Syd collapsed, sobbing, into Emma's arms, while Izzy clung tightly to her aunt's leg. But Emma knew if Sydney had the knowledge of what Jamie had made Isabella do a couple of nights before she wouldn't have shed a single tear.

Without having to overact, Emma gave a commendable performance of being deeply concerned. Her housemates had come to depend on her as the responsible one, and her calm, serious demeanor at this moment was not out of character. She consoled Sydney for a while before taking Izzy upstairs to give her a shower while the others remained downstairs, mourning the pathetic pedophile they had all regarded as their friend. People were so sensitive about shit, she thought disapprovingly. Jamie had been a fucking asshole drunk who had staggered around and annoyed everyone most of the time. He had often fought with the other housemates and had certainly crossed the sane line when he made Izzy whack him off. Emma couldn't understand why all of them were so upset at his death. He had been a prick.

As Izzy showered, Emma sat on her bed, smirking, satisfied that she had taken care of one more asshole in the everlasting procession of scum that seemed to come her way. In her world, people who fucked with children were scumbags and shouldn't be given a second chance.

To add to her contentment that he had deserved what he'd gotten, the headline in the local paper the next day read:

"Unidentified Man Mauled to Death by Pit Bulls in Kensington."

According to the report, the dead man's alcohol level, when tested, revealed his severe state of intoxication at the time of his death. He was presumably in no condition either to heed the warning sign about the attack dogs on the premises or to realize he was trespassing on private property. Apart from a fake Pennsylvania driver's license, no other identification was found on the dead man, leaving the police clueless about his real name and origin.

A few months after Jamie's death, Emma took Sydney and Izzy out for dinner at Tracy's Restaurant on Kensington Avenue. After a satisfying meal, they decided to walk a little farther for ice cream. Dusk had fallen and the three chatted as they hurried toward the 7-Eleven to get their much-desired treat. Having bought their ice cream, they stood outside eating it and enjoying the autumn air. Emma teased Sydney about her crush on one of the boys in the house, who she herself didn't think was good enough for her.

"Hey, ladies," a voice rang out, sending icicles up Emma's spine, "how are you doin' tonight?"

Emma looked at the stranger, her green eyes icy. "We're doing fine and we aren't interested in anything you have to say," she shot back.

"Whoa, bitch!" the man smiled, liking the stunning blonde instantly for her spirit. She would be an asset to his team of hookers, he concluded. "Easy does it," he went on. "No need for you to get all jacked up. I was only saying hello."

Emma watched him eyeing up Sydney and then Izzy. She stood protectively in front of her niece, who had dropped her ice cream on the sidewalk in panic when she recognized Rock. Izzy was clearly terrified of the man and Emma could see the fear in Sydney's face as well.

"Let's go, girls," Emma urged them, pushing past Rock.

"Now hold up a minute," he said with a smile that revealed several gaps from missing teeth. "If you ever need some cookie, well, then I'm the man you'll want to see."

Emma stood tall. "We will never want some 'cookie,' as you put it. Don't ever let me catch you coming around my kid again pushing your fucking crack! You stay the fuck away from us and we'll stay away from you!"

"Well, how about you, Syd? You change your mind yet? I still have an opening for you on my crew anytime you're ready," he hissed in a sleazy, perverted tone.

Sydney shook her head and followed Emma as she hustled the two girls away, hearing Rock laughing behind them.

"Fucked-up bitch," he remarked to one of his usual customers, referring to Emma. "She doesn't know who the fuck she's talking to! When she comes around, I'm going to tap that fine piece of ass for a month before I turn her out on the streets."

Emma didn't look back, although she was very tempted to. She was conscious of Izzy being there with her and she had to think of the child's safety first. Besides, the bastard was a big guy and probably carrying a gun.

When they finally turned down a street a block away, Izzy asked, "That's the scary man we saw before, right, Syd?"

Emma shot her friend a scathing look that made her squirm. "You've met him before?" she asked Izzy. "When?" Then her laser gaze focused on her friend. "How does she know him, Syd?"

Intimidated by Emma's tone, Sydney decided to be upfront. "The last time you were living with us in the house," she explained, "Izzy and I went down to Kensington Avenue and he came up to us wanting to know if I wanted to sell for him. He was my father's partner and he's been after me to work for him for the past couple of years. It scared the shit out of us and we never went back again. We went home that day and locked the doors and windows. Rock is a mean bastard, Em. You don't fuck with him. He's the biggest drug lord out here. Most of the pushers and prostitutes work for him. So you need to be careful about what you say to him."

"Oh, so that's Rock!" The pimp, Emma realized. Then she chuckled, "I know exactly who he is. My friend Maggie at Doubles works for him. He might be all big and mighty around here, but I don't give a flying fuck who he is! Nobody fucks with my family and definitely not some overgrown asshole with a name like Rock! I better never hear that you talked to him again. You get me?" She looked at Syd pointedly.

"Yeah, Em. I get you. Let's just get home."

They walked the rest of the way in silence. Emma again thought about Salvatore—knowing that if there was any trouble with Rock that she could always call him. When they were back at home, Izzy finally looked at her aunt. "I'm sorry you were mad at us for talking to that ugly man," she said. "It's wasn't our fault, really. He came up to us, just like he did tonight."

Emma had a jab of guilt for being so harsh, "I'm sorry too, for being so pushy," she said sincerely. "I just don't want anything to happen to either of you. Now how about if we go upstairs, get into our pajamas, and play Monopoly Junior?"

"Yay!" Izzy squealed, running up the stairs ahead of them.

Chapter Ninety-Six

As time passed, a constant flow of people seemed to move in and out of the house. Everyone had just voted in a new girl who would be joining the herd. She would share the bedroom with the three girls, and they all agreed to clean it up a bit before her arrival the next day.

Sydney asked Emma, "Um, do you think maybe it's time to go through those boxes in the corner? Shit, for all we know, there could be stuff in them we could use."

Emma agreed and while Sydney took Izzy downstairs to find something to eat for lunch, she stayed behind and started sorting through the contents of the boxes. The first one was packed with all of Isabella's clothes that she had clearly outgrown. There were a couple of Gracie's possessions that Emma couldn't bear to part with and some of her own clothes that were in decent enough condition to share with some of the other girls in the house.

The second box was filled with old bills and papers and a mishmash of things from all over her old apartment that didn't have a specific purpose: magnets from pizzerias and pens with company names on them, the common things that people collect over time that never had either purpose or value. It was clearly a box of junk. Nonetheless, Emma went through every bit of it to be sure that she wasn't missing anything she might need.

When she opened the last box, an overwhelming sense of happiness swept over her. Inside were many of her old costumes from Doubles. Had she remembered they were there, she would have used them earlier. She sorted through them and kept a couple. The remaining costumes she would cart off to Doubles to see if they might come in handy for some of the other girls, especially the ones just starting out.

At the bottom of the box she found the duffel bag she had used to carry her costumes to work when she lived with Ethan. She opened it up and found a large bag of cosmetics that she also wished she'd known about. As she dumped the rest of the contents on the floor in front of her, out fell Gracie's journal. She had forgotten all about it and felt an overwhelming sense of shame that she had forgotten something so important to her. The thought made her feel like a bad sister. In reality, she was in such a frenzy at the time to get away from Ethan that she'd left behind Gracie's journal.

She picked it up and opened it to a random page so she could gaze at her sister's familiar handwriting. She gently closed the journal and put it under her mattress. She wanted to read through it again, but knew Izzy would be coming back upstairs soon. She reminded herself to take a look at it later.

As she picked up the duffel bag to put the other items back into it, she noticed how heavy it still felt. She looked into it again, closely examining its interior, and unzipped the inner pocket. Inside was a white cloth with something wrapped in it. As Emma took it out of the bag, her excitement peaked. She knew exactly what the object was, even before she had unwrapped Ethan's gun. She did a happy dance inside her head. That stupid asshole had left the gun inside the bag! A gun was what she had been wishing for, ever since they'd run into that slime ball, Rock. Now she had one of her very own that no one else knew about.

There was one other manila folder inside the bag, filled with various papers that Emma knew had belonged to Ethan. She forced herself to go through the folder and found useless bills and old pay stubs from the time he had actually held a job and hadn't yet resorted to sponging off her. At the bottom of the folder was a lone document with the following words printed at the top: "DNA Paternity Test." As Emma quickly scanned down the sheet of paper, she found Isabella's and Ethan's names at the bottom. The results of the test were 99.8 percent positive that Ethan was not the father of Gracie's child.

"Fuck!" Emma exclaimed.

Her mind raced with thoughts, some of them angry, others bitter. It infuriated her to think that the motherfucker had blackmailed her into going back to the apartment by threatening to legally take Izzy away from her. All the events that had led up to Emma being back in Kensington had followed from her mistaken assumption that Ethan was her niece's father. Then her head pounded with gut wrenching questions: if Ethan wasn't Isabella's father, then who was? Why would she lie to me about who she slept with? Or was I so burdened by my own hardship that I had missed signs that my little sister was looking for love from other people?

She had so many questions that would have to remain unresolved, because the only person who knew the answers to them was Gracie. It didn't really matter to Emma who Izzy's father was, because as far as she was concerned, she herself was the only parent in the child's life. The little girl was as content as she could possibly be in their current situation. She had people around who cared for her and loved her deeply. Emma had stopped being the praying type for a long time, but if she had still believed in the power of prayer, she would have prayed for forgiveness for failing to be there when her sister had needed her most. All the lies her sibling had resorted to, all the secrets that were slowly being unveiled told Emma that more had been going on in Gracie's life than she could ever have imagined.

Emma slipped the paternity test report into Gracie's journal and shoved it back under the mattress. She turned and picked up one of her costumes, the one Alessa had given her when she was just starting out at Doubles. Holding it in her hands, she decided to drive over and see her old friend before the end of the following week. At least when she was with Alessa she gained hope that her own life would turn out better.

Chapter Ninety-Seven

The following week Emma put Isabella in the car and drove to West Philadelphia. She had planned a surprise visit for Alessa. It was early on Friday evening and Emma was hoping to find her friend at home. As she parked in front of the row house, she saw Remo standing on the porch with a glass of wine in his hand. As she and Izzy made their way up to the porch, her face lit up with a smile of anticipation at the prospect of seeing her old friend who had helped get her started at Doubles. Remo gave them both a warm, welcoming look.

"Remo, it's so good to see you!" Emma said. "I was hoping to find you guys home tonight."

Something in his demeanor told her that all wasn't well, although he smiled pleasantly and said, "It's good to see you, Emma. You too, Izzy. Man, you've really grown, haven't you?" His expression turned solemn as he looked at Emma again before turning to her niece. "Izzy, why don't you run upstairs and say hello to Lucy," he suggested. "I know she'll be happy to see you."

After Isabella had disappeared into the house, Remo turned his attention to Emma. "Alessa is gone," he announced, his face lined with worry. "She's been missing for three days now."

"What happened to her?" Emma asked, making a heroic effort to conceal the turbulence of her own emotions.

"We're not exactly sure, but we suspect that Harlin, the guy she lived with in North Philadelphia, has taken her," he explained, his voice cracking.

Overcome by the anguish of not knowing where Alessa was or if he would ever see her again, Remo could hold himself back no longer. His face crumpled and his hands shot up to mask his grief. As his shoulders shook, Emma wrapped him in her arms. She felt terrible, remembering the time she'd actually contemplated killing Harlin but had thought better of it because she wasn't sure if she could contend with the wrath of his whole gang. She now regretted her decision bitterly. If she had just thought it through and shown a little more courage at the time, Harlin would no longer have posed a problem and Alessa would be here with them now.

"I remember Harlin," she now said in a voice dripping with hate. "Someday he'll get what's coming to him. I'm sorry about Alessa, Remo. How's Lucy doing?"

"She's trying to remain hopeful. She keeps telling me that any day now the police will find Alessa or she'll come strolling back through the door. Alessa is the only mother Lucy has ever known. She was living on the streets when Alessa found her and she managed to get themselves both a home. Alessa is the most important person in Lucy's life. Mine too. We're both hanging in there as best we can. The police are still looking for her."

"I'd like to see Lucy, if that's okay with you," Emma said tentatively.

Remo nodded and they made their way up to the apartment, Emma's anger spurred by further hostile thoughts about Harlin. When they reached the door to the apartment, Remo paused.

"Lucy's a very strong person, but she may break down when she sees you," he warned her. "Alessa talked about you often, wondering how you were doing and where you'd ended up."

Emma nodded and prepared herself to be brave for Lucy. They found her and Izzy cuddled together on the sofa, watching Barney on TV. Lucy looked up at Emma and stumbled to her feet, running up to give her a long, tight hug. Both of them were crying.

"I'm so sorry, Lucy," Emma said with feeling. "But I'm pretty sure the police will find her. I wish there was something I could to do to help, though. I didn't know about this or I would've come sooner. Is there anything I can do for you now?"

"No," Lucy said. "Alessa really liked you. She told me how much fun the two of you had when you worked together." She pointed to Izzy and tried to lighten the moment. "Well, this one sure got a lot taller," she quipped. "What are you feeding her?"

Izzy didn't know what was going on, but sensed that something had happened to Alessa. Why else would everyone be crying? But she went ahead and answered Lucy's question. "She feeds me Cheerios," she chimed in. I'm going to be tall, just like my Aunt Emma!" She beamed with pride as she uttered the words.

There is nothing like an innocent child to lighten a dark moment, Emma thought.

Remo went into the kitchen and came back out to hand Emma a glass of wine. "Will you stay for dinner?" he asked, grateful for the company and the diversion it offered from his dreary thoughts.

"Are you kidding me?" Emma responded, winking at him. "I haven't forgotten what a good cook you are!" Then she turned to her niece. "How 'bout it, Iz? Should we stay and eat dinner with Remo and Lucy?"

"Are you making macaroni and cheese?" Izzy asked, seriously considering the offer.

"Well, it just so happens that I am," Remo replied. "Chicken cutlets too. Is that all right with you, Miss Isabella?" he couldn't resist teasing her.

"Yeah!" Izzy answered excitedly, then turned to Lucy. "Can we have ice cream for dessert?"

"Of course!" Lucy told her, matching her enthusiasm. "You know me. It's not a meal unless ice cream is involved."

They spent the evening enjoying their meal and catching up on each other's news. Emma told Remo about Salvatore, but refrained from mentioning his Mafia connections. She did confide, however, that he was married and had a son. Remo felt truly sorry for her. He and Alessa had always thought of her as a terrific person and had hoped her life would turn out well. He knew that Alessa would also be sad for her when he told her the news.

When Emma left after dinner, she exchanged phone numbers with Remo, promising to call and check in. "Don't worry," she reassured him, "the police will find her."

Driving back to Kensington with Izzy, she reminisced about Alessa and how helpful she had been when the two had first met at Doubles. They hadn't been the closest of friends, but Alessa had been the first person to help her without asking for anything in return.

Emma's thoughts drifted to Harlin and the way he had harmed Alessa and her family. Her hatred for him flared up again and she wished she knew his whereabouts so that she could kill him herself. She wondered if people were just born mean or turned that way because of the way life had treated them. She remembered being an innocent child, but time and the ordeal of living with her father's cruelty had robbed her of empathy for other people. No one is ever born mean, she decided. Life turns them that way.

Chapter Ninety-Eight

The next afternoon, Emma felt tense and restless before going to Doubles. She tried to relax, but she knew it was impossible. She couldn't stop obsessing about Alessa and the uncertain fate that awaited her and her family. The disturbing news about her missing friend fueled her aggression toward those sadistic people who walked the earth and took pleasure in ruining the lives of others. In an effort to distract herself, she reached under her mattress and pulled out Gracie's journal.

Emma sat on her bed and looked at the journal in her hands, suddenly reluctant to open it. Eventually she did and fanned through its pages. It was about three-quarters full with Gracie's thoughts, and as she continued to rifle through the diary, feeling the soft breeze from the turning pages on her face, she noticed an entry on a page toward the very back of the book that she hadn't noticed the first time she'd read it. She flipped back the pages until she found the entry. As her mind absorbed the words, her gut twisted.

> **I didn't think my life could suck any more than it already did. I wasn't able to sleep for days because of what Ethan had done to me. So my friend gave me five of her mom's Valiums. I was so happy when I felt my body relax as I became sleepy from the pills. Then I woke up to find Pete having sex with me. I had been in such a deep sleep from the pills I hadn't even felt him taking off my underwear. When I tried to scream, he jammed my panties into my mouth. I tried fighting him, but I couldn't make him get off of me. He told me he'd kill**

me if I kept it up. So I stopped fighting him and let him do what he wanted. When he was done, he told me he would much rather have fucked my sister. He laughed and said that all the time he was having sex with me, he had to pretend it was Em, because I was an ugly little freak who got all the bad genes from my parents. He said if I told anyone about what he had done to me, he would deny it and everyone would think I was lying. He said Ethan would stick up for him, anyway. When I got up to go to the bathroom, I was bleeding. He hurt me really bad, even more than Ethan ever had. Pete had just kept pushing himself inside of me and it had taken forever for it to be over, even after I had stopped fighting him. God, how I hate him! I hate both of them!

Emma shook with the rage that flooded her body. To think that she had defended Pete when Salvatore was threatening to kill him for raping her! She had, in fact, talked Salvatore out of the idea, claiming it was Ethan who had egged his friend on, and had even suggested that Pete was, at heart, a decent guy who just had too much to drink.

But now she saw him for the person he was—a scum-sucking maggot with a twisted sexual appetite. The journal entry made it all too clear to Emma. She now realized with a shock that Pete was Isabella's father. She now understood why Gracie had lied to her all along about one of the boys from school being Isabella's father. Since the paternity test results showed that Ethan wasn't Izzy's father the only other logical answer was that Pete was the father of her niece. Emma's resolve hardened: she was going to make Pete pay for what he had done to Gracie.

By now she was pacing the bedroom, wracked by a thirst for blood that was no less intense than that of a vampire you read about in young adult fiction. She pulled the duffel bag out of the closet and reached for the cloth that concealed Ethan's gun. She removed it from its covering and clicked open the chamber. It was loaded. Emma was no longer in control of her thoughts or actions as she put the gun into her purse and walked towards the front door without a single thought about Izzy.

"Are you leaving already?" Sydney asked, looking up from the book Izzy was reading to her.

"Yeah, I gotta go. I got called in to work early," she lied.

Izzy ran over and gave her aunt a kiss. "Be careful," the child advised her wisely.

Emma didn't respond. She was too consumed by her thoughts of getting even with Pete to consider the child whose future she might be jeopardizing by embarking on a mission of this kind and endangering her own life. She walked briskly to her car and spun off toward Ambler. Half an hour later, she was parked down the street from Pete's house. She shut off the engine and waited. At ten o'clock, she watched the pig strut from his house, get into his car, and drive off. She followed him in her own car to a small bar twenty minutes away. She parked in the rear of the lot so he wouldn't see her, then watched him get out of his car and enter the bar.

As Emma walked through the entrance of the bar soon after, she didn't notice any of the customers who crowded the place, although they were drinking heavily and shouting to be heard above the music playing through the old, fuzzy-sounding speakers. She spotted Pete standing among a group of men and watched one of them hand him a beer. As he lifted the beer to his lips, Pete froze; he had noticed Emma approaching. He hadn't seen her since the night of the rape well over a year ago, and the sight of her made him nervous.

She eased up beside him with fluid grace. "Well, look who it is!" she said, leaning in close to Pete.

"Listen, Emma," he babbled, "all that shit that happened the last time I saw you, that was all Ethan. I never wanted to do that to you."

Emma cut him off before he could utter another word, knowing that if she allowed him to continue telling his lies, she just might kill him before she had a chance to say everything she wanted him to hear.

"Pete, say no more," she said reassuringly. "I know you're a decent guy and that Ethan was a bad influence on you. See, part of the issue that Ethan and I had was my attraction to you. He sensed it, and it made him jealous. I knew it would only be a matter of time before you and I hooked up." Then she slid her hand over his bicep.

"Wow, for real?" Pete asked in disbelief. "I mean, I've always had a crush on you. Look at you!" he exclaimed, gesturing with his hand down her body. "You're gorgeous! Who wouldn't want you?"

"Good, now that we have that settled, how about buying me a drink?" Emma suggested seductively.

They settled themselves on two seats at the bar. Emma was going through the motions possessed with revenge for Gracie and no longer in control of her emotions. Meanwhile Pete's friends couldn't help gawking at the incredible creature talking to him. With her sexy blond hair hanging loose down her back, her skin-tight jeans outlining her perfect curves, and her firm breasts peeking over the top of her blouse with its low "V" neckline, they thought she was exquisite and all of them envied Pete.

After they had finished their second drink, Emma slid off the bar stool and moved close to Pete so that she was standing between his legs. She put her hand on the back of his neck and moved in to kiss him.

"God, Em!" he muttered. "Do you know how long I've wanted you to be mine? I never thought Ethan was good enough for you."

"I know, Pete," Emma replied calmly. "I've felt the same way about you. It was always you I wanted. I think Ethan sensed how attracted we were to each other. Now there is nothing to stop us from being together, is there? What do you say we get out of here?"

Pete pulled a twenty-dollar bill from his pocket and slapped it down on the bar. Turning to her, he said, "Let's go," before getting to his feet and leading her out of the bar.

Emma took his hand. "Where's your car?" she asked.

"Over there," Pete replied, gesturing in its direction.

Once he had unlocked the car doors, they slipped into the backseat. Emma lay on top of him as they kissed passionately. As he began roughly unbuttoning her shirt, she reached sneakily into her back pocket, diverting his attention from what she was about to do by using her other hand to rub the crotch of his pants. Distracted by his lust for her, he couldn't think clearly.

"How's that feel, Pete?" she murmured.

"Great, Emma..." he managed in a voice hoarse with desire. "It feels...just...great. Don't stop!" he implored in a demanding voice and pulling hard at her breasts, his sexual appetite for her rising as he began to get more forceful with her.

When the blade of her knife had sliced through his jeans and was embedded in his erection, the pain finally wiped out the sensation of his arousal. Pete snapped back into awareness and his eyes focused on the knife sticking out of him. It was then that he realized what she had done to him. He screamed, going into panic mode, as the pain signals reached his brain and the horror of what Emma had done sank in.

"You fucking cunt!" he screamed, trying to reach up and grab her neck.

It was at this precise point that she reached into her purse, pulled out Ethan's gun, and placed it against Pete's head. He lay on the backseat of the car, perfectly still, beads of sweat forming on his forehead.

"You know," she began softly, "it was just a couple of hours ago that I read an entry in Gracie's journal. She wrote it the night you raped her."

Then she sat in silence, watching him.

"Please, I'm sorry. I was drunk. I didn't know what I was doing," he said, hoping for mercy, but she cut him short.

"Oh, there's no point begging, Pete," she said evenly, as though they were engaged in a polite conversation. "There's nothing you can say that will help you now. You raped my little sister and you are Isabella's father."

He saw the madness in her eyes. She was like a beast that had stalked and cornered its prey and he knew there were more horrors in store for him. He tried to reason with her again. Emma's persona had changed. This time her contempt overpowered her ability to be calculated in her actions.

"Emma, please," he whined, "I was drunk."

"Emma, please," she mimicked, her manner and voice unnaturally composed. Then her expression changed and she twisted the knife in him viciously, watching him scream from the unbearable agony she was putting him through. "You thought you'd got away with it, didn't you?" she murmured. "You assumed your horrible little secret had been buried with Gracie. By the way, she also wrote in her journal that you had told her she was ugly. You hurt her. Do you hear me, you fucking loser?!" she yelled.

Pete's survival instincts kicked in. He knew now that it was a matter of life or death—his own. He began struggling to push her off him. If he could manage that, he thought, he would be able to pull out the knife she had stuck in him and use it on her.

It seemed as if she had read his mind. "No, Pete, I don't think so," she said, her tone malicious.

Before he could react, Emma yanked back her index finger and coolly shot him in the face. Fragments of his skull and bits of brain matter flew out and clung to the car's windows and backseat. At the sound of the gunshot Emma was jolted back into reality. For the first time in hours her thoughts went to Izzy. Her heart raced as panic rose and a lump formed in her throat. Oh fuck! What have I done? Why wasn't I more careful? Then as if she were outside of her body looking down on herself, all of the destruction that surrounded her came into clear view and she grimaced at all the blood in the car. Her mind shifted into overdrive as she searched for something to wrap around her hand so she didn't leave finger prints in the blood. On the floor she spotted a pair of Pete's work gloves. She picked them up and shoved her hands into them and proceeded to exit the car. Just before she got out, she pulled the knife out of Pete's body and looked down at what was left of his mangled face.

"Now who's ugly, motherfucker?" Emma asked feeling conflicted by the fear of getting caught and the satisfaction of avenging Gracie's honor.

Then she quickly stepped out of the car, strode briskly to her own, and sped away. Inside the bar, Kid Rock's song American Bad Ass blared so loudly that it drowned out the noise of the gunfire and none of the drunken patrons heard a thing.

Chapter Ninety-Nine

As she drove fast through Ambler heading toward Double Visions, Emma pulled her cell phone from her purse, found the phone number she needed, and pressed "send."

A moment later, Salvatore answered. "Emma?" he asked with anticipation.

"Salvatore, I need your help," she stated, the sound of her own heart drumming in her ears. "Can you meet me at Doubles?"

"Of course, Bella. Are you okay?" He sounded genuinely concerned.

"I'm fine. Just get there as soon as you can," she told him, a note of urgency creeping into her voice as she dwelled on Isabella and her lack of consideration.

For the remainder of the drive Emma was traumatized by her own behavior. She was irritated with herself for acting with reckless abandon. She had always been so careful and patient, but this time her self-control had betrayed her and now she was worried. Ten minutes after Emma parked her car at Doubles, Salvatore pulled into the parking lot with Tony and Vincent. She stayed in her car and watched them approach.

Salvatore leaned down to look at her through the open car window. "What the fuck?" he blurted out, seeing that she was covered in blood. "Have you been hurt?"

"No, I'm fine. But do you remember Pete? Ethan's friend," she reminded him.

Salvatore nodded.

"Well, he's not doing too good anymore. I need to clean up and get rid of a gun and a knife. Can you help?" She already knew what his answer would be.

"Of course," he said in a businesslike manner.

Emma followed the three men back to Salvatore's apartment in her own car. Having showered and dressed in a jogging suit she had left behind when she moved out, she walked into the living room and handed Tony the plastic bag they had given her earlier. Inside the bag were both weapons, her clothes, shoes, and purse.

"You'll take care of this, right?" she inquired.

Tony nodded, took the bag, and left the apartment. Emma turned her attention to Salvatore, who offered her a gin and tonic.

"No, thanks," she told him, declining the drink. "I have to get back to Doubles. My shift starts in two hours."

"What happened, Em?" Salvatore inquired. "Why didn't you call me to take care of this for you?"

"I found out that Pete raped Gracie. Isabella is his daughter," she said expressionlessly. "I really lost it this time. After I read her journal, all I could think about was how I was going to kill him. I just flew on impulse and that just isn't like me. I should have planned things so it wasn't so blatant. Salvatore, it was like I was possessed. After all that time I protected Izzy from Ethan and now I go and lose all control of myself. I let my rage get the better of me. I never even stopped to think about Izzy, not once until after it was over. This has never happened to me before."

"I see," was all he said, but he regretted that Emma hadn't called him to handle this for her. She had made an epic mistake. She pulled off a sloppy kill and he suspected there would be a price to pay for her lack of self-control. "Here's what we're going to do. I have a friend who can get you another car in less than an hour. We'll take care of your car. With all that blood you were covered in, we can't take any chances of the cops finding the car. Do you get my point?" Salvatore asked her.

"Yes," she said, a bit surprised that she hadn't thought about it herself.

"How is Izzy?" he asked fondly.

"She's fine, Salvatore. Can you call that guy about the car now?" she persisted, unwilling to be diverted from the matter at hand.

An hour later, she was standing at the door of Salvatore's apartment, ready to leave. She turned to face him, stepped into him, and put her hand on his shoulder.

"Thanks for your help tonight," she murmured.

He responded firmly, "You are never to act impulsively again. You call me before you do anything radical. Anytime you need me, just call. Understand?" he said.

It was more a statement than a question, she reflected. For the first time since she'd known him, he sounded like a real mobster.

"I promise, I will." She kissed him on the cheek and headed out.

She arrived for her shift at Doubles twenty minutes early. She was in the dressing room talking to one of the other dancers when Jay came in with two police officers.

"Emma Murphy?" one of the officers inquired.

"Yes," she said without any change in her demeanor.

"We need to take you in for questioning, Ms. Murphy," the officer stated.

"Questioning for what?" Emma asked innocently.

"The murder of Peter Somers," he replied coolly.

"Who?" she asked, feigning incomprehension.

"Peter Somers," the officer repeated before directing her to put her hands behind her back. Then he began to read her the Miranda rights.

As the cold metal of the handcuffs tightening around her small wrists, Emma took a moment to rejoice secretly. The police officer had confirmed that Pete was dead. On hearing it for the first time, she felt victorious. Sure, she was disappointed with herself for not planning his murder, but she couldn't deny the wonderful feeling of getting revenge.

As they led her out of the bar and to the police car, Emma noticed some of the girls standing with Jay and watching the scene in fear and confusion. Of all the dancers, it was only Maggie who wanted her friend to be okay again. However, she sensed that things were about to get much worse, and she wondered what would happen to Emma.

Even knowing that Izzy's future was in question, Emma was completely at peace on the drive to the police station. Like a drug addict injected with their heavenly nectar, she felt whole. She had taken care of all the people who had hurt Gracie.

Chapter One Hundred

The next few hours seemed to go by in a blur. The moment she entered the station, Emma was taken into a room behind the front desk. A female officer turned her to face the wall and asked if she had any sharp objects, needles, or knives on her body or in her clothing. After Emma confirmed that she didn't, the officer frisked her and led her over to a counter. Emma was fingerprinted, and photographs of her were taken from various angles. Finally she was led into a small holding cell, where she sat alone. Later, she was taken to another room where she was interrogated. When the officer questioning her asked for the names of her parents, Emma realized that resorting to a lie in this situation wouldn't help her case. She gave them her parents' names and her mother's address. Then she was led to another small cell, where she was locked in, alone.

Hours later, after she'd relived the moments following the pulling of the trigger and watching, as if on a movie screen of her imagination, the bullet shattering Pete's face and reducing it to pulp, Emma allowed herself to think about Izzy again. She had not mentioned her to the police. She saw no reason to volunteer information they didn't ask for. She planned to keep the existence of her niece a secret for as long as possible; forever, if she could. She had seen enough on television to know that if the police found out about Izzy, they would immediately hand her over to Valerie, the child's grandmother and her only living relative. Emma knew her mother would ruin Isabella's future. She might even try luring more abusive men into her life by using Izzy's beauty and charm as bait. No, she thought, she wouldn't speak of Izzy to the police. Nor would she tell them where she was, even if they did find out about her.

When Emma was finally allowed to make a phone call, she dialed Sydney.

"Syd, it's Emma. I don't have a lot of time to talk. I'm in jail and I'll be here for a while. I need you to take care of Izzy for me, all right?"

"What do you mean, Em?" Sydney shrieked into the phone.

The girl was rattled not only because she was afraid of what lay in store for her friend, but also because Izzy would be her responsibility for an indefinite period of time. The seriousness in Emma's voice told Syd that something really terrible had happened.

"Calm down, Syd," Emma told her. "Just do what I say. I'll be in touch, but for now, just make sure that Isabella is taken care of. Don't let her out of your sight for even a minute. I swear I'll call you again as soon as they let me and we can figure things out. Will you do that for me? Please?" she ended on a pleading note.

"Yes, I'll keep Iz with me," her friend promised. "But call me as soon as you can." Then she couldn't help asking, "What did you do to end up in jail?"

"I didn't do anything, Syd," Emma lied. "I've been accused of killing Ethan's friend, Pete. I have to go now. Tell Izzy I love her."

As the line went dead and Sydney's gaze traveled around the room, the enormity of what had transpired within those few moments came crashing down on her. She looked over at Isabella who was sleeping soundly in her bed. What the fuck was she going to tell her? She lay down on her own bed, curled into a ball, and cried silent tears of fear and sheer helplessness. She was desperately afraid of what would become of Emma and more so of what would become of Izzy. She loved the child, but at the end of the day, she belonged to Emma. Sydney lay awake all night, terror of the unknown seeping into her body until she felt ill.

At the police station, Emma sat locked in her cell. It was utterly silent but for the distant sound of barred metal doors being occasionally opened and shut. She had no regrets at all for what she had done. She would do it again in a minute if the situation arose. She considered Pete's death a matter of righting a wrong that had been done to Gracie and her.

The next morning, a woman officer Emma hadn't seen the night before unlocked her cell door and informed her that she needed to go for her informal arraignment. The proceedings were simple. Emma was informed that she was being charged with murder and apprised of her right to counsel. Since she was being held as a murder suspect, the judge decided to hold her without bail after reviewing the statements given by those present at the bar that night.

Emma asked for a court-appointed attorney and, eight days later, went for her preliminary hearing. Based on Emma's point-blank answer when questioned—"I didn't kill anyone"—her attorney, Alexis Fairburn, stated that her client was pleading not guilty to the crime.

The prosecutor, Elliot Lawes, produced a dozen eyewitnesses from the bar who claimed they had seen the accused leaving the bar with the murder victim. From the facts available, it was decided that her case would go to trial. Elliot intended to go for first-degree murder and did his utmost to establish a watertight case against Emma. Once the police had discovered the victim's connection with Ethan, Emma's late ex-boyfriend, the motive for the murder was thought to be some kind of psycho-vendetta. Alexis, a young female lawyer only two years out of law school, approached the trial with caution. She knew she would have to proceed carefully if she intended to gain the respect of her more senior colleagues and be taken seriously.

Emma called Sydney to check on Isabella and inform her friend about the latest developments.

"How is Iz? Everything okay?" she gushed, desperately wanting to hold Isabella in her arms.

"She's fine, Em," Sydney assured her. "We're both fine. But Izzy's been crying a lot. Keeps asking me when you're coming home."

Emma sighed, knowing she was about to drop a bomb on her young friend. "They've set my pre-trial conference thirty days from now, Syd. They're going to take the case to trial. This could take a really long time."

"Fuck, Emma! Izzy's lost and confused and I need to tell her something. Another thirty days is like a fucking eternity!"

Emma recognized Sydney's familiar whine. "Okay, Syd," she said briskly. "Just put Iz on the phone."

A moment later, the small voice penetrated the silence. "Aunt Em?"

"Yes, sweetie, it's me. How are you?"

"I miss you!" Isabella sniffled. "When are you coming home?"

"I don't know, Isabella," Emma told her honestly. "I need to stay where I am for a little bit. But while I'm gone, Sydney is going to take care of you and make sure you have everything you need. What have you two been doing?"

"Begging during the day and reading or playing games at night," Izzy told her aunt sadly.

Emma felt as if she'd been kicked in the stomach. It hadn't occurred to her how Sydney would earn money to take care of Isabella while she was locked away behind bars. To hear that they were begging on the streets of Kensington again gave her pause.

"Okay, Iz," she sighed. "Put Syd back on the phone, will you? I'll call you again soon. I love you, baby."

"I love you too, Aunt Em," the child said yearningly. "Please come back soon."

The moment her friend came back on the line, Emma told her, "Syd, you need to be careful. I'm truly sorry I didn't think about the money you might need. You can sell my stuff, okay? I don't want you guys out there on Kensington Avenue, begging for money. Maybe you can get a job until I know what's going to happen. You know, at a local restaurant or something? Or how about a job at a daycare? You love kids."

Sydney's irritation flared and she made no attempt to hide it as she snapped, "What the fuck do you want me to do? I didn't ask for this. I've begged for money all my life and now you want me to go out and get a job. You know what? How about trusting someone else with taking care of Izzy? I love her and all, Em, but I never signed up to be mother of the fucking year! I've been totally stressed out trying to keep her belly full for the last eight days. Now you're asking me to figure out how to take care of her for thirty more days!"

There was a moment of strained silence between them.

Then Emma said quietly, "You're right, Syd. I just want you to be careful. In the meantime, I'll try and think of some way to get you some money."

By the time Emma hung up the phone, she knew that Salvatore was the only person who could help them. She hoped that if asked, he would give Syd the money she needed to take care of Izzy. After several hours, she asked the guard if she could make another phone call.

"Not tonight, hon," she told her. "We'll see if you can make a call tomorrow, though. Now settle down and try to sleep."

But Emma had a difficult time quieting the thoughts that cluttered her brain. The prosecutor was determined to bring her down. He had already established her former relationship with Ethan. What if someone had seen her getting out of Pete's car after she had killed him? She had thrown caution to the wind and was annoyed with herself for being so reckless. She lay sleepless now, tossing and turning, obsessing over what more the prosecution could unearth that might incriminate her. There had been so many people at the bar when she'd left it with Pete that night. Acknowledging the possibility of a long prison sentence ahead of her, she knew her first priority would be to ensure that one of the people in her life would take care of Izzy.

Utterly frustrated, Emma sat up and swung her legs over the edge of her cot, blaming herself for creating a situation that might jeopardize Isabella's life. Now, she couldn't forgive herself for failing to plan Pete's death to the last detail, instead of killing him so rashly, for allowing her desire for revenge to override her common sense.

She knew she needed to make long-term plans for her niece. She would call Brianna and Katie first to see if either of them could help her. If that didn't work out, she would get in touch with Salvatore. Exhausted by her nightlong bout of self-recrimination, Emma drifted off to sleep, feeling hopeful that in the end, one of her friends would come through for Isabella. She knew that all three of the people she had thought of loved Isabella very much and told herself that the answer would be waiting for her in the morning, or so she hoped.

The next morning, feeling tense and wound up, Emma set out to make her calls. The first call she made was to Brianna, who was still living in Germany, as it turned out, with a guy who was no less abusive than Ethan had been. She herself needed an escape plan from a desperate situation and was in no position to help anyone else. Emma wished her luck and urged her to run as fast as she could to get away.

When she contacted Katie, her friend explained with deep regret that Bryce would never allow her to take in another child. Things were working out better for them in Nevada than they had in Ambler and she didn't want to rock the boat. She felt terrible about having to refuse Emma, but she really had no choice.

Both of the girls were, of course, shocked and concerned to hear that Emma was in prison. Katie was surprised that she was a suspect in Pete's murder. She had always believed that Salvatore had something to do with Ethan's murder, but now she wondered if Emma hadn't instigated him after the rape. Brianna found it less shocking that Emma was accused of killing Pete. She had known, although never confirmed, that Emma was connected to the deaths of Pepper and Jake. She was also aware of what Emma had done to Valerie before they fled their respective homes. But both were loyal friends and understood that Emma would never hurt those that she loved.

Emma's despair deepened at the discovery that neither of her friends could help her, but in all fairness to them, she acknowledged that what she had asked for was beyond reasonable.

The last call she made was to Salvatore. Emma quickly filled him in on her situation and asked him if there was anything he could do to help them out. He offered to send five hundred dollars to Sydney so that she could buy the things Izzy needed to live for a while. He told Emma solemnly that he would have loved to take in Isabella, but knew his wife would never give her consent to such an arrangement. He refrained from disclosing that it was, in fact, his father who would forbid him from giving refuge to a child who didn't belong to the family.

True to his word, Salvatore sent five hundred dollars to Sydney that very day and planned on sending her money regularly. It was something he had in plenty, and using it was the only way he could help Emma now. And she did need help very badly. He feared that she would be handed a long prison sentence for the crime she had committed.

Chapter One Hundred One

T he first day of the trial began with the prosecutor calling Ethan's family in as witnesses. His mother and sister both testified that Emma had been a bad influence on their son and brother. In fact, Elliot Lawes suggested slyly, she might even have been responsible for Ethan's violent death.

Emma sat at the table next to Alexis listening quietly as her character was ripped to shreds. Much was made of the fact that she was a stripper by profession, the insinuation being that it automatically made her a person of inferior moral character. Not flinching even once, Emma watched the circus unfold before her. She couldn't believe that Elliot Lawes, a supposedly educated person, could pass such harsh judgment on working at a strip bar. After all, the money she made at the bar was what had helped her to survive.

She didn't see the point in stirring up the bullshit that was irrelevant to her case. She had killed that bastard, Pete, for hurting Gracie and her. End of story. Who the fuck cared if she was a stripper or not? But it quickly became apparent that the stupid little jurors cared. She observed the women among them cringe as this fresh bit of information about her profession was tossed around and did not miss the second once-over the men gave her, probably fantasizing about her in costume, she mused.

The next day, the defense brought in witnesses from Doubles. They needed to face the stripper accusation head on and prove to the jury that women in the business were no different from those who sat in the courtroom. Shiver and Jay both testified in Emma's favor. They answered questions about her character and personality. They spoke briefly of her personal life, of which they knew little, since Emma rarely shared those details. Shiver gave the court an emotional performance when she talked about Emma losing Gracie in a car accident and the impact it had had on her friend.

When Elliot's turn came to question Shiver, he asked only one question: "Did anyone die during the time that Miss Murphy worked at Doubles Go-Go Bar?"

Stunned by a question for which she was not prepared, Shiver paused. "Well," she finally said, "yes, one of our dancers died."

"That's very interesting," Elliot observed, rubbing his chin with his fingers. "Do you know how she died?"

"She was found dead in her car," Shiver told him. "It was parked in her garage and it was still running when they found her."

"In fact," Elliot stated, turning to the jury with a dramatic gesture, "the deceased, whose stage name was Jade, died of carbon monoxide poisoning. The coroner's report shows that she was very, very drunk at the time of her death. Allegedly she pulled into her garage, shut the door, and passed out at the wheel. Now we've heard of this happening before to other people. But we followed up Jade's case and talked to her two orphaned children," here he paused and looked directly at Emma, "who informed us that their mother had gone out with Miss Murphy that night. You see, no one suspected foul play until now. The children were never asked if their mother went out with anyone that night and if she had, to identify that person—until just a couple of days ago. That, ladies and gentlemen," he directed his words at the jury now, "is just another person Miss Murphy knew who died of unnatural circumstances. Is it a coincidence? I think maybe it isn't a coincidence at all."

Alexis Fairburn kept objecting to the kind of conjectures being made, but the judge wouldn't give her a break and continued to overrule her. Shiver's face had gone deathly pale on the witness stand. She kept looking over at Emma for reassurance that the lawyer was nuts and just making it all up. Emma remained stoic as they tore her character down, bit by bit. She knew there was no way they could prove beyond reasonable doubt that she had anything to do with Jade's death. It just wasn't possible. When Shiver stepped down from the witness stand, she looked at Emma, who nodded to acknowledge her appreciation for her help.

By the end of the second day, Emma's attorney was secretly beginning to suspect that her client might be more sinister than she had imagined. It wasn't until the third day of the trial that she began to see her defense strategy as hopeless. For the prosecutor had called Emma's mother, Valerie Murphy, to the witness stand.

Chapter One Hundred Two

O nce she was seated, Valerie removed her sunglasses, scarf, and hat and turned to face the jurors. This was a deliberate dramatic action that Elliot Lawes had instructed Valerie to do once she was seated in the witness chair. The entire courtroom gasped at the appearance of the woman who now sat before them. Even with her facial injuries healed, she looked like a character from a horror film. Without the means to afford cosmetic surgery, Valerie was doomed to live the way her daughter had intended her to. The scars from the slashes on her face, both vertical and horizontal, now made the corners of Emma's lips turn up in a barely perceptible smile of malicious pleasure. She stared at Valerie with contempt, waiting for the imbecile who had given birth to her to tell the whole world how her daughter had sliced up her face with a kitchen knife and ruined her life forever. She wondered, though, if her mother would be as truthful about her own savage behavior to her younger child.

Emma leaned over and whispered to Alexis, "We need to talk. There's a reason why my mother looks that way."

Alexis nodded. "After the prosecutor is done questioning her, I'll ask the judge for a break," she whispered back. But her eyes were intent on Emma's mother, anxious to hear the story she was about to tell them.

"Mrs. Murphy," the prosecutor began, "could you explain to the court how you got those scars on your face?"

Valerie was visibly uneasy as she tried not to meet her daughter's scorching stare. "Emma was mad at me," she said without wavering. "So she knocked me unconscious and cut my face up with a knife."

"Why would your daughter do such a horrible thing to her own mother?" the prosecutor went on. "Surely you must have done something to provoke her?"

"She...she was angry because her little sister had been punished and she decided to take it out on me," she stammered.

Valerie now looked at Emma, her resentful eyes taking in all of her beauty, the kind of beauty she herself had been robbed of. Something in her daughter's character reminded her so much of Pepper. But she knew she need no longer be afraid of her daughter. The prosecutor had promised her that Emma was going to prison for a very, very long time.

"Mrs. Murphy," Elliot began again, "you told me that Emma ran away from home as a teenager. And before she left, she butchered your face." The man now turned to the jury, holding up a photograph of Valerie taken shortly after Pepper's death. "This," he said with a flourish, "is what Mrs. Murphy looked like before her daughter mutilated her face."

The jurors shook their heads sadly, appreciating the irony of how beautiful this physical wreck of a woman had once been.

"Mrs. Murphy," the prosecutor persisted, "did anyone in your home die while Emma was living with you?"

"Yes," she said, leaning forward into the microphone, "her father died. One day he was healthy, and in less than two months, he became really ill and died."

"Died of what?" the prosecutor pushed.

"I don't know. We just thought it was natural causes," Valerie said.

"Did anyone else die during the time Emma was living with you?" he asked.

"Yes. After Pepper's death, I met a man named Jake. He moved in with us, but he died too."

"And what was the cause of his death?" Elliot persisted.

"The police told me he had too much to drink and fell into an empty pool at a hotel in the area. He died from the fall," she sniffled.

Valerie now glanced in Emma's direction, knowing that if her daughter could, she would get out of her chair at that moment and beat her to death.

Elliot Lawes turned to the jurors. "As you can all see, while Miss Murphy is being tried for the murder of Peter Somers, there are three other people we know of—either living in her home at some time or somehow acquainted with her—who have died untimely deaths." He turned to the judge. "Your Honor," he said, "if the pattern that seems to be emerging here can be established with proof to support it, I think we may have before us a serial killer."

Emma was enraged at the way she was being portrayed. She was the one who had been abused and violated. Granted, Jade had never harmed her personally, but that bitch had been beating her helpless children, and when Jade's daughter asked her to help, she couldn't deny her responsibility to step in. Emma's jaw clenched, and under the table, her hands balled into tight fists on her lap.

This didn't go unnoticed by Alexis Fairburn.

"Objection, Your Honor," she yelled, jumping to her feet. "The prosecution has no proof whatsoever that any of these other deaths are connected with my client. This is all circumstantial and, in my professional opinion, mere coincidence. Besides, Miss Murphy is being tried for the murder of Peter Somers. I fail to understand why the prosecution is wasting the court's time by bringing these other people into the picture."

"Sustained," the judge finally ordered. He turned to the prosecutor. "Counselor, you should know better than to project your opinion on the court without sufficient evidence to back your claims."

"My apologies, Your Honor," the prosecutor mumbled and sat down.

But Elliot's expression was triumphant. He had connected the dots for the jurors. The seeds of doubt had been planted in the minds of the jurors. He could see their thoughts churning and could tell from their body language that they were inclined to believe him.

During the break they were granted, Alexis took Emma to a separate room. Then she shut the door and turned to her.

"What the hell happened?" she hissed. "Did you really do that to your mother?"

Emma remained calm. "Yes, I did."

"How could you?" the young lawyer demanded, shocked. "What could she have done to you to warrant retaliation of this kind?"

"Her boyfriend, Jake, buried my little sister in a shallow grave in our basement to punish her. My mother knew about it and left Gracie there for days. In fact, my mother allowed my father to do horrible things to both my sister and me ever since we were little girls. Do you need to know more?" she asked, challenging Alexis to pass judgment now that she knew the truth.

"Fuck! How much more is there that I don't know about?" she yelled at Emma.

"How much time do you have?" she retorted calmly. "This is going to be a long, long story."

Chapter One Hundred Three

O ver the weekend, Emma sat with her legal team and gave them the details of her life. She talked about her childhood and the abuse she and Gracie had suffered at the hands of Pepper and Jake. She discussed the kind of life she had shared with Ethan and the cruel indignities he had inflicted on her, but was careful never to reveal Pete had raped Gracie and her. And she didn't utter a word about her involvement in the deaths the prosecution had tried so hard to link her with. That was something she intended to take to her grave.

When Emma came to the end of her story, Alexis and her assistant sat in silence, gravely contemplating the facts that had been laid before them. They now had the vital information they needed to set the stage anew so that the judge and jury could examine the case from a different perspective altogether. Emma's defense lawyer began planning the line of questioning they would use to cross-examine Valerie Murphy about the real reason that had driven her daughter to disfigure her face. They needed to evoke the jury's sympathy for Emma before its members decided her fate.

On Monday, when the court reconvened, Valerie was called back to the witness stand. Alexis Fairburn repeated the account of the events the witness claimed had led to her daughter's attack on her. Then she turned to Valerie and asked gently, "Mrs. Murphy, is it a fact that Emma hurt you in retaliation for refusing to rescue your younger daughter, Gracie, from a shallow grave in the basement of your home where she had been buried for several days, although you knew that by doing so you were putting her life at risk?"

Valerie sat silently for several moments, stunned at the question. Then she started to cry. "I was afraid to defy Jake's orders," she whimpered. "He's the one who did those horrible things to Gracie, not me! I couldn't do anything about it, because I'm not like Emma. She never seems like she's afraid of anything."

Alexis now found her chance to hone in on her target, turning relentless as she questioned the witness in detail about the atrocities Pepper had inflicted on Emma.

Valerie now burst into sobs. "My husband was a good man!" she blubbered. "It was his drinking that made him so mean. I always reassured my girls that their father loved them. It was just that his life hadn't turned out the way he'd planned."

"So you did nothing to prevent these two men in your life from physically and verbally abusing your daughters?" Alexis persisted.

"Objection, Your Honor," Elliot Lawes intervened. "Mrs. Murphy isn't on trial here. Let's remember this is a murder trial and the line of questioning adopted by the defense has nothing to do with the murder in this case."

The judge considered for a moment. "Overruled," he finally said. "While I agree that the line of questioning isn't directly related to this case, I believe it's important for the jury and me to understand the character of this witness."

Without losing her composure or coming across as discourteous, Emma's attorney proceeded to humiliate and belittle Valerie for her role in the systematic abuse of her children. By the time she left the witness stand, Valerie Murphy's involvement in the abuse of her minor daughters had been irrevocably established and her integrity as a witness was in serious doubt.

Only two days earlier, most of the jury had perceived Emma as a ruthless rogue assailant, but within hours, Alexis Fairburn had established her point convincingly enough that there was more to her client's story than met the eye. The jurors now felt compassion for the woman they had regarded as unfeeling as she sat through the trial without a change in her expression. The women jurors, in particular, were not only horrified by the ordeals the accused had endured from a tender age, but moved enough by her suffering to blame her choice of career as a stripper on her childhood tribulations.

A day later, in her closing argument, Emma's attorney pointed out that the prosecution had failed to produce in court the weapons allegedly used to kill and mutilate Peter Somers. The police had not recovered the gun and the knife purportedly used in the slaying. She further reminded them that there was a reason for Emma's fingerprints in Pete's car and strands of her client's hair being found on the victim's clothes: Emma Murphy had never denied being at the bar with the victim on the evening of the murder. She had also stated that she accompanied him to his car later, where she kissed him, a fact that had been corroborated by witnesses at the scene. That did not, however, prove that her client had killed the victim.

Alexis Fairburn walked across the courtroom and stood directly in front of the jurors.

"Ladies and gentlemen," she said, gearing up for her closing speech, "I will ask you to consider the following facts: first, that no murder weapon has been recovered; second, that no one actually saw Miss Murphy kill Mr. Somers. My client left him in the backseat of his car, after they had, as she put it, 'messed around for a while.' She has admitted in court that they didn't have intercourse and, in fact, stopped 'fooling around,' because she realized that Mr. Somers wasn't ready for the long-term relationship she had been looking for. Now the decision is in your hands—and yours alone. You need no reminder, of course, that as jurors in this case, it is your duty to be absolutely certain that my client did, indeed, commit this murder. If there is even a shadow of doubt in your mind, it would be a grave injustice on your part to convict her. I repeat that my client is innocent. She has suffered much injustice from the time she was a small child, as you are now aware. Please ensure that you are not responsible for doing her yet another injustice. Please don't destroy an innocent young woman's life by sending her to prison."

Two weeks later, after the jury had considered all available evidence and the testimony of witnesses, Emma was pronounced not guilty. During the trial, the local and national media had gone to town with the story. With the catchy label of "serial killer" having come up, the media had stayed riveted to the case, "improving" on the available tag and describing Emma as the "Serial Stripper—a killer who sought her own type of justice."

Even though she had not been convicted of murder, the infamy of the trial would continue to haunt her long after the verdict had been delivered. But now that the facts from the case were public knowledge, Emma was praised for the resilience she had displayed in persevering through the dismal circumstances of her traumatic childhood and taking care of her younger sister. True to its unpredictable nature, the media now turned its venom on Valerie, portraying her as the most vicious mother that ever lived. Emma quietly enjoyed her mother's disgrace, savoring every word she read in the newspapers about how society viewed her as an utterly despicable person.

As the bedlam surrounding the trial subsided, all Emma could think about was her need to get back to Izzy. Sydney and the herd had watched some of the highlights of the trial on the news. None of them could believe what was being said about Emma. And hard as she tried, Syd couldn't shelter Izzy completely from the facts. When Emma was declared innocent, they all cheered and hugged each other and Sydney was finally able to announce to Isabella that her aunt was coming home to her.

Infected by the excitement of the teenagers around her, Izzy looked at her and asked, "So when will Aunt Em be here?"

"Soon, Iz," Sydney promised, secretly relieved to be free of the responsibility of caring for the child. She shuddered to think what she would have done if Emma had been found guilty and given a life sentence.

Later that afternoon, Emma walked out of the prison gates, a free woman, to find that Salvatore had a cab waiting to pick her up and take her back to Kensington. She called him when she got home.

"Thank you," she said. "Now, Isabella and I can start over."

"Good idea, Bella," he said encouragingly, wishing that he were a part of Emma's new beginnings, but respecting her need to figure things out on her own.

Emma recognized the sadness in his voice. "I'll be in touch with you soon," she promised him.

Chapter One Hundred Four

I t was nearly two months to the day Emma was released from prison that she left Izzy with Sydney, explaining that she needed to run an errand. She was on her way to fulfilling a promise she had made to herself while counting the long hours in prison, often lost in contemplation of what awaited her. Emma had known that if she were found innocent, she would have to go and face her mother. It was a chore that she could no longer avoid.

She parked on Chain Street and approached her childhood home on foot, noticing the slight changes that had taken place in the neighborhood while she'd been away. A lot more children lived on the street now compared to the time she was growing up there. She climbed the rickety steps and knocked lightly on her mother's front door.

Valerie opened the door, peeked out, and froze.

"I don't need any shit, Emma," she said coldly.

"It's okay, Mom," her daughter reassured her. "I understand that you did what you thought was right at the time. It's taken me all these years to realize that you were just too scared to help Gracie and me. I'm not here to start any trouble, I promise. I'm here to find out if you wanted to give our relationship a second chance." Emma's voice was tender with a new understanding.

Valerie looked at her suspiciously. "Why the change of heart?" she asked, her tone still skeptical.

"Well, for starters, you have a granddaughter. Gracie gave birth to her before she died," Emma told her, remembering her sister with a twinge of sadness.

"I do?" Valerie perked up. "I have a grandchild! Oh, all of my friends will be so jealous of me! They all want to become grandmothers, but now I'm going to be the first! What's her name?" she exclaimed.

The fact that Valerie had exhibited no signs of grief over Gracie's death had not gone unnoticed by Emma. The news of Gracie succumbing to her injuries from a fatal car accident years ago had come up during the trial, but the death of her younger child seemed to have left Valerie unmoved.

Emma pushed herself to keep talking. "Her name is Isabella. We call her Izzy. So how about if I bring her over to see you tomorrow? Would that work?" Emma asked, looking for a commitment from her mother.

"Yes, of course," Valerie assured her. "That'll be fine. I'll need to go out and buy some things. Why don't you come for lunch? What does Isabella, I mean Izzy, like to eat?" she persisted, her mind on the phone calls she would make to her friends as soon as Emma left.

"Lunch would be great!" Emma said warmly. "Izzy likes pizza or macaroni and cheese. Either one will make her very happy."

As she walked back to her car, she wondered how she would explain Valerie to Isabella. Her niece didn't even know what a grandmother was, let alone that she had one.

Emma was back at her mother's place the next day with Izzy in tow. She knocked on the front door and Valerie, excited about meeting her granddaughter, flung it open. She was delighted to notice how beautiful the child was. She also observed what a strong resemblance she bore to Emma.

"Well, hello there!" she smiled at Izzy. "I'm your grandma."

"What's wrong with your face?" Izzy asked with the directness of a child, backing away fearfully from what was a frightening sight to her.

Valerie looked nervously at Emma. "Grandma had an accident, honey," she explained to Izzy.

"If you want to come in, I'd like to show you a picture of what I used to look like before my accident," Valerie offered, glancing uneasily at her daughter.

"Okay," Isabella agreed hesitantly, her hand going up to clasp her aunt's in a firm grip.

"We're having homemade macaroni and cheese for lunch," Valerie told her granddaughter, trying to win her over.

"I love that!" the child said simply. Then she turned to her aunt. "Aunt Em, is this where you grew up?"

"Yep. In this very house," Emma replied. "Want to see the room I shared with your mom when we were kids?" she asked, trying to divert the child with something she thought would interest her.

Isabella nodded, and the two of them climbed the stairs to the second floor together, while Valerie went off to the kitchen to tend to last-minute chores. Up in her old bedroom, memories of Gracie flooded Emma's mind.

"This is where your mom and I would pretend we were princesses," she told Izzy. "We imagined having beautiful clothes and lots of servants to order around. It was a lot of fun."

Emma gave the child a tour of the rest of the house before finally entering the kitchen, where Valerie was waiting to serve them lunch. Izzy chatted about her books and games, telling her grandmother all the things she'd read about. Valerie listened attentively, taking it all in so that later, after they had left, she could call her friends and brag about having such a smart granddaughter.

She also asked Emma routine questions about where she'd been and what she'd done with her life since she left home. Then she quickly turned the focus of the conversation on herself.

"I've been really lonely since everyone left me," Valerie said in a self-pitying tone. "My looks don't exactly pull the men to me like they used to, if you know what I mean. And I still don't sleep too well at night."

"I know," Emma said sympathetically, "I understand now how you feel. I'm real sorry about that. I was young."

"Yes, I understand that," Valerie said gently. "And I'm sorry for testifying against you in court. That attorney told me it was the right thing for me to do. But I was scared to death that you would come after me if they let you off. But now I can see that you have finally matured enough to understand that if you had just not been such a little rebel when you were younger things may have been different for you."

"Well, I guess we learn as we get older," Emma said, swallowing the lump that had gathered in her throat at her mother's statement. "I was hurt that you testified against me. But now I see that you didn't have a choice. Well, it all turned out good in the end and I think we can make a new start together."

The idea of not being alone anymore appealed to Valerie. "Why don't you two move in here with me?" she offered. "I have plenty of room. We can share the expenses and I can look after Isabella while you're at work."

"I don't know," Emma said hesitantly. "I'll need to think about it. I mean, it's awful soon and, well, Isabella and I will need a little time to think about it. I can let you know in a couple of days."

Valerie was visibly disappointed. The prospect of not living alone anymore had given her hope.

As they were leaving, Emma promised her mother she would call in the next day or two. Valerie was eager to have people back in her life. She needed others to live with her again and help drive away the loneliness that had fallen over her life like a heavy wool blanket. With the prospect of having family move back into the house, she was optimistic about life getting back to normal. Just as it used to be, she thought, when they had all lived together and Pepper was the man of the house. After all, she reflected, whatever others might think, everything she had ever done in her life—all her sacrifices—had been for an unselfish purpose: to keep her family together. Valerie lived in deep denial of who she really was, and of the heartache that she had heaped upon her daughters, all for the sake of keeping a family around her. This was a personality flaw that no one would ever change.

Driving back to Kensington, Emma's thoughts lingered on her mother. She hadn't changed much in the years since she'd been gone. In many ways, she was just the same. A little more pathetic, perhaps, now that her beauty was gone and in its place were the gruesome scars on her face that would remain a permanent reminder of her past mistakes. Deep down, Emma knew that she would go back and live with her mother. She and Izzy needed to start over, and she wanted to get the child out of Kensington. She decided to call her mother in a day or two and let her know they were coming home. She smiled, thinking how delighted Valerie would be at the news.

Chapter One Hundred Five

E mma and Isabella moved back to Chain Street a week later. They found an excited Valerie eagerly awaiting their arrival. She had baked chocolate chip cookies for Izzy as a special treat. Emma looked on, reminding herself that her mother had never done anything special for Gracie and her. They settled in quickly, and within a week, Emma had painted the room she and Izzy shared, bought furniture, and even installed new lighting so that her niece would have no difficulty reading. Isabella spent most of her time in her "new" room, now that it was painted and decorated the way she liked it.

It was less than two weeks after they had moved back to Chain Street that Valerie went to Friday night bingo with her friends and returned ecstatic.

"Oh, Emma!" she exclaimed, "I met a man. He's just wonderful! He's asked me to go on a date with him tomorrow night. He didn't even seem to notice what happened to my face!" she gushed.

"Wow! That's great, Mom," Emma said, echoing her enthusiasm. "Did you say yes?"

"Are you kidding?" Valerie retorted. "Of course I said yes! I haven't been asked out on a date in years. Who in their right mind would turn a man down for a date?" she rattled on.

Over the next two weeks, and to Emma's delight, her mother went out with this new man almost every night. This gave Isabella and her time to spend alone in the quiet of the house. They were able to read and play games without Valerie's incessant jabbering about herself.

One night, after a date at the movies, Valerie boasted, "My boyfriend, Ted, has a house on the beach in Florida. He wants me to move there with him. He's also promised to take me to his plastic surgeon so that I can have my face fixed." Then her voice dropped to just above a whisper, as if she were letting Emma in on a divine secret only meant to be known by special people such as them. "I suspect he's filthy rich."

Valerie was the happiest Emma had ever seen her. All of her mother's dreams were coming true. A knight in shining armor had come in to save the day. Emma was beyond thrilled that her mother was willing to give her new relationship a go. With Valerie gone, the idea of having the house just to the two of them indefinitely seemed very appealing. She was well aware that her mother lived for male attention. Valerie's beauty had been her greatest asset in attracting that attention. That was precisely the reason why Emma had mutilated her face. But now, watching her mother behave like a giddy young girl, Emma laughed quietly to herself. She was about as different from her mother as one could get. Unlike Valerie, she was independent-minded and wanted nothing more than to be self-sufficient. Besides, after Salvatore, she didn't know if she would ever be able to love another man again, and certainly not in the way she had loved him.

"Mom," she suggested while Valerie was busy packing her bags, "now that you're moving to Florida, I was thinking that Isabella and I could live here and pay the bills and mortgage for you. Does that sound okay? I really don't want to uproot Izzy again."

"Of course that's okay, darlin'!" Valerie cooed, ready to be generous now that she had something better to move on to. "My home is your home. I think it's a wonderful idea!"

"Good. So when are you moving?" Emma asked, flashing Valerie a smile so bright that it reminded her of the beauty she'd lost and stirred envy in the older woman. But she shook it off after remembering what Ted had promised about the plastic surgeon.

"Next week! Can you believe it? My friends are just going to die! I'll miss them, of course, but now they can come and visit me at my house on the beach! Everything is finally turning out the way I wanted. I have my daughter back and a new granddaughter. And to top it all off, I have a rich, handsome boyfriend! See, Emma, my sacrifice has been worth its weight in gold. Good things come to those who wait," she declared.

Over the next week, Valerie quit her job at the grocery store, said her good-byes to her friends, and packed her belongings. It was Friday night and Ted was coming to pick her up early the next morning. Emma had cooked a farewell meal for her mother that the three of them shared.

After Emma put Izzy to bed, she went back down to the kitchen to help her mother clean the dishes. She chatted easily with Valerie about her new adventure as they worked together to tidy up after dinner. Valerie yapped nonstop about her new life with Ted, while Emma talked about enrolling Izzy in school the following Monday. Drying the last frying pan, Emma looked at her mother with pity. She was the dumbest person on earth, she thought, lifting her arm and whacking Valerie on the side of the face with the heavy metal pan. As her mother slipped out of consciousness, the last thing she saw was Emma standing over her, her green eyes blazing.

Chapter One Hundred Six

O n Saturday morning, Sydney arrived at the house on Chain Street to watch Izzy for the day. Once they were playing a game in Izzy's room, Emma went into the bathroom to change. She put on one of her mother's "going-out" dresses that was two sizes too big and a pair of old sneakers. She tucked her hair under a brimmed hat and put large sunglasses on. One would never imagine how beautiful Emma really was under the unattractive camouflage she was wearing. It was exactly what she'd intended. As she descended the stairs she yelled, "See you this afternoon, girls. Have fun."

Forty-five minutes later, Emma walked into Dunkin' Donuts in West Philadelphia. She looked for a man wearing a green baseball cap and walked up to him, "Ted! Right?" she asked joyfully.

"Yeah, that's right," he replied. "I was instructed to come here and pick up my five hundred bucks. I assume everything went as planned with that Valerie woman. Man, she gave me the willies with that face of hers! She is one fucked-up broad. Ewww!" He flailed his arms, as if he were trying to shake a bug off himself. "She's one foul chick," he went on, "but hey, five hundred bucks to tell some homely woman I love her and we're going to live in Florida and I'm gonna pay to fix that fucked-up face of hers—that's the easiest money I've ever earned!"

Emma pulled the envelope from her pocket. "Here's the money," she said. "Thanks for everything."

"Sure thing!" he responded, accepting the envelope and leaving right away, an expression of satisfaction plastered on his face.

Emma waited for him to drive away before getting into her own car. She quickly pulled out her cell phone and made a call. "Thanks, Salvatore," she said. "Everything worked exactly as planned."

"Good. I'm happy to hear it went smoothly. I am very happy you called me. I'll talk to you soon?" he asked hopefully.

"Yes, I'll call you. And Salvatore...thanks again," she said with deep affection in her voice.

In the End . . .

W hen Valerie woke up in the middle of the night, her excitement over moving to Florida flooded her with a sense of immense pleasure. What time is it? She wondered drowsily, puzzled as to why she had woken up so early. She came fully awake when she tried rolling over to look at the alarm clock next to her bed and couldn't. She realized then that something was preventing her from moving. She couldn't see a thing through the shroud of darkness, and as her senses jolted alive, she smelled dirt. She put her hand out in front of her and felt plywood. Terror surged through her body as she began to push at the object on top of her but it would not budge.

She felt the dirt, cold against her arms and the back of her neck. In a panic now, she scratched and clawed at the plywood with her fingernails. Then she began screaming at the top of lungs, until her air started to grow thin and her breathing became labored. She knew then exactly where she was and how she'd gotten there, as her fate wrapped itself around her in that suffocating space. She realized how she had been fooled and that Emma would never come for her. The realization made her lose all self-control. Sobbing and shaking uncontrollably, she contemplated the reality of what lay ahead. The grimness of what was to come engulfed her in horror as she felt the bugs crawling on her lower legs and feet. Valerie tried to swat them off, but the tight space in which she was confined would not allow her to. All she could do was lie there and wait for death to come.

In the late afternoon, after Sydney had left, Emma sat watching television with Isabella. She felt blissfully content as her mind wandered momentarily to her mother, now lying in her shallow grave in the basement. The same grave Valerie had left Gracie to die in. The dimwit hadn't even bothered to fill in the hole after they'd left home. Emma's demons were finally laid to rest.

"Aunt Em, is Grandma ever coming home?" Izzy asked suddenly.

"No, baby. She moved to Florida, remember?" she reminded her niece.

"Oh yeah, that's right. But it's okay. She was weird. I didn't like her that much anyway," Isabella confessed.

"Me neither, sweetie, me neither," Emma stated with heartfelt honesty.

Continue reading . . .

The First Twelve Hours of Captivity

Read more about Maggie Clarke in **One Among Us.** Maggie is kidnapped and forced into human sex trafficking. **Read a sample of One Among Us here . . .**

Eleven-year-old Maggie threw up when the man behind the camera demanded that she remove her jeans. "What the fuck," Vic, the photographer, mumbled as he walked over and pushed her down on the bed in the makeshift studio. Then he ripped her jeans off with so much force that it felt as though a layer of her skin came off with the denim. Vic threw a towel at her. "Now wipe up that slop and take your fucking shirt off," he ordered.

Maggie was sobbing; she was stricken with an overwhelming sensation she'd never felt before, a feeling that she was going to die. She had no control over her emotions as she tried not to piss off the man with the camera any more than she already had. She removed her T-shirt slowly. "Good," Vic huffed. "Now lie down on the bed and take your underwear off."

Maggie shook her head. "I don't want to do that. Please don't make me do that, mister." Her small voice quivered.

"That's it," Vic screamed. "John William, get the fuck over here and handle this. I don't have all day for one kid. We have a fuckin' business to run, here."

John William thudded over to the bed where Maggie sat huddled, trying to cover her body, and he backhanded her across the face. Blood dribbled down her split lip and into her mouth, its coppery taste threatening to excite her gag reflex again. Before she could regain her senses, he pulled her panties off. Maggie pulled her knees up to her chin and wrapped her arms tightly around her legs as she sat naked on the bed with the two strange men watching her.

She was alone and terrified. All of her senses were heightened by the evil surrounding her. She didn't know what they were going to do to her. Her parents had warned that no one should ever touch her private parts. But here, in this crumbling cement room, she had no choice. Maggie had an overwhelming feeling that the two men were going to do things to her that they shouldn't, and this intensified the vulnerable feeling that gnawed at her gut, jeopardizing her ability to follow their instructions.

Vic looked at Maggie, his face devoid of any kindness. "I'm going to tell you this one time and one time only. I want you to spread your legs apart so I can take some pictures. Just drop your knees to your sides. Do you understand?"

Maggie nodded, not wanting to be hit again. Once Vic was back behind the camera, he looked over at her. "OK, spread your legs like I told you to."

Maggie dropped her knees to the sides, and he began to snap pictures. "Now, I want you to reach down and touch yourself."

Maggie froze, not knowing what to do. John William stepped in, grabbed her hand, and placed it roughly between her legs. "That's it. Put your fingers inside," Vic coaxed her.

Inside where? Maggie wondered, feeling filthy and ruined. Not knowing what she was supposed to do, she remained motionless. Vic strode over briskly, grabbed her hand, and shoved her fingers inside of her. Fear mixed with adrenaline coursed through her body—she thought they had broken her. She had no idea there was a hole between her legs before that moment. They had just started sex education at school, but nothing could have prepared her for the horrible acts she would be expected to perform to her body.

Vic turned to John William. "The next time you bring a new kid in here, make sure they're ready for me. You understand?" he demanded.

John William nodded and glared heartlessly at Maggie. The look was so demonic that it was almost blinding. She shrank away from him, and a deeper level of fear ran uncontrollably through her body, seizing her muscles, paralyzing her.

After Vic took several more pictures, he told her to put on her clothes and leave. As Maggie quickly dressed, she wondered if they had gotten what they wanted and would take her back to the mall now. She was certain that her mother was still at the mall, searching for her. Maggie decided that when the two men let her go home, she would never tell anyone about the pictures they'd taken. Maggie feared that she would be in trouble if her parents found out what she had done.

However, ten minutes later, John William pulled Maggie into her cell and pushed her toward a cot. When he reached the doorway, he turned. "You have a lot to learn. I suggest you pay attention and do what we tell you to do. I'm going to cut you a break since it's your first night, but if you ever embarrass me like that again, I'll bash your brains in."

Maggie's hope of going home quickly vanished as his words bounced inside her head. Since it's your first night. She instantly understood that they weren't finished with her yet. Her heart beat faster as she tried desperately to hang on to the hope that they would let her go.

He raised his voice. "You are to obey everything that you are told to do! If you weren't worth so much money, I'd fuck the shit out of you right now."

Maggie was shaking. She didn't know exactly what he was talking about, but she knew enough to understand that John William wanted to do bad things to her, dirty things. She clung to the cold block wall of the cell, unable to wrap her mind around what was happening to her.

"Take off all of your clothes," John William instructed.

Maggie did as she was told quickly this time.

He looked at her with lust. "Now bring me your clothes."

She quickly scooped them up and carried them to him. John William grabbed them from her arms.

"For causing such a scene tonight, you can sleep naked. So you can get used to it, you little whore," John William taunted.

After John William left her and locked the heavy door behind him, Maggie sat on the dirty cot. She wept from the very depth of her soul. The unrelenting fear was suffocating and inescapable. This had been the hardest day of her young life. She had only been missing for twelve hours, but it felt like a year to eleven-year-old Maggie.

She cried herself to sleep that night, thinking of her family, and when she woke the next day, her nightmare continued.

One Day Prior: The Capture

Maggie was only thirty feet from the line of people at the pizza counter in the food court inside the Plymouth Meeting Mall. As she walked by the large glass doors that opened to the parking lot, she saw two teenage girls standing just outside the entrance. They were talking to a man with a puppy. She watched as the girls took turns holding the dog. Then, as they passed Maggie on their way into the mall, she heard them talking about how adorable the puppy was. "Wasn't that man nice?" one of the girls said. "I wish my dad felt that way about dogs and would let me get a puppy."

Maggie looked out the glass doors at the man holding the puppy; he turned the dog in her direction and lifted a paw, as if to wave at Maggie. She stood glued to the glass door, smiling at the tiny pile of fur in the man's arms. She opened the glass door just a couple of inches. "He's so cute. What's his name?" Maggie asked.

"I just got him today, and I haven't named him yet. I'm taking ideas, though. What do you think I should call him?" John William asked sweetly.

"I don't know," Maggie said shyly, not able to take her eyes off the fluffy mound of fur.

"Would you like to hold him?" John William offered.

"I would, but I really shouldn't. I can't leave the mall," she explained.

"You're not leaving the mall. I'm standing five feet away from the door. What's the difference whether you're standing five feet inside or outside of the door? Besides, I'm not allowed to bring him inside," John William said.

Just then, the puppy gave a small bark at Maggie.

"See, he likes you. I think he wants you to hold him," John William told her.

Maggie looked around and then over her shoulder across the food court at McDonald's. She saw her mother and brother in a long line waiting to place their order. Deciding they'd be quite a while, she agreed.

"OK, but just for a minute. If my mom finds out I went outside, she'll ground me for sure," Maggie explained.

She stood next to John William, and he handed her the puppy. It immediately started to lick her face.

"See, he loves you already. What's your name?" he asked.

"Maggie. He's the cutest puppy ever." She kissed the top of the dog's head and handed him back to John William. "I have to go back in. Thanks for letting me hold him," she said.

John William took the puppy from her and set him on the ground. To his delight, the dog did exactly what he'd hoped. It ran off toward the parking lot.

"Oh my God," John William exclaimed, pretending to be worried. "He's gonna get killed by a car. Please help me catch him!" he yelled to Maggie as he ran in the direction of the dog.

Without thinking it through, Maggie darted off to help rescue the puppy. She was running behind John William when he turned. "You run down that lane, and I'll meet you at the far end. That way, he can't get away," he rasped.

Maggie ran between two cars and down the lane to the very end, where she stood behind a red van. When John William met her, he was carrying the puppy. "Thanks for your help. He could have been killed," he said and handed the puppy to her.

She took him into her arms again. "Pup, you could've been killed. You have to be more careful," she cooed.

"This is my van," John William told her as he opened the back door.

Maggie looked inside and saw a small dog crate.

"Why don't you put him in the crate for me, and I'll get his bowl from the front seat. I want to give him some water. He must be thirsty from all that running around," he said with a smile.

Maggie watched as John William started toward the front of his van. Only then did she climb in to put the puppy in the crate, but before she made it that far, she was wrapped in an overpowering embrace. She panicked; the desire to flee surged through her body.

John William shoved her toward the crate, and she quickly scurried to find her footing. He was right next to her when he yanked a rag doused in chloroform from a small bucket on the floor of the van. He grabbed her around the waist and put the rag over her mouth and nose. She was unconscious in seconds.

When Maggie woke up, she was lying in the back of the van, hog-tied and gagged. Her head was pounding and the motion of the van churned the nausea that swirled in her belly. As her vision began to clear, she saw a young boy lying next to her, bound and gagged in the same way. The boy was much younger than she was—five or six, she guessed. He lay lifelessly, and she hoped he wasn't dead.

Maggie started to weep. She thought about how stupid she was to follow the man outside. Her mother had warned specifically about adults using pets to lure children in so they could steal them.

Then she thought about her mother. Why had she insisted that she was old enough to get pizza by herself? Her mom had said no at first, but Maggie had begged, "Come on, Mom. I'm not a baby. I'm eleven years old. I can walk to the other side of the food court by myself."

Lorraine, Maggie's mother, wanted to show her daughter that she trusted her and finally agreed. When Maggie headed to the pizza line, her mother took her younger brother, Keith, to McDonald's for a happy meal.

Maggie wanted the other kids at the food court to think she was cool. The fifth-grade girls from her class, who always left Maggie out, were celebrating a birthday with a pizza party at the food court. She wanted to show them that she had independence and was too good to join their stupid little group.

Still, in the back of the van with a man she didn't know, she tried to keep herself calm. The little boy lying next to her finally woke up. He looked at her pleadingly, but there was nothing she could do to help. She tried to keep her eyes from revealing her own fear, but it was a wasted effort.

Suddenly, the van came to a stop, and the back doors opened. John William reached in and clamped his large hand on one of Maggie's ankles. Then he reached down with a knife and cut the thick rope that kept her legs and arms tied together. He pulled her out of the van and into a field, putting one of her arms behind her back. She felt the handcuffs fasten on her right wrist and then her left. The cold steel of the cuff cut into her flesh, and she looked at John William for mercy.

Ignoring her, John William did the same to the small boy, who was crying and squirming in an attempt to escape. John William slapped the boy, and after the child fell to the ground, he put his dirty white sneaker on the child's back while he handcuffed him.

Maggie looked around frantically for someone who could help them. Since it was dark outside, she knew they had been in the van for a long time. John William took each of them by the arm and dragged them down a dirt path with high grass on either side. Maggie could see a stark, stone building ahead. The building was as frightening as the man who had taken her from the mall. It stood like an abandoned castle against the moonlit night sky.

Maggie's New Home

J ohn William led the children through a heavy steel door and down a hall with jail cells on either side. It was obvious that no one else was there. "Where are we?" Maggie squeaked through the gag that was tied at the back of her head.

"Silence," John William demanded.

Her mind raced as they walked through the decrepit prison. Oh my God, how will I find my way home? After he took them through a block of cells, he stopped to grab a flashlight from a stool next to a small steel door. John William pulled the two children along, down two long flights of rusted metal stairs, deeper into the bowels of the building.

Finally, they were walking down a dark, narrow hall. The flashlight threw off a spooky yellow haze, and Maggie knew that her abductor had delivered them to hell. On either side of them were tiny cells. Mounds of dirt poured into the hallway from some of the cells, where the building's foundation had given way to the force of the earth pressing in from the outside.

Unlike the cells two floors above them, these cells had solid steel doors with small, rectangular openings in the middle. John William stopped midway down the hall and took them both into one of the cells. He made the little boy lie down on the cot. Then he removed his gag and handcuffs. "Don't you move," he ordered.

Shutting the door behind them, he led Maggie to the cell directly across the hall. After her gag and handcuffs were removed, he abruptly left. Maggie began to pray that whatever was happening to them would end quickly. That someone would come and rescue them.

Maggie heard the small child whimpering. Then she heard John William ask the child, "Why were you such a bad little boy?"

"I not bad," the child insisted.

Maggie heard the first couple of slaps and the child begging John William to stop. "You will not be disobedient to me."

Maggie heard the sound of whipping as John William's belt flew across the boy's back. The boy screamed as each lash landed, and then suddenly, he went silent. Maggie paced in her small dark cell. She willed the child to make a sound so she would know he was still alive. Then the door to her cell was unlocked and John William stood before her like a giant. He stared down at her with an icy expression. "Why were you such a bad little girl?"

Maggie's survival instincts kicked in. Having heard what John William had just done to the boy, she whimpered, "Because I was jealous of the other girls in the mall. I'm sorry. I won't do it again."

John William paused and sized her up. "Good girl. Now are you willing to accept your punishment?"

"Yes," she muttered, beginning to cry. "But I swear I'll be a good girl."

For the first time, John William smiled. His crooked, yellow-brownish teeth were twisted and looked sinister. "OK then."

He sat on her cot and told her to come over to him. She stood next to him shaking, her arms crossed over her chest. He pulled her down across his lap and spanked her with his open hand. After three hard whacks on the ass, he forced her to her feet again. "Tonight, you go to bed without dinner."

"OK," Maggie responded, humiliated from the spanking. Maggie had learned her first lesson: whatever happened, she always had to agree with John William if she wanted to live to see her family again.

BUY NOW: One Among Us (Home Street Home Series: Book Three) **The HOME STREET HOME SERIES is a collection of novels that can be read in any order.**

More books by Paige

Home Street Home Series:
Believe Like A Child
When Smiles Fade
One Among Us
Mean Little People
Never Be Alone
My Final Breath

Rainey Paxton Series:
A Little Pinprick
A Little High

A Note From Paige

Dear Dearth Reader,

I want to take a moment to thank you for reading and supporting my work. I appreciate you spreading the word about my books to family, friends and co-workers. If you enjoyed this book please go to Amazon and leave a short review so that other readers can determine if this is the right book for them . . . great reviews mean so much to me and keep me writing. Thank you!

~Paige

Made in United States
Orlando, FL
06 January 2023